A THOUSAND ROADS HOME

2013 and Romantic eBook of the Year 2013. Her books have captured the hearts of readers worldwide and have been translated into eight languages to date.

Previous novels include *The Woman at 72 Derry Lane* and the official ITV novel *Cold Feet: The Lost Years*.

Carmel is a regular panellist on TV3's *Elaine* and *Midday* shows. If that wasn't enough to make the juggle struggle real, she is co-founder of The Inspiration Project and Chair of Wexford Literary festival.

Carmel loves to chat to her readers, so do get in touch.

www.facebook.com/happymrsh/
@HappyMrsH
www.carmelharrington.com

Also by Carmel Harrington

Beyond Grace's Rainbow
The Life You Left
Every Time a Bell Rings
The Things I Should Have Told You
The Woman at 72 Derry Lane

CARMEL HARRINGTON

A Thousand Roads Home

HarperCollins*Publishers*

HarperCollins*Publishers* Ltd
1 London Bridge Street,
London SE1 9GF

www.harpercollins.co.uk

First published by HarperCollins*Publishers* 2018
This edition published by HarperCollins*Publishers* 2019

1

A catalogue record for this book is available from the British Library

ISBN: 978-0-00-827658-4 (TPB)
ISBN: 978-0-00-827661-4 (B)

This novel is entirely a work of fiction.
The names, characters and incidents portrayed in it are
the work of the author's imagination. Any resemblance to
actual persons, living or dead, events or localities is
entirely coincidental.

Set in Sabon LT Std by Palimpsest Book Production Limited,
Falkirk, Stirlingshire

Printed and bound by CPI Group (UK) Ltd, Croydon, CR0 4YY

MIX
Paper from
responsible sources
FSC™ C007454

This book is produced from independently certified FSC™ paper
to ensure responsible forest management.

For more information visit: www.harpercollins.co.uk/green

For Ann Murphy, my person. You've been making my life better for nearly thirty years. Thank you.

There are a thousand ways to kneel and kiss the ground;
there are a thousand ways to go home again.

Rumi

PROLOGUE

Then

Ruth fastened the seat belt around her newborn son's car seat. She tugged it twice to double-check it was secure. Little DJ puckered his lips and smiled as he chased his dreams, the way babies do.

She switched the engine on and drove away from the only world she knew. But she was not sorry. It was just her and her son now. Whilst there was fear, there was excitement, too. It was time for a new beginning. She looked in the rear-view mirror to ensure her sleeping son was as he should be. She would do this many times until they arrived at their new flat in Dublin.

Ruth Wilde had always been a person with obsessions: *Odd Thomas*, who was both her imaginary best friend and the main character from her favourite book written by Dean Koontz (she would soon finish this book for the hundred and fourth time); Westlife, her number-one favourite band, whose song 'Flying without Wings' helped

1

her drown out the white noise and anxiety whenever it threatened to overcome her; mashed potatoes, white sliced loaf, bananas, ice cream – in fact any food that was white in colour; counting steps, always even.

Yes, Ruth Wilde did obsessions very well.

And now she had a new one. The most important one of all.

Her son.

She would be a good mother. She would fight for DJ when he could not fight for himself. She would keep him safe from the dangers that lurked in the dark shadows. She would make him laugh at least once a day. And she would love him as she had never been loved herself.

Yes, it was time. Ruth was ready to leave Wexford to make a new home for her family.

'Just the two of us against the world, DJ,' she whispered. She hit play on her CD player, letting Shane from Westlife's voice fill the car. The words from, 'Flying Without Wings' had never felt more apt. For as long as Ruth had thought, she too had been looking for that *something*. Something to make her complete. She glanced at DJ again in the rear-view mirror and felt joyful satisfaction bubble its way up inside her.

If she had not chosen that exact second to do this, she might have noticed instead the man she'd just passed, walking with a rucksack on his back. And she might have stopped.

Tom did not notice the red car pass by him either, as he walked along the Estuary Road towards the N11. His head was full of the warnings his friend Ben had made earlier. They nipped and taunted him, whirling around in his brain, tangling everything up, until he could no longer make sense of anything.

'If you don't find something to light up the darkness, Tom, you'll get lost in the shadows.'

But what if that was what he wanted? Tom didn't believe he would ever feel peace again. He was bone tired from weeks of sleepless nights. Despite this, he kept on walking, putting one foot in front of the other. His pace was steady and a few hours later he arrived in the town of Enniscorthy. Tom's feet were beginning to protest about the long walk. A throb in his right little toe and left heel set up residence. He welcomed the pain.

He walked over the Seamus Rafter Bridge, leaving the banks of the River Slaney behind him. He glanced at Enniscorthy Castle on his right then made his way towards Main Street.

It was late, the last of the daylight now swallowed up by the night. He didn't plan to end up here, but somehow he'd found himself in the grounds of St Aidan's Cathedral. He walked to a small clearing in the shadow of the big church and sat down, his back against the cold stone wall.

For in that sleep of death what dreams will come. That's what Shakespeare had written. Tom hoped he was right. Because if so, Cathy was living the life they had dreamed they would have. The life that had been cruelly snatched from them. Wouldn't that be something?

Close your eyes.

– *Cathy?*

Yes, my love.
– Are you here?
Remember what I told you. If you close your eyes, the dreams will come.
– I don't know how.
Yes, you do. We're waiting for you, Tom. Come home to us.

Tom didn't make a conscious decision to sleep outdoors. The night just crept up on him. To his surprise, on the hard, concrete ground with the cold brick of the Cathedral to his back, he finally found a different kind of peace and the sleep that had eluded him for weeks.

And in that sleep the dreams did come.

Cathy stood a few feet away from him, carrying Mikey. He ran towards them and pulled them both into his arms.

Daddy's home. I'll never leave you again.

1

RUTH

Now

'Err, what's it supposed to be, Mam?' DJ asked.

Ruth flicked on her tablet and pointed to an image on Pinterest. Their eyes flicked back and forth between the green chequered fondant perfectly encasing the square Minecraft cake on screen, and the mound of brown, black and green smudged squares that covered Ruth's cake in front of them. Four hours of baking, dyeing fondant, cutting, moulding. And for all that effort she had what looked like a patchwork quilt made by a four-year-old. Ten candles leaned to the left, perilously close to a sugary grave.

It was DJ's tenth birthday. A milestone that deserved celebrating. And not with a big mess of a cake. *Was he cross with her?* She peered at her son's face, trying to determine his mood, as he contemplated the cake in front of him. His face broke into a big grin and he pointed to the tablet screen, then back to Ruth's cake, and said, 'Nailed it!'

Ruth repeated his words with relief and then they both said it together, 'Nailed it!', each time making them snort a little louder. This went on until they clutched their sides, the pain from a laughter stitch doubling them over.

'Thanks for trying, Mam. It probably tastes all right. But don't give up the day job!'

Ruth felt a rush of emotion for the boy DJ was now and the man he was on his way to becoming. The past ten years had gone too quickly. One moment a baby in her arms. Now, on the brink of opening a door to adulthood.

'You have to blow out the candles,' Ruth said.

'Aren't I too old for that?'

'Never too old for candles and wishes.' Ruth lit the wonky wax sticks one by one.

His nose scrunched up as it always did when he was thinking. His father had done the same too. She remembered that much, even if some things had become a bit faded with time. A shared mannerism between father and son despite the fact that they had never met.

'Make a wish, DJ,' Ruth whispered.

With one big puff, DJ blew out the ten candles all at once, as Ruth sang 'Happy Birthday To You'.

She reached under the kitchen table and pulled out a basket of gifts all wrapped prettily in blue paper with a perfectly formed red bow tied on top. DJ quickly counted them. Ten. His mam always bought him a gift for each year, even though he always told her she shouldn't.

'Thanks, Mam,' he said, ripping the paper from the first parcel.

Ruth's eyes never left him, drinking in his every reaction

as he opened the gifts one by one. A football jersey, a journal, a Rubik's Cube, a book, artist's pencils, a sketch pad, a bar of Galaxy, a new T-shirt, and a pair of bright, stripy socks.

'I know what this one is,' DJ said, as he pulled the paper off the last gift. He nodded in satisfaction when it revealed a book of raffle tickets. A sticker, with a message written in Ruth's neat handwriting, covered the front of the book: *One strip can be redeemed for a hug at any time.* He didn't have a birthday memory that didn't include a version of this gift. He had never spoken about this arrangement with his friends in school, suspecting, correctly, that they would find it strange. It was just the way it was with him and his mam.

DJ felt her eyes on him, as he picked up his new football shirt, and a lump jumped into his throat. His mam must have been saving for ages to get him that jersey. It was the real deal. Not a cheap copy from the market. He pulled a strip out of the book and handed it to her.

Ruth folded it in two, then placed it in her jeans pocket. She opened her arms to her son and held him close in her embrace, breathing in his unique smell. Mud, milk, bananas and tonight, because of his earlier treat, pepperoni pizza.

Ruth knew that there would come a day when raffle tickets would no longer be needed. Previous years she had to buy new books halfway through the year, such was the demand for her cuddles. But when she had checked her son's bedside locker last week, she realised that a quarter of his ninth birthday book was unused. She closed her mind to that. Because right now in this moment, she was his and he was hers.

'Hey! How did you do that?' DJ asked when the lights in the flat went out.

Ruth's stomach sank. *Not again.* She stood up and counted her steps to the kitchen. She continued counting until she got to eight, then pulled open a drawer, reaching for her torch. She flicked it on and investigated the ESB box. *Please let it be a trip switch.* Her silent pleas fell on deaf ears. All switches were upright and correct. 'We have been cut off.'

'It doesn't matter,' DJ said by her side, reaching for her hands that had begun to fly in frustration at this turn of events. 'We can watch the movie another time.'

'I get paid tomorrow. I was going to pay the bill then.' Ruth popped her knuckles in frustration. Her phone pinged to let her know she had a text message, its blue light flashing on the kitchen table. It was from Seamus Kearns, her landlord.

I will be calling at the flat next Friday at 6pm.

She turned her phone upside down.

'All OK?'

Ruth nodded and pushed aside a niggling feeling of unease. This was DJ's night. Ruth would deal with the landlord tomorrow.

'We can still eat cake, even in the dark!' DJ said, pulling two plates from the cabinet.

Ruth held the torch over her son as he cut a large wedge of the cake. Then he reached up into the larder press and felt his way until he found his target. Rice cakes. He took two out and put them on the second plate. Ruth grabbed a bag of tea lights and lit a dozen of them, placing them around the sitting room. They sat side by side on the small sofa, balancing their treats on their knees. With a mouthful of the cake, DJ said, 'Knew it. Tastes great.'

Ruth shuddered just thinking about putting a mouthful of that green mess into her mouth. Knowing how hard it must have been for his mother to touch food that wasn't white, DJ said, 'I can't believe you made this cake for me, Mam.'

'I would do anything for you, DJ. Always remember that.' And they inched a little closer to each other.

His eyes, now accustomed to the near darkness, took in the birthday banners that hung from each corner of the room. The multi-coloured balloons that seemed to dance in the candlelight. The empty pizza box. The gifts. *His mam*. And while he didn't know it yet, this birthday was the one that, for the rest of his life, he would look back on as his best.

2

RUTH

The day Ruth Wilde and her son, DJ, became homeless was just an ordinary day in Dublin. The sun poked its head through the grey clouds of an autumnal sky. Cars drove by at a snail's pace, bumper to bumper in their early morning commute.

One, two, three . . . Ruth began counting steps to herself as she walked down the driveway in front of her flat.

For most, it was just another thank-crunchie-it's-Friday morning in the suburbs. For Ruth it was a day of despair. Her world, her normal, was falling apart. She was not prepared for the unknown future that lay ahead. With every change that was flung at her, she felt like she was moving closer to the edge of an abyss.

. . . ten, eleven, twelve . . .

And for Ruth, who lived her life in quiet, isolated order with her son, the abyss looked impossible to cross. Taking a leap of faith was not in her psyche. Ruth needed to prepare, to understand, to know before she undertook anything new. That way she had time to build a bridge, if you like, that would take her safely to the other side.

. . . nineteen, twenty, twenty-one . . .

She looked up and down the road, seeing it with new eyes that told her danger lay ahead.

. . . twenty-five, twenty-six, twenty-seven . . .

The end of the driveway. She took one more step, then breathed the last number with relief.

Twenty-eight. As it should be; as it had been for four years now.

Ruth placed two black sacks beside the ugly but serviceable suitcases she'd left there moments before. Not much to show for her thirty years in this world. Running her hands over the cases, she felt a moment of sympathy for them. When it came to the luggage lottery they lucked out. While other suitcases got to travel the world, hers were used only to transport meagre possessions from rented house to rented house. So many moves over the past ten years since they arrived in Dublin. The plan had been to stay here until they were given a council house. Now there was a new plan. She just did not know what it was yet.

Ruth felt her son's presence before she saw him. He had this weird energy lately that filled the air between them: a mixture of disappointment, anger and, she supposed, fear. None of which she knew how to alleviate.

'You should be in school,' Ruth said, watching the patterns of the cracks in the pavement. She had dropped him there earlier this morning, then went for her usual early morning run. She never needed the escapism running gave her more than she did today.

His response was to kick the concrete path with the toe of his scuffed runners. He'd had another growth spurt over the past couple of weeks. School tracksuit bottoms were almost at the point of embarrassment for him, barely grazing the tops of his shoes. She would have to get to Penneys at some point to pick up a pair. And then a thought hit her hard. *How will I clean his uniform if we have no home of our own, no washing machine?*

She felt guilt flood over her again. She had let him down just as her mother had predicted she would. A spectacular failure of a parent. She cracked the knuckle on her ring finger and felt tension release as she heard a familiar *pop, pop, pop.*

'Sorry,' she said, when DJ made a face. She knew the noise irritated him. But this quirk had been embedded in her for as long as she had a memory. It proved hard to say goodbye to.

'Why are you looking all weird at the cases?' DJ asked. He gave the one nearest to him a kick.

'I feel sorry for them,' Ruth said, pushing them away from DJ's feet, which were hell-bent on causing damage right now.

'That's weird. You do know that, right?' DJ asked.

'Yes.'

You used to like my weirdness. Please do not stop.

'Is that it, then? We're really leaving now?' DJ said.

'Yes.' Her culpability crippled her. She had promised him that they were done moving around when they had found this flat four years previously. But she made that promise without the knowledge that eviction lay in their future.

13

'I never liked it here anyway. It's a dump,' DJ lied.

'I liked it,' Ruth answered softly. 'And while it was not much, it was our dump.'

'So what next?' His voice made a lie of his earlier bravado, the tremor showing his truth. He was a scared kid who didn't want to leave his house, his bedroom, his life.

'Right now you need to go back to school. We have talked about this. I will collect you later on. After my meeting with the council in Parkgate Hall. I will come and get you. You have my word,' Ruth said.

'I'm not going to school today.' DJ was matter-of-fact, and when she didn't answer him he turned to her. 'You can't make me go in.'

'Yes I can,' Ruth replied.

'Well, maybe, but you need me with you, Mam. You know how you get when you're stressed. Let me help. Let me go with you to the council.'

'I will not say the wrong thing.'

DJ had heard his mother rehearse possible scenarios for this day dozens of times. He'd watched her struggle to stay calm, with the sound of her pops cracking in the air, as her knuckle-cracking habit exacerbated. The fear that the council would not have somewhere safe for them danced around them both. But DJ could not give in to that. He was no longer a baby. He had to be strong for his mam. She needed him.

'It's not fair to expect me to sit through double maths when all I'm thinking about is you and where we will sleep tonight,' DJ whispered.

Ruth nodded in agreement. 'None of this is fair.'

Her reasoning that it was better for him to miss all of this was perhaps misguided. She took in every part of him, from the frown on his face to the hunch of his shoulders, and felt her love for him overtake everything else. 'Do you need a hug?' Ruth asked, taking a step backwards.

If he said yes, she would pull him into her embrace and whilst she did so, she would count to ten, before letting him go. That's just the way it was for them, and on a normal day that didn't bother him. But today was not normal. For once, just once, DJ wished she would hug him without question. Without a raffle ticket.

'It's OK.' DJ turned away from the look of relief on her face.

'You can stay with me. I will write a letter for your teacher tomorrow morning,' Ruth said.

'Thanks.' He felt some of his irritation slip away.

Their Uber arrived and the driver jumped out of the car, looking at their luggage with dismay. 'This all yours, love?'

'Correct.'

'We'll be doing well to fit this in the boot,' he complained, picking up the black sacks. 'You should have ordered a people carrier.'

'Put the suitcases in first and you will have adequate space,' Ruth pointed out what seemed startlingly obvious to her.

'Listen to my mam. She's good with stuff like this,' DJ said, when the driver ignored her. DJ helped him do as Ruth suggested. With one last shove, the boot closed with a loud bang.

'Told you,' DJ said. He liked proving his mother right. Had she even noticed? He didn't think so.

Ruth and DJ turned to look one last time at the home they had lived in for the past four years. Anger flashed over DJ's face once more and Ruth shuddered as his features changed. Cold. Angry. Disappointed.

'Stop staring at me,' he complained.

Ruth ignored him and only looked away when his face returned to normal.

That's better. He looked just like his father again. They got into the car and she turned her head to look out the window. Had things been different, if she had never met DJ's father, his namesake, they might not be in this situation. But then she would have no DJ – arguably a fate much worse, because without her son, she had nothing.

As the car moved away from their old life, she said, 'I am so sorry.'

'You keep saying that,' DJ said.

'Because it is true.'

DJ sighed, something that Ruth noted he did with increasing regularity. The stress of the past month had made sighing part of his new normal. It was funny how sounds could bring you back to another time. Back to her childhood home where life had been full of sighs. The thing was, despite their regularity, they had the power to cut her each and every time.

The first sigh she could remember was at her four-years-old developmental check-up in the local health centre in Castlebridge, Wexford. Her mother had dressed Ruth in her best dress, a burnt-orange tweed pinafore. She had thick black tights on underneath, which scratched her legs and made her cry. Her mother had sighed and asked, 'Why must you always be so difficult?'

Ruth did not like seeing her mother upset so she pinched herself hard and tried to make the tears stop. She wanted her mother to look at her with different eyes. With love.

On the way to the health centre, her parents coached her. They were second-guessing what the nurse would ask Ruth. She had tried to listen to her parents' instructions, determined to succeed, to win, to not be a loser again. But with every question they threw at her and every answer Ruth offered up, she saw her parents throw furtive glances at each other. She could sense that something was not quite right. She wanted to be at home again in her bedroom, wearing her soft pyjamas that were made of pink fleece. She liked how they felt on her skin. They did not itch or scratch like her tights and dress, and they made her feel safe. She wanted to go back to her picture book and read about Angelina Ballerina. Instead she had to sit in a cold waiting room with hard plastic chairs and dirty floors while her parents told her to act like a normal child.

'I want to go home,' Ruth decided, and she felt her arms begin to fly. She wished she was a bird so she could disappear into the blue sky. Back home. Back to safety. Back to her normal.

Her mother's exasperated sigh filled the air with tension. 'Oh, Ruth, stop that right now. People will stare! Why must you always be so difficult?'

Ruth had sat on her hands, shamed, scared and tearful.

A lifetime of sighs and sorrys. Now her son was in on the act, too.

'DJ,' she whispered, and her hand hovered in the centre of the car, in the space between them. Only a few inches away from each other yet it felt like an unbridgeable gulf. She let her hand drop into her lap and she looked back out through the window.

3

RUTH

'It's not your fault,' DJ said, finally, in a voice that was older and more knowing than it had any business to be. 'It's Seamus Kearns. I hate him. The . . . the . . . fucker.'

Ruth looked at her young son in shock. Had he just said that? DJ's honest, innocent face jarred with his foul language. She was not naïve enough to believe that he had never used bad language before, but this . . . this really was out of character. One of the rules of their family was that they had a swear-free home. As much for her as him because, in truth, she enjoyed a good expletive.

Ruth wanted so much for DJ: an education, friends, social acceptance, a life without offence. Because offending people had been, and still was, a regular occurrence for her.

'Hate is a strong word, DJ,' Ruth said. Had it been any other day, she would have been cross with him. But she had to concede that on a day that involved losing your home, a few concessions had to be made.

'You hate him, too,' DJ said.

'That is incorrect. I would say I abhor his actions. But hate is a negative, angry and all-encompassing emotion. He is not worthy of taking up that much space in my head. Or yours.'

DJ's resentment filled the air between them, contaminating their close unit. She felt at a loss, knowing that she must, as the adult, find a way for them both to get through this. She turned to face him, then moved her hand an inch closer to his, letting her fingertips brush the top of his. He looked down and she saw a ghost of a smile inch its way back onto his face. He squeezed her hand for a moment then released it back to her lap.

It was a start. She would find a way to do better.

DJ turned his attention back to the blur of Dublin as they drove through the city. Their taxi came to a halt at a pedestrian crossing. Ruth looked up and watched an old man, unshaven and dirty, wearing a long grey overcoat, begin to cross the road. By his side was a dog with a long and silky strawberry-blonde coat. The man raised his hand in small salute to the taxi driver, thanking him for waiting. He walked slowly, with a slight limp on his right leg. He had a rucksack on his back and something about him – his clothes, his hair, the collar of his coat turned up to protect him from the chill in the air – brought a lump to Ruth's throat.

Where is he going? Does he have a home?

Then a car behind them blasted its horn, impatient to get on with its journey. They all jumped in unison, including the dog, who stopped suddenly, causing the old man to crash into it. Like a deck of cards, he tripped and fell to the ground, his rucksack spilling its contents onto the road.

'Probably pissed,' the Uber driver said, looking with annoyance in his rear-view window at the car behind, whose driver continued to blast the horn.

'His dog tripped him up,' Ruth said, feeling the need to defend the old man. She watched a red-and-white flask escape his rucksack and roll towards their car.

'Where you going?' DJ asked in surprise when Ruth opened her door.

'To help.' She ran over to the flask and picked it up before it disappeared under their car.

'That's mine!' the old man shouted at her, back on his feet again.

Ruth shook the flask gently to see if it had broken, relieved to hear only the swoosh of liquid inside, not broken shards.

'It is unharmed,' she said, handing it over to him. His boots were brown. Scuffed and worn. Like him.

He stuffed the flask back into his rucksack, looking at her curiously. Was she imagining it or did he look surprised? Without any further comment, Ruth counted the steps back to their Uber.

'I don't know why you bothered, love. His kind would stab you as soon as look at you,' the taxi driver said. 'Only last week I saw one of his lot robbing a handbag from a woman. Witnessed it from this very car.'

Ruth glanced towards the man still standing on the side of the road, watching her intently, his head tilted to one side. For a split second their eyes met and he raised his hand and saluted her. And in that gesture, Ruth had the

21

strangest feeling she knew him. She had seen that salute before, she was sure. The memory teased her but refused to show itself. It was gone. And so was he when he turned away and walked in the opposite direction, his dog by his side. Her imagination was playing tricks on her.

'Why did you do that?' DJ asked.

'Because it was the right thing to do,' Ruth replied. She nodded towards the back of the Uber driver's head. 'Do not write off people based on how they present themselves to the world. You should know that better than anyone. Everyone has a story, if you take the time to listen.'

As their car moved on, the old man disappeared from her view but not from Ruth's mind. She supposed he could have a home. But something about the way he retrieved his fallen items and put them back into his rucksack made her think that his home was in that bag. His face looked weathered in a way that suggested it had been exposed to the outside elements twenty-four-seven. Had life changed as quickly for this man as it had for her and DJ? In only four weeks, they had gone from home to homeless. Four short weeks that had been the longest of her life. When their landlord, Mr Kearns, gave them notice to leave their two-bedroomed flat, he set their life into a tailspin. Ruth was never late paying the rent, even by a day, which meant some months were leaner than others. But Mr Kearns did not care about that.

He had walked into her kitchen and opened up a cupboard above the sink, two months previously. Then pulled out a mug, laughing as he said, 'It's a mug's game, this landlord malarkey. I'm getting out. Selling up.' His eyes narrowed as he turned to look at Ruth. 'Make me an offer if you like. Can't say fairer than that.'

Ruth knew when someone was making fun of her. She recognised the tone, one that she had heard many times in her life.

'I can't maintain the rent. Not at the levels they are at,' Mr Kearns said, in a manner that implied he was talking about the weather, not their eviction.

'You raised the rent by twenty per cent only a year ago,' Ruth interjected.

'You can blame our government for the mess they've landed us all in. I can't raise the rent for another two years, because of these new laws they've made,' Seamus replied, picking up cushions on their sofa and examining them, before tossing them back.

Ruth had been relieved when she'd read about the changes to the Irish rent laws. Naïvely, she believed it meant that she would not have to worry about a further increase until 2020. By then she would have a council house. Only she realised now that although they were on the housing waiting list with Fingal County Council, they were as likely to win the lottery as they were to get a house. Ruth had heard the phrase 'You are only two pay cheques away from the streets.' As it happened, for them, the number was one.

Ruth felt panic begin to mount inside her once again, as she sat in the back of the car. Then Odd Thomas's voice whispered to her, as it had done for over a decade whenever she needed help, calming her, supporting her:

Perseverance is impossible if we don't permit ourselves to hope.

It was his name, 'Odd', that made her choose the book in the first place at her local library in Wexford. She had been called that on more than one occasion in her life. For different reasons from his, she found out soon enough. Odd could see and talk to dead people, and used this skill to help the Chief of Police in Pico Mundo to solve murders. Odd's world in the USA became as real to her as the one she herself lived in in Ireland. She read the book in one glorious sitting the first time, then picked it up to read again the following day. Then something extraordinary happened on a damp, grey morning in spring. She watched her classmates playing basketball in the school yard, chatting in groups of twos and threes, happy cliques. A thought crept into her head, insidious and mean. If she disappeared, faded to nothing, who would miss her?

And that was when Odd Thomas spoke to her for the first time. *Be happy. Persevere.*

That very line was one of her favourites from the book. And she knew immediately what it meant. Ruth would have to work extra hard to be happy. But if she never gave up hope, she could find happiness. *Thank you, Odd.*

And so their friendship began: she trying her best to be happy; he reminding her that perseverance was necessary to achieve that end. Of course, Ruth knew that Odd was not real. She was neither stupid nor delusional. Just alone.

She looked across the seat to her son. For him, she would fight. She would find them a home again. He would never feel alone.

4

TOM

Bette Davis nuzzled Tom's hand again, her apology for knocking him off his feet earlier. 'It's OK, girl,' he said to his dog, ruffling her coat behind her ears, the way she liked. He leaned back into the curve of his park bench. His home now, he supposed, as it was where he spent most of his nights. Bette rested her head on his feet. Tom closed his eyes. His breathing slowed down and his lids flickered, heavy, until every sense lost its place in the now and went back in time to his dreams, to his happy place, to his home . . .

Tom stretched his aching muscles upwards, knowing that a locum was a priority. He couldn't keep this pace up for much longer. His bones ached, older than his forty years. His small general practice had grown to the point that Tom had to turn new patients away. And patients were beginning to complain that the usual twenty-minute waiting time for their appointment was stretching towards an hour. That didn't sit well with him.

His receptionist, Breda, poked her head through his door. The sound of the Spice Girls singing their Christmas hit 'Too Much' drifted in towards him. He stood up and heard his knees click in protest. He needed to get out for a run. He'd been saying that to himself for the past two months. But somehow or other, another day would go by and he'd find himself falling onto his couch, tired and hungry, exercising his fingers with the TV remote.

'What's the plan for the weekend?' Breda asked.

'Not listening to the Spice Girls. That's for starters,' Tom said.

'Would suit you well to find a Spice Girl for yourself.'

'Would be a lucky lady to get me,' Tom said, smiling. 'But if she's out there tonight she'll have to wait. Because my only plan is to head to Tesco. I need to replenish my poor cupboards, then it's home to catch up on some sleep.'

'It's no life you have,' Breda said. 'Good-looking man like you.'

'Stop flirting with me,' Tom joked.

Breda waved her hands at him and grinned, 'Oh, you, you're such a messer.'

'What are you up to this weekend, Breda?' He watched her tidy her reception desk, switching off the computer. She looked as tired as he felt. Was he expecting too much from her? Probably.

'I'm going dancing. Don't laugh. I told you not to laugh!' Breda said when Tom's face broke into a grin. 'Himself has it in his head that we should learn how to ballroom dance. I'm not sure I'll ever be Ginger to his Fred, though.'

Tom walked over to Breda and grabbed her hand,

spinning her around 360 degrees. 'I don't know. I reckon you have all the moves.'

She laughed as she pushed him away. 'Get away out of that! Maybe thirty years ago. But I'm nearly sixty now!'

'Never, you don't look a day over forty!' Tom didn't miss a beat and she beamed. They had formed their mutual appreciation society nearly fifteen years previously, when he'd opened the practice. He would be lost without her.

They both groaned when the doorbell rang. Who on earth was calling at this late hour? They had cleared all appointments and it was now twenty minutes past their closing time.

'Is it Ben, maybe?' Breda asked. Sometimes Tom and his solicitor friend had a drink together after work.

'Not tonight. He's got a hot date with a new woman called Orla. Right now he's dousing himself in aftershave.' He unlocked the front door to a young mother with a young child in her arms, wrapped in a blanket.

'Siobhan!' Breda exclaimed, walking towards the woman.

'I saw the light on. I hoped you were still here,' Siobhan replied.

'We were just about to walk out the door,' Breda answered.

Siobhan's face clouded with anxiety. 'I'm worried. Daniel's chest is really bad. His wheeze has gotten worse.'

Breda looked at Tom, ready to take his lead. Technically they were closed. Surgery hours were explicit on the sign at the front of their office.

'You did the right thing coming,' Tom said, shrugging his jacket off. Daniel looked smaller than his four years, his face bleached white.

Breda was unsurprised. Her boss had a big heart. It was one of the reasons she loved him like her own son.

Once they got into Tom's office, Daniel climbed off his mother's lap and stood in front of the doctor. Daniel knew the drill – he'd been here so many times before. He lifted his top up before he was asked, so that Dr Tom could listen to his chest.

'Good man. Big deep breath for me. Hold it. And exhale,' Tom said. 'You're a great fella. Do that again for me.'

Tom took his temperature, which was high, and looked in his ears and throat. 'His left lung doesn't sound good. The wheeze is particularly bad there.'

Siobhan wrung her hands back and forth. 'I knew I should have brought him in earlier today. But Lulu has a bad cold. And I didn't like to bring her out. She's been so bad-tempered with it all. Gerard was away working. As soon as he came home, I told him I had to bring Daniel to see you. I rushed here as fast as I could. I'm so sorry . . .'

Tom put his hand up to stop the apologies. The woman would have a heart attack if she didn't let herself off the hook. Nothing like a mother's guilt. Unnecessary in this case. Her children were idolised and well looked after. 'You were right to come to me.'

An hour spent on Tom's new nebuliser made Daniel a new boy. Tom walked them both to the door with a prescription in hand. 'If anything happens during the night that worries you, just go straight to A&E. But I think he's going to be OK at home with the steroids.'

'Bye, Dr Tom,' Daniel said. He looked better already and was walking beside his mam now, holding her hand.

Seeing how much improved the little fella was made the late night worth it. He locked up and jumped in his car. With a bit of luck, with traffic on his side, he'd make the supermarket before it closed.

The store announced its imminent closure as Tom raced up the escalators. He grabbed a trolley, ignoring the look of annoyance on the spotty-faced store assistant, who was restocking the baskets and trollies. The last thing he wanted was a last-minute trolley dasher like Tom to delay closure of the store. 'Sorry, buddy,' Tom said. 'Promise I'll be quick.'

He went straight to the pre-packed meal counter to cut out any procrastination on what to buy or, indeed, cook. Not quite home cooked but marginally better than living in the chipper all weekend. If he was fast he could hit the booze aisle to grab some beer too. It was Friday night, and while he was planning a weekend of little else but a book and maybe a bit of TV, alcohol would play a part, too.

His parents would be horrified if they knew he wasn't going out this weekend looking for love. They were obsessed with his social activities and he found himself making up events that he'd been to just to satisfy them. Not that he was short of social opportunities. He just didn't want any of them right now.

Tom was one of those people who always had lots of friends. He was born with charisma. His mother used to say that from the moment he arrived into the world people would stop and stare at him. He would lock his big brown eyes onto theirs and they were putty in his hands. In school kids loved him. His easy-going nature, coupled with a quick wit, made him good company. Children and teachers alike gravitated towards him.

This aura that surrounded him followed him through to university. His best friend, Ben, would watch him sail his way through his classes, making friends and finding new girlfriends without breaking a sweat. Whereas he always had to try harder. And whenever he complained, asking him what his secret was, Tom would answer, 'I'm a charming fecker, that's how.'

And he was. People liked him.

But even charmers like him need a chance to recharge batteries every now and then. The savage hours in work were taking their toll.

But, if Tom had finished his day at 6 p.m., as was originally planned, he would never have met Cathy. And that would have been the greatest tragedy. Cathy liked to think that something else governed their destined meet-up that day. Fate. Tom thought it was dumb luck. Either way, it was the start of everything.

In the shadow of the bench, Bette Davis looked up when she felt her master shift to the right. Even though he had his eyes closed, he was smiling. He was happy. He was home.

5

RUTH

Ruth was never late for an appointment. If she made a commitment to be somewhere, you could rely on her. Even with the unscheduled stop for the old man and his dog, Ruth and DJ were waiting outside the front entrance of Parkgate, ready to see the council, five minutes early. At 10.01 a.m., Ruth began to feel agitated.

She willed the door to open, wondering how many steps there were between the door and their scheduled appointment. When the door swung open moments later, she said to the brown-lace-up-loafer man, 'You are two minutes late.'

'Not by my watch, missus,' the man replied, not one bit put out by her comments.

'Excuse me? Are we in the 1950s? I am neither Mrs, Ms, nor Miss. I am Ruth.'

His bewildered face gave DJ a fit of the giggles.

Ruth and DJ picked up a black sack each, balancing it on top of a suitcase. Then they wheeled them into the hall following the signs for the Central Placement Service. *One hundred and two steps*. Ruth and DJ placed their bags against a wall on their left, which seemed as good a place as any to leave their worldly goods. Then they settled down to wait. From previous interactions with the council, Ruth expected that to be at least thirty minutes. She came prepared and placed her headphones on, hoping Westlife's harmonies would block out the hundreds of horror stories she'd read online in support forums about other families who were in the same predicament as her. They were difficult to silence and over the past twenty-four hours had been, lingering inside her head.

I slept in my car for nearly two weeks. Gas thing is, I woke up at three o'clock every morning, at the exact same time. The cold woke me, or the nightmares, maybe both.
    Laoise

We left the kids with my mother. She doesn't have room for us all. But I can't have them in the hostel. It's not right. Not for anyone but definitely not for them.
    Jude

They can't find us emergency accommodation. Hotels won't take our family of six. We're too big. They want to separate us. But without each other, what's the point of anything?
    Gerry

I gave away all our clothes and possessions, except for one bag each. Not because I didn't want them any more. But because I had nowhere to put them.
    Ursula

The desperate words of these families kept her awake at night and haunted her during the day.

Plan B was one she could not contemplate. Could she do it? Ask her family for help? Which of them? Her mother, her father or Mark?

Pop, pop, pop.

'Mam.' DJ nudged her, unease pinching his face. 'You're crying.'

She wiped the tears away, surprised to feel their wetness on her cheeks.

'Ruth Wilde,' a voice called out.

They stood up and turned to look at each other. DJ's head now reached her breastbone. He was getting tall and she surmised that within a few years he would overtake her. But despite his physical appearance, despite the fact that his emotional intelligence was far older than his years, he was just a kid. And she was letting him down. *Shame on you, Ruth. Shame, shame, shame.*

'It's going to be fine, Mam,' DJ said, sensing her anxiety.

'Ruth Wilde?' the voice shouted again.

Not everyone is cut out to be a mother, Ruth. That's what her mother had said. Had she been right all along?

Eight steps till she reached the counter, and with each one Ruth vowed to make this right for DJ. But as she walked, she looked around the small waiting room that was now almost full. She felt the eyes of the room follow her, judging her, questioning her story. She wrung her hands. Ruth felt blinded by an imaginary spotlight, one that was focused on her inadequacies.

Shame. Shame. Shame.

She wanted to run. Run, leaving behind her suitcases and black sacks. Leaving behind her shame. DJ moved a step closer to her and she felt the warmth of his hand on her back, steadying her. She was not alone. For her son, she summoned every ounce of strength and she focused on the job at hand.

They each took a seat side by side in front of the clerical officer. Ruth looked at the desk in front of her and saw a photograph of a family, taken at a child's First Holy Communion. Mum, dad and two smiling kids, one of them dressed in white. The woman in the photograph beamed and her hands rested on the shoulders of her two children. She had a kind face and she was a mother. That had to be a good sign. Because right now this stranger in front of them held their fate in her hands.

DJ's hands covered hers as Ruth began popping her knuckles one by one. She unflexed her hands reluctantly. *If I just get through this interview, I can go home and be myself in private* . . . The thought hung unfinished in her mind. She no longer had a home to go to. She forced herself to look up at the woman in front of her and silently begged her to help them. The woman's eyes were locked on her computer screen and she hit the keyboard a few times, before looking up at them both and smiling.

'Good morning! I'm Gillian. Nippy out there today, isn't it? My car nearly skidded on black ice when I left our estate. Put the heart across me!' She spoke fast, her smile bright and honest, reaching her eyes. Ruth had not been expecting a summary of Gillian's journey to work and was thrown by it. She had rehearsed what to say all morning and this had not been part of any scenario. So she ignored Gillian and repeated her rehearsed statement in one long breathless sentence.

'I have a job I always pay my rent on time but our landlord has evicted us as he is selling our flat I have tried everything in my power to find another home for us but there is nothing in my price range we have nowhere to go we are homeless I have a job that I am going to lose if I do not have a home and I have a son who needs a home.'

'It's OK,' Gillian interrupted. 'Breathe.'

'I am breathing. I would be dead if I were not.'

Gillian could not work out if Ruth was joking or not. She decided that she was. 'Good one! Well, don't worry, I'm going to help you. OK?'

Ruth nodded, looking closely at the woman in front of them whose face only showed sympathy and kindness. She could not see her shoes and that disappointed her. She guessed she was a black-mid-heel-court type of woman. She decided she could trust her.

'Do we get a house with a garden?' DJ asked.

'I can't guarantee that, I'm afraid. But I'm going to do my best to make sure you have somewhere to go today, until we find you something more permanent. And we need to ensure that you don't lose your job, Ruth. Let me just double-check that your information on file is still correct.'

'I cannot lose my job I have worked very hard not to lose this job.'

'I'm sure you have. You work from home as an online customer advisor?'

Ruth nodded.

'Your annual salary is 18,000 euro.'

Another nod.

'You are a single mother. You have one child – DJ, who is aged ten. You do not receive maintenance from his father. All correct?'

Three nods in a row. Ruth felt like one of those nodding dogs in the back of a car.

'And there's no family you can call on for help? Somewhere you can stay until your name comes up on the housing list?'

Her family. What would this woman think if she knew the truth about her mother?

'I have no family support,' Ruth confirmed. She felt DJ's eyes on her and looked towards him. She knew what he was thinking. *Why?* She wished she had an answer to that.

'I'm going to make a few calls to find emergency accommodation close to DJ's school. But I must stress that I can't guarantee that. It's been a busy month – hell, it's been a busy year,' Gillian said.

'It's OK if I miss school for a bit,' DJ said helpfully.

Gillian laughed at this, but stopped when she realised Ruth wasn't joining in. She was such an odd woman, so serious.

'We have no car to sleep in. Or friends' houses to sofa surf. Please help us. I do not want my son to sleep on a bench. Please,' Ruth said.

Pop, pop, pop.

Gillian leaned in and said, with utmost sincerity, 'I told you that I would help. And that's what I plan to do. Try not to worry.'

Twenty minutes later, Gillian looked up from her computer screen and said, 'I've pulled some strings and found you a room in a hotel. It's a little bit away from DJ's school, which I know was a priority for you both location-wise, but it's all I have at the moment. Like I said earlier, it's been a hard year for many people,' Gillian said.

'Thank you. We will take it,' Ruth said, breathless with relief. She wanted to dance with joy. No park bench for them. They would be safe.

'I'll keep the pressure on for you, to try and get your house. You've been on the waiting list for a long time. Your turn has to come soon,' Gillian promised.

'What's the name of the hotel?' DJ asked.

'The Silver Sands Lodge. It's small. Really a guest-house or, as Erica, the owner, likes to say, a boutique hotel. We've housed a number of our families there over the past couple of years. I think you'll be comfortable. It's all booked with Erica, who is expecting you. You mentioned you have no car?'

'No. I sold our car a few years ago to pay for a deposit on the flat we've just been evicted from,' Ruth replied. She scribbled down Erica's name and hotel details into her notebook. Fairview. She did not know the area, but knew it was close to the city centre.

'Just as well maybe. The Silver Sands Lodge does not allow social housing residents to park in their car park,' Gillian said.

'That makes no sense. A car park is for cars.'

'It's small, so they prefer to keep the spaces there for their paying guests. You understand.'

Ruth did not understand, but thought she'd better keep quiet in case the room was taken from her as quickly as it had been offered.

Gillian turned to DJ, who was listening to their exchange with eyes wide. 'My priority is to get you that garden, DJ. I promise I'll do my best.'

DJ's face was alight with excitement. 'I've never stayed in a hotel before! This is going to be so cool. Our first holiday!'

Gillian looked at him, pity turning her kind face sad. She had visited too many families squashed into one hotel room, with little privacy and no comforts to make themselves a home. Gillian wished she had the power to stop that harsh reality sinking in for DJ. He wasn't much older than her own kids. Glancing at the photograph of her beaming family, snapped at home, she realised how lucky they were, to live the life they did. And when she got home, she would tell them so.

6

RUTH

Then

Ruth slipped a navy sleep mask over her eyes, smiling in satisfaction when her brother, Mark's, small kitchen disappeared into darkness. Armed with her bowl of chopped fruit, she moved eight steps to the small dining-room table, which sat at the edge of the open-plan kitchen and living room. She had considered eating standing up, against the sink. But the thought was fleeting. One, her lower back ached and she needed the welcome relief of sitting. Two, more importantly, the sink was not the correct place to eat.

Ruth liked to do the correct thing. Follow the rules.

'Sorry, little baby. Be patient,' she whispered.

A third kick under her ribcage made her jump and elicited a loud bellowing laugh. 'Not afraid to look for what you want, that's my fierce little one.' In delight, she rubbed her round tummy.

The baby responded by kicking her once again, its

target the top of her pelvis. She lowered the bowl onto the table, ignoring the stabbing pain, then sat down. The relief was immediate. She felt her body celebrating the respite from hauling around the additional weight she now carried on her slight frame.

Reward for her efforts was immediate when Ruth popped a large slice of mango into her mouth. The sweet, tangy juice spilled from the soft flesh in an explosion that set her taste buds alight. She laughed out loud again as her jubilant baby began a victory dance, its craving for bright-orange mango fruit quenched. 'If there is a sweeter taste, then I do not know it,' she whispered to an empty room. But her little one answered, with another sharp kick to her ribs.

'I will always do all in my power to give you what you want, little one,' Ruth whispered to her unborn child.

Not everyone is cut out to be a mother.

Ruth stuck her tongue out to the voice of her mother, which loved to peck, peck, peck at her. If she could fulfil the wishes of her baby, even now, before it was born, maybe her mother was wrong.

Then a monstrous thought crept up on her, threatening to ruin what had been a perfect moment. Irrational fears about consuming food that was not white began to fill her head. What if she turned her breast milk orange, from all the mango juice she had been relishing? What if the baby decided that it did not want to drink her milk or formula? What if the baby only wanted juice? The mango syrup changed from a vibrant orange to blood red and her head began to pound. What if . . . what if . . . what if . . . Ruth felt dizzy with the unanswered dangers that were hidden in the what ifs of her mind. A familiar flip of panic turned her stomach upside down and as it grew stronger, feeding on her fear, it snaked its way around her insides, exploring her body, poisoning her.

She pushed the bowl of fruit away from her and stood up, taking off her mask.

Why must you always be so difficult?

It was no use. Her mother may not be here, in this flat, but she lived in her head and would not leave her alone.

'*Do you think the starving children of Africa get to choose the colour of their food? Oh, for pity's sake, Ruth. You are trying my patience. Just EAT YOUR DINNER!*' Marian shouted to her ten-year-old daughter.

'*I am sorry, Mama, I am trying,*' Ruth whispered.

'*Yes you are. Very trying.*'

Now she reached for a napkin and threw it over the discarded fruit in disgust. Her baby thought about protesting, even gave a small kick but, in a moment of solidarity, quietened down.

Sweat trickled from her forehead, sliding down her cheek, disappearing under her chin. She wiped it away with the back of her hand, feeling contaminated and shamed. Always just below the surface, ready to jump up at a moment's notice, self-reproach returned. She *was* bad. She let people down. Shame, shame, shame.

Ruth lay her hands on her protruding tummy and felt love move between her and her baby. It was a tangible thing – an energy that was palpable. Had her mother ever felt that energy herself, when she carried Ruth in her tummy? Her memories said no. But maybe she remembered her childhood incorrectly. Was it possible that she had distorted her childhood into something ugly, something untrue? A confusion of dreams with reality. Maybe right now, her mother was in her childhood home, baking bread and smiling as she thought of her daughter and the grandchild that was soon to come to this world.

Sometimes Ruth thought her head would break into hundreds of pieces. Dangerous scenarios crashed around her skull. But even Ruth's vivid imagination could not have predicted how far her mother would go to take her baby from her.

7

RUTH

Now

Ruth and DJ stood side by side in front of the small hotel. Painted in a garish canary yellow, it stood at the end of a small complex of shops. Ruth noted there was a café, a chemist, a newsagent and what looked like a beauty salon included in the row.

She looked to her left and then to her right and saw rows of red-brick semi-detached houses. Their driveways were in the main empty, waiting for their owners to return home from their working day.

'Is *that* our hotel?' DJ asked, disappointment lacing his words. His dream of a fun holiday hotel, with a swimming pool, maybe even a Jacuzzi, faded with every mediocre angle of the building in front of them.

'Yes, it appears it is. The size would suggest that it is more a guesthouse than a hotel,' Ruth noted.

'The sign is crooked,' DJ said, pointing to the blue wooden sign that said, 'The Silver Sands Lodge'.

Ruth had noticed the lopsided sign the moment the taxi pulled up outside. If a ladder was in her eye line, she would have climbed up and straightened it. Instead she pointed to their surroundings.

'They have put us in a hotel that is falling apart,' Ruth said, looking at the fallen sign.

'I don't want to stay here!' DJ raised his voice with deliberation. He wanted to upset Ruth. He wanted to cause her pain. Maybe that would stop him feeling so bad. Maybe that would keep the tears away.

'We have no choice.'

'I want to find my dad,' DJ said, kicking the road with such ferocity that a haze of dust rose up to obscure him. He hoped this time the whole hotel collapsed in front of them.

'You choose now, in this moment, to say that,' Ruth said.

'I want to know where he is,' DJ repeated, knowing that his question was unfair. Knowing that Ruth could not answer him. But he was sick of being fair, of under-standing, of helping. He was sick of it all.

'I do not know where your father is. You know that,' Ruth said, taken aback by her son's outburst.

DJ ignored this statement and said, 'He might be able to help. If we can find him. I want to find him.'

Ruth thought about DJ's father. His large, round, earnest face only seconds away from laughter at any time. *If we kiss, that will be it*. That's what he'd said. They had kissed, they had done a lot more than kiss, but it turned out that it wasn't it, after all. Over the past ten years Ruth had gone over and over their last moments together. She believed him when he said he would be back. She had waited for him. She supposed she was still waiting.

'Come on, it is time to check in. We shall talk about this another time,' Ruth stated. She picked up her case and sack and began counting the steps to the front door.

One, two, three . . .

'You always say that,' DJ complained, but he followed her all the same.

. . . *nine, ten, eleven* . . .

This was wrong. There were twenty-eight from kerb to door at their old flat. Only eleven here. She took a step sideways. Twelve. Better, but not right.

DJ sighed, watching her.

A bell tinkled as they opened the double front door. Ruth wiped her feet and nudged DJ to do the same, trying to put the bothersome number twelve out of her head.

'It's dirtier than our shoes!' DJ said, nodding down towards the doormat that had years of mud ingrained into it.

A woman looked up from her computer screen with interest and studied them both up and down, taking in their suitcases and black sacks.

'Ruth and DJ Wilde?' She smiled as she spoke, but it was without any real warmth.

'Yes,' Ruth said. She noted the woman's name badge: 'Erica'. The owner.

'How did you know it was us?' DJ asked, impressed by the woman's correct assumption.

'My guests don't normally bring black sacks with them. Don't just stand there, you're making my entrance all cluttered up!' Erica said. Then she tutted, loudly, in case

45

they were in any doubt as to her distaste about their appearance.

Ruth and DJ moved in quickly without a word.

'Now, as it's your first day, I am making an allowance, letting you use our front entrance.' She smiled as she informed them of her generosity.

'I do not understand,' Ruth said.

'We have a side entrance reserved for our social housing residents,' Erica explained.

DJ and Ruth looked at each other, confused.

'That's rule number one,' Erica stated, 'but it's one I am most particular about.'

'Excuse me?' Ruth was still at a loss.

'The front entrance is for our normal guests,' the woman replied, her smile still in place, but her eyes narrowed.

Normal. That word again. How many times had Ruth heard people say that she was not 'normal', and here, once again, she had been labelled. There was no getting away from it.

'But we *are* guests, too,' Ruth stated.

'Of course you are. But you must also know that you are different to our paying guests. It was my Billy's idea to make an entrance just for you. It's just down the lane to the left of the hotel. You'll be far more comfortable using that.'

'I am quite comfortable using this entrance,' Ruth insisted.

'Are we going to have an issue here?' Erica's voice was sharp now. All pretence of a smile gone.

Ruth and DJ shook their heads in unison. The thought of a park bench put paid to Ruth's annoyance.

'We might be safer using the side entrance anyhow,'

Ruth said. 'Your sign looks like it is about to fall off. That is a health-and-safety issue.'

'That blasted sign!' Erica said with irritation. She beckoned them over to the front desk and turned a large red hardback book towards them. 'Our register must be signed every night to let us know that you are in the hotel. If you would please do so now . . .'

Signatures were listed beside room numbers, day after day until they blurred into one big hot mess.

Ruth's hand shook as she picked up the pen and added her autograph to the list of names. *Big Brother is watching us*.

'We've placed a laminated list of all the rules in your room. They have been drawn up by the council and ourselves to help make your stay as comfortable and safe as possible.' Erica's voice had taken on a singsong quality that Ruth suspected she reserved for new guests like them.

'Your curfew – that's rule number five, by the way – states that you must return to the hotel by 11 p.m.,' Erica continued.

'Why?' Ruth asked. She could not remember the last time she was out later than nine or ten, but that was not the point. To be dictated to like this felt intrusive.

'For the convenience of our guests. It's just better this way,' Erica sighed, her patience growing thin.

DJ moved closer to his mam. The adventure of hotel living was wearing off and they hadn't even seen their room yet.

'Now, to your right is our restaurant. Breakfast is included in your room rate and I think you'll be very happy with it. We have quite the reputation for our hot buffet. We do three types of eggs,' Erica boasted. 'Served between 7 a.m. and 9.30 a.m. We also have a bar, located next door to the restaurant. But residents are asked not to use these facilities after breakfast. The communal areas of the hotel are out of bounds, as they are reserved for our . . .'

Ruth cut in and finished her sentence, '. . . normal guests.'

Erica sensed trouble. 'I suggest you read all the rules when you get to your room and if you have any further questions you can direct them to your housing officer in Parkgate.'

Erica walked past a lift near the lobby down a long dark corridor, to a second smaller lift. She pointed to a sign for the car park and said, 'That's where you will enter and leave the hotel from now on.'

The difference between the double-fronted entrance and this emergency fire exit was stark.

'Are your normal guests allowed to use this entrance?' Ruth asked, and DJ sniggered into her back.

Erica chose to ignore her and said, 'Your room is on the first floor. All our social housing guests are there.'

They followed her into the small lift, dragging their luggage behind them. They each found a space in a different corner, the wait for the doors to close feeling like an eternity.

Ruth had never felt so claustrophobic in her life. Her hands were full so she couldn't even pop to alleviate the pressure. She kept losing count of her steps because Erica would not shut up. *Ninety-four. Yes. Ninety-four.*

Once they got to the first floor Erica pointed to her right. 'The communal kitchen is down there. It's small, but I think you'll find it has everything you need. Your room is at the other end of the corridor.'

Two kids, young boys that looked no more than four or five, came running around the corner onto the hallway at great speed. The looks on their faces as they slammed hard into Erica and Ruth were comical.

'Hey, you two, watch it. You know the rules,' Erica shouted at them both.

The two suitcases Ruth and DJ had been pulling along behind them fell to the floor with a thud.

'Oh, shit,' one of the boys said. DJ started to giggle, which made them both giggle even louder.

'Sorry, 'Rica. Sorry, missus. Don't go off on one,' the taller of the two boys said, panting from his run. He offered them both his biggest smile, all teeth and a wrinkled-up nose, then grabbed his brother's arm, pulling him out of the way so they could continue on theirs.

'You don't look one bit sorry, but you might be when I tell your mother about this!' Erica's words were lost on them. 'Just slow down, lads. It would be good if we could all get to the end of the day without someone ending up in A&E!'

'We will,' the boys shouted back.

'Oh, for goodness' sake!' Erica exclaimed, watching them take off again. She wiped a trickle of sweat that was making its way down the side of her face onto the back of her hand. 'The heat in this place. I must talk to my Billy about the air conditioning.'

'Carrying extra weight causes the body to work harder and could be at the root of your unwanted perspiration. It is only eight degrees outside after all,' Ruth said.

'I beg your pardon!' Erica exclaimed.

Ruth replied, 'I said, it is unlikely that the temperature outside is causing your perspiration issue.'

'I know what you said!' Erica said, then marched off down the corridor. DJ and Ruth picked up their cases and black sacks, then followed Erica's retreating back once more. They weren't heavy, but they were big and cumbersome. DJ's little hands were red from his efforts. Yet he never complained, not once all day. Ruth was so proud of her boy and grateful she had listened to him when he insisted he stay with her.

Her eyes drifted downwards to their preferred position and DJ's too-short jogger bottoms taunted her. Where was the nearest Penneys to here? One hundred steps already. Erica's black Skechers shuffled their way over the busy red-and-gold carpet that was underfoot. It was showing signs of years of wear and tear. *One hundred and nine.* Parts of it were shiny from the thousands of feet that had walked on it, the edges beginning to fray. Ruth felt her head buzz as a ringing sound bounced its way between her two ears. It was making her cases feel heavier than they actually were, slowing her down. For a large woman, Erica moved at great speed. Ruth tried to focus on the retreating back of Erica and not give in to her dizzy spell.

One hundred and thirteen. Erica stopped in front of a white door that had a gold number, top centre. 'Here we are. Room 129. Your new home. Had Parkgate called yesterday we would have had to turn you away. We'd a nice couple in this room until this morning. They fell on hard times and were a genuine case that needed help. Not like most of the wrong 'uns that we see in this place.'

'We're not wrong 'uns, Mam,' DJ said.

'No we are not,' Ruth replied, then turned to ask Erica, 'How long were that couple here for?'

'About six months, I'd say. Not that long,' Erica said.

Six months. Ruth felt DJ's eyes on her. She could not bear to look at him, to see the reproach and fear that she knew would be there.

Erica placed the key card in the slot and smiled with satisfaction when the light turned green. 'These can be buggers. The amount of times I've had to go back down to reception to reset the key. Don't put your card in the same pocket as your phone. That's my top tip. It wipes them, then makes them redundant.'

Ruth replied, 'That is correct. Anything with an electromagnetic field transmitting from it, such as a mobile telephone or TV can cause a mag stripe to demagnetise.'

Erica's mouth dropped open in surprise, making DJ laugh. *Go, Mam!*

'However, due to the frequency of the problem you are encountering, it is instead more likely to be caused by the faulty encoding equipment. I would suggest your machine in reception needs a service,' Ruth said, matter-of-factly.

Erica pushed the hotel-room door wide open and walked in, keeping her eyes on Ruth all the while. In realisation that her mouth was agape, she shut it quickly. 'Well, I never. I'll tell my Billy that. Maybe you've got something there. You're full of surprises, aren't you?'

DJ said, 'My mam knows a lot of stuff.'

Ruth remained silent. If she was that clever she would not be standing in the doorway of a small hotel bedroom that was the only roof over her and her son. It felt like she had just been issued a prison sentence. But for what crime? Living?

'Aw, that's nice that your boy is so proud of you,' Erica said.

DJ continued, 'She can add up numbers in her head, better than a calculator.'

A thought struck Ruth that would be funny if it was not so tragic. *The woman who is so good with numbers has now become one. A statistic. One of the many thousands homeless in Ireland.*

'Well, enough of our gabbing, go on in. Here you go, home sweet home,' Erica said.

They looked into the tiny room, which looked like it belonged in the 1980s. Magnolia walls, heavy red-and-cream checked curtains, with matching duvet covers and pillow shams on twin beds, and pine furniture. The woman was wrong. This wasn't home to Ruth. And it never would be.

8

TOM

Over the years Tom had moved around Dublin quite a bit but he kept finding his way back to Fairview Park. He liked its proximity to the sea. In fact, the twenty-hectare park was once part of the North Strand, reclaimed in the 1900s. During the day, he would sit on his park bench and listen to the sounds of the children playing in the distant playground. Their laughter and squeals of delight as they spun faster on a roundabout, or climbed one rung higher on the rope ladder, lifted his spirits. Bette Davis, his dog, his friend, liked to watch the kids do tricks in the skateboard park. They'd stop for a while and watch in awe. No fear, those kids. They would fly through the air, from ramp to ramp. Sometimes, in the amongst the noise of children having fun, he could hear Mikey.

His knee was aching again. He knew that one day soon he would have to get it looked at. His guess, which he reckoned was fairly accurate, was that the cartilage was gone. He'd walked more miles than he could even begin to hazard a guess over the past ten years. And it had caught up on him.

Sleeping rough in the cold winters doesn't help either. He liked to ignore that voice in his head. It irked him because it spoke a lot of sense. And he wasn't interested in sense. He liked his life the way it was, just fine. Out here. It was his choice.

He'd slept on the same bench every night since he took up residence in this park. And the Fairview Park regulars agreed that it was unofficially his. Lash and Bones, fellow rough sleepers, slept in the park most nights. And while they weren't friends, it was nice sometimes to pass the time of day with them. Bones loved telling stories about Fairview's most famous resident, Bram Stoker. The coastline beyond the park was eerie at night and it was easy to imagine, when the fog came down, how it had played a part in inspiring Stoker's stories.

Tom sat down on his bench and Bette Davis fell asleep at his feet almost instantly. His sandwich was limp and uninspiring. But he wasn't complaining. He'd had it in his rucksack since last night, when the volunteers from the Peter McVerry Trust did their rounds handing out food and hot drinks. He sat back, feeling every day of his sixty-one years. Bette had the right idea. Time for a nap. *I'm coming, Cathy.* He closed his eyes and remembered back to that first evening his wife and he had spent together . . .

Cathy rented a one-bedroom apartment that turned out to be only a mile or so away from Tom's place. How had he lived so close to such an incredible woman and never seen her before?

He felt big and awkward in her small kitchen, bumping into her as he tried to help unload the groceries, on that first night they met. She told him to sit. He watched her fry their steaks and chop tomatoes for their salad, her every movement a symphony. Her grace bewitched him.

He wanted to know everything about her life. He couldn't get the questions out quickly enough. She was from Donegal, one of three children, and a carer for adults with disabilities.

'Tell me about your work. What's an average day like?' Tom asked.

'We offer supportive services to help meet the needs of adults with disabilities.'

Tom looked at the tiny woman in wonder. He'd known her only a few hours yet she had surprised him several times in that short time. He couldn't lie, it was a physical attraction at first. But the more she shared about herself, the more he found himself struck by her beauty, not just on the outside.

'We're there for help with both the physical and emotional wellbeing of our attendees and their families too. Parents and carers get a break, and the adults themselves keep some independence when they come in to us. In the main they return home each evening, relaxed. That's crucial.'

'I have a patient who is a full-time carer for her son. When I ask who looks after her, she just shrugs. I can't get her to recognise the importance of having some time off, taking care of her own needs,' Tom said.

'There's huge guilt for most carers. All self-imposed, but real none the less. You should tell your patient about

our programme. We might be able to help. You can change the world by helping one person at a time. That's what we try to do at the centre. One at a time,' Cathy said.

Tom felt a lump in his throat, catching him unawares. Her words moved him profoundly. He would never forget that statement. Ever.

His appetite disappeared and it seemed hers did, too.

'Maybe I should have bought tofu,' Cathy joked, pointing to Tom's uneaten steak.

'I'm sorry. It's delicious,' Tom said, quickly spearing a piece to prove the point.

She reached over and her fingers brushed his and they both felt another jolt. 'There's no need.'

Their eyes locked. Time stood still. Cathy put her glass down, the crystal tinkling as it hit the glass top table. The sound bounced around the kitchen and his eyes could not leave hers. They moved to her bedroom and they made love. He could not call it anything but that. It was tender, every touch a promise.

'I didn't expect this,' Cathy said afterwards, when they lay in each other's arms.

'Breda, my receptionist, is forever saying that I am one of Ireland's most eligible bachelors. Sure you couldn't resist,' Tom teased.

'She's right. A good-looking man and a doctor. At least in the top one hundred,' Cathy joked back.

'Thank you, young lady.' Tom pretended to tip his cap to her.

'I bet patients fall in love with you all the time.' She started to laugh when she saw him blush. 'I knew it! Spill!'

'Well, there was this woman last year who kept making appointments, saying she was unwell. Breda used to tease me that she had a crush on me. But I thought that was preposterous. Then one day, she came in with a bad chest infection.'

'Oy oy! That old chestnut!' Cathy laughed.

'I remember thinking she was looking very well for someone who needed a doctor. Then before I had a chance to so much as take her temperature, she had her blouse unbuttoned.'

'Her blouse,' Cathy snorted in response. 'How old was she?'

'About thirty, why?'

'No one wears a blouse under the age of fifty!'

'Well, she opened her . . .'

'Her top, just say top,' Cathy advised.

'She opened her top and had on this red lacy thing that left nothing to the imagination!'

'Oh my goodness, I am scarlet for her! What did you do? Actually, scratch that question. I'm not sure I want to know.'

'I jumped up and called Breda in. I told the woman that I had to have Breda in with me for any consultation that involved chest investigations.'

'Ah, the poor woman.'

'Poor woman my hat. Funnily enough, she stopped coming shortly after that.'

'I bet she did!' Cathy laughed again. 'Go on, tell me more. How many hearts have you broken . . .?'

'I'm afraid that's it, really. I did meet one of my patients out in a bar last year. She was pretty drunk and she made *a bit of a clumsy pass at me. I made a joke about being resolute to stay single. Then I ran home!'*

'Are you resolute to stay single?' Cathy asked, leaning into him.

'I've always been open to meeting Miss Right. She was just tricky to locate. No matter how many women I dated – all lovely, or at least most – I never felt "it".'

He looked at her silhouetted against the fading evening light. And realised something. She was it.

'So, what is "it" for you?' Cathy asked.

'"It" is that undeniable, unfathomable, unmistakable feeling of knowing that what you have is something special. I think "it" is you.' He finished on a whisper.

'Oh. That "it",' Cathy said, and they beamed at each other for the longest time.

The next evening, they moved to his flat above the surgery for a change of scenery. 'It's double the size of mine!' Cathy said, walking from room to room.

'I've the top half of the house. Downstairs is the surgery . . .'

'Do you mind living above work?' Cathy asked.

'The commute is hard to beat.'

'Are these your parents?' She picked up a photograph of Tom in his graduation cap and gown, standing in between a couple who were bursting with pride.

'Yeah. It was a good day. First in our family to graduate.'

'Do you see much of them?' Cathy asked.

'They died last year, within a month of each other,' Tom admitted sadly.

'I'm so sorry,' Cathy said, wishing she'd known him

then to help him through the pain, which still lingered on his face.

'My parents were obsessed with the idea of me settling down. They spoke about this subject often and at great length. They hung around until their eightieth and eighty-second birthdays respectively, before dying within weeks of each other.'

'A proper love story.' Cathy felt tears in her eyes.

And Tom and Cathy looked at each other and both silently wished for the same thing. A lifetime together, just like Tom's parents had.

For a split second, when Tom woke up, he forgot. He reached across the cold pavement for Cathy. But she hadn't been by his side for a long time. He gently stroked Bette Davis and wished for the one millionth time in his life that he could wake up and find happiness in the now, not just in the then of his dreams.

9

RUTH

As they walked into their hotel room another dizzy spell hit Ruth and she clutched the door frame.

'Are you OK?' Erica asked, frowning as she spoke. 'You don't look very well. You're not going to get sick on the carpet, are you? You'll have to clean it up yourself if you do. Housekeeping are gone for the day. You'll see that in the rule book. Rule number nineteen.'

Ruth shook her head in an effort to reassure Erica that she was not about to contaminate her room. She was not sure that she could trust herself to speak, to say the words out loud that she was OK.

'Mam?' DJ saw the colour drain from her face.

'I am fine,' Ruth lied. She just wanted to give in to panic, fall into the darkness.

Erica looked dubious but she was a woman on a mission. She had a tour to give and she was going to deliver it. 'This door to your left, that's your en-suite bathroom.'

Ruth and DJ looked into the small room, which had

a shower, bath, toilet and sink. 'It's dirty,' Ruth said with dismay. The room was clad in white tiles, with greying grout that looked like it had not been cleaned in years.

'It most certainly is not. I pride myself on the cleanliness of this hotel,' Erica said, smarting at the insult.

'Awkward,' DJ said, not bothering to hide a snigger.

'You can bring your luggage in here.' Erica swung her arm around, like she was a hostess on the QVC shopping channel showcasing a roomful of beautiful baubles and silk scarves.

DJ and Ruth both sucked in their breaths as they took in the scale of the room that was to become their home – their bathroom, living room and bedroom. Where would DJ do his homework? Perhaps she could move the lamp and small radio alarm clock off the locker.

'Are we supposed to take turns sitting on that?' Ruth asked, pointing to a single armchair that sat alone under the large bedroom window. Ruth blinked when the curtains morphed into bars. Their room became a prison cell. *Your imagination working overtime, that's all,* Odd whispered. She blinked again and the sad grey curtains were back.

Erica pursed her lips together. Opposite the two beds was a long vanity table with drawers, on which sat the TV and a phone.

It's all wrong. Everything is in the wrong place.

Ruth pulled at her hands.

Pop, pop, pop . . .

'We have all the channels. Not that I look at much regular TV any more. It's all Netflix and chill for me!' Erica said, laughing at her own joke.

DJ started to flick through the channels before Erica had finished speaking.

Ruth counted the steps to take her from her bed to the bathroom. *Six. Wrong, wrong, wrong. It should be fourteen steps.* For four years, it had been fourteen steps.

'Your accent, I can't quite place it. It's not a Dublin one, anyhow,' Erica stated. She stared at Ruth, taking in her short hair, cut like a boy's, which she wasn't sure she cared for. Her face was white as a sheet, without a scrap of makeup on. And she had two piercings in each ear. She'd put money on the girl having tattoos. She had that look about her. She was what her Billy would call 'alternative'.

'I'm from Wexford originally. But Dublin has been my home for ten years,' Ruth answered.

'Oh, a beautiful part of the world. But as I often say to my Billy, half of Wexford is living in Dublin and half of Dublin are down in Wexford. Funny old world we live in, all topsy-turvy,' Erica commented.

Ruth picked up one of her suitcases and placed it on one of the beds. She had placed some cleaning products in this case and wanted to start scrubbing the bathroom.

'The rules of the hotel are listed on this.' Erica pointed to an A4 laminated sheet. 'There's nothing too major, but if we didn't have them, chaos would ensue. And if you have a problem with any of them, take it up with the council, not me. My Billy says I'm too good-natured.'

'Mam?' DJ whispered loudly.

Ruth turned her back on the woman and faced her son. 'Yes?'

'Where's my bedroom?' he asked.

Ruth said, 'We will be sharing this room.'

Erica tutted loudly, so that they both heard her. 'I don't know. The phrase "beggars can't be choosers" springs to mind. You're luckier than most. You could have been given a sleeping bag and left to your own devices outside.'

DJ looked mortified. Ruth held the laminate up in front of her. 'My son was simply asking a reasonable question. And from a cursory glance at this laminated sheet of paper, refraining from asking questions is not listed as one of your rules.'

Before Erica had a chance to splutter a response, Ruth added, 'For the record, you will never know how grateful this "beggar" is for a hotel room.'

Erica's face softened at those last words. 'Maybe my choice of words was a bit harsh. There's no point looking back. That much I've learned over the years. Your old home is gone. This is your home for the foreseeable. Make the most of it.'

Ruth re-counted her steps to the bathroom. Still six.

She felt another wave of dizziness overcome her. *One, two, three, four.* She sat down on the nearest bed before her legs gave way.

'Are you always that pale? You're like one of those goths,' Erica said, looking at her closely. 'I hope you're not coming down with something. Keep out of the communal areas if you've a bug. I don't want any viruses going around the hotel, thank you very much! All I need is another bad TripAdvisor review . . .'

She took a step backwards and covered her mouth, as if Ruth's germs were about to march their way towards her right that minute.

'I am not sick. I am tired.' Sleep had not played much of a role in the last nightmarish forty-eight hours. Could Erica take this room away from them, if she suspected Ruth was carrying a virus? She felt panic join into the myriad of emotions that were running around her body.

Please leave. Just let me lie down on the bed and close my eyes for five minutes. Please.

Erica groaned, ignoring Ruth's silent pleas, then sat down on one of the single beds, making it bounce as her body hit it. 'I'm shattered myself. And while I don't know your story, you seem like a nice family and I wouldn't wish this situation on anyone. I've said to my Billy, over and over again, we should count our blessings. We own this beautiful hotel. Boutique, I like to say. And we have our own mews out the back. It has three bedrooms. With a lovely garden back and front. And we have our mortgage paid for over five years now. Yes, we really should count our blessings.'

DJ pretended to put a gun to his head behind her back.

'. . . there but for the grace of God go I . . .' Erica's voice continued to drone on.

'I do not believe in God,' Ruth said, moving towards the door.

'An atheist? I thought you had the look of one of those all right,' Erica said.

. . . *five, six* . . . Ruth had reached the end of her patience and could take no more, so she opened the door to their room and said, 'Goodbye.'

'Well, I do beg your pardon,' Erica sniffed, before heaving herself up from the bed with a wobble and a creak of her knee.

Human beings can always be relied upon to exert, with vigor, their God-given right to be stupid, Odd Thomas whispered as Ruth slammed the door shut behind Erica.

Never a truer word, Odd.

Every nerve in Ruth's body felt frayed, exposed and tender. With a frenzy, she began to empty the contents of her two suitcases and the black sacks onto the bed. She doubled things up on hangers but still was unable to fit everything into the wardrobe. She hung their coats on the back of the one chair they had, looking around, trying to work out how she could turn this room into a home.

Who was she kidding? This would never be a home for them. It looked exactly like what it was: a small hotel room, crammed full of nothing. How had they come to this?

She grabbed her bleach spray and began to scrub the sink in the bathroom, frantically trying to remove years of inbuilt grime and dirt. And she felt herself sink into a vat of sadness and anxiety. Every bone in her body ached. Her eyes felt heavy. If she could just sleep. But then the sound of a drill on the street below filled their room. She checked the windows to make sure they were closed. But the noise kept coming. The lighting in their room was too bright and hurt her eyes, so she pulled the grey curtains tight.

'Mam?' DJ asked, hovering close to her. Like a car with no brakes, his mam was going to crash. He had to be ready to rescue her.

One, two, three . . .

Her bed was in the wrong position. It should be facing the other way. But she had no more energy.

Pop, pop, pop.

DJ watched her hit the wall, head on. Ruth's anxiety spilled over until her body shook in response.

Ruth felt her arms and legs go heavy, her head buzzed until the pain became unbearable and she fell into a ball on the bed. She could feel DJ's eyes on her, watching her, as he always did.

DJ's voice whispered in her ear, 'It's going to be OK, Mam. Go to sleep and it will all be better when you wake up.' He had been only three years old the first time he helped to calm Ruth down. He didn't understand why his mama had got so upset when they were shopping and the fire alarm went off. He thought it was really cool when the big fire engine came. But he did understand that she was scared. And he loved her so very much, he would do anything to take away her fear. He knew she liked listening to her music through her headphones, so he gently placed them on her head and said, 'DJ make Mama better. There, there, Mama.' He wrapped his arms around her and snuggled into her back. She was warm and soft. He loved snuggling with his mama.

Ruth closed her eyes as she felt her son's soft hands gently place her headphones on her head, as he had done hundreds of times before. And while she could not thank DJ at this moment, she was grateful more than he would ever know. For now, she let the music take her to her safe place, away from the pain, away from the chaos, away from here.

10

RUTH

Ruth woke up feeling disorientated. She heard muffled sounds coming from either side of their room. For a moment, she forgot where she was. She blinked her eyes twice to get used to the darkness and make out her surroundings.

She was in The Silver Sands Lodge.

'DJ?' she called out to the darkness. Silence.

Once her mind had again caught up to her new normal, Ruth reached over to locate the light switch. Bright lights filled the room, eliminating the darkness. She looked at her watch. It was nearly 4 p.m. She had been asleep for over three hours. She could not remember the last time she had slept during the day. She was not a good sleeper at the best of times but she supposed this was new territory.

While she slept, DJ had made efforts to make their room look more like home. He had placed her favourite soft green chenille throw over her. At the end of the bed was her green velvet cushion. DJ had also placed his

Liverpool FC throw and cushion on the bed beside hers. *Oh, DJ.* She was wrong earlier. This room could be their home. Because home was wherever DJ was.

She needed to see him, to tell him that. She picked up her phone, knowing he would have sent her a text message, letting her know where he was.

Going out to explore. Back soon, DJ.

Where are you?

Her stomach reminded her that she had not eaten since breakfast. It appeared she had lost her appetite around the same time she lost her home. Her jeans felt looser this morning when she slipped them on. She could not afford to get ill. She had to be strong in mind and in body if she was going to get them both through this.

Back in five, DJ pinged back to her. She would have to talk to him about taking off like that. He was streetwise, but he did not know this part of Dublin.

He would be hungry, too. She scanned through the list of rules on the laminate sheet until she got to the one regarding the kitchen.

There is a small kitchen at the end of the second floor, beside the fire exit, available for use for all residents, who are part of the emergency housing scheme. The kitchen consists of a small fridge, a cooker, oven, toaster and microwave. All cups, plates and utencils must be washed up after use and kitchen MUST be cleaned after use.

Please note that no microwaves, toasters or hobs are allowed in your hotel room or bathroom.

Ruth walked over to her handbag and took out a Sharpie, then circled the word 'Utensils'. *If you are going to the trouble of laminating rules, at least make sure they are correctly spelled! And who on earth would put an electrical item in a bathroom?* Sometimes the stupidity of people amazed Ruth. She hoped the kitchen was clean. Not having her own kitchen was going to cause her a lot of problems and was perhaps the hardest challenge she would have to face.

While she waited for DJ to return she scanned the other rules once again.

No running in the hallway.
No guests in your room.
A communal room is available on the ground floor. Guests ask reception for the key.
No hanging laundry on the balcony.
No smoking in the room.
No hanging of pictures on the walls.
Parents must look after their own children. No babysitting of other guests' children allowed in hotel.

A thump in the corridor outside made her jump. She got off the bed and walked to the door, peeping out the small glass hole.

'Hey, Jason, hey, Barry,' DJ said, high-fiving the two boys from earlier, who were still running up and down the hall.

Ruth marvelled at how quickly he had made friends in the space of a few hours.

'Where have you been?' Ruth asked, when he walked into their hotel room.

'Nowhere,' he answered, flopping down onto his bed.

'Well, that's impossible. You must have been somewhere,' Ruth said.

'Exploring,' he mumbled. 'You OK again?'

'Yes. Thank you.' Ruth looked at her son and tried to gauge how he was doing. She was not good at reading people's emotions. 'Are you OK?'

He shrugged.

'Does that mean you are OK?' Ruth asked.

'I'm OK. But hungry. Can I watch TV?'

'I will go to the shop, buy some groceries and make us something to eat,' Ruth said.

'What are we eating, and please don't say mashed potatoes?' DJ said.

'Depends what choice there is in the shop down the road. But noted on the potatoes.'

DJ turned back to the football match that had just started. As Ruth reached the door, he called out, 'Just remember to say hello if anyone speaks to you. And take the sunglasses off when you are inside. You're not one of the Kardashians.'

'I could think of nothing worse. No potatoes. Speak. Sunglasses. Got it,' Ruth replied, with more confidence than she felt. She threw the sunglasses onto the bed to avoid temptation.

It was her brother, Mark, who gave Ruth her first pair of sunglasses when they were kids. Her classmates had begun to call her a weirdo. Mark did not like other kids making fun of her. Not because he was worried about Ruth, but because he was worried about how it would reflect on him.

*   *   *

'People think you are being shifty, hiding something, if you don't look at them. And then they think that you don't like them,' Mark explained.

'I am not hiding anything,' Ruth said. 'And I like them all. Except for Mary Lawlor and Tadgh D'arcy, who laugh at me a lot.'

'Just try eye-balling them when you are in conversation with them. Look at them for five seconds, then you can be all weird and look at the ground again.'

'But I do not like eyeballs,' Ruth said.

'Don't look at their eyes then. Jeez, Ruth, help a guy out here! Cheat. Look in that general direction. It will be grand,' Mark said.

'I can do that. I will try it,' Ruth said.

And try it she did. It went spectacularly wrong. When Mary Lawlor asked her for help with page 190 of their maths homework, it was the perfect opportunity to try out her new skill. People often asked her for help at maths and she was happy to do so. She liked solving problems. Ruth looked up at Mary, who was a few inches taller than she. She lowered her gaze to avoid eye contact and hoped for the best.

'You big fat lesbian!' Mary Lawlor screamed. 'Did you see that? Ruth Wilde is looking at my breasts!' She covered her chest with her arms, delighted to see that she held the class's attention.

Ruth did not know what a lesbian was. She suspected it was not said as a compliment.

Mark was not happy when they walked home together after school. 'How on earth did you manage to make them all think you were a lesbian in the space of

73

only a few hours? I can't leave you on your own at all, can I?'

'What's a lesbian?' Ruth asked.

'Ask Mam,' Mark replied, making a face.

So when she walked into their kitchen, she asked Marian, 'Mary Lawlor said I was a lesbian. Am I a lesbian?'

Marian's face told Ruth that she'd done something wrong again. 'In the name of all that's good in this world, what is wrong with you, child? Are you trying to kill me? That's all I need on top of everything else.' Then Marian sighed again.

And that was why Mark bought Ruth a pair of sunglasses. That was the thing about her brother. He spent most of their childhood ignoring her or making fun of her. But every now and then he surprised her with a random act of kindness.

Twenty minutes later, armed with a small bagful of groceries, she made her way to the kitchen for the first time. She crossed her fingers that it would be empty. Her hopes disappeared when muffled sounds of fellow residents creeped out into the corridor as she approached. She braced herself for interactions and hoped that the people in the room were friendly. She reminded herself that she was actually a good communicator. She could enjoy a conversation for an hour or two at a time. Unless it was boring, of course.

A sign on the door stated:

Please avoid prime times in the kitchen:
8–9 a.m., 1–2 p.m. and 5–7 p.m.

As it was now four o'clock she hoped that meant it was a good time to make their dinner. A man and a young boy were sitting down at the kitchen table, tucking into fish and chips. A woman stood at the hob literally watching water boil in a pan. Then another woman stepped out from behind the door and said, 'Don't get any ideas about skipping the queue. I've been waiting nearly ten minutes already.'

Ruth shook her head quickly and took two steps away, until her back hit the wall.

'Leave her alone. She's the new one I was telling you about,' the man said. 'I saw you arriving earlier. I'm Kian. This handsome young fella with me is Cormac, my heir apparent.'

Ruth nodded in his direction. She did not recollect seeing him in the lobby earlier. She was pretty certain it was empty. She would learn that Kian was like a silent ninja. A pro at hiding in places he was not meant to be.

Kian continued, 'One fridge, one cooker, one microwave, ten families and five hundred bleeding rules about how you can use them all. Welcome to the kitchen.'

This made the woman beside Ruth laugh, but hob woman replied in a tone that was decidedly frosty, 'Rules that some in this establishment don't seem capable of following. I'm Ava, in room 124. That's Aisling hovering to your right.'

Say hello, remember to say hello.

Kian saved her by continuing his rant. 'Bleeding bureaucratic bullshit. There's more rules on the lists in The Silver Sands Lodge than in a bleeding jail. What gets my blood boiling is that they don't make sense at all. I mean, take

75

a look at the notice on the door. The so-called rush hours to be avoided create rush hours in the quiet times. Do you get me?'

His little boy, who looked no more than eight or nine, started to laugh, delighted with his dad's rant.

'Ignore our resident ray of sunshine,' Ava said. She threw a look of disdain in his direction. He happily threw an equally disdainful one back at her, then scoffed the last of his chips.

'They need to add a new rule to the laminate. No stealing food. That way I wouldn't have to be here. Cooking again,' Ava said loudly.

Kian pretended to play the violin behind her back, making Cormac snort with laughter. Aisling looked uncomfortable with the conversation between them both.

'When Brian hears that someone has stolen our food again, he's going to lose his shit. There should be cameras in here to catch the thieving bastards,' Ava said. 'I wouldn't mind but I used extra-lean mince in that lasagne. It was bloody lovely.'

Aisling turned to Ruth and said, 'I wish I could say it's not like this every day. But . . .'

Ruth felt like she had stepped into an episode of a bad daytime soap. And she did not like it one bit.

Aisling continued, 'I'm sorry if I sounded snappy when you walked in. It's just I've left my daughter, Anna, on her own. We're in room 127 down the other end of the corridor. Her asthma has been playing up this week and I don't like leaving her.'

Ruth could not imagine what that must be like, dealing with a sick child on top of everything else. She felt Aisling's eyes on her, waiting for a response. She looked up and quickly scanned the room. *Damn it.* They were all staring at her. She had forgotten DJ's advice.

'Hello hello hello hello,' Ruth burst out in one breathless sentence to each of them, one by one. She looked down at the floor again and hoped they would stop talking to her.

'Hello, hello, hello, hello to you, too,' Kian said. The room swelled with merriment and Ruth felt her skin prickle with heat.

She was messing this up, like she always did.

But to her surprise Aisling moved a little closer to her and said with warmth, 'I won't be long. I'm only frying up a few sausages for Anna. Her favourite, and you'd give them the world when they're sick, wouldn't you?'

Ruth nodded to Aisling's pretty pink pumps. She had small feet, dainty. Which looked at odds with her large frame.

'Here, Aisling, I've finished with the second hob. You can cook beside me.' Ava shuffled over to make room for the woman. Aisling pulled a frying pan out of the cupboard beside the cooker and stuck it on the heat. She sprayed the pan with Frylight, coating the base. The sausages sizzled and spat as soon as they hit the pan. The smell made Ruth nauseous and reminded her of Saturday mornings when her mother cooked the full Irish fry-up for them when all she wanted was porridge.

Ruth was two seconds away from breaking rule number six and running out of the kitchen and down the corridor back to their room. They could eat rice cakes for their supper, with bananas on top. She felt the eyes of the kitchen on her. She wished she had left her sunglasses on, ignoring DJ's advice. She could not win. You got looks from people if you wore sunglasses indoors; you got looks from people if you preferred to keep your eyes to yourself. People were tricky. People passed judgement all the time.

People are fierce judgemental. To hell with people, that's what I say.

Ha! You're funny, Odd.

I've been told that once or twice before.

Me too . . .

Kian and his son, Cormac, stood up, the sound of their chairs scraping the floor bringing Ruth back from her chat with her imaginary friend.

'Will I do the dishes, Da?' Cormac asked.

'Do, son,' Kian replied, then they both sniggered some more when Cormac threw their paper plates into the bin.

'A regular double act, those two,' Ava sniffed, keeping her back to them. 'I queued for an hour yesterday to use this oven. And the large lasagne I made was supposed to last for two days' dinner.'

'Did someone take it off yer?' Kian asked, his face a picture of innocence.

Ava ignored him and said to the others, 'It's not good enough. I'll be sending an email of complaint to the council and Erica when I get back to my room. Some people have a bare-faced cheek.' She thumbed towards Kian, who whistled as he walked out of the room, his sidekick right behind him.

'Did you see the cut of them both? The fecking bastard!

I know it was him,' Ava spluttered out. 'We're eating in our room tonight. And so help me, if there is any leftovers, it's going in the bin.'

'They looked a bit shifty all right,' Aisling reluctantly agreed. 'I've seen Cormac running in and out of here a lot, checking to see if the kitchen is empty. I gave up leaving yoghurts in the fridge months ago. Always swiped. He's a divil for those.'

Ava nudged Aisling as she turned the sausages over, nodding towards Ruth. 'You don't say much.'

'Hello,' Ruth said again. They continued to stare at her, so she added, 'I am not here to steal anyone's food or to skip any queues.'

Aisling and Ava laughed in response and Ruth breathed a sigh of relief.

'My son and I arrived at 12.07 p.m. today,' Ruth answered. 'It has been quite the day.'

Aisling reached out to touch Ruth's arm in a gesture of support, causing Ruth to jump back and knock one of the chairs onto the floor.

'Sorry,' Aisling murmured. The room went quiet, except for the sound of water as it reached boiling point and the splash of pasta as Ava threw it into the water with a slosh. Steam filled the air around her. 'It's fresh, not dried, so I'll be done in a jiffy.'

'Fresh pasta is 3.45 times more expensive than dried,' Ruth stated.

'Well, I like fresh. And for the sake of a few cent . . .' Ava said.

'Assuming you eat fresh pasta twice a week, then your saving per meal for two people, is 0.94 euro. Over a year that will be just under 98 euro,' Ruth replied, eyes still on the ground.

Ava and Aisling looked at each other, then back to Ruth again, a little startled by her quick maths.

'Wouldn't it be nice if, for once, we didn't have to be thinking about things like the cost of every little thing we need to buy?' Aisling said. 'I spent a day yesterday trudging around Penney's, Heaton's and Tesco, comparing prices on a tracksuit for Anna. And everywhere I looked I saw all these cute outfits in, ready for Christmas. I'd have given anything to buy her a whole new wardrobe.'

'Anna always looks beautiful,' Ava said with kindness.

'Hand-me-downs. Thank God for my friend. She sends down a bag of clothes every six months or so. It's like Christmas for Anna.' Tears threatened to spill from Aisling's brown eyes as she flipped her sausages again. 'Just once, I'd like her to have her own outfit. Brand new with labels. Chosen just for her.'

Ava squeezed Aisling's arm in sympathy.

Ruth wanted to say to them both that she knew what it was like to juggle her finances so that she did not have 'too much month at the end of her money'. She wanted to tell Aisling that she needed to do a similar exercise to find DJ new tracksuit bottoms and trainers. But the words were getting jumbled in her head again, the way they did. She was making a terrible first impression but she felt powerless to change it. They would see her continued silence as an insult and she did not want them to think she was rude.

Tell them you are shy. Be honest. People always respond well to honesty. This advice was given to her over a decade ago by her doctor and it often popped into her head. Funny how some words stick while others disappear into nothing. Maybe it was time to take this advice.

'I am shy, not rude,' Ruth blurted out.

'Ah, I've a younger sister like that,' Ava said, nodding in understanding. 'Crippled with shyness, has been ever since she was born. She spent most of her childhood hidden behind Mam's skirts!'

'And there I was, thinking the cat had your tongue! I'm sure it's been a tough day for you,' Aisling said, smiling.

'I never thought I would end up in a place like this. In this situation,' Ruth said.

They both understood that.

'Hotels are meant to be about leisure, rest, holidays. But this is hell on earth,' Ava said, her eyes filled with tears.

'Maybe this will be your month to get a house,' Aisling added, patting her hand.

'We said that last month and the month before, too. When we moved into this hotel, we thought it would be temporary. Couple of weeks, max. Six months later it's getting harder to be upbeat,' Ava replied. She pulled the pot of pasta off the stove and drained it over the sink. 'I don't think my husband, Brian, can cope much longer.'

'It will be your turn soon, you wait and see,' Aisling said.

'That is most unlikely. Twenty per cent of those on the housing list will remain on it for five years,' Ruth interjected in an effort to join in.

Ava and Aisling both turned towards her, Ava in distress, Aisling in irritation.

'Read the room!' Aisling said. She made a face, nodding her head towards a tearful Ava.

Ruth looked at the floor, wishing she was an Aisling, someone who knew automatically what to say, how to make Ava feel better. Why did she always find her voice just in time to say the wrong thing?

You have really gone and done it this time.

You ruined all our lives when you were born, and this pregnancy will be the final nail in my coffin!

Ruth would block out her cruel taunts by looking at a slip of paper with a fortune printed on it. A memento from her lost weekend with her soul mate. He had loved her. He would be back. Her old friend Odd whispered to her that she must always hope and persevere. But nevertheless, conclusions had to be made.

Dean was not coming back to rescue her.

She was having this baby on her own.

She needed to do as Mark had said and get the fuck out. Not just for her sake. But for the sake of her unborn child.

She moved from the village where she grew up and hitched a lift to Wexford town. Fate was on her side, because Pat from the arcade in Curracloe pulled up beside her in his beaten-up Jeep. Ruth did not have any friends, but she had gotten to know Pat over the many summers she had spent on Curracloe beach, buying ice cream from him in the arcade. He did not waste her time offering raspberry or chocolate syrup, as he did with the other kids. Or sprinkles or hundreds and thousands. He took the time to know she liked hers plain, in a tub, not on a cone. That was her way.

And Pat liked Ruth. She was a good kid once you took the time to get to know her. Not like her older brother, Mark, the little prick. He was forever in the arcade kicking the machines, trying to get them to cough out money. Trouble. Always looking for trouble. And he watched other kids pick on Ruth, letting them call her names. That's no way to be about family. Pat had had to step in once or twice.

As Ruth climbed into his jeep, Pat realised that she wasn't a kid any more. Short cropped hair, not a scrap of makeup on, wearing oversized dark sunglasses. He didn't think he'd ever seen her without them. They'd been too big for her for many years, like she was playing dress-up with her mama's things. But now they suited her perfectly.

'Where you off to?' he asked.

'I am pregnant. I have to leave home.'

And Pat felt heart sorry hearing this. He remembered all the times Ruth had put coins into the fortune-telling machine in the arcade. He wasn't sure what she hoped would come spitting out of it. But if Pat could rig it so that it gave her whatever it was her heart desired, he'd do it. He told her he would take her anywhere she wanted to go.

'I am going to Mark's in Wexford.'

Pat was pretty sure that Ruth was jumping from the frying pan into the fire, but he held his counsel. Before she said goodbye he pressed a fifty-euro note into her hand. 'Come back sometime with the baby to see me. Always an ice cream for you and the little one in my arcade. OK?'

She nodded but she had a feeling that she would not be licking ice creams in the arcade any time soon. She made her way to Mark's flat, which was at the end of Wexford Quay, opposite the railway tracks. She had been there just once before, when he first moved in and had asked her and their mum around. But he had never asked her to visit since and she was not sure how he would react now.

His response – 'Oh, for fuck's sake!' – when he answered the door was problematic. She stepped inside, taking it as a good sign that he had not told her to go away.

'I have left home,' Ruth said to his Nike trainers. They were new and brilliant white. He usually wore Adidas.

'Good for you. Didn't think you had it in you,' Mark replied.

In the end, he let her stay. He did not have much choice, she supposed. She loved Wexford town. A place that was big enough that she could get lost in it, where she could go days without meeting anyone who knew her or thought she was strange. She liked that. She liked that a lot. His flat, without the oppressive disapproval of her mother, was a welcome relief.

For the first time in her young life, Ruth felt like she was in control. And it was a feeling that she very much approved of.

12

TOM

Now

Bette Davis growled at the two kids who stopped to snigger at the sleeping Tom, who lay on his park bench, in his sleeping bag.

'Bum!' they jeered, until Bette growled a little louder and they ran away laughing. The dog moved closer to her best friend, keeping guard while Tom dreamed some more . . .

When one of Tom's patients died, a young mother who had been battling breast cancer for years, Cathy was the only person he wanted to see. He didn't want to talk about it. He didn't want to analyse why it had happened. He just wanted to be with her. And Cathy instinctively got that. She simply fed him, held him and asked no questions. The following day, one of her day-care patients lost his temper and threw a chair through the patio window to the garden. Tom drove over to help her clear up the mess. While he understood that there were times that things happened that were beyond your control, he was terrified that she might ever be in danger. This terror clarified everything for him.

There were no longer any questions in his mind. He loved this woman and he wanted the world to know it. He plotted and planned the perfect proposal. He wanted to make it memorable, worthy of the woman he loved. But in the end, all his plans fell in disarray back in the deli aisle of Tesco where they'd first met.

'This is where it all started!' Tom said, looking at their single trolly this time.

'One clash of our trollies and that was it,' Cathy remembered with a smile.

'You could never resist me. Me being such a charming fecker,' Tom joked.

'That is true,' she answered, kissing him lightly. 'Now, goat's cheese-and-spinach pizza, or the triple meat feast?' She held them both up, waving the goat's cheese one in front of his face, which he duly pointed to.

'Marry me,' he blurted out. He couldn't for the life of him see the sense in hanging around one more moment.

'What?'

'Will you marry me?' He moved in closer. 'I have been planning the most beautiful and perfect proposal, but I can't wait a moment longer.'

'Yes,' she whispered.

'Yes?' he asked in disbelief.

'Yes!'

He spun her around, lifting her off her feet. When he put her back down he realised they had gathered quite a crowd around them. 'She said yes!' he shouted loudly and they all cheered and whooped for him.

They had a small wedding a few months later on 18 October, the date they had met.

'I only want people who love us in the church,' Cathy stated. With just immediate family and friends, they exchanged vows in Cathy's hometown of Donegal. She walked down the aisle on the arm of her proud father, to the sound of 'Nella Fantasia'. There was a lot of love in that small church that day.

Cathy had invoked a speech ban for her father's sake, a shy man, who hated any public speaking and was more at home on the farm. Tom should have been taken aback when she appeared on the stage, holding a microphone. But he wasn't. His wife was unpredictable.

'We said no speeches. Well, I said no speeches!' she conceded when Tom raised one eyebrow. He walked close to the front of the stage, their guests moving in behind him.

'There's not enough love in this world, is there?' Cathy asked the small group. And they all nodded in agreement. 'I sometimes wake up at night and think, what if Tom hadn't been in Tesco that Friday night, where would we be now? I am astonished that we found each other that night. I am astonished that we fell in love as quickly as we did. I am astonished that despite the whirlwind nature of those first few days, we never stopped in regret, realising we had been swept away. And I am astonished that despite my compulsive cleaning habits, my need to be right, my snoring – yes, my snoring – that Tom still loves *me. I cannot wait for a lifetime of astonishments with you, Tom, my love, my friend, my confidant.'*

In his sleep, on the cold, lonely park bench, a tear rolled down Tom's cheek. Bette Davis's ears pricked up, her sixth sense telling her that her master needed her. She moved in closer, licking his hand. She would never leave his side.

13

TOM

Tom didn't like to make plans. He preferred to see where life took him. Over the past ten years it had been full of surprises. He looked up to the grey sky and thought to himself that it was highly unlikely that this beautiful world was done surprising him yet. Take today. On a whim, he hopped on the 41C bus. And on another whim, he jumped off in Swords village and decided to sleep there tonight. It had been years since he'd done that. He preferred to stay close to Fairview Park, the place he called home now. It was getting late. He walked over a stone bridge in the centre of this historic town, looking down at leaves drifting along the inky-blue water of the River Ward with its green grass banks on either side. Bette Davis sniffed an empty Coke can that poked its head through a cluster of weeds that sagged towards the river, as if in protest at the intrusion.

The sun had shone all day, a fine day for an Irish autumn, but even so, he pulled the collar of his grey overcoat upwards to form a barrier between the breeze and the back of his neck. He'd had a haircut last week and the hairdresser had been scissor happy. The haircut was a trade with Winnie, a woman he met in the Peter McVerry Trust. She was a semi-regular there like himself and they often chatted in the dining hall, both enjoying a good debate. As they discussed the horrific shooting that had occurred that month in Las Vegas, he'd noticed a gash on her hand, red and angry. Winnie was a proud woman and she would not allow him to clean and dress her wound unless she gave him something in return. A haircut was agreed.

Tom remembered another evening, years before, when he had driven over this same bridge in search of a petrol station. Cathy and he were on a road trip to Belfast and long before Applegreen Services were built to feed and water the travelling nation, diversions to small towns to hunt for fuel were the norm. The car radio was on. Cathy was singing along to a song with Gary Barlow and his Take That pals. *What was it?* Tom started to hum, trying to remember the lyrics, knowing it would irritate him for days until he remembered what it was.

Tom looked to his left where the ruins of a castle lay and where he'd spent a large proportion of today. Then to his right where shops and flats lined the path. The town was still busy, cars whizzing by the Main Street pavement. End-of-the-day shoppers and pedestrians moved fast with their heads down. He walked in the opposite direction. Away from all of that. He wanted a quieter area to settle down for the evening. As he explored the estates that surrounded the town the sun began to set. Headlights flooded the roads as cars made their way home after a busy day at work. He wandered into a large housing estate, which had a small cluster of shops in the middle of it. He looked at every doorway and entrance to see if he could find just the right spot to make his own for the night. *Bingo*. A doorway with a deep inset. Perfect. It belonged to a pharmacy that was now closed for the evening and would give him and Bette great shelter. He laid his rucksack down, guessing he'd walked nearly five or six kilometres today in all. They were both bone tired.

He heard footsteps before the shadow of their owner appeared around the corner. Bette's ears pricked up and she whined. 'Ssh,' Tom commanded, and she laid her head down on his feet.

Tom watched a slender figure, dressed in black, walk their way. It had a hoody pulled up over its head. It covered half of the face so it was difficult to decipher gender. But there was something about the swagger that told tales on its owner. It was all boy, that swagger. A nervous one, at that, the way he looked around every few seconds as he walked.

Tom pondered his next move. He'd just found this sweet spot. He was warm and content exactly as he was. But experience had taught him that it was sensible to be upright when a young fella in a hoody walked by. He hated stereotypes with a passion, but as he'd had four different incidents with 'hoodies', all of which Tom came out of the worst, he felt he was justified. Before he had a chance to stand up, the figure walked by. He glanced towards where Tom stood with unseeing eyes. Tom realised that the shadowy inlet hid him.

Where was the hoody going? He watched him walk

across the street and then stop in front of a block of flats. Maybe he was meeting some friends who lived here. If that was the case maybe it was time for Tom to make a move, find somewhere else to sleep for the night.

The boy had now come to a standstill in front of the long brick wall that surrounded the small concrete yard which sat in front of the flats. His rucksack now pulled off his back, he did another jerky scan of his surroundings. Every move was angry. He placed two spray-paint cans onto the ground beside him.

Tom felt the tension seep away from his shoulders. This boyo was likely working on his own. He'd do his thing, then with any luck piss off and Tom could start his evening meal. One he'd been looking forward to for hours now.

The trouble was he found he couldn't take his eyes off the boy, who was staring at the walls of the flats, his head cocked to one side. Then when a car backfired from somewhere in the estate, the kid jumped at least two feet off the ground, landing with a thud and a clatter, dropping his cans. He glanced Tom's way, again unseeing, but this time Tom managed to catch a look at the boy's face. He was no more than ten or eleven. He looked scared. Something told Tom that he wasn't watching a seasoned graffiti artist.

Without plan he was on his feet moving out of the dark shadow of his doorway. Bette jumped up and walked by his side, ready to defend her master if she needed to. The boy sensed he had company and spun around, his body tensed, two hands in fists, raised to his side ready for a fight.

'What you want?' the boy croaked, all bravado.

Tom stopped a few feet from him. He thought about

that for a minute. What did he want? He was breaking all his own rules about keeping out of trouble, not getting involved. It had taken years for him to work out that best practice was just to turn round and walk away.

But there was something about this kid . . . He took another step forward as he said, 'I'm just here to enjoy the show. Not often I get to see a young Banksy doing his thing.'

'A what?' Hoody replied.

'Banksy.'

'What's that?'

Tom despaired of the youth sometimes. 'He's probably the world's most famous vandal.'

This grabbed the attention of the kid. 'Never heard of him.'

'Well, I'd suggest you look him up. He's a street artist at the top of his game.'

'What makes him so special?' Hoody asked.

'He's a political activist. He's a commentator on culture. Some say a legend. He's an enigma. As I said, you should look him up.'

The boy shrugged, then turned back to inspect the wall. He looked back with suspicion to Tom.

'Don't mind me,' Tom said.

Hoody paused then shook the can with vigour, moving closer to the grey wall, ready to make his first mark.

'Before you do that, do you want to smile for the camera?' Tom asked.

Hoody spun round. 'What camera?'

'The CCTV. Well, there's actually four cameras on this street, by my reckoning. It's one of the reasons why I chose this spot to sleep tonight. It's safe.' Tom pointed to where the cameras lay.

'Cameras don't bother me,' Hoody responded, but Tom noted that he'd not raised his spray-paint can again.

'You're right not to care. Banksy never did. A political activist, sure he never worried what anyone thought about his street art.'

Hoody looked at Tom a little closer. 'What kind of stuff does this Banksy do?'

'He uses stencilling. Strong images, but always coupled with even stronger messages. There's a lot about his work to learn from. Like, for instance, his ape with a sign on him, that says, "Laugh now, but one day we'll be in charge." To me, that's all about respect.'

'For who?'

'For everyone and everything. It's telling us to be kind to each other and our environment. And really another way to say what my mam always used to preach: be careful who you step over on your way to the top, because you might need them, when you stumble back down again.'

The boy laughed. 'I like that.' Then his face changed and anger contorted his features into a grimace. 'There's someone I know who I'd like to see stumble on his way down.'

Tom wondered what had happened to the lad to cause him so much upset. 'What message are you planning on sharing with the world today?'

Hoody shifted from one foot to the other. 'Seamus Kearns is a fucking tool.'

'Ah. That's disappointing.'

'Why?'

'It's lazy just shouting expletives, without giving any context to back them up.'

'I never said I was a political activist!' Hoody shouted.

'No. That's true, you didn't. I'll probably regret asking, but what did this Mr Kearns do to you?'

'That used to be my bedroom.' Hoody pointed to the upstairs window.

'Used to be?'

'Seamus Kearns was our landlord. He evicted me and Mam. And we couldn't find anywhere else to live, so now we're homeless.'

Tom felt his heart sink at this news. 'And you want to graffiti his flat because he evicted you?'

Hoody nodded. 'My mam, she's scared, but she's trying so hard to be brave. We're in this hotel, which is a joke because it's nothing like the hotels I've seen on TV. They have more rules than I have in school. And I have to share a room with my mam.'

Ten years on the streets of Dublin and Tom had watched more families than he could count go through exactly what this kid was going through right now. Emergency housing was not the Ritz, that was for sure.

'Listen, I don't know anything about your life, but I do know that getting arrested won't do either of you any good. You said your mam was scared. Well, if you do this, it will make things worse for her.'

'I have to do something,' Hoody said.

Tom nodded. 'I get that. You want to be the hero. But real heroes know when to walk away. And trust me, this is not the way.' He nodded towards the CCTV cameras again. 'It's late. I suspect your mother is worried sick.'

'I told her I was going to a mate's this afternoon.' He looked at his watch and frowned.

'And did you go to your friend's?'

'For a bit. But he kept asking me when he could call over to my flat to watch YouTube. Over and over, banging on about it being my turn to have him come to my home. So I bailed.'

'You didn't tell him about your current situation?'

'What do you think?' The kid pulled a face. 'I don't want anyone to know.'

'A good friend would understand,' Tom said.

'Maybe he's not that good a friend,' the kid said. He looked at his watch again. His mam would be looking for him. He said he would be home by seven o'clock and it was past that now.

He sighed then placed his paint can back into his rucksack. He turned to walk away, then stopped for a moment. 'Thanks, mister. For the heads up about Big Brother watching. I owe you one.'

'Do you know any Take That songs?' Tom asked.

'Nope. Mam likes all that golden oldie stuff, but not me.'

'It's going to annoy me until I think of that bloody song Cathy was singing,' Tom muttered. 'You're going home?' He realised he cared that this kid got back to his mother in one piece.

'I don't have a home. Not any more.'

'Ah, but you do. Home isn't a place. It's a feeling. It's what is up here and in here.' He pointed to his head and heart. 'Promise me you'll try to remember that.'

The kid pulled his hoody up over his head and moved off into the night.

14

RUTH

As Erica had boasted, the hot buffet at The Silver Sands Lodge was substantial. DJ had been on a mission to try everything on offer each morning. Sausages, bacon, scrambled eggs, mushrooms and tomatoes were in large silver hot dishes, with steam rising from them into the dining room.

Today was a big change for them both. DJ's usual five-minute stroll to school was to be replaced with a one-hour, two-bus commute. Things were strained between them still. She was not happy that DJ had stayed out too late after a play date at a friend's house on Saturday.

Ruth went to the porridge station and filled a bowl full of the steaming gloopy cereal from the black pot that stood at the end of the buffet.

They had just taken their seats when Aisling and her daughter, Anna, walked into the dining room. They sat down at the table beside Ruth and DJ and began working on their bowls of cereal.

'I am glad to see your daughter is feeling better,' Ruth said.

'Thank you! That's the gas thing about asthma. You can be in a heap one minute, unable to breathe, and then jumping around, not a bother, the next day,' Aisling replied.

'When I was a baby, I was very sick,' Anna said, joining in the conversation. She was small for her age, Ruth noted. She looked no more than seven or eight years old. 'My chest hurt so bad.'

Aisling reached over to caress the top of her daughter's blonde curls. 'But you are all good now.'

'Yep, and guess what – I'm hungry,' Anna said.

'She's always hungry,' Aisling replied with a laugh. 'Or at least she is when she's well. She went right off her food last week.'

'DJ is the same. At home, when he was hungry, he would just jump up and make himself something. I do not feel comfortable with him doing that here in the communal kitchen.' Ruth was a little scared of Kian. He seemed to be angry all the time.

Aisling leaned in and whispered, 'I have a little portable fridge in our room. Technically it's against the rules. I got it for nothing in the "Free to a good home" Facebook page last week. It's bloody brilliant.'

Ice-cold milk and vanilla yoghurts at her disposal twenty-four seven. That sounded blissful. 'I might look into that myself. Thank you for the tip.'

'I've loads more of them. We've been here for four months so I'm all, been there, done that, wore the T-shirt. You know yourself. I'm trying to make sure we eat healthier. We've both put on weight since we lost our home. Too many takeaways and sandwiches. Sometimes it's easier than queuing for hours to use that cooker in the shared kitchen. I was overweight to start with, but Anna, she was just a slip of a thing.'

DJ arrived back to his table with a plate piled high with the full Irish. Anna and DJ eyed each other up silently, trying to decide if they liked each other.

'Make sure you grab some fruit and yoghurts before you go. I stick them in with Anna's lunch. I make her sandwich here too before we go,' Aisling said.

'Is that allowed?' Ruth asked.

'Well, it's not on their list of rules, and goodness knows, there's enough of those!' Aisling said.

'Can I take a muffin for school break later?' DJ asked.

Ruth nodded her consent. Once DJ had finished his cooked breakfast he went back to the pastry section. Ruth marvelled at where he put all the food he ate.

The only plus DJ could see about their situation was the breakfast. The pastries were his favourite: sticky, sweet and unlike anything his mam usually let him eat.

As he piled his plate he shivered, feeling eyes on him. Then he heard a voice behind him: 'He's one of those homeless kids. Look at him, filling his plate like he's never had a decent meal in his life.' A second voice chimed in, 'I blame the parents. I mean, how could they let themselves end up here?'

For a moment DJ forgot that he was homeless. That it was *him* that the voices were talking about. But only for a moment. With his face flaming red in shame he turned round to face the two women who had been talking about him. He wanted to tell them to shut up, to go away, to stop being so bloody horrible. But he couldn't find the words. Ruth was on her feet, walking towards him, angry and ready to take on the two women. She too had heard their loud commentary.

Aisling stood up and grabbed her arm, 'It's not worth a row.'

'I want to go,' DJ said, his head low, red cheeks telling tales on his embarrassment. He placed his plate filled with pastries onto the table. He no longer had the appetite to eat a thing.

'How did they know?' Ruth asked.

'The uniforms are a dead giveaway. It's well known this hotel is used for social housing. Been in the papers a few times,' Aisling said. 'You get used to it.'

In silence they went back to their room, taking turns to brush their teeth, grabbing their bags and leaving through the side entrance. 'I don't want to go to school.' DJ was the first to speak. They stood a few feet apart at the bus stop. Their first bus was due in five minutes.

'It is not negotiable,' Ruth said.

He moved a few feet away from her.

'You need to tell me how you are feeling,' Ruth said.

'I don't want people to know I'm homeless. But they do. There's no hiding it,' DJ replied. Then he turned his back to her, waiting for the bus to arrive.

How did she deal with that? Embarrassment she understood. She had spent a large part of her life feeling like that. Before she had a further chance to discuss it, their bus came into view. DJ's issue had to wait because Ruth's stomach was a spiralling mass of nerves. She normally avoided public transport. They were a hotbed of germs and bacteria. They smelled bad. Usually of stale body odour and farts. People never followed the rules about personal space. And they were noisy. She pulled on her headphones, allowing Westlife to block out the sounds of commuters as they began their day. She opened up *Odd Thomas* and continued with Chapter Eighteen. With every word, she soothed herself as her mind roamed the streets of Pico Mundo, alongside her best friend, Odd. It was when they had to change buses for the second part of their journey that her anxiety levels began to spike out of control. Ruth tried her best to ignore the hustle and shoves of fellow commuters around her. DJ continued to sulk in silence, occasionally moaning that he wanted to go back to the hotel. Ruth was tempted to say yes, let's get off this bus, turn round and go back to our hotel room.

When the bus braked suddenly, Ruth was jostled forward. Her book fell to the ground, lost between a sea of feet. Time slowed down for Ruth and she felt the all-too-familiar trickle of fear take over all rational thought. The bus was too crowded. People pushed into her, invading her space, her imaginary circle that she placed around herself, that nobody was meant to enter, except for DJ. *If one more person was allowed on the bus, the strain would be too much. The wheels would buckle. What if they crashed? None of them had seat belts on. They would all die.* And over and over her mind spiralled into fearful chaos until she could not think straight.

'I've got to go, I've got to go, go, go, go, go . . .' Ruth shouted from the floor of the bus as she tried to retrieve her book.

'Shit,' DJ said, realising what was happening. He should have copped this sooner. He jumped up to push the bell, alerting the driver that they wanted to get off.

'Mam, come on, get up. People are looking. Please.' DJ tried to pull his mother up but Ruth remained on the floor, kneeling down, repeating over and over, '. . . go, go, go, go . . .' DJ watched strangers around them back away and judge his mother for the millionth time in his life.

'What are you looking at?' he confronted a man in a suit who was rubber necking. DJ hated his life. He hated this bus. He hated the women in the restaurant who whispered and judged. And as the last cruel thought jumped into his head – that most of all, right now he hated his mother – the bus shuddered to a halt.

DJ grabbed Ruth by her arms, pulling her upright, and pushed the doors open so that they could get off. Once they were on the pavement, Ruth gasped in long breaths of air.

DJ stood back and watched his mother wrap her arms around herself. Then flap her arms like a bird trying to fly away, before popping her knuckles one by one. He felt tears prick the back of his eyes, making him want to cry in a way he hadn't done since he was little.

'Mam,' he whispered. 'It's OK. You're OK now.' *I don't hate you. I'm sorry I thought that. I take it back. I'm sorry. I'm sorry. I'm sorry.*

'No. No more bus,' Ruth said, gradually calming down. She was safe. She was on the pavement. The pavement was good.

'No more bus, Mam,' DJ agreed. 'We can walk the rest of the way.'

It took them twenty minutes to reach the school gates. They were fifteen minutes late.

'I'd better go in,' DJ said, but he was looking worriedly at Ruth. 'Maybe I should stay. Walk back to the hotel with you.'

You will do the right thing for your baby. Because that's what mothers do. Ruth clung to words her kind doctor had told her before DJ was born. She had to do the right thing.

'I will explain to your teacher what happened,' Ruth said. She could not let DJ get into trouble for something that was outside of his control. Her fear slipped away but in its place was ugly, ugly shame. The shame of letting her son down. The shame of being Ruth, someone who got things wrong. Over and over again.

'No!' he said, a fraction too loudly. 'I don't want anyone in school to know about this.'

'About what part?' Ruth asked.

'That we're homeless. That we had to take two buses to get to school. That you had a meltdown in one. That we live in a hotel now that doesn't let us use the front door. That you don't know my father's surname.' DJ blurted every hurt, angry feeling in one long tirade. He could no longer hold it all in.

'I can make them understand,' Ruth replied, feeling her guts churn at every word he uttered. She had done this to him. This was all on her.

'No! Promise me, Mam. You are not to say anything,' DJ begged, tears in his eyes.

'Yes, I promise,' Ruth said, knowing she was defeated. She could not add anything else to his obvious distress. 'I will be here to pick you up again at 3 p.m. OK?'

She watched him leave and began her long walk back to the hotel. The luxury of a taxi was not hers to take. She ran into the hotel lobby, her mind full of commutes to school. They would have to leave every morning by seven o'clock, before it got too busy. She would practise. Make it normal. Make it right. Yes. That's what she would do.

'Rule number seven,' Erica's voice called out, stalling her. 'Remember, Ms Wilde, you have your own entrance.'

Ruth turned to her and said, 'Laws and rules should be recognised as only an approximate guide to actions by the people. They are never meant to enslave us. Just a guide.'

A ruffle of newspaper behind Ruth made her start. Kian revealed himself from behind the palm tree where he was hiding. 'Yes, sister! Preach. At last someone else who understands!'

'Rule number fifteen, Mr Furey!' Erica shouted out. 'You are not allowed in the hotel public areas during the day. That newspaper is for the sole use of our normal guests, as well you know!'

'Arbitrary rules are meant to be broken,' Kian replied with a wink. He sauntered out of the lobby, almost kicking his heels in delight.

'Let's be complete rebels and use the lift for the normal guests,' Kian said to Ruth.

Ruth backed herself into a corner of the small lift. Seconds went by until Kian spoke. Softly. His words falling onto the floor of the lift between them. 'I received my fourth Dear John today. "We're sorry but the position has been filled by another. We wish you well in your search for a new job, blah, blah, blah."'

She peeked up at him but this time it was he who was looking at the floor. His shoulders hunched.

Say something, anything, tell him you are sorry.

No words came out. It had been a horrible morning and she was hanging on by a thread.

'If I can't get a job, how can I afford to get us out of this hell? I've tried. I really have. But the rents are jacked up so much. The landlords blame the government. The government blames the landlords and the builders. Meanwhile, poor fuckers like me and you are left here in limbo, or on the streets, if we don't like it. And don't get me started on the fact that even if we can find a landlord who is happy to take a tenant who is on the council's long-term rent supplement list or the new Housing Assistant Payment scheme, then it's like finding a needle in a haystack to find a flat or house we can afford!'

Two thoughts struck Ruth at once, causing a flush to run through her from her head to her toes. One, she had misjudged Kian. Her assumption that he was a lasagne-robbing layabout shattered into pieces. Two, she had a job and she was supposed to be online by 10 a.m. With the episode on the bus she had forgotten completely about it. She should have taken a taxi home, no matter the cost.

As the doors to the lift opened, Ruth said to Kian as she ran out the door, 'I would like to offer my sympathies on your current situation, but I do not have time right now. But I will revisit this conversation with you at a later time. I have to go.'

Once she entered her room she scrambled to switch on her laptop.

Where was the bloody wi-fi?

She typed in the hotel password and clicked *Connect*. *Come on!* As another minute clicked on the bedside clock, Ruth felt a scream build up inside of her. *Why wouldn't it work? She was now over an hour late.*

She dialled 0, her hands shaking by now.

'Good morning from The Silver Sands Lodge. Your friendly neighbourhood boutique hotel. This is the manager, Ms Erica Rossitor speaking.'

'The wi-fi is not working,' Ruth said.

'Who is speaking, please?' Erica replied.

'It's Ruth Wilde, in room 129.'

'Just one moment, please.' Then she put the phone down.

Ruth heard the shuffle of her feet as she moved out of the reception desk.

Come on, lady, hurry up! Over the past month, she had been late for several of her shifts. But only because she had to queue to see potential flats to rent. Which all turned into wild-goose chases, as they were all out of her reach in the end. This was not her fault. *Come on!*

'Do you . . . ever have one . . . of those mornings?' Erica said, breathlessly. 'Wi-fi was switched off. One of the cleaners must have knocked it when . . .'

'Is it fixed now?' Ruth asked.

'Why yes, it is. As I was saying, when the cleaner—'

'Thank you,' Ruth said, then hung up. She clicked *Connect* again and prayed to a God that she didn't believe in that the wi-fi icon would turn green.

Yes!

Her joy was cut short when she saw several missed messages on the chat forum from her supervisor.

Where are you Ruth?
Your shift started half an hour ago, please get in touch.
Calls are queuing up, this is NOT acceptable!

She typed a message back.

I'm so sorry. I had a family emergency. Here now. Ruth.

I'm sorry to hear that. However, this is your third
non-show. I'm afraid this is not working out. We have
already given you a written warning.

It will not happen again. Ruth.

No, it won't. We have terminated your contract
Ms Wilde. An email with full details has been issued.
Wishing you the best of luck in the future, but perhaps
another role, with less regular hours would suit you.

An ever-increasing feeling of hopelessness and shame threatened to choke her. No home. And now no job. What else did she have to lose? Her son? Her mind . . . yes, her mind would be the next to go. The small hotel room shrank in size and she felt her chest constrict, as she struggled to breathe. She ran to the window and unlocked the latch. She inhaled large lungfuls of air, trying to calm the storm that was brewing inside her. Ruth counted the cars as they passed by her window. *One, two, three, four* . . . Then the number 17 bus stopped and a woman exited, lighting a cigarette as soon as her feet hit the pavement. The red tip glared bright and Ruth's head was filled with another time, another woman, another cigarette. *Marian*.

15

RUTH

Then

Marian arrived unannounced at Mark's flat where Ruth was staying now. Her unmistakable scent of nicotine and Chloé perfume filled the air as she walked into the room. She looked around her, taking in every detail of the small two-bedroomed flat, disappointment and vitriol in every glance.

'Would you like a cup of tea, Mother?' Ruth asked, moving towards the kettle.

Marian looked at her in surprise. 'Since when did you start making tea for anyone? You've never done that before.'

Ruth let the sound of the running water cover the sound of the sigh that her mother was inevitably making. Then, once the kettle was switched on, she replied, 'My new doctor has been helping me manage my food issues.'

'You have a perfectly good family doctor. What will he think about this betrayal?'

'I am sure he will care little,' Ruth replied, rearranging the mugs in the small cupboard over the sink. Mark must have messed them up earlier this morning. They were all wrong.

'You can't have this baby,' Marian said, cutting straight to the chase.

That was one thing that mother and daughter shared. They said it like it was.

'Who says so?' Ruth replied.

'I do. With good reason, too. You are not mothering material. You never will be.' She leaned in, as if they were friends whispering secrets together and continued, 'Not everyone is cut out to be a parent.'

Ruth remembered the distress and isolation of her childhood and realised that her mother was speaking a truth. And Ruth knew that there were many times that she unintentionally hurt people with her bluntness. Her mother, on the other hand, showed no remorse.

Ruth watched a crack on the wall behind her mother and popped a knuckle. It helped. She couldn't explain why, but when she did, she felt a release. And she needed every bit of help right then. 'You are right. Not everyone is cut out to be a parent. You and Dad are proof of that.'

Marian's response was a slap that landed hard on Ruth's left cheek. The sound of skin on skin bounced around the room, and when the room fell silent all that was left was a red mark on Ruth's face. And heart. Ruth reached up and touched the bruised spot. Shock at the assault changed to acceptance faster than it should. Marian had battered her daughter with words for years; this was just another form of abuse.

'I shouldn't have hit you. But sometimes, Ruth, you just drive me insane.' Marian made sure that her apology was an excuse. The fault was all on Ruth.

'Did you ever love me, Mother?' Ruth asked.

Marian answered without missing a beat. She had asked herself this same question many times, when guilt niggled her conscience. 'You were difficult right from the start. I watched other mothers in the ward with their newborn babies in their arms. And I was envious of them, because when I picked you up, you cried. Even back then you preferred to be in your cot, on your own, rather than in my arms.'

Ruth was puzzled by this revelation because her childhood memories were peppered with moments where she reached out to her mother for an embrace, only to be pushed away.

'And on top of that you cried incessantly as a child. From the moment you came into the world you screamed your anger at the world, at me, at your father. Always so angry. It was frankly all rather exhausting,' Marian said.

'I was a baby!' Ruth shouted, the injustice of her mother's accusations making her angry.

'A baby who tore our life apart. A baby who broke my heart when she refused to breast-feed. No matter how hard the nurses tried – I tried – you would not latch on. Always the same with you: your way or the highway!'

Ruth was staggered by the degree of hatred in her mother's voice. How had they come to this? Her earlier question about her mother's love was answered in every recrimination that Marian fired at her.

'Mark was so easy as a child. Always smiling and

kissing his mama. Then you came along and everything changed . . .' Marian said. She stood up and took her Marlboro Lights out of her small grey clutch handbag. She tapped the top of the box, then extracted a cigarette, letting it dangle between her ruby-red lips. Then, with a look of disgust at Ruth, she said, 'I can't even have a cigarette.'

'You need to stop smoking; they will kill you,' Ruth said.

Irritation flashed across Marian's face. 'I gave them up when I was pregnant with you and Mark. When Alan left, I swear they were the only things I had in my life that gave me relief from dealing with . . .'

Dealing with ME, Mother, we all know that is how the sentence ends.

'My marriage ended because of you. We would still be together if it wasn't for you.'

Ruth tried to remember a time when her parents looked happy together and failed. The weight of that responsibility sagged her down as a child. A sudden surprising niggle of doubt took root in her head. Was it really her fault that her father left?

Everyone's lives are destroyed just because they know me.

Irritation took up residence beside doubt. Ruth was fed up being the scapegoat for everything that went wrong for the Wildes.

'We never had a happy family,' Ruth said.

Marian paused before she replied, 'You've had your fun playing house. But I've no doubt that by now the realities of your situation have hit home. Correct?'

When Ruth remained silent, Marian opened her

handbag and pulled out a brown manila folder. She tapped it with one of her manicured red nails. 'Don't start flapping. I need your hands here, to sign these forms. I've filled out the details. Although you changing doctors is most irksome. I've the wrong name written down now.'

Pop, pop, pop . . .

'Oh, for goodness' sake. That sound is like fingernails on a chalkboard, Ruth. I don't know what is worse, the flapping or the knuckles.' She waved her cigarette towards Ruth's stomach, then with a sigh, finished, 'These forms will start the adoption process for your . . . baby.'

Ruth felt her arms begin to fly and watched Marian smirk as they made their way upwards. Ruth focused her attention on her knuckles and willed her arms downward again.

Marian's voice changed. Became softer, each word wrapping itself insidiously around Ruth's neck. 'It's time you came home, to me, then we can draw a line under all this nonsense,' she said.

It is not nonsense, it is my life! Leave me alone, Mother, leave me and my baby alone!

'For goodness' sake, say something. You're just staring at me like an imbecile!' Marian's voice was back to its usual snappy self.

'I. Am. Not. Giving. Up. My. Baby!' Ruth screamed.

Marian's laugh rang through the apartment, mirthless and cruel. 'What happens when the baby fusses over food like you did? Because it will. And if it has your stubborn streak . . . You refused to eat a single thing I prepared, not one thing. Do you have any idea how that made me feel as a mother?'

Marian was lost in the past and, like a can of worms spilling open, she continued her tirade. 'It was impossible to dress you. You refused to put on the clothes I laid out each morning for you to wear. It had to be the same thing every day. And Lord knows, if there was a label on the back of your top or skirt you would have a meltdown. You complained incessantly that your socks hurt your feet. And don't get me started on your school jumpers, which you insisted scratched you.'

'I am sorry,' Ruth whispered. She could not deny any of these accusations. Was it really that big a deal to cut the labels out of her clothes? Now, she put a long-sleeved T-shirt underneath her jumpers, so that they did not itch. Marian always refused to find a solution to help Ruth as a child. Instead they fought, Ruth cried, flapped and popped while Marian sighed.

'I grew up feeling the weight of that finger pointing at me,' Ruth told her mother. 'I wish you would believe me when I say that my intention was never to aggravate or upset you or Dad. Or Mark.'

Silence filled the room again, save for the tip-tap of Marian's nails on the cigarette packet in her hand as she planned her next missile to launch.

'To be honest, Ruth, we could never get things right with you. Your father gave up trying. Maybe it's time I do the same.'

16

TOM

Now

It had been a quiet day for Tom. Neither Lash nor Bones stopped by for their usual chat. Maybe they had gone into one of the shelters for the night. He began the task of setting up his bed, pulling things from his rucksack, first unfolding a large sheet of cardboard, which he laid on the ground for Bette. Then laying his sleeping bag and cushion on the bench. While he found his park bench comfortable, it lost its charm on a wet night. Thankfully, predictions of a mild night looked likely to come true. But there was no getting away from the fact that winter was coming. He'd been in Pearse St. Library earlier today. One of the librarians there, Jackie, was a dog lover and turned a blind eye to Bette Davis, who in fairness was always an exemplary guest. Tom liked to read the newspapers and catch up on the news and weather online.

Earlier this evening a couple of volunteers from the Peter McVerry Trust stopped by to see him. They did most nights.

Walking angels, they were. They gave him sandwiches, hot tea, dry socks and blankets. More than that, they chatted to him. And tonight the main topic of conversation was the impending bad weather that was making its way towards them. He promised he would go into the shelter for a few days once the weather changed. The noise there made it hard for him to reach his family. Here, on his own with nature, his family were only moments away. He was eager to get back to them.

He whispered to Bette Davis, 'You stay here, girl. I'll be back in a minute.' She barked her consent and Tom walked towards the back of the park to the public toilets. He was gone only a few minutes in total. His pace was quick despite the painful knee, because Bette didn't like to be left on her own.

Hoody boy? At first he thought his eyes were playing tricks on him. Surely not the same kid that he'd seen in Swords? That was miles away. What was he doing here too? There was something about the way he moved . . . Tom watched him for a few moments. He was making his way towards his bench. The kid paused and looked at Bette. Tom's first instinct was to run over but he stayed a few feet away, stepping behind a tree to watch him. He'd seemed harmless enough the last time they spoke, though angry at the world and wanting to express himself the only way he thought he could. But appearances were often deceptive, that he knew for sure. Tom had made mistakes with kids before, taking them under his wing, seeing something in them that he fancied could be Mikey from a different life.

The kid shivered. His shoulders were hunched up like

an old man's. He shoved his two hands into his sweatshirt pockets. What was he doing wearing jeans and a hoody in the middle of winter? Where was the boy's coat? Tom pulled his long overcoat closer to his body, grateful for its protection. It might not look much but it was functional.

Surprised, he saw Bette nuzzle the kid's hand. She didn't usually do that with strangers. Tom stepped out of the shadows of the trees.

If the kid was startled to see Tom he didn't show it. He smiled when he saw him walk his way. Was it because he recognised Tom or that he just didn't think he was a threat?

'Hello.' The kid's smile was wide and instant, the kind that lit up a room. It changed his face. Tom resisted the urge to smile back. He didn't want to make friends with this kid. He wanted to eat his supper, close his eyes and go home to Cathy and Mikey.

'Hope you're not thinking of giving my bench a makeover,' Tom said.

'Maybe I am. Was thinking about writing, "Keep your coins, I want change."'

The kid had just quoted Banksy. 'You looked him up,' Tom said, impressed.

'You were right, he's cool.'

'I'd still rather you left my bench alone. And don't be mauling Bette Davis, either. She doesn't like it if you do that.'

Bette Davis panted with delight as the kid petted her, making a liar out of Tom.

'That's a weird name for a dog.'

'She's named after a Hollywood legend. Someone else for you to look up,' Tom said.

'I looked up Take That songs. Was it "Patience", "Shine", "Relight My Fire" . . . em, or "A Million Love Songs"?'

Tom shook his head at each suggestion.

'"Back For Good"?'

'Bingo! That's the one,' Tom said, delighted. 'Thanks, kid.'

Two men walked by, takings swigs from a bottle of cider, held in a brown paper bag. 'Howya, Doc,' the taller of the two said. His words came out in a slurring rush.

'Bones. Lash.' Tom nodded at them each. Normally he'd be glad of their company, but they'd been drinking and he was worried about the boy.

Bones moved on but Lash stopped and walked towards the kid, growling at him, 'What you looking at?'

The kid, to be fair, stood his ground and lifted his chin defiantly. 'Nothing much.'

His bravado only made him look younger than his years.

'You snotty-nosed little bastard,' Lash said.

Tom stepped in between the two and growled, 'Feck off, Lash! You'd start a row with a paper bag when you've had a few ciders. Don't be picking on the kid. He's doing nothing but minding his own business.' Bette Davis stood to attention, ready to defend her master and new friend if necessary. She threw in a growl just in case Lash took a notion. Bones, always the peacemaker, dragged Lash away, calling, 'Sorry' over his shoulder.

Tom ignored him and he turned back to the kid. He didn't seem so cocky any more.

'You're a puzzle to me,' Tom said. 'One minute I find you about to break the law and then I see you're wandering around parks way past your bedtime.' Tom took a closer look at the boy. He had said he was staying in a hotel with his mam. Had that changed? The kid was clean. He looked healthy. There was no sign of drink or drugs on him. Whatever was going on, it was time he had a stark wake-up call. This park was no place for him.

'That tall guy, the thin lanky one. He called you Doc. Is that your name?' the kid asked.

'To some, yes.'

'I'm DJ.' He sat down on the bench and ruffled Bette behind her ear. 'Do they live on the streets, too? Those men.'

'They do. In the main they are harmless enough. Well, Bones is, anyhow. Lash gets contrary with drink on him.'

'Why is he called Bones?' DJ asked.

'I gave him that nickname when he broke his arm a few years back. It's as good a name as any.'

'Why is the other fella called Lash?'

'He's always on the lash,' Tom replied.

'Which means he's always contrary,' DJ said.

They both laughed at this.

'As funny as you are, kid, you need to go home,' Tom said.

'I told you. I don't have a home.'

'And I told you what I thought about that.' Tom touched his head and heart. 'You have a mother. You told me that too. She'll be worried.'

'No, she won't. She was asleep all afternoon. She probably doesn't even know that I'm gone,' DJ said.

Tom thumbed in the direction of the street. 'You can't stay here. It's not safe. Lash could be back to finish off the argument he's been having in his head with you since I sent him running. Go back to your hotel. I assume it's The Lodge up the road you're in?'

DJ made himself as tall as he could and replied, 'I'm not scared of Lash. Or anyone. I can take care of myself. And how'd you know that's the hotel I'm in?'

'I know a lot.'

The kid had a fair set of balls on him for one so scrawny. Tom almost smiled. It was time to put an end to this though, send him back to his mother. 'Word of warning, don't make me repeat myself. That turns me from being an old man into a grumpy old man.'

DJ didn't move.

Tom continued, his voice firmer this time, 'Go back to your hotel.'

Bette Davis barked once and moved closer to the boy, placing her head on his knee. And when he smiled, something inside Tom shifted.

17

TOM

*What am I going to do with this kid, Cathy? I can't
seem to shake him. Everywhere I look he's there. What's
that about?*

'I will go back to the hotel, I promise. But let me stay
for a bit. Please, Doc. I don't want to go back to that room.
Not yet.' His eyes pleaded with Tom's to let him stay.

For feck's sake. Why did he feel responsible for this kid?
'You think we're gonna have a bromance or something?
Become best buddies? You picked the wrong bench, kid.
Don't be expecting any neighbourly chitchat from me.'

DJ pretended to zip his mouth, that big smile of his once
again taking over his face.

Tom felt his stomach growl. His supper had already
been delayed by this kid. Bette Davis nudged his rucksack
with her button nose.

He pulled her bowl from his rucksack and filled it with
water from a bottle. Then he took out his flask and
unscrewed the cap. Aware he had an audience, he put on
a little show. He elaborately poured himself a cup of

coffee. The smell of the nutty roast filled the air around him and he breathed in the scent with loud appreciation.

'I prefer tea. Well, if I had the choice, I'd go for hot chocolate. But coffee is good, too,' the kid said, subtle as a brick.

A cold breeze ruffled Bette's coat and she moved closer to her master.

'It's cold,' DJ stated the obvious.

Tom looked at him and said, 'You're not very good at that whole zipping-your-mouth, are you? I can see what you're thinking. This is going to be coffee time over the garden fence. Dream on. This here is no Hollywood movie. You want coffee, go get your own. I've been looking forward to this all afternoon.' He moved his two hands around the plastic cup to warm them. 'And this sure is a mighty fine cup of Java.'

'Real mature,' DJ said, his lips in a cartoon pout.

'Yep, that's me, Mr Mature, sipping *his* cup of coffee. Keeps the chill out of a night,' Tom chuckled, and stroked Bette's silky ear, the way she liked. Tom realised he was enjoying himself.

'So how long have you been homeless?' DJ asked.

'Who says I'm homeless?' Tom asked.

'You're living on a bench,' DJ said, pulling a face.

'I've been sleeping outside for ten years or so now, on and off. That's true.'

'That's a long time,' DJ said, pulling the hood of his sweatshirt up over his ears as a gust of wind whipped by them.

'Things aren't always black and white. You should remember that,' Tom said, taking another sip of coffee. 'Tell me about your mam.'

DJ shrugged. 'Nothing to tell.'

'Humour me. What's so bad about your mother that you'd rather be out here in the cold, talking to me than sitting with her?' Tom asked.

DJ remained tight-lipped.

The kid had said she was asleep on the bed. 'Is she fond of the gargle? Does she drink a lot? Too much gin or wine? Passed out from it?'

'Sometimes she has a glass of white wine on Saturday nights. But she says it's a waste of money because she only has one glass, then the rest goes down the sink,' DJ said.

'Then what has she done that's so bad?'

'She's on my case morning, noon and night. I've a pain in my arse listening to her, she never lets up.'

'Sounds like an awful mother. What is she on your case over?'

'Everything! Nothing I do has ever been good enough for her. I don't keep the place tidy enough for her. But it's impossible to do that in our hotel room. There's no room for anything,' DJ said.

'That sounds unfair. Out of interest, could you do more?'

'I do plenty,' DJ said.

'Oh, well then, I'm not surprised you are so pissed off. Nothing worse than if you put the work in and nobody appreciates it,' Tom said.

'I just want to be my own boss. Like you. Nobody to tell me what to do,' DJ said.

'Before you go packing your bags and leaving, I have to tell you I'm not buying any of this. There's something else going on. Every parent nags their child to tidy up. It goes with the territory. What's really annoying you so much?' Tom asked.

DJ sighed. 'I'm just tired of . . .' He didn't finish. He placed his head in his hands and ruffled his hand through his hair until it stood up on end. 'I love my mam. But sometimes I don't like her.' He felt tears rush to his eyes as he uttered the ultimate betrayal.

Tom pulled a second plastic cup from his rucksack, then poured coffee for the kid.

DJ took a sip and closed his eyes as he said, 'The other week, I tripped and fell in the yard at school. My own fault. Was running towards Mam with my laces untied. I hit the ground hard and skinned my two knees.'

'Ouch.'

'Yeah. Mam asked me if I could get up. I said yes, so she waited and watched until I got onto my feet again.'

'What did you want her to do?'

'To help me, to put her arms around me without me asking her to, to put a plaster on my two knees. Stop the bleeding.' He stopped abruptly, feeling embarrassed that he had opened up to this old man, this stranger.

'Is she not the maternal type?' Tom asked.

'She's not like most mams,' DJ sighed.

'Does she hurt you?' Tom asked in a low voice. *Was the kid being mistreated?*

DJ quickly shook his head. 'Not like that. She's just different.'

'How?'

'She's not one of those touchy-feely mams. My friend

Dylan in school, his mam is always hugging and kissing him. Drives him mad. Mine will only hug me when I ask her for one. Hugs make her feel restricted.'

'Maybe you and Dylan should swap mams,' Tom joked, making the kid laugh.

'I don't think Dylan would be able, for all the mashed potatoes,' DJ said.

Tom raised his eyebrows in question.

'She only eats white food. Her favourite thing being mashed potatoes. With real butter. When we studied The Famine in school I kind of wished a blight would hit the country again.'

Tom laughed at this. 'That bad?'

DJ sighed, the injustice of his diet restrictions evident in every word uttered: 'Porridge, bananas, milk, potatoes, white fish, mayonnaise. I've had them all cooked in a variety of ways. Some days, if she's in good form, she will let me eat anything I like. But her food always has to be white.'

'At least she tries to be flexible with you. That doesn't sound like someone who doesn't care,' Tom said.

'I know she loves me. That's not the issue. She doesn't say it much. But I don't mind that. And last night she brought home a big tub of vanilla ice cream. We ate as much of it as we could, then she wrote this sign, saying "Eat me!" and stuck it on top of the lid.'

'Why?' Tom asked.

'We have a communal kitchen in the hotel and food is always being stolen. She said that if people are going to rob the food anyhow she might as well give them permission and let them enjoy the ice cream guilt free.'

'Respect.' Tom liked this woman already.

'Yeah. She's kind of cool. And funny, too. But most people don't bother taking the time to see that. They just think she's weird 'cos she talks funny.'

'How does she talk?'

'It's hard to describe. She likes proper English and will never use slang. She likes to follow rules, I guess. And slang breaks all the rules of English.'

'I think a lot of kids could take a leaf out of your mam's book. Use more formal English in formal settings, keeping the slang for the playground.'

DJ looked at Doc with respect. This old homeless guy seemed to get it. Get him. He liked him.

'You said people think she's weird. I think what's more important is if you do too,' Tom said.

'Sometimes. No. Not really. Maybe the odd time.'

Tom laughed. 'Thanks for the clarification.'

'When people meet her, they think she's rude because she gets all tongue-tied and can't speak. She hates noisy places and crowds so we have to avoid those.'

'That must be tough for you, seeing her go through all of that?' Tom asked.

'I hate it when she cries. Sometimes she has to lie down when things get too much for her, sleep it off. When she was little, she used to put a blanket over her head so everything went dark. So I put one over her, too. It helps, I think.'

Silence fell, DJ's words hanging between them. Tom felt an emotion he had not felt in a long time. Tenderness. Followed by respect, awe and, if he was honest, pity.

'You're a good kid,' Tom said to him.

DJ shrugged. 'No, I'm not. Because sometimes I hate my mam and our life. And then I feel so bad.'

18

TOM

It was time for a change in subject. The kid looked like he was about to cry. And while there was no doubt that he had more than most to be upset about, there were always worse off out there.

Tom took out his chicken sandwich from his rucksack, passing half to the kid.

'You sure?' DJ asked, the guilt of taking the man's food fighting his growling stomach.

'I'm sure.'

'Thanks. Where do you get your food from?' DJ asked as he shoved half of the sandwich in his mouth in one bite.

'I've a few delis and cafés that hook me up with food and coffees. Plus the food runs done by the Peter McVerry Trust every night. Helps to be as charming a fecker as I am.' He grinned. 'Tell me something, DJ. You ever been hungry?'

'Course I have. Today. Now.'

'OK, how does hungry make you feel?' Tom asked.

'Shite.'

'Don't be so lazy with your words. Think, then articulate. Perhaps once you have finished chewing,' Tom said.

DJ giggled, then frowned as he tried to find the right words for Tom. 'I felt light-headed. Weak. No energy. My stomach kept growling.'

'There you go. Amazing how articulate you can be when you try. Well, imagine if you hadn't eaten breakfast this morning. Imagine if that feeling carried on into tomorrow and then the next day, too.'

'I'd go mad.'

'You would. A craziness sets in when you're hungry. It's mental torture. You might be shocked to hear that there are six hundred thousand people experiencing food poverty in Ireland right now.'

'No way!'

'Way. A new generation of food poor,' Tom said, shaking his head in regret.

'Mam used to say that when things were tight, food was the flexible item,' DJ replied, remembering times when he saw his mam eat nothing else but a banana sandwich for the day.

'That's the thing, kid. You don't need to be homeless to be hungry. Many of those six hundred thousand have a roof over their heads, but don't have a scrap in their fridges. It makes me so angry to think about the kids who go to school hungry every day! That's not right. Not with the amount of food wastage in the word. Tons and tons of food thrown in the bins every day, while children are starving.'

'I never thought about that before,' DJ said. He wiped his mouth with the sleeve of his hoody.

Tom nodded, satisfied that he was beginning to get into the kid's head.

'Mam used to make porridge for us both every morning. Mine with currants, hers plain. She said if we eat nothing else, we'll have that to set us up for the day. Now we eat in the hotel restaurant every morning. There's so much food on their buffet, Mam said she reckoned they must throw out loads.'

'Your mam is probably right about that. Isn't it a wonder, though, how mothers always know the intricate details of their children's likes and dislikes? A mother's love knows no bounds,' Tom said. His mind drifted to Cathy and Mikey, a dull ache making its way to the pit of his stomach.

DJ nodded and his earlier irritation at his mother began to feel trivial and unjust. Maybe he didn't have it so bad after all.

Tom changed the subject abruptly. 'What's your favourite subject, kid?'

'English,' DJ answered.

'Ah, you're a dreamer so.'

'Maybe. I think I'd like to be a journalist when I grow up. Or write a book like Dean Koontz.'

'Noble ambition,' Tom approved. Cathy used to have one of his books.

'I've got this idea bouncing around my head about an island where you get sent to when you mess up,' DJ said.

'What happens there?'

'You have a chance at redemption there, kind of like a do-over.'

'Wow. What happens if you don't take that?' Tom asked.

'Then you die on the island. You never leave. It's like a prison, but it's not. Because you live outside in hammocks. There's no way to escape. You have to forage for your own food. I'm not explaining it right. But it's all in my head,' DJ said.

'I'd read that,' Tom said. 'Seriously. I would.'

'Mam always says the same to me when I tell her about it.' DJ sighed. He started to shift and fidget on the bench, then lowered his eyes to the ground. 'I've been a bit shit to Mam lately.'

'That goes with the territory. Boys are little shits ninety per cent of the time. But here's the thing: for your mam, you're her little shit, so no matter what, she will still love you. It's part of her DNA as a parent. They can't turn that off.'

'Sometimes I think she'd be better off without me,' DJ said.

'Don't ever say that, you ungrateful little . . .' Tom stopped, shocked by the strength of the anger he felt at DJ's words.

'Chill, old man,' DJ said, alarmed by the change in his new friend.

Tom took a deep breath, trying to chill, as the kid said. 'Listen to me, kid, there will always be times that you upset your mother. But you need to remember something. She loves you unconditionally, which means she will forgive you all your transgressions as long as you learn from them and are sorry.'

'Why are you getting so worked up?' DJ asked, unsure as to why Tom was so agitated. He didn't like to see him upset. He liked talking to him. Tom listened to what he had to say, like he was an adult, not just a silly kid. And the last thing he wanted was to do anything that might make Tom tell him to go away again.

'I hate seeing you waste your life, throwing it away when there's people out there who would give anything to swap places with you, people who would give anything to have a family like you . . .'

'Who said I was wasting my life?' DJ said. 'You're going all crae-crae there, Doc.' He watched Tom's eyes glaze over as he became lost in his own thoughts. 'Doc? You all right?'

Tom pulled himself back from Cathy and Mikey, to the kid in front of him.

'Sorry. I was thinking about someone, that's all.'

'You have a wife or something?' DJ asked.

Tom nodded. 'As it happens I do. Cathy. As beautiful as a summer's day. I don't mind telling you that I was punching above my weight with her.'

DJ said, with a grin, 'But you being such a charming fecker . . . not a bother to you!'

'Ha! You catch on quick. That's right. And I have a son. Mikey.' Tom closed his eyes for a moment to gather his thoughts.

'Do you miss them?' DJ asked.

'Every single second of every single day. Not much time goes by that they are not the centre of my thoughts.'

DJ held his phone out. 'I've got credit left. Go on, Doc. Call them.'

'I'm not sure that there's a phone out there that can make the kind of call I'd need to reach them. If there is, kid, I'd like to find it.'

DJ said, 'I have some money from my birthday left. You can have it so you can buy a train ticket to go see them.'

Tom looked at the kid in wonder. 'Thank you for that offer. But I don't need your money.'

DJ stood up and said, 'I didn't have you pegged as a coward! No matter why you left them, they'll be glad to see you. Remember what you said to me, about my mam unconditionally loving me? I bet they feel the same about you!'

Tom looked at DJ and smiled. 'Oh, they loved me. I've never doubted that. I felt the blanket of their love every day we were together.' He paused for a moment and looked away. 'I didn't leave them, kid.'

'Then what? I don't get it.'

'They left me.'

Bette Davis moved to her master's side and nudged his leg in sympathy. Then she raised her ears and sat up. They heard footsteps approaching them.

Bloody Lash, back for a row. Tom jumped up and stood in front of DJ. He should have sent the kid back to the hotel as soon as he saw him.

But it was a woman who came into view. She stopped when she spotted DJ sitting behind the old man on the bench. 'DJ!'

'That's my mam.' DJ jumped up to greet her. He was in trouble, it was way past his time due back to the hotel.

Ruth ran towards him and they stopped a few inches away from each other. 'Are you all right? Where have you been?'

Tom watched the woman's face go through several

emotions: fear, relief, then fear again. She turned to take a better look at the man who had been sitting chatting to her boy in the park.

Years fell away like leaves from the trees, as recognition sparked between them.

'Hello, Ruth.' Somewhere in the back of his mind Tom already knew that it would be her. Their lives were connected, always would be, by the kid.

DJ looked between his mother and his new friend, puzzled. How did Doc know his mam's name? Ruth looked at the man in confusion. She didn't recognise him, yet his voice and his eyes reminded her of someone. *I know you. But how?* She moved closer to him, keeping her son behind her.

'Who are you?' Ruth demanded.

'He's my friend,' DJ said. 'It's the Doc. He's really cool.'

The Doc?

Tom saw fear change to shock as their eyes locked once more. 'It's good to see you again, Ruth Wilde.'

The world shifted for Ruth and she felt unsteady on her feet. She did not trust her eyes, her ears. She grabbed DJ by his arm and pulled him after her.

'See you tomorrow, Doc,' DJ shouted over his shoulder.

Ruth looked back one last time, feeling the old man's eyes on her. He raised his hand in salute in the way that he always did.

Dr O'Grady. She would not be a mother if it had not been for this man.

And now he was here, standing close by, almost unrecognisable.

19

RUTH

Then

'It is time to see how you are doing in here,' Ruth said, patting her bump. There had been several phone calls from Dr O'Grady's surgery. She had missed her last appointment in Wexford Hospital. She had also put off going to see her GP because she knew he would bring up vaccinations again. Everything was quite complicated now that she was carrying a baby. Strangers felt they had a right to tell her how she should behave, what she should do.

She grabbed *Odd Thomas* and shoved it in her satchel. Dr O'Grady knew she did not like to be kept waiting and to his credit, she rarely was. But it was prudent to be prepared for all eventualities.

Ruth liked Dr O'Grady. He was a big man in every way. Tall, broad, with a face that instilled trust. He was a Converse trainer man, or heavy boots if it was a wet day. Today the sun shone. He would be wearing Converse.

He was around her father's age, she guessed. But the polar opposite to the man who was her father in name only. When Dr O'Grady smiled in her direction, she felt his support. She believed that he was on her side and wanted the best for her and her baby. Sometimes she wished he was her father and she daydreamed about a life where someone cared for her and her wellbeing.

She found her new doctor listed on the Medical Council website. She did a Google search to double-check that nothing untoward was reported about him. She could walk to his surgery on Spawell Road from Mark's flat, which was a plus.

Her first appointment with him had not been without issue. Despite the fact that she arrived five minutes early, she was irritated to find three patients still awaiting their consultation in front of her. And that caused her a problem. Not the waiting part – she had been accused of much in her twenty years, but impatience was not one of them – but the waiting room itself. Like Russian roulette, you never knew what dangers were lurking in a doctor's surgery waiting room. It was a potpourri of bacteria and viruses. Ruth knew that a visit to the doctor's with a simple cold could result in far-reaching consequences. Teeny tiny organisms that cause pneumonia, diarrhoea, meningitis, tuberculosis, septicaemia, lingering in the air, would delight in a new host. She was not going to be that host.

Ruth was prepared for this possible issue. She took out a surgical mask she had the foresight to bring with her as a precaution. She was surprised by the reaction of the other patients. They seemed uncomfortable by her prudence. One woman pulled back her small son, who wandered over to examine Ruth more closely. When he sneezed, Ruth was grateful for the mother's over-protective arms and her own forethought.

'Why the mask?' an elderly man shouted, poking her hard on her side with the end of his walking stick.

Ruth answered truthfully, 'I walked into this healthcare facility virus free and I fully intend walking out in the same condition. You, sir, sitting here amongst the potential septi-caemia bacteria, will likely be wheeled out on a trolley.'

She had not expected her statement to cause him so much distress. How could she have known that he was highly strung and prone to dramatics? His reaction caused mass hysteria in the small waiting room. She was quite taken aback by his agitation. As she told Dr O'Grady when he walked into the room, if he insisted all patients wore masks none of this panic would have occurred. She was, however, impressed by Dr O'Grady's finesse as he handled the situation. He was calm and quickly quietened the room down.

After their first consultation, which was most satisfac-tory, he suggested that she might prefer to attend her prenatal appointments directly after lunch. That way she could have the first appointment. She would avoid un-necessary waiting if a patient (inexcusably, as far as she was concerned) was late and messed up the whole schedule.

Right now her swollen feet were causing her problems. Ruth peered over her bulging stomach, which appeared to have grown overnight, taking in her feet, which refused to squeeze themselves into her flat moccasins. This situ-ation took her by surprise because only this morning she had worn them when she went out to buy her milk in a nearby newsagent's.

The speed in which her feet could swell, doubling in size, alarmed her. She could go from Cinderella to Anastasia or Drizella, in an instant, trying to shove a glass slipper onto her huge bunioned feet. She made a mental note to start researching books to read to her baby, when he or she arrived.

Ruth shook away the memory of her mother reading to her as a child. It had been weeks since they had last spoken, months since she had seen Marian in person. And she liked it like that very much. Right now, she had to concentrate on shoe options. To her dismay the only footwear that fitted this Cinderella was either a pair of slippers or a pair of sandals. Each objectionable. She tried once more to place her moccasins on, but realised it was a fool's errand. Time was slipping away and if she did not leave soon she would be late, which was unacceptable.

Reluctantly, she reached for her slippers and realised that already her baby was changing her. Before this pregnancy, she would have just stayed at home rather than wear inappropriate shoes. She peeked out the window of the flat and noted that while it was May, the weather was still in a December frame of mind. Dry, but cold. Sandals just would not do.

Maybe she should cancel again. A kick in her abdomen from baby was like a kick to her conscience. *OK, I shall go.*

Her gait was slower than normal so she estimated that her usual eight-minute walk would take at least double today. Despite her unscheduled mishap with shoes she should still arrive five minutes before her appointment. As she closed the apartment door behind her, she placed her headphones on and began to hum along to Westlife's 'Flying Without Wings', which she had set to play on loop. She held on tight to the banister as she walked down the stairs from Mark's flat to the ground floor. Ruth was careful to keep her eyes focused firmly on the road ahead, concentrating only on the lyrics. She had created a game that helped her get from her flat to the doctor's. The rules were simple. She must avoid making eye contact with anyone between each mention of the word 'Flying' that Westlife sung. She was very good at this game and won nearly every time.

Ruth was so lost in the music that she nearly ran into a large double buggy that took up half of the pavement in front of her. *Damn it.* Now she had lost that round. She looked at the smiling woman with irritation, who moved her buggy to one side to let her pass. The woman seemed disappointed when Ruth continued forward without stopping for a chat. This was a new phenomenon for Ruth. She had spent most of her childhood and teenage years on the periphery of the various clubs that were formed in school. By choice in the main. She preferred her own company. And eventually the kids in her class stopped asking her to join in. Her pregnancy puzzled her. It was like a golden ticket, and had opened the doors to a sisterhood of mothers who all nodded, smiled, spoke to her, no matter how hard she tried to avoid them. It was most disconcerting.

She felt her baby squirm inside of her, fighting to find space in what was already a crowded room. She was breathless by the time she walked through the surgery doors. Her heart beat so loud that even the headphones could not protect her from its sound. With regret she slipped them off, ready to face Dr O'Grady's receptionist, Breda.

'Hello, Ruth,' Breda said, smiling when she noticed her slippers. Ruth liked her a lot, despite the fact that she could sometimes be overly familiar. 'How are you doing? Not long now! I think this must be the quickest pregnancy ever, eh? I bet you don't feel like that, though! I remember when I was pregnant with my two, at the end every day felt like a week. People told me that pregnancy was a joy, but it was pure penance for me. Didn't suit me at all, I don't mind telling you. The heartburn, it just lifted me out of it every day. Sure you'd know all about that, wouldn't you?' She reached in to rub Ruth's stomach.

This Ruth could not allow. She pulled away and said, 'I have a right to my privacy. I have a right to my space. I have an appointment at quarter to two. It is now twenty minutes to two.'

The receptionist gave her a look that she'd received many times in her life. It was the triple whammy of looks: a mix of disappointment, reproach and pity. Ruth knew she had upset Breda and she regretted that, but she did not like to be touched.

When Dr O'Grady walked out, Ruth was not sure who was more relieved, her or Breda. *I knew it! Converse!*

'I can always rely on you to be on time, Ruth. I wish all of my patients were as punctual,' he said, leading the way into his surgery.

'Being late is rude and inconsiderate. I would never

place a higher premium on my time than on yours,' Ruth replied.

'I'll remember that next time someone rocks up here twenty minutes late for the last appointment of the day!' Dr O'Grady said.

'Better late than never, but never late is better,' Ruth said.

Dr O'Grady laughed out loud at that. 'How are you today?'

'I am quite well, thank you,' Ruth replied. 'How are you?'

He looked up from his computer screen and replied, 'I'm very well, too, Ruth.' He tapped his mouse twice, then scrolled down the screen. 'Right, here you are. Let's see how far along you are today.'

'Two hundred and seventy-seven days. Of course this is just an approximation. Only four per cent of babies are born on their due date,' Ruth stated.

'For sure. In my experience that's true.'

'And as a Caucasian woman under thirty, statistics show that it is extremely unlikely that I will be part of that four per cent,' Ruth added.

Dr O'Grady laughed out loud again and said, 'You are a ticket, Ruth. I like a woman who has done her research. My wife is just like you. She likes to have all the facts herself.'

Ruth was pleased with the comparison. She did not know the doctor's wife, but she imagined she was quite lovely, just like he was.

'I'm happy to see that you turned up for the last scan. I was getting worried there. Thought I would have to drive you to it myself.'

'I do not care for hospital appointments. They keep changing my registrar. I liked the first one; the second and third, not so much.'

'I understand it's tricky for you not to have the same people take care of you and the baby at each hospital visit. But as I explained before, the registrars work on a four-week rota. But I can assure you that they all have your notes in front of them. So you are in perfectly safe hands, no matter who sees you.'

'I did enjoy seeing the baby on the scan,' Ruth conceded, gently rubbing her tummy.

Dr O'Grady smiled. 'I have your notes from that hospital visit and baby is coming along nicely. Do you know what you're having yet?'

'I am having a baby,' Ruth answered, puzzled.

His laugh bellowed out into the room. 'Yes, that you are. And that's all you need to know, right? May I have your permission to touch your tummy? I promise to be quick.'

'Yes,' Ruth said. She appreciated him asking her for permission. It was the unsolicited strokes of strangers that made her want to scream.

Dr O'Grady rubbed his hands together briskly and said, 'You're going to feel a slight pressure as I palpate the baby.'

Ruth grimaced. She did not like this one bit.

'Ah, that all feels perfect,' Dr O'Grady said. 'I'm very happy.'

Ruth felt pride explode inside her at this statement. Perfect. He said her baby was perfect. *Take that, Mother.*

'There is no nicer sound than that of a good, strong, steady heartbeat,' Dr O'Grady said. 'Now it's time to check you out.'

He placed the strap of the blood-pressure unit around her arm and began to squeeze the pump. 'Sorry about this. It will be all over in a jiffy.'

Ruth closed her eyes and thought about the baby that would soon be in her arms. She wondered if it would like Westlife as much as she did. She read that babies liked listening to music. They could listen to hers together. And she would read *Odd Thomas* to the baby, too. Cutting out the scary bits until it was old enough to understand.

'You look happy,' Dr O'Grady said in approval. 'Penny for them.'

Ruth answered, 'I was thinking about reading to my baby.'

'Well, it won't be long before that happens, I suspect. This baby is a big one. I reckon he or she will be coming out to say hello to you any day now.'

'I am ready. I have packed my hospital bag. And I have rehearsed my route to the hospital several times. If Mark is at home, he will bring me. But I also have three taxi companies on standby. I have inspected their cars and all seems in order.'

Dr O'Grady looked up from his notes, where he had scribbled down some more information. 'And how have you been doing food-wise?'

'Your gift is still working,' Ruth said, referring to the blindfold that he had given her a few weeks back when she confessed how much she craved oranges. 'I've been eating mango and oranges every day. Once I cannot see their colour, as you predicted, I can cope.'

Dr O'Grady nodded in approval. 'Good for you. You know, that blindfold has been at home for years unused.

My wife, Cathy, got it as a present at some point but she never used it. She doesn't like the dark. Has to have a small chink of light in our room each night or else she cannot sleep. It was her idea to give it to you, I can't take credit for it.'

'I prefer the darkness myself,' Ruth said.

'Well, you should be very proud of yourself. I know how hard it is for you to eat anything that isn't white. But you are doing what is best for the baby. And that's what being a mother is all about. Lucky little baby, having you.'

Ruth had made many decisions purely on the basis that Dr O'Grady said it was the right thing to do for the baby. She fought hard against taking the flu and pertussis vaccinations he recommended for pregnancy. But as soon as he told her to think of the baby's needs, she found she had the strength to cope with the intrusive needles.

Her mother's angry face flashed into her mind again; the very last thing she screamed at her, when she walked out the door of her childhood home. *You have to get rid of it. Before it's too late. You can't keep this baby. For goodness' sake, you don't even know the father's surname.*

'Are you OK?' Dr O'Grady noticed the pain on Ruth's face. She nodded.

'Have you thought any more about who you want with you when you deliver the baby?' he asked gently.

I want Dean.

She tried not to think about him too much, because when she did, it threatened to undo her. For a second – just a split second – she visualised him standing beside her in the delivery ward, holding her hand, waiting to meet their first child.

'Thinking of holding your baby again?' Dr O'Grady said. 'You were smiling again.'

She pushed all thoughts of soul mates from her head and said, 'I shall be on my own for the delivery.'

'There's nobody?' Dr O'Grady asked, clearly worried about this information.

'No. But that is fine. You see, I am used to being on my own. In fact, I do alone quite well.'

'Not for much longer, Ruth. Soon you will have a family of your own,' Dr O'Grady said. Ruth began to dream of a different future for her and her baby and thought that maybe, just maybe, everything was going to be all right.

20

TOM

Now

It took him hours to get over the shock of seeing Ruth. A ghost from his past, standing in front of him, in this park. Just under one million people lived in Dublin. And yet somehow he and Ruth had stumbled across each other. Because of DJ. She looked well. Hardly changed from the last time he'd seen her. Life had continued to give her knocks, it seemed. Living in emergency housing. But that kid of hers. She had loved him before he was born. He understood that, because it was the same for him and Cathy. His eyes stung, it was late and his memories haunted him. His head was jumbled with images of Cathy and Ruth, each with a baby in her arms. Bette was out for the count already, snoring softly beside him. He had to give his head peace, so he closed his eyes and let the dreams take him away . . .

*   *   *

They never had a big discussion about whether they wanted children or not. They just fell into their conversations, a shared hope that one day their family would grow. At forty, Cathy had some concerns that she'd left it too late to have a family. Tom wouldn't hear of it and shut down her worries as quickly as she raised them. As a GP he had dozens of consultations with couples who wanted to conceive and were finding the process tricky. There was nobody better to answer Cathy's concerns and reassure her. But aside from the science, from his experience as a doctor, there was something inside of Tom that was convinced that children were going to be part of their future.

Months passed and became a year. They celebrated their anniversaries with joy that their life was good. But it was also tinged with some disappointment. Fertility tests gave good news – no underlying issue for either of them. The bad news came with every pee on the stick resulting in a big fat no. Tom watched Cathy begin to lose hope. Each new birthday, she fretted about stark statistics regarding chromosomal abnormalities.

One night, late, in the darkness of their bedroom, when they should have been asleep, but were both overwrought from another failed pregnancy test, Cathy confessed, 'I don't think we will ever have children.'

'Yes we will,' Tom replied firmly.

'There is a chance, a big chance, that children are not in our future. Have you considered that?'

'Not really,' Tom admitted. He could not explain it. He just had a strong conviction that she was wrong.

'*All these hormones I'm taking, all they do is make me fat.*' *Cathy looked down at her gut.*

'*You're not fat,*' *Tom said.*

'*I am nearly thirty pounds heavier than the day I met you, Tom. Fact.*'

'*I haven't noticed,*' *Tom lied without missing a beat.* '*I've put some weight on myself.*' *He lied once more as Cathy looked at his lean physique.*

'*I'm scared,*' *Cathy whispered.*

Tom had never heard his wife say this in all their time together. She was the fierce one, strong, unflappable. He whispered back, '*Of what?*'

'*That you'll leave me. That we'll not survive this.*'

Anger came fast. He'd never felt like that about a single thing she had said or done. Until now. '*Is that how little you think of me?*'

She shrugged.

'*Cathy, I love you. And our life is enough for me as it is.*' *Undeterred he continued,* '*If we don't get pregnant, it's shit. It's heartbreaking. It's not what we wanted. But it doesn't mean it's the end of us, of our life together.*'

'*I'm just so tired from it all,*' *Cathy said. Her face, which normally was only moments away from a smile that made his heart sing, was clouded with self-doubt and recrimination.* '*It's like a full-time job with no pay cheque at the end of the month.*'

'*Darling, it's not your job to get pregnant for us. Nor is it my job to get you pregnant. We have spoken to the experts, we've gotten their advice, we're following it. We hardly drink any more, we are an organic household and I let it all hang out in my boxers every day. We have to wait.'*

'We wait,' she whispered.

In the end, they were both right.

21

RUTH

Then

Ruth was now 284 days pregnant. She was tired, she was fed up and she was not sure she could last another week, which Dr O'Grady predicted was likely.

'My mother thinks I should not be a parent,' Ruth said while Dr O'Grady took her blood pressure.

That would explain the elevated blood pressure. Dr O'Grady looked at the young girl in front of him in concern. She had been coming to him now for almost five months. And in that time he'd grown fond of her. Worried about her.

'Never mind what your mother thinks. What's important is what you think.' Dr O'Grady asked, 'Can you be a good parent?'

Ruth looked down at her bump and felt a reassuring kick to her ribcage. 'Yes.'

'That's all you need to remember.'

'I like your stethoscope,' Ruth said. Dr O'Grady always

wore it around his neck. Something about the soft black leather strap was reassuring to her.

'It was a gift from my parents the day I graduated. It's precious to me.' He turned the stainless-silver chest-piece over and showed her the engraved words that ran around the circle: 'A fine doctor but an even finer son.'

Ruth could not imagine her parents ever calling her 'fine'. She suspected it was a nice feeling to be loved like that. And she knew that she would do everything to ensure that her child felt that same love, too. Maybe one day he or she would grow up to be a doctor, like Dr O'Grady.

'Has anyone ever suggested to you that there might be a reason why you find certain things more difficult than others?' Dr O'Grady asked.

She shook her head. 'Other than to say I have quirks or I'm highly strung, no.'

'I'd say that you are the least highly strung person I know,' Dr O'Grady answered. He put his pen down and leaned in towards Ruth. 'I hope you don't mind but I spoke to my wife about you.'

Ruth was surprised to hear this. 'I'm not sure anything about me is worthy of discussion, outside of this office.'

'I disagree. I think you have no concept of how lovely you are. My wife, Cathy, runs The Rainbow Centre in Wexford. Do you know it?'

Ruth shook her head.

'It's a place for adults with additional needs to go during the day. There are a number of adults who go who are on the spectrum. The autistic spectrum.' Dr O'Grady's voice was low, gentle.

Ruth realised that she had not blinked since he

started to speak. Her eyes felt dry and itchy. She allowed herself to blink three times in rapid succession, keeping her eyes on the doctor's boots. It was raining outside.

'I wonder if there is a possibility, a strong possibility, that you might be like them?'

Ruth looked at him in shock. Why was he saying this to her? She placed a hand over her tummy, protecting her child from his words.

Dr O'Grady continued, 'Please don't be alarmed, Ruth. I believe that you are just perfect as you are. The world would be a better place with more Ruth Wildes in it. But I always think that knowledge is power. If you had a diagnosis, it could help you understand and work through some of the things that you find difficult . . .' Dr O'Grady paused to let the words settle in.

'I am not giving up my baby,' Ruth stated, pushing herself up to her feet.

Dr O'Grady reached his hand over towards Ruth's and clasped hers between his own, surprised when she did not take it away. 'No one is going to take this baby from you. I just want to help you prepare for the little one's arrival and afterwards make sure you have all the support you need.'

'I will not give up my baby. Not to you, not to my mother, not to your wife or her centre,' Ruth insisted.

Dr O'Grady held his two hands up, in surrender. 'I believe you! I wouldn't dream of taking your baby from you. I would just like you to meet Cathy. Together, you can take it from there.'

'What is your wife like?'

'She's the best person I know. Kind. Smart. Funny. And

she doesn't bullshit anyone. I suspect you two will get on like a house on fire.'

So twenty-four hours later Ruth found herself sitting in the centre, face to face with Cathy.

'I'm so pleased to meet you,' Cathy said. There were two chairs side by side, in front of the desk. To Ruth's surprise Cathy chose to sit beside her, rather than at the desk.

Behind which was a wall of books. Ruth liked that. She could not see any Dean Koontz on the shelf. That was a disappointment. Soft music played on a CD player. Also a disappointment, as it was not Westlife. She did, however, approve of Cathy's pink, sparkling Skechers runners.

'Dr O'Grady talks very highly of you,' Cathy said.

Ruth nodded. 'I am very pleased to know him, too.'

'I'd like to help you. If you would let me,' Cathy continued.

'I am not giving up my baby,' Ruth stated once more for the record. Better to have no misunderstandings, she always believed.

'I'm glad to hear it. I wouldn't give up my baby either,' Cathy replied.

'I would think that it is highly unlikely that you are pregnant, given your estimated age. However, the oldest non-IVF mother recorded is an American woman who was fifty-seven at the time. So with that in mind, I apologise if indeed you are also pregnant.'

Cathy replied, with only a ghost of a smile, 'Oh, you are kind that you would think it even a remote possibility. I'm afraid I've a few years on that wonderful American lady. No more babies for me.'

Ruth looked around the room, then settled her attention on the bookshelf behind the desk once again.

'Do you like books?' Cathy asked.

'Yes,' Ruth replied.

'What kind?'

'I love Dean Koontz,' Ruth replied without hesitation. 'And Stephen King. J. K. Rowling.'

'I don't know Dean Koontz, but I like the *Harry Potter* books, too,' Cathy said. 'Tell me, Ruth, do you ever memorise passages or quotes from favourite books?'

Ruth looked at her with suspicion. She should have known her parents were involved in this meeting. They must have told Cathy about her habit of quoting Odd Thomas. They hated that.

Cathy said, 'I've spoken to nobody about you with the exception of Dr O'Grady. I promise. But I would like you to answer me. Please.'

'From time to time, I do consider that I might be mad. Like any self-respecting lunatic, however, I am always quick to dismiss any doubts about my sanity,' Ruth said.

Cathy laughed. 'I like that.'

'It's not mine. It's written by the genius Dean Koontz,' Ruth replied.

'Funny and clever. I can see why my husband likes you so much. Which book is that quote from?'

'From my favourite of Mr Koontz's books, *Odd Thomas*.'

'Do you know many parts of that book off by heart?' Cathy asked.

'I just quoted one, so that is a redundant question,' Ruth replied.

'You are quite correct. I'll rephrase. How many times have you read it, would you think?' Cathy asked.

'One hundred and three times,' Ruth answered without hesitation. Her first time was in 2003. Since then, it was rare that a day passed when she had not read at least a couple of chapters.

'What a tribute to the author. I am sure he would love to know that his words mean so much to you,' Cathy said.

'*Odd Thomas* is misunderstood and at times mistreated by many. I understand him.'

'Well, you've sold me on it. I think I'd better pick up a copy of this book. And soon.'

'I have also enjoyed the sequels, *Forever Odd* and *Brother Odd*. But so far neither has eclipsed the first, which remains my favourite,' Ruth added.

'Noted.'

'How long have you been married to Dr O'Grady?' Ruth asked.

'Nearly twenty years.'

'I like Dr O'Grady,' Ruth stated.

'Me, too,' Mrs O'Grady said, smiling. 'He told me about the first time you went to his surgery. Is it tricky for you when there are crowds?'

Ruth nodded. 'I do not like shopping centres in particular. They are too noisy. Unless it is really early. Then it is tolerable. It was different at the surgery. I did not care for the germs that were most likely to be airborne there.'

'That makes sense. How do you like social situations, like, say, parties, with families or friends?'

Moments in Ruth's life from early childhood to now, flashed through her mind.

Her fifth birthday party where she sat in the corner of their sitting room, alone, watching her classmates play together without her. Various clubs her parents forced her to join where her only survival technique was to tune out, by thinking about her favourite books and TV shows, rather than join in. And the numerous attempts – all disastrous – in clubs and bars with Mark, who was forced to bring his sister along in an effort to normalise her. But for every girl he charmed, she managed to offend someone with her awkwardness.

'Are you OK?' Cathy asked, her voice soft with concern.

Ruth said, 'People do not like me very much. I think I make them uncomfortable. I wish I knew why, so I could change it.'

'Well, I like you very much just as you are. I don't think I'd like you to change at all,' Cathy said. With sincerity. She slid a clip board towards Ruth with a pen attached to it. 'This questionnaire will take about twenty minutes to complete, but it will really help us to understand you better. I'll make us a cup of tea while you complete it.'

'I do not drink tea. But a glass of cold milk would be acceptable. Anything less than ice cold and I will not drink it,' Ruth warned.

'I think I can manage that,' Cathy said.

Ruth picked up the pen and began to answer the questions, one after the other, until her eyes swam and blurred. She ticked 'YES' in most boxes. She completed the questionnaire in under ten minutes and accepted her drink from Cathy when she handed it in.

'Is that cold enough?' Cathy asked.

'Acceptable,' Ruth replied. By the time she had emptied the glass, Cathy said, 'Ruth, based on these answers and our chat earlier, I'm pretty certain that you are on the autistic spectrum.'

Images of stereotypical autistic characters jumped into Ruth's mind. *She thinks I'm like Raymond Babbitt in* Rain Man.

This thought triggered a memory, a row she'd had with Mark when they were children. She idolised her brother and, despite his indifference to her, she remained steadfast in her appreciation of him and his ease at life. Her mother's favourite catchphrase, 'Why can't you be more like Mark?' made her wish that she could swap her social awkwardness for his charm. And one day an idea crept into her head. She could copy him. Then people would like her as much as they liked him. She watched him, mimicking his movements, repeating his words. Imitation may be the sincerest form of flattery, but for Mark it was the opposite. His rage when he shouted at her, 'Leave me the fuck alone, you freaking rain man!' left her shaken for days. But it also curbed her habit of copying him.

'Ruth?' Cathy asked. She leaned in, her hand hovering near Ruth's.

Ruth told Cathy about the incident. 'I could not forget the insult. I began to question myself, was I like him? So I asked my parents. They were angry. At both Mark and me.'

'That movie has a lot to answer for,' Cathy said. 'Stereotypical traits like maths genius are not in my experience the norm for those on the spectrum.'

Ruth shrugged. 'My maths skills are excellent.'

Cathy laughed. 'Good for you! I suppose the way I see it, though, there will only ever be one Raymond Babbitt. Just like there is only one Ruth Wilde.'

Ruth liked that. *And there will only be one of you, little one.* She stroked her bump.

'It's such an exciting time for you,' Cathy said. 'But it must feel overwhelming at times. Dealing with all the changes in your body. And preparing for what comes next. If you'd like, I can help you understand what this diagnosis means. It doesn't need to be the end of the world. In fact, I hope it might be the beginning of a new one.'

'Given my heritage and the ordeal of my childhood, I sometimes wonder why I myself am not insane. Maybe I am,' Ruth said.

'*Odd Thomas* or Ruth Wilde?' Cathy asked.

'*Odd*,' Ruth replied.

'I really am going to buy a copy on the way home tonight. You should be on commission!'

Ruth leaned in closer to Cathy and whispered, 'Can you make me normal?'

Cathy shook her head. 'Normal? I tried being normal once. Worst ten minutes of my life!'

Ruth loved that. 'I shall steal that joke. It is most satisfactory.'

'It's all yours, Ruth. The point is, you don't need to change, you just need some help discovering who you really are. I suspect that person is pretty spectacular.'

'I am afraid that my mother will tell people that I am a bad mother and then I'll lose my baby,' Ruth whispered, her eyes not leaving her bump.

'Then you must *be* a good mother. Then it doesn't matter what your mother or anyone else says,' Cathy said.

'That's what Dr O'Grady said, too.'

'Well, you have to believe it. I have faith in you, Ruth.'

Her logic was sound. Ruth smiled at her, feeling like she had walked into this room alone, but would leave with a friend. 'I want to leave Wexford. Start again somewhere new.' She told Cathy about her father's money and her plan to move to Dublin.

'Good for you. I think that is a great idea. And I'll help you. But before you move, before your little baby arrives, would you spend some time with me here in the Centre. I'd love to get to know you a bit better.'

'That would be most acceptable.' Happiness sparked its way around Ruth. *I'll be a good mother, I promise, little one.*

Sometimes life throws a curveball your way. Because while Ruth walked back to Mark's flat, her head full of plans for her future, her mother was waiting. And Marian was not leaving until Ruth agreed to give her baby up. No matter what she had to do to persuade her.

22

TOM

Now

Tom avoided his usual Thursday haunts. He told himself that his knee was playing up, and that was why he did not call into Pearse Street Library. When of course the truth of the matter was he was really staying close to the park entrance in case Ruth came by. He could not pretend that he was not shaken by her appearance the previous night. This connection he felt towards her son had been unfathomable. From that first moment when he saw him with a spray can in hand. Ruth . . . His eyes flicked back to the entrance gate to the park. Maybe she wouldn't come.

But somehow he knew that if she was going to come on any day, it would be this.

The eighteenth of October.

The day he met Cathy. The day he married Cathy. The day of so many firsts . . .

And then she was in front of him, holding two paper cups.

'How do you know my son?' Ruth asked.

Straight to the point, just like he remembered. 'You should be very proud. He's a fine young man,' Tom replied.

'I did not ask you for your opinion of him. How do you know him?'

Tom replied, 'I met him last Saturday. He was outside your old flat in Swords. I happened to be camping out in a doorway close by.'

Ruth was thrown by this. How had she not known this? When DJ had got back that evening he'd looked guilty, but she put that down to the fact that he was late home and she was cross with him.

Tom continued, 'He was about to get his revenge on your landlord but he didn't do anything. Honestly.'

'Tell me everything,' Ruth said.

'He was going to graffiti the flat with some spray cans. I pointed out the CCTV that was on the street, suggesting it would not be a wise move. We had a chat. He left. No damage done. I promise.'

Ruth exhaled in relief. Then she looked at Tom, alarm once again in her eyes, and said, 'Did you follow him here?'

Tom held his hands up. 'No! No! I swear!' He had not thought of it from a mother's perspective: that she might add two and two and get six. 'DJ left Swords that night and I thought no more of him or the incident.' That wasn't strictly true though was it? He felt a connection to the kid from the get-go. He thought at first it was because the kid reminded him of Mikey. But he was wrong. He was there when the kid took his first breath. It had created a bond it seemed, that pulled them back together again, all these years later. 'Last night he was here, in the park, sitting on my bench. I'm not sure who was more surprised, me or him. When you came along we were chatting. I told him to go home too.'

'You just happened to be here? I find that hard to believe,' Ruth asked, her head telling her that the co-incidence was unlikely, but her heart reminding her of the countless times she'd sat in Dr O'Grady's surgery and felt safe. And the time when he'd saved her and DJ. She knew without further confirmation that he was speaking the truth.

'I'm here most days. Every now and then I move around. Like last Saturday. I've not been in Swords for years, but the urge took me for some reason. Other than that, I'd never have met DJ there. This is my park. It's where I live. Honestly.' Tom looked at her and hoped she believed him.

'This is very strange . . . Dr O'Grady.' And then she realised something else. 'I saw you on the road. Last week. I picked up your flask.'

'I realised that too, last night. I thought you looked familiar. Thank you for that. It was kind of you. Call me Doc or Tom, by the way. I'm not Dr O'Grady any more.'

'I shall stick with Dr O'Grady,' Ruth replied. She handed him one of the paper cups.

Tom hoped that meant she believed him. 'I didn't think you were going to give me that. Thank you.' He smelled the coffee in appreciation.

'Five minutes ago I contemplated throwing it over you,' Ruth said.

Tom knew she was one hundred per cent serious.

'So you live here? On this bench?' Ruth asked. He nodded. She looked around her in shock. 'What happened to you?' She moved herself a few inches away from her former doctor and the musty, damp smell that he emitted.

He ignored her question. He didn't have an answer for her. Not one that made any sense.

'What were you and DJ talking about last night?' Ruth asked when the silence stretched between them.

'Life, moving here, you, his friends . . . that kind of thing. I had no idea that DJ was your son, Ruth. I got just as much of a shock as you did when you walked over.' Tom turned towards her and he said, earnestly, with truth, 'But I've thought about you on and off, over the years.'

'And I you. I preferred your Converse, by the way,' Ruth said, looking down at his clumpy brown hobnail boots.

'I haven't worn a pair of those in a long time. How are you, Ruth? You look well.'

'I am well. Thank you. More than I can say for you,' Ruth replied.

His answer was a low rumble of laughter.

One boot was dirtier than the other. That was curious. 'I went back to the surgery to look for you. Before I left Wexford.'

He watched her pop a knuckle and felt a flush of shame. Once or twice he thought of the patients he had left behind ten years ago. But he would be lying if he pretended that it had kept him awake at night.

'It stopped making sense for me to work there,' he said.

'I still do not understand why you are living in this park.'

Tom had spent most of the day trying to work out how to answer this inevitable question. Unsuccessfully. How do you explain something to someone when you don't understand it yourself?

'Hello, Doc,' a voice called out, a welcome interruption. Bones walked towards them leading a heavily pregnant young girl by her arm.

'Doc, this is Sheila. She's up the duff.'

'You don't say.' Tom's sarcasm was lost on Bones.

'I told her you'd check her out.' Bones turned towards the young girl and reassured her, 'Doc's sound as a pound. You can trust him.'

'Hi, Sheila,' Tom said. 'Take the weight off your feet.'

Ruth moved further along the bench, making room for the young girl. Her poor feet were swollen, almost bursting out of the green runners she wore.

'How old are you, Sheila?' Tom asked.

'Twenty,' she replied, lifting her chin in defiance, daring them to question her obvious lie.

'You look no more than fifteen,' Ruth said, taking the dare. Tom shared her scepticism. This was just a kid and she was in a world of trouble.

'How many weeks pregnant are you? Do you know?'

The girl shrugged. 'Maybe eight months. Maybe more.'

'Have you been to see a doctor before?' Tom asked. *Please say you've had ante-natal care.*

She shook her head.

Damn it.

Bones inched his way in closer. 'Her fella doesn't trust doctors, but that's not right. My mam swore by the

169

Rotunda Maternity Hospital. Had all of us there. But she won't go in. She needs your help, Doc.'

'Where are you staying at the minute?' Tom asked. *Say a hostel. Don't be outside.*

'We're squatting in a house down by the quays. No electricity, but we've got a little camping stove. And a mattress,' Sheila said.

When she saw the look of pity that flew across his and Ruth's faces, she said quickly, 'Bobby and I are gonna get our own place. And we'll fix it up and make it special for the baby. I have a cot. I found it in a skip. I'm gonna paint it up and make it real pretty.'

'Good for you,' Tom said. 'And where's Bobby now?'

Bones mimicked sniffing a line of cocaine behind her back. No further explanation needed.

'Where are your parents?' Ruth asked.

Sheila said, 'I ain't got no parents. Not any more.'

'Dead?' Tom asked.

'To me they are. My da's a fucking pervert. And my so-called mother turned a blind eye and ignored it when he crept into my room and my pants. I left a year ago. I'm not going back.'

'No one is going to make you do that,' Ruth said. *The poor child. What a life to lead.*

Tom pulled out his black leather doctor's case from his rucksack. Then took out his Littmann stethoscope.

'You still have it. That's the same one you had when I was pregnant with DJ,' Ruth said, seeing a flash of the inscription under the silver chest-piece.

'One of the few things I've kept since I left Wexford. I've had it since my first day as a junior doctor. I dare say I'll have it with me the day I die. My mother said when she gave it to me, "All a doctor needs is a stet and pen and he's set." She was right,' Tom replied.

'What's the pen for?' Bones asked.

'To write prescriptions. But I don't do much of that lately. Comes in handy for the crosswords, though,' Tom said. 'I need to listen to the baby's heart rate, Sheila.'

They all held their breath as he placed the silver chest-piece on Sheila's abdomen. And exhaled in relief when he smiled. 'That's a strong heart rate. Good. Very good. Would you like to listen?'

Sheila's eyes filled with tears as he placed the stetho-scope in her ears and she heard her baby's heart beating inside of her. *A new life.* She had created this.

Filled with wonder she whispered, 'I think this is the first time I've properly been happy in my whole life.'

Bones wiped his eyes furiously, then turned away.

Ruth looked at the young girl and realised their lives were not so different. 'Wait until you hold your baby in your arms. It will change everything, I promise you.'

Tom took out his cushion from his rucksack and placed it on the bench. 'Lie down there, Sheila.' Once she was as comfortable as she could be on a metal bench, he began to palpate Sheila's abdomen. 'Well, you're at least thirty-seven weeks, by my reckoning. The head is engaged.'

'Does that mean the baby is coming soon?' Sheila asked, her voice so low they could barely hear it. She wasn't ready.

'I would say within the next week or so. Your boyfriend might not like doctors but for the baby and your safety you need to be under the care of a hospital. You can't have this baby in a squat.'

171

'Bobby said no hospitals. No doctors. They'll take the baby from me. They'll send me back to my parents,' Sheila said, tears welling up in her eyes again.

'You cannot let that happen!' Ruth exclaimed.

'There are charities that will give you assistance in finding a home, support in caring for your baby. You don't have to do this on your own. There are people I know that will help,' Tom said.

'I'd rather die than go home. What if Da did to this baby what he did to me?' Sheila said.

'Whatever happens, you are not going back to him. But you need to trust me. Let me get you help,' Tom said.

Sheila wrung her hands like she was squeezing water out of sheets. Her heart hammered in her chest. She hadn't met an adult who she could trust. What made this guy any different from the rest of them? Bobby. He loved her. He swore he would take care of her.

'I met Bobby the first week I arrived in Dublin. He saw me nicking some chocolate from the Spar and he knew that I was a runaway. He left home the previous year. His dad used to beat the shit out of him for sport. He understands what it's like because he's been through it before. He takes care of me. He'll take care of the baby, too. I know he will.'

Tom looked at Bones, who shook his head just the once. So this Bobby was not all Sheila built him up to be.

Ruth turned to Sheila and said, 'I left home when I was pregnant. I was scared just like you are now. My mother told me that I had to give my baby up for adoption. But Dr O'Grady helped me. You can trust him.'

'Did you keep your baby?' Sheila asked.

Ruth nodded. 'He's ten years old now, in school. And my life is changed because of him. Dr O'Grady helped me back then. He can help you, too.' She looked at Dr O'Grady and said, 'You saved DJ's life. You saved me, too.' And with that acknowledgement, Ruth knew that it was now her turn to help him. She did not know what had happened to him, but no matter what, he now had her on his side.

'Please let me help you too,' Tom said to the young girl.

Sheila wanted to trust the Doc. She wanted someone to swoop in and save her and the baby; tell her what to do.

'I'm not really twenty,' Sheila said. 'I'm fourteen.'

Ruth felt a tremor of fear run from the tip of her head down through her body. This girl was only four years older than DJ and dealing with so much. How could that be fair?

'Do you see your parents now?' Sheila asked Ruth.

Ruth shook her head.

While Tom was not surprised by this news, he was disappointed, and angry too. He had hoped that with time and the joy at being grandparents, they would have stepped up. Ruth had been on her own all this time. Damn them to hell.

'I need to get back. Bobby will be looking for me.' Sheila stood up, pulling her jacket around her.

Ruth stood up and took a deep breath. She wanted to help this girl, like she had been helped by Dr O'Grady. She reached over and touched her hand, lifting her eyes to reach the girl's. 'You are about to become a mother.

You have to put the baby first. This is not about you any more, Sheila. It is bigger than that. Let Dr O'Grady make some calls and find you some help. For the baby's sake if you will not do it for your own.'

The young girl nodded and walked over to Bones, who was shuffling from one foot to the other. He wanted a cider. He wanted a smoke. But not until he taken Sheila back to the squat.

'Come back here tomorrow, same time. I'll have a plan in place for you by then,' Tom said.

'I'll bring her back, Doc,' Bones promised.

'Take care of her, Mr Bones,' Ruth said.

With a half-bow to Ruth, he offered his bony, grubby arm to Sheila.

'That baby doesn't stand much of a chance if she doesn't find a way to get back into the system,' Tom said.

They both sat back down on the bench side by side. The smell did not bother Ruth as much any more. 'How will you make calls? Do you need to use my phone? I have a pay-as-you-go. It even has credit on it!'

'I'll need Peter McVerry's help for this one. I'll head into the shelter tomorrow to ask their advice; use their phone. But thanks for the offer. I'll remember that, if I need one in future.'

'Life has changed a lot since we last saw each other,' Ruth said.

'It has.'

'Yet you are still a doctor,' Ruth said.

Somehow or other, over the years Tom was on the streets, his doctoring crept back up on him again. It wasn't a conscious decision, it just kind of happened. 'This bench is my surgery now. I've patched up a few here over the years. And I do the odd house call.'

Ruth was surprised until Tom continued, 'House calls to homes under bridges, in doorways, in a squat, behind wheelie bins in the back of supermarket car parks, at the ends of dark alleyways.'

Most of his street patients had neglected themselves for years so their symptoms were more acute and pronounced.

'Yesterday, a man, a young fella, came to see me here, barely able to walk. Seen him around over the past twelve months. He sometimes drinks with Bones and Lash over the road. I watched him go from a cocky know-it-all to a shadow of his former self. The street has a way of shutting the most exuberant of people up,' Tom said.

'What was wrong with him?' Ruth asked.

'He had pneumococcal pneumonia,' Tom replied. 'His lungs were fecked. I'd say he was walking around outside with that for days. It took me a while to persuade him to go to A&E. But I got him there in the end.'

'You saved him,' Ruth said.

Tom shrugged. 'I do what I can. We're all in this together, the way I see it. Life has let us down in some way. So I listen to their hearts and sometimes to their stories. Both usually broken. I do what I can.'

He is still a good man, I knew it. 'You are helping the invisible, Dr O'Grady. But who is helping you?' Ruth whispered.

Bette Davis whined and laid her head on his knee. He ruffled behind her soft ears and felt a great sadness envelop him. Tom didn't need help. He was exactly where he wanted to be.

'How's The Lodge?' he changed the subject.

'I am adjusting to it. It could be worse. I could be on the streets.'

They sat in silence, her words fluttering around the two of them. She glanced at him every now and then, taking in every line on his face, eyes that were once brown, now watered down and grey. Bushy eyebrows with long hairs tangling their way over his lashes, with a shock of white hair and beard. He was the same as he had been ten years ago and yet he wasn't.

'What happened to you?' Ruth asked for the third time.

'I lost everything,' Tom finally admitted.

'Me, too,' Ruth said.

For now, that was enough questions.

23

RUTH

Then

'How did you get in?' Ruth asked her mother, who was waiting for her in the flat.

'Mark. He's gone out with a friend for the evening.' Marian took a sip from a bottle of soda.

'What do you want?' Ruth was tired from her walk back from The Rainbow Centre.

'Where were you?' Marian hated not knowing what was going on in her daughter's life.

Ruth replied, 'It is not your business any more, Mother.'

A flash of anger flew across Marian's face. She did not like this version of her daughter. Insolent. More than that. Independent.

'Be careful Ruth. I'm here to give you the chance to apologise. And then you can come home. You are not equipped to live on your own. You need me.'

Ruth said, 'You might be surprised by how well I am

coping without you. And I am not alone. I have friends. And right now, I need to rest. So please leave.'

Marian moved towards her daughter and waved her bottle at her as she said, 'You will come back home to me. With your tail between your legs.' Then she walked out, closing the hall door behind her.

Ruth closed her eyes and started to count, right up to eighty-seven, when she heard the slam of the front door at the foot of the stairs. But she could not rest until she was sure that Marian was gone.

For someone who spent most of her time looking at the ground, it was perhaps the cruelest trick of fate that in this very moment Ruth's eyes were facing straight ahead when she walked onto the landing. She didn't see the puddle of soda at the top of the stairs. Her legs slipped from under her. She hit the floor hard and rolled down the stairs, one, two, three times until she finally landed with a thud at the bottom.

A pain shot from the bottom of her spine and made her cry out loud.

My baby!

Her abdomen became hard and a dull ache began to form in her back, followed by an uncomfortable pressure in the pelvis. She had read about these. *Contractions.*

She lost track of how long she lay on the floor, hoping that they would go away, that she was not in labour, that soon she could get to her feet and go back upstairs to rest.

But they did not stop. They got stronger and closer together. She felt panic threaten to overtake her, but remembered Dr O'Grady's question: *Can you be a good parent?* This was her first test. She had to save her baby. She scrabbled into her coat pocket and pulled out her mobile phone. She knew who to call. Dr O'Grady had given her his mobile number for emergencies and she believed this to be a perfect example of one.

He must have driven ever so fast, because he got to her before the ambulance did, kicking in the front door with one of his converse runners.

'I can feel the baby's head and this hall is most unsanitary,' Ruth cried.

'I'm here now. It's going to be OK, Ruth. Trust me. I shall take care of you both.'

Dr O'Grady calmly delivered DJ into the world. He pulled his sweatshirt off and wrapped the tiny infant in it before placing him into Ruth's arms.

'I was not on my own after all. You were with me,' Ruth sobbed.

She looked in wonder at her son and felt emotion unlike anything she had ever felt before. Love, tenderness, joy and, most of all, hope.

As the baby took his first breath, cried his first cry, a connection formed between the three of them. And even though they did not know it right then, it would last for ever.

24

RUTH

Now

Kian stood up to stretch, rubbing his belly as Ruth walked into the kitchen. She opened the fridge, peered in and took out her milk. Someone had been helping themselves again. The bottle was a third less full now than last night.

'Saw you in the park yesterday,' Kian said to Ruth's back. 'Talking to some old fella in a long grey overcoat. I've seen him around with his dog. Homeless, I'd say, by the cut of him.'

Ruth poured herself a glass of milk, then replaced it into the fridge. She then began to make a couple of rounds of chicken sandwiches.

'Are those for him?' Kian asked, looking over her shoulder.

'As it happens, yes.'

'Be careful with him,' Kian advised.

Ruth looked at him in surprise. 'Why?'

'You're a nice woman. And I'd hate you to get taken

in, hurt. His kind would rob you blind as soon as look at you.'

'His kind? What do you mean by that?'

'Homeless!' Kian said.

'But we are homeless, too. So does that mean that I need to be wary of you?' Ruth replied.

Kian shook his head. 'No. Totally different. You see, he's a rough sleeper. That's a whole other kettle of fish than us lot in here.'

Ruth said, 'The only stealing I have witnessed recently happened in this kitchen. Not out on the streets.' Ruth forced herself to look at him, right in the eye. *One, two, three, four, five.* She felt a bead of sweat form on her upper lip, but despite how much she wanted to look at the ground, she kept her eyes locked on him.

He was startled by her comments and his mouth dropped open in cartoon-like reaction. Then he bellowed laughter and said, '*Touché.* Well played, Ruth, well played.'

She felt a flash of satisfaction. She had stuck up for her friend. She had not backed down.

Kian asked, 'You had any more run-ins with herself downstairs?'

Ruth shook her head.

'She's losing her head with me. She doesn't like me sneaking into the lobby to read the paper. It's only for her . . .' he used his fingers to make inverted commas, '. . . normal guests.'

They both laughed at this. How many times had they heard that phrase?

'Here, stick the kettle on, I'll have a cuppa with you,' Kian said.

Ruth was startled by the suggestion. Did this mean he wanted to spend time in her company? She flicked the switch on and told him, 'I do not drink hot beverages.'

'But you do drink milk. I've seen you. Have another glass of that. Your pal in the park can wait five minutes for his sambo.'

'I believe he can,' Ruth agreed.

'I hate it when me young fella isn't here. Fecking lonely without him. But he has to go to school. Education is important. I know that. And I don't want him ending up somewhere like this when he's an adult. He's got to be the one to get out, leave this fucking country,' Kian said.

'Hours feel like days in this hotel, I find. The weekends are better when DJ is here,' Ruth said.

'Same for me too. Sit down and rest your legs,' Kian said, pulling back a chair for her. And to her surprise, she did as he asked. She was sure that he was the kind of man that she could not converse with. Yet here they were.

'You seen Aisling today?' Kian asked. He tried to sound casual, but failed.

'Not since breakfast,' Ruth replied.

'Listen, I only took the lasagne from Ava for the craic, you know. I wonder if Aisling is annoyed with me over that. It was meant to be a wind-up. To pass the time of day here. Didn't want to upset her husband Brian. The poor fecker.'

'I try to remember that when DJ is older he will follow my example, not my advice,' Ruth said.

He repeated her words to himself. 'I'll remember that, Ruthie girl. I'll talk to Cormac later. Might be time to lay off nicking food. Jaysus, I hope my number comes up soon. This place would put years on you!'

'What is your number?' Ruth asked, referring to his place on the housing list. It was funny, but in the short time since Ruth had been in The Lodge, she'd heard all the residents of the first floor talking about their number, like others talked about the weather.

'There are twelve months in the year, twelve days of Christmas. My Cormac is twelve years old and let's not forget I've about twelve bleeding euro in my arse pocket! Twelve is my number.'

'You are funny,' Ruth said. 'How is Cormac doing in school?'

Kian's eyes darkened once more, this time with emotion, and he pounded the table with his fist in frustration. 'It's not fair on the young fella. He has to get two buses to school every day, traipsing across the city to his old school in Templeogue. Long enough day for anyone, just going to school, but add the commute . . . sure he's bollixed by the time he gets home. I'd drive him, but the bus lanes are quicker. And then every night we have a row about homework. He didn't want to go in yesterday and I hadn't the heart to force him. So he stayed here with me. But that's no good either. Had to send him in today, kicking and screaming.'

They each took a sip of their drink, lost in thought about their boys.

'Hello.' Aisling walked into the kitchen and Ruth noted the smile that lit up Kian's face.

He jumped up and said, 'Take a load off. I'll make you a cuppa.'

'Why not? I was going to prepare a meal for later while it's quiet, but tea first of all would be great,' Aisling said. 'What you talking about?'

'Our numbers, life, the universe. Usual kitchen chitchat,' Kian said.

'I'm still fourteen,' Aisling replied, shaking her head in disbelief. 'Feels like I've been stuck on that number for ever.'

'I am still eighteen,' Ruth said. 'I rang Gillian today and expressed my concern over the speed I am moving.'

'Good for you. Well, looks like I'll be first out the door then. Don't think that's ever happened to me before!' Kian said, placing a mug in front of Aisling.

'You settling in OK?' Aisling asked Ruth.

'It is difficult. I do not have enough space for everything in my room. I like everything to have its place,' Ruth replied.

Kian jumped in, 'In a space this small there's no room for clutter. I've most of our stuff stored in me ma's. We stayed with her for a while when the landlord kicked us out, the aul' bollix. No notice. He just told us we had to leave. Just like that. Said he was moving back in himself. And wouldn't give me the deposit back either, saying there was damage to the wallpaper.'

He stood up and began pacing the small room, fury darkening his eyes. 'The fucking wallpaper had no choice but to come off, because of the damp! But it was the only place we could afford. I spent weeks looking for another place. But if there's a flat out there in my price bracket, I'd like someone to show it to me.'

Aisling reached a hand out and her touch brought him

back from his tirade to them both. He smiled his thanks, then sat down again. Aisling blew onto the top of her tea, then said, 'If you gave me a thousand guesses as to where I might end up, I would never have said this. When Anna's dad, my ex, lost his job, he went to the UK to look for work on a building site that a friend of his managed. But he never came home. And I think it's fair to say that at this stage he never will. To add insult to injury, I lost my job soon after. Sure it was no wonder things spiralled out of control. I couldn't afford the mortgage. Fast forward two years and they repossessed the house.'

'I can't get over that. What kind of man would leave a lovely woman and child like you both behind?' Kian said.

'I don't miss him any more. But I do miss the house,' Aisling said, trying to lighten the atmosphere. It worked, they all giggled along at her joke.

Somehow, for Ruth, hearing their stories, knowing that she was not the only one in this situation, helped. They were just as trapped as she was.

'What's your story, Ruth?' Kian asked.

'Similar to yours. Landlord evicted us and I could not afford to rent anywhere else. I tried so hard to find somewhere. This morning, out of 1,678 properties available to rent in Co. Dublin, only three were in my price range. Two were rooms to rent in an owner-occupied house. They stipulated no families and no pets. And the last one was gone when I rang it.'

'Soul destroying,' Kian said.

'I had no choice but to ask for help. Here we are.'

'Here we are,' Kian repeated.

'Here we are,' Aisling agreed.

Then Aisling added, 'It's hard watching others leave. The ones that have gotten a call saying a house has become vacant. You try to be happy for them, but sometimes . . .'

Kian jumped in, '. . . you want to just shout out, "You jammy fecker, that should have been my house!!!"'

'Yes!' Aisling said. 'Exactly that.'

'Tell you what, ladies, when I get the call I give you both full permission to throw obscenities at me.'

They clinked mugs to seal the deal. And the three friends smiled at each other, in the way you do when you begin to recognise something of yourself in the person in front of you. A kinship. A tribe.

25

TOM

A plan had begun to take shape for the pregnant kid Sheila. With the help of the Peter McVerry Trust, they had formed solutions for both emergency housing and pre-natal and post-natal care for Sheila and the baby. But Bones sent the plans crashing to the floor like a deck of cards in the wind, when he shuffled up to Tom and said, 'She's not coming back. Bobby went mad when she told him about you.'

Tom felt like he'd let the girl down. He should have handled things differently. Taken her to the Rotunda Hospital last night and insisted she see someone there and then. He was so lost in recriminations he didn't hear Ruth's arrival until she said, 'I thought a picnic lunch might be nice.'

He felt light-headed with a sudden burst of happiness. He brushed down his hair with his hands as he moved to make room on the bench for Ruth. Bette Davis yelped in excitement, too.

Ruth pulled out a tea towel from a large black tote

bag. She laid it on the bench between them, then placed a flask in front of Tom, unscrewing the plastic cup. 'I had to guess how you would like your coffee. I made it strong and black, but I have milk and sugar. If you tell me how you like it, I will make it that way the next time.'

The next time! Tom felt tears spring to his eyes. *Damn it. What is wrong with me?* 'I drink it exactly as you have made it, Ruth. Thank you.'

She then unwrapped a tin-foil bundle of sandwiches, made in white bread with the crusts cut off. 'I made chicken. I hope you are not a vegetarian.'

'I'd be a vegetarian if bacon grew on trees,' Tom joked. Thirty years ago he made Cathy snort with laughter when he told her that joke on the first day he met her, in the deli aisle of Tesco . . .

Cathy had reached inside a cold fridge to grab a ready meal.

Tom lied and said, 'I was about to get the same.'

'Oh, wow you're a vegetarian, too?' She waved a tofu lasagne at him. 'I would have thought you were more of a steak-and-chips guy.'

Tom licked his lips and protested no, who didn't love a good tofu?

She laughed, seeing straight through him. That was her superpower. She threw back her pack, then picked up a steak and some oven chips with a side of petit pois. 'My favourite dinner for one!'

'Oh thank God. I'd be a vegetarian if bacon grew on trees,' Tom said, and when she laughed he knew he loved her.

*   *   *

'Dr O'Grady?' Ruth's voice brought him back to the bench, to her. 'You were miles away.'

'Sorry, I got side-tracked. I was thinking about Cathy.'

Ruth passed him a napkin with two sandwiches enclosed.

Tom said, 'The day I met her, I made the same joke about bacon. It made her laugh.'

'I thought it was without any comedic merit, as it happens,' Ruth said.

'My humour has always been dubious! But Cathy laughed and that was the beginning of the end for us.'

'I do not understand what you mean by that. Can you explain?' Ruth asked.

Tom closed his eyes again and there she was, his Cathy, tumbling curls escaping from her ponytail, dark-brown eyes that were brimming with humour, her cheeks red from her last-minute dash and the echo of her voice, which trailed off singing along to the Spice Girls' 'Too Much'.

He opened his eyes and said, 'When I looked at her, I felt a sudden hit of recognition. I'd never met her before in my life, but I *knew* her. This was it for me. I never understood what *it* was before, but once I felt it, understanding floored me.'

Ruth watched him, her sandwich held mid-air, as she was captivated by his words. He articulated how it was for her with Dean. A weekend when she felt the same way. A weekend when she knew that the person in front of her was her future.

'I understand now. Thank you,' Ruth said.

'This is a damn fine sandwich. If I had a death-row

191

meal to choose, chicken would be included,' Tom said. He poured coffee into his plastic mug, sniffing the roast in appreciation. Ruth took a carton of milk out of her bag and poured some into a second plastic mug.

'I used to play "the last meal you ever ate" game with DJ when he was small. He loved choosing his favourites, especially when it meant he could have chocolate for a starter, main course and dessert if he so desired,' Ruth said.

'Sounds good to me! What would you choose?' Tom asked.

Ruth answered without hesitation. 'I would start with a cauliflower-and-brie soup. No garnish. With one slice of white crusty baguette, salted butter. Full fat. Then I would like a chicken risotto, *al dente*, followed by a banana-cream pie.'

'Nice,' Tom said in approval. 'To drink?'

'A vanilla milkshake.'

'That's a fine choice, Ruth.'

'I have given it some thought over the years. And I believe it to be the best option. What would you order?' Ruth asked.

'Vegetable soup. With a dollop of cream in it. Then Cathy's roast chicken, with her famous crispy skin and home-made stuffing. All the trimmings. No one could make a roast dinner like the way Cathy did. Her gravy . . .' He put his fingers to his mouth and blew a kiss of appreciation.

'I shall have to take your word for that.' Ruth shuddered at the thought of brown congealed sauce covering any of her food.

'I still have the blindfold you gave me,' Ruth said. 'It has been used many times over the years.'

Then they finished their sandwiches in a companionable silence. It surprised them both, considering it had been a decade since they had been in each other's company. Bette Davis nudged Tom with her nose, reminding him that she needed food, too. Tom broke off part of his sandwich and gave to her.

'Have you seen Sheila today, or Mr Bones?' Ruth asked.

He shook his head. 'Bones came by earlier. She's not coming back.'

Ruth was disappointed for her. 'I really wanted her to give herself a different ending.'

'Maybe she will change her mind again. Bones said he'll keep an eye on her and try to get her to see sense. Surviving on the streets is a full-time job, and Sheila, I suspect, is not thinking straight. She's found some level of "safety" by living with her boyfriend, Bobby, in that derelict building, away from the harsher realities of her previous life. I've seen it before many times.'

'How bad it must have been at home that she would choose to live like that, rather than go back,' Ruth said.

'Was DJ surprised that we knew each other?' Tom asked.

'He was astounded. I still cannot quite believe we are sitting here, right now.' She looked at her watch. She would need to make her way to collect DJ from school in twenty minutes. Would he be any happier this afternoon than he was this morning?

'DJ does not smile any more,' Ruth whispered.

Tom looked at her in surprise. He thought about the

handful of times he had been in DJ's company and realised that he'd only smiled a few times.

'His life now is either commuting back and forth to school or being cooped up in a small hotel room. Already I can see our new normal is sucking the joy out of him,' Ruth said.

'A child needs space,' Tom said.

'And it is the autumn, so if the evenings are wet, like last night, I cannot allow him to go out. He was angry with me that he could not come here to see you.'

'I went to the Peter McVerry shelter last night,' Tom said. 'I usually do when it rains. Tell him that, if it helps.' Tom felt happiness nip him. He liked that DJ wanted to see him. 'And do you have things to smile about now, Ruth?'

'I am the adult. It is my job to take care of DJ. My smiles are of no matter. And right now I am letting my son down.'

'You are doing your best. And from where I am sitting, that is more than a lot do.'

'Did you have a happy childhood, Tom?' Ruth asked.

'Yes, as it happens I did. My parents were older when they met and married. And I always knew that I was considered a blessing in their lives. I had a charmed childhood. They told me often that I was a loved child. And because they showed me with their actions, I believed them.'

'I am worried that the memories of this difficult time will be the ones that stay with DJ. The good ones will be squashed out of his brain by the mess we are in here.'

'He'll remember the happy times,' Tom said.

'How can you be so sure?'

'Because every night I lose myself in my happy memories,' Tom replied.

'Do you ever think about the bad stuff too?' Ruth asked.

He shook his head. 'Not if I can help it.'

'Sometimes all I can think about is the bad stuff,' Ruth said.

He thought about that for a moment, taking a sip of his coffee to buy time. 'I think that by remembering it all, the odd time, you can see how far you've come. The trick is not to get lost in the bad stuff. Don't let it become the dominant voice in your head.'

As if bidden by their conversation, one of the bad memories came to visit Tom. The thundering silence when Cathy was lost in her private hell. Unable to speak. Unable to connect with anyone. He pushed it aside, refusing to let it take root. Some things were best left in the past and right now, he wanted to enjoy the present, with Ruth.

26

TOM

DJ visited Tom and Bette as soon as his homework was finished, bringing two new friends with him. Cormac and Anna from the Lodge. They were all charmed with Bette and the feeling was mutual. They sat and chatted for a few minutes, then disappeared off to play on the swings in Fairview Park.

'Hey, Doc.'

Tom looked up and saw a couple of the volunteers who helped the homeless heading his way. Whenever he faced the bad in this world, he thought of those who gave up their time every night, for no reason other than to help others.

'Soup? Or a sandwich?' they offered. He wasn't hungry but he took both all the same. He'd learned over the years that it was better to accept food when it was offered and keep it until he was hungry. 'Do you want to come back to the shelter? We're heading in soon, so we can give you a lift.'

'No, thanks. I'm exactly where I want to be,' Tom told them.

'All right, mate. We'll be back tomorrow. Sleep well.'

They walked on, scouring the park as they looked for more of the invisible. Those who most people ignored and walked past.

The evening soon changed to night, and the park changed, too. Trees cast dark shadows on the ground and every sound seemed electrified as it bounced around the near-empty place. It had been a big day. Lunch with Ruth, then DJ and his friends. A good day. Yesterday, for the first time in years, he had welcomed the day, waiting to see what it unfolded. He sensed that it had surprises for him, like it used to. Back then. With Cathy. He set up his bed, climbed into his sleeping bag, and closed his eyes to the now.

18 October, a date of significance for Tom and Cathy. The day they met, Tom's proposal, their wedding day.

'Happy Anniversary,' Tom said, and they swapped cards with hearts and flowers on the front.

'No baby talk today,' Cathy promised. It was her attempt to bring back normal. 'Or tonight when we go out for dinner.'

Just before Tom saw his last patient before lunch, Cathy called him. 'Come upstairs. Now. Please.'

Tom didn't ask why, he simply jumped up, shouting to Breda, 'Back as soon as possible.'

Ever unflappable, Breda told him to go on up, that she would keep the last patient in their waiting room happy with tea, if need be.

He ran upstairs taking two steps at a time, calling out Cathy's name. His heart hammered in his chest and he found himself crossing his fingers on both hands behind his back, in the way he had done as a young boy, when he made a wish. There had been something in her voice. He was sure he'd heard a tremor in it when she called. It was not one of upset, it was one of excitement.

Please let me be right. Please.

She was standing in the centre of the living room, her back to him. And when she heard him approach she turned around slowly, keeping her arms behind her. His eyes searched her face and he knew without the need of any words of confirmation from her.

'I'm breaking my promise not to talk babies today.'

He held his breath.

'You see, it appears you were right all along,' she whispered.

'I usually am,' Tom replied. He took a step closer.

'I'm especially glad you're right about this.' Her eyes danced with joy and she held up three pregnancy tests. 'I would have done more, but I ran out of pee.'

Tom laughed. Or maybe he cried. Probably both. He knew that he would never again feel joy like they were experiencing in their flat right now. They had done it. They were going to have a family of their own.

'I knew my boys could swim!' Tom said as he grabbed Cathy and he danced her around the room. Their laughter filled the air, their flat swelled with happiness.

'We are literally dancing for joy,' Cathy said.

'You have really excelled this year at the whole anniversary present giving,' Tom said.

'This is your early Christmas present, too!' Cathy joked.

'You need never buy me another gift again. Nothing could ever beat this, my darling,' Tom said.

Wait and see.

They did just that and look!

When Tom went back downstairs he ran into the waiting room, unable to help himself. He stood in the middle of the square room, with a big goofy grin on his face. Breda followed him into the room, standing beside him.

'Are you OK? Is Cathy OK?' she asked.

'I'm going to be a daddy!' he screamed, and she laughed with him.

'Luckiest day of my life, this day,' Tom said.

Breda was crying and he pulled her in for a tight hug.

'Lucky, lucky baby, having you and Cathy as parents.'

Tom wasn't sure how he managed to get through the rest of the day. He would find himself daydreaming about the possibilities of their future. Would they have a boy or a girl? He didn't care. Either way, he would spend every day of his life working at being the best possible father he could be.

When his last patient walked out of the surgery, Tom sat down in his office and for a moment, felt a rush of overwhelming fear paralyse him. His wife, his beautiful wife, was pregnant. As a doctor he had seen so many complications that being pregnant caused. The thought of her health being compromised in any way scared him.

'I'll lock up. You go on up,' Breda said, walking into the room. Then taking in his face, she walked over and sat down on a chair opposite him. 'Oh, you got there quickly.'

'Got where?'

'To the "Oh no, I'm terrified" stage! It took my husband a little longer.'

'That obvious?'

'The unflappable Mr Cool finally flaps,' Breda teased.

'Most children are loved even before their arrival, right?' Tom asked.

'Yes. Thankfully, in the main that's true.'

'I know it's unfair to say that this child is wanted any more than anyone else's. But it feels like that to me.' His eyes filled with tears and he shook his head to stop them.

'You've been dreaming about this day for a long time,' Breda said. 'It's no wonder you are so emotional.'

'I've wanted to be a father long before I ever managed to persuade Cathy to be my wife. I can't believe it's finally going to happen. I'm scared I'll mess it up.'

'Listen, Tom, no father or mother knows what the hell they are doing when they become a parent. You just make it up as you go along and do the best you can. You and Cathy are far better placed than most parents. You're a doctor, Cathy is a social-care worker. Between you both, I have no doubt you'll do beautifully.'

Tom relaxed with each word Breda spoke. It was going to be OK.

'I have so much to do. I need to buy a house. And my car is totally unsuitable and unsafe for a baby.' He glanced out the surgery window and took a look at the battered old Volkswagen he'd owned since university. It was held together with rust and dirt, but he loved it and up to now had refused to change it.

'Maybe. But that can wait. Your wife, however, will

be upstairs wondering where you are. You need to get ready for your anniversary meal.'

He stood up and kissed Breda lightly on her cheek. 'I'd be lost without you.'

'I know. You can be a right eejit sometimes.'

'Good job I'm a charming fecker . . .' he answered with a laugh then he ran upstairs to Cathy.

He found her lying on the couch fast asleep, a magazine on her lap, opened on a page showing a mother cuddling her baby.

First trimester tiredness. A rush of tenderness overcame him. His darling, beloved Cathy. Carrying their child. He needed to cop the fuck on. He had a job to do now. He had to protect them both. Pulling a throw from the chair beside him, he gently laid it over his wife.

27

RUTH

Now

Ruth and DJ had finally cracked the commute. By leaving thirty minutes earlier they got a quieter set of buses to the school. And like everything for Ruth, once she had time to adjust she just got on with it. She began running home each day, too, unless it was raining heavily, doing the same in reverse when she went to collect DJ. It saved money, plus Ruth loved to run. It helped her ease some of her fears and anger about the situation she was in as she pounded the footpaths.

She arrived at the school gates a few minutes early today. A personal best, she realised with satisfaction. Ruth leaned against one of the walls that surrounded the school and took a number of deep breaths. She was fit; years of running barely caused her to break a sweat. But the breaths were needed to steady herself before she entered what felt like the gates of hell.

Very little had changed at the school gates since she

was a child. Back then when she walked through them she entered into a world of mean girls and boys. They made fun of her and sniggered behind her back and even to her face. And, unfortunately, mean girls and boys often grew up to be mean mums and dads. She looked around the school yard for potential monsters lurking in dark corners, ready to intimidate those who were a bit different. As is often the way with monsters, once you think about them they materialise. Striding towards her was Denise Donnelly, the chair of the parents' council. Complete with a clipboard in hand.

Denise flicked her long shiny hair and smiled, displaying a row of straight, white, veneered teeth. 'Good afternoon, Ruth. Aren't those sunglasses just darling?'

Ruth pulled at her sweatshirt and smoothed down her short hair, which hadn't been brushed yet today, feeling Denise's eyes burn their way up and down her body.

'Will you be joining us for our AGM next week?' Denise asked.

Ruth could think of a dozen reasons why the answer to that question was no. *Where was DJ?*

'It's so disappointing, the lack of civic duty in a large percentage of our parents. This school is our school. And it is up to us parents to ensure that it is run to our satisfaction. I always think serving on a committee is such a worthwhile thing to do, isn't it? I like to give back, where I can,' Denise boasted, clearly delighted with her selflessness.

Ruth became a nodding dog and looked around her to see if there was any hope of salvation from another parent. She didn't have any friends here, but there were one or two mothers who at least gave her the time of day. She waved at Siobhan, one such parent. But when Siobhan spotted the Queen Bee Denise, she scurried away to the other side of the playground. *Coward.*

'I'll add your name down as a yes,' Denise said, scribbling something onto the clipboard.

The bell rang out and children began to march out of their classrooms. First came the senior infants and the first class, in single rows, their large school bags pulling their shoulders down, hats and scarves wrapping them up warm.

'Aren't they so cute at that age?' Denise asked. They watched a little girl with long curly hair in bunches skip into the arms of her mother. 'That's Susan Walsh's little one. Do you know her?'

Ruth shook her head.

'Well, between you and me they've been having lots of problems at home. As I said to Susan, there is no shame in your marriage ending in . . .' She looked around her, from left to right, before mouthing the final damning word, '. . . divorce.'

What an utter bitch. Had she said that out loud? No. Denise was still fake smiling.

Denise shouted out, 'Mary, Sinead!' to two women passing by. They ran over to join her and all three bounced up and down with excitement.

'That was such a great night,' Mary or Sinead said. Ruth could not tell who was who.

'The best,' Denise agreed.

'Were you busy on Friday night? I didn't see you there,' Mary or Sinead asked Ruth.

Ruth thought about the previous Friday night, sitting

on her hotel bed with DJ, watching Ryan Tubridy do his thing on *The Late Late Show*.

'No, I was not busy,' Ruth said.

'It was the annual school mammies' night out! Did you not get an invite?' Denise asked in mock shock. The Queen Bee knew how to sting with style – Ruth had to give her credit for that. She had been coming to this school gate for five years now and was comfortable that she was not part of any of the cliques. Yet despite this, the snub hurt her, as it was intended to.

Thank goodness, there's DJ.

'Hello,' Ruth said. Her heart flipped when she saw him. Who cared about these wagons at the school gate when she had him?

'Mam, Mr O'Dowd wants to talk to you,' DJ said.

Denise, Mary and Sinead inched a little closer, practically salivating at the potential drama that might unfold.

Ruth asked, 'Did something happen today?'

DJ shrugged.

'DJ, is there something you want to tell me?'

'He's a dickhead,' DJ said.

She heard the women behind them gasp.

'Not helpful,' Ruth said. 'Come on.'

'Hope everything is OK,' Denise said, following her as they moved towards the school.

Ruth stopped and said, 'Would you like me to ask Mr O'Dowd to have the meeting out here so that you do not miss anything to gossip about later on?'

'You try to be friendly and you get this!' Denise said in shock.

'Don't mind her,' Mary or Sinead said, and they closed ranks, throwing daggers at Ruth with their eyes.

Utter wagons.

Imagine the torture of spending a whole evening with them.

Ruth and DJ walked to DJ's classroom, passing a small cloakroom, pegs now empty of coats and bags.

And suddenly Ruth was a child again, waiting in her classroom for the other kids to put their coats on.

'It's better this way, Ruth. You can do yours on your own when they have gone outside. And we'll all avoid any unpleasantness,' her teacher, Mrs O'Leary, said.

'Mam?' DJ asked and she shook the memory away as she knocked on the grey classroom door.

'Come in, Mrs Wilde,' Mr O'Dowd said.

Did he call her that on purpose? 'It's just Ruth. I am not married,' Ruth answered. She looked down at DJ, who was kicking her surreptitiously. He mouthed, 'Told you. Dickhead.'

'Take a seat.' Mr O'Dowd gestured towards a kid's-sized chair that sat in front of his desk. He swivelled towards her in his normal-sized, leather, lording-it-over-you chair.

'Is everything OK at home?' Mr O'Dowd asked, leaning in towards her.

'Everything is fine,' Ruth said.

'DJ has been late several times over the past month,' he pointed out.

'He has been on time every day this week,' Ruth countered.

'Even so, his timekeeping is an issue. Plus his homework is leaving a lot to be desired.'

Ruth looked at DJ, who was staring at the floor, a scowl on his face.

'What is the issue with his homework?' Ruth asked.

Mr O'Dowd pulled open an exercise book of DJ's and said, 'Look at this work from earlier this year.'

Ruth smiled as she read his short story about a cat who got lost in the woods. His writing was so neat and she felt pride swell up inside of her. 'He worked very hard on that piece.'

'And it showed,' Mr O'Dowd replied. 'But look at this piece he handed in on Wednesday.' He flicked through the pages, stopping on two pages that bore no resemblance to DJ's earlier work.

'That is DJ's handwriting?' Ruth asked, trying to decipher the scrawl in front of her.

'Yes.'

She scanned the words that were scattered with spelling mistakes. His writing was unrecognisable as from the same person as the earlier work, with pencil stubs all over the page.

'You can see the difference,' Mr O'Dowd stated.

Ruth nodded. The evidence was irrefutable. But there were extenuating circumstances. She once again looked at DJ, who continued to ignore the situation unfolding and was staring at the floor in an uncanny resemblance to Ruth.

'So once again I'll ask, is there something going on at home, *Ms* Wilde.'

Does he really need to emphasis the 'Ms' like that?

'Everything is fine at home,' Ruth stated again. *Maybe DJ was right.*

'It's just I feel that DJ is not making the progress he should be. He seems tired all the time. I would hate him to continue this trend of moving backwards rather than forwards,' Mr O'Dowd continued.

Was it just the trick of the lights or did he look exactly like her fifth-class teacher, Mrs O'Leary? *Ruth is moving backwards, rather than forwards.* She had said the very same thing to her parents at the annual parent–teacher meeting. Memories of another time, of another school came rushing back to her. The isolation she felt at being told she must sit on her own every day.

'Ms Wilde?' Mr O'Dowd said once again.

Ruth looked up and saw concern on Mr O'Dowd's face. She pulled at her hands, frantically.

Pop, pop, pop.

'Are you OK? Would you like a glass of water?'

'Mam. You're crying,' DJ said, alarmed.

Ruth had not noticed the tear that was chasing its way down her cheek, or the fact that she was rocking back and forth on her small chair. To stop herself cracking her knuckles, she sat on her hands, the wood biting into her fingers. No flying, no popping, she had to be normal for DJ.

'DJ, please go to the staff room and get a glass of water for your mother,' Mr O'Dowd instructed.

'Mam?' DJ asked, only leaving reluctantly when Mr O'Dowd shooed him towards the door.

'I never intended to upset you. I apologise. I've always been too heavy handed. It's one of my many faults.'

Ruth looked up and saw regret on his face. He did look sorry.

'I do want to help. I see such great potential with DJ. His imagination is wonderful. May I help you?'

She shook her head. This was her mess; she had to fix it.

'Is there something happening at home?' he asked for the third time. He was like a dog with a bone.

Home. She didn't know whether to laugh or cry at that. 'It is not DJ's fault. Do not take this out on him.'

He looked horrified at the suggestion. 'DJ is a great kid. I like him. It's only because I am worried that I asked to see you. Because I care.'

'We . . . we became homeless recently,' Ruth whispered to his beige loafers.

A silence laden with questions filled the air.

She heard the scrape of his chair. He stood up and moved around from his desk to sit beside her on DJ's small chair. 'What happened, Ms Wilde?'

'Our landlord evicted us. I tried to find somewhere else but there was nothing we could afford. At the moment we are in a hotel in Fairview in emergency accommodation.' Ruth heard her words and saw Mr O'Dowd's reaction. But she felt oddly removed from it all. It was as if someone else was talking to him, not her.

The sound of a glass crashing to the floor made them both look around. DJ was watching them both, horror on his face. 'You promised. You said you wouldn't tell!'

There was no answer to that. She had promised. And she had broken that promise. Not someone else. Her.

'I hate you!' DJ screamed. Then he turned on his heel and ran from the room.

Mr O'Dowd was quick to reassure, 'I had no idea. But I can promise you, this stays in this classroom between us.'

'I have to go,' Ruth said, jumping up.

'I'm here. Talk to me. Anytime,' Mr O'Dowd said, following her to the door.

But she was gone, running after her boy, whose heart she had just broken, when she broke her promise.

Denise was waiting outside with Mary and Sinead, fake concern etched on their faces. 'We saw DJ run out. He looked upset. Is everything all right?' Denise asked.

'Oh, go fuck yourself,' Ruth said.

28

TOM

DJ had been kicking his football about for an hour or so. Every now and then he glanced over at Tom but when their eyes locked he turned away. His face was scrunched in anger at his annoyance at the world. It reverberated with every kick he made. The wind began to pick up. The weather was due to take a turn this week and Tom's knee felt it. As good a predictor as any weatherman.

DJ's ball rolled its way to Tom's feet. 'Bette Davis likes playing fetch. Problem is, my knee is giving me gyp today. Would you do me a favour and take her out for a bit?'

DJ shrugged his acceptance. He took the stick that Tom produced. Bette jumped up, alert at once to the fun ahead. DJ threw the stick, watching it sail through the air. Bette's eyes never left it either and she took off at speed to catch it. And when she returned the stick, dropping it at his feet, the frown disappeared from DJ's face and a hint of a smile appeared.

Work your magic, Bette Davis.

It was impossible to stay mad when playing catch with

an excited dog. Tom thought about his first few years spent on the streets. Days would turn into weeks and he would realise that he had barely moved more than a few feet, he was so weighed down by his pain and misery. But that all changed when he rescued Bette. He found her lying in a muddy puddle, stunned from a head-on collision with a car. Tom had seen the accident happen and was incredulous that she survived. At first, he thought the dog was deaf, because she was so quiet and seemed unable to hear a word that he said. But he realised twenty-four hours later that this was not true. The dog was in shock. He tended to her injuries, bathed and dressed her cuts and bruises like he was taking care of a child. By the third day, she accepted some chicken and began to make improvements. Then on the fourth morning, he woke up, feeling the warm weight of Bette's head on his feet. She looked up at him with such love in her eyes that it took his breath away. They had not left each other's side since. And he knew that Bette had saved him, just as he had saved her. Within a week of their being together, Tom noticed a strength returning to his body. And to his mind too, if he was honest.

DJ's laughter rang through the park when Bette somer-saulted head over paws trying to catch the latest stick he threw.

DJ ran back to Tom with Bette by his side ten minutes later. 'She's so fast! Did you see how quickly she caught the stick that time?' he gushed. He was not worrying about a single thing in this moment. Simply living fully in the moment with Bette.

'I did. And you would be doing me a huge favour if

you played with her a bit each evening. Assuming it's not raining, that is. You can't be out in the rain. And either ways, I'll not be here myself,' Tom said.

'If it's raining, where do you go?'

'During the day, either the library on Pearse Street or Anne's deli and coffee shop. She's a nice lady. She lets me stay inside with Bette for a few hours. When it gets cold, I head to one of the shelters for the night.'

'Where are they?'

'There's a few of them in town. The one I go to is on Richmond Street.'

'Is it nice there?'

'Like the fecking Ritz, with fluffy bathrobes and cute slippers for all who enter,' Tom said.

DJ wasn't sure if he was joking or not. 'Can anyone just check in?'

Tom replied, 'Oh, aye. They'll give you a key card and a doorman will even carry your little rucksack to your room!' He watched the penny drop for the kid, who took it well, smiling with good nature.

Tom reached into his rucksack and pulled out his sandwich. He held it up to show the boy and said, 'You hungry? I don't mind telling you, this is what some might call hitting the sandwich jackpot. Chicken tandoori with a lime mayonnaise. From Anne's deli. Hmmm, hmmmm. Still cold from the chiller.'

'Like you are gonna share anything with me!' the kid said, thinking he was teasing him again.

'So young and so cynical already. As it happens, young man, I am more than happy to share. Call it payment for playing so nicely with Bette,' Tom replied. 'Plus, I've a pain in my head listening to your fecking stomach growling like a big old grizzly bear.'

Tom took half of the sandwich out of its plastic container and handed it to the boy.

DJ took a large bite and sighed. A long, loud, no-business-coming-out-of-a-kid's-mouth sigh. 'I haven't eaten since lunchtime.'

'Are you going to tell me what had you looking so vexed all afternoon?' Tom asked.

DJ's face went dark again. 'I hate my mother.'

Oh, we are back to that again. What had Ruth done?

'You think I'm wrong to say that, don't you?' DJ accused. He didn't wait for an answer, but continued with his tirade. 'She doesn't give a shit about me.'

Tom raised an eyebrow. 'You know I don't like it when you are lazy with your words. If you are going to give out about your mother, at least be articulate while you are at it. And you and I both know that Ruth loves you.'

'You don't break promises with people you love! She told my teacher that we're homeless.'

'Will your teacher tell the rest of your class? Is that what you are worried about?' Tom asked.

DJ shrugged.

'Why did she tell him?'

'He called her in to complain about the state of my homework. Which is not my fault, either. You should try doing essays on a bed.'

'It seems to me that your mam was stuck between a rock and a hard place. Your teacher was having a go at you. And she wanted to explain that it wasn't your fault. She broke her promise for all the right reasons.'

DJ looked unsure. 'A promise is a promise.'

'Yes it is. Did your mam tell you about Sheila, the pregnant girl we met here recently?'

DJ nodded.

'Well, she's someone who has a reason to complain about her parents. She's only a few years older than you. And believe me when I say that no kid belongs out here on the streets. But not every kid has a home and people who love them like you do. The truth of the matter is, if Sheila stays on the streets she'll be a crack head within a year. That's if she's not found dead in a ditch beforehand.'

DJ shivered as Tom's words reached their target.

'I know Mam wasn't being mean on purpose. But she doesn't know what it's like for me. Kids at school have only just stopped slagging me about the last incident.'

'What was that?' Tom asked.

'At last year's cake sale she made a scene. All she had to do was come along, be nice to the teachers, say hello to the other parents, then go. Instead she started a row with my friend Dev's mother. She even made Dev cry. And then, after all that, had a meltdown, so I couldn't even get annoyed with her.'

'So all in all, it went well,' Tom said.

DJ ignored the sarcasm and continued his story. 'First of all, Mrs Delaney came over and asked her what she wanted to drink. And I could see her panicking because she didn't know what to say. Mam hates too much choice – freaks her out. I ran over to help her out, but Mrs Delaney was hell-bent on offering her every possible option: water, still or sparkling, fizzy drinks, diluted orange, juices, tea, green or breakfast, coffee, decaffeinated, blah, blah, blah! With every choice Mrs Delaney rattled off, Mam went a shade whiter. Which in itself is hilarious because all she wanted was something white . . .'

'A cold glass of milk!' Tom interjected. 'That list would stress me out, never mind your poor mam.'

DJ nodded. 'We barely got over that when Mrs O'Brien came over. She's Dev's mam.'

'And Dev is your friend?' Tom said.

'Yes. I'm pretty sure Dev has got what Mam has.'

'Autism?'

DJ nodded. 'Dev had a freak-out in music the week before. I mean, I find that class torture, thirty kids all playing different instruments – badly – but he went off on one.'

'Poor kid,' Tom sympathised.

'It was me who asked Mam to talk to his mam in the first place. But Mam was freaked out already about the drinks and was popping her knuckles like a madwoman. And Mam being Mam, was too blunt. She just blurted out that Dev had Autism.'

'Oh.'

'Mrs O'Brien was horrified at the implication that her son had learning difficulties. She was so cross,' DJ said. 'Then Dev came over to see what the shouting was about. Mrs O'Brien said that just because Mam was mental that didn't mean everyone else had to be, too. Dev started to get really upset then. Annoyed with me for blabbing. Mrs O'Brien pulled him away saying that she would not let her child be stigmatised. Now he doesn't talk to me any more.'

Stigma. Fear.

Tom said, 'It's catch-22 and no easy solution. I feel for your friend. And his mam. But it's always been like that. My generation had a hard time accepting a lot of things, too. Gays, blacks, people with disabilities, mental health issues. I can remember my father, who was a good man, a fair man, making a mean statement about a kid in my class who had dyslexia.'

'That's horrible.'

'It is,' Tom agreed. 'But things are getting better. I would never have believed that same-sex marriage would be allowed in Ireland. Or the Eighth Amendment repealed. We've become a Yes generation. Progress.'

'I marched with Mam for both of those. Even though she hates crowds, she still went.'

'I marched too,' Tom replied.

'I wish I had met you ages ago,' DJ said. 'I like talking to you. It's different than when I'm with Mam.'

'And I you, kid,' Tom said. Then he watched the kid's face scrunch up in a frown. 'What's wrong?'

'I sometimes wonder what it would be like to just chat like this with my dad. But I don't know who he is,' DJ said.

'I know.'

'Or my grandparents. Did you meet them when you lived in Wexford?'

'No. I've never met them.'

'I think they were afraid, too. Of the stigma. Like you said. Sometimes Mam has this look on her face – scared – and I know she's thinking about them.'

Tom knew that Ruth had reason to be scared of her mother.

'We've got to hope that each generation learns from

the previous. One day, if you have children they'll know more than we do now. That's the way the world works.'

'I just wish that sometimes people knew how hard Mam tries to fit into their world,' DJ said. 'She may not look you in the eye but she sees everything.'

The kid was clever. Tom clasped his shoulder and squeezed it. 'She sees you. Who you are. And loves you.'

'I know. And that makes me feel shit when I get angry with her. Because even though she hates hugs, when she hugs me, she does so with every part of her. And if I ask her for anything, she'll do all in her power to get it for me. I've always felt her love.' DJ felt a tear escape. His mam was right now lying on her bed, curled up into a ball with her headphones on, trying to escape the pain she was in. And he left her like that because he was angry.

'You need to go back to The Lodge now, kid,' Tom said, reading his mind.

'I like talking to you, Doc,' DJ repeated. Bette moved over to lay her head on the kid's foot in solidarity.

'One of my favourite parts of the day, when you stop by,' Tom said. 'See you tomorrow. I'll be here.'

DJ disappeared out the park gate into the dusky evening.

Ruth was as he had left her earlier when he got back to their room. He felt shame and guilt. He had every right to be annoyed with her. She broke a promise. She told. But he shouldn't have shouted at her. She was his mam. And he loved her. He kicked his runners off. Then he climbed into his bed in his clothes just as he was. He lay there listening to her shallow breaths, in and then out. He wanted more than anything to feel her arms around him. He felt lost and alone and scared. He turned his body so he was facing towards her and she opened her eyes. Their eyes locked, hers glistening with tears. He smiled and she nodded once before she closed her eyes again. She moved her hand a fraction to the right so that it was closer to the edge of her bed. Closer to him. He moved his hand until his fingers tipped the top of hers. He waited for her to pull away. But she didn't move an inch. The room remained silent. Then suddenly he felt the warmth of her fingers as they laced around his.

A million silent sorries fluttered around the room as they held on tight to each other. Ruth for putting her son in a position where he might be made fun of. DJ for getting angry with a mother who always accepted him for what he was. For hating her for being what she was.

And together they found their way back to each other.

29

TOM

The aroma of good coffee hit his nostrils. Tom peered in the window of the coffee shop, trying to decide if he should go in or not.

'Hello,' Ruth said, walking towards him.

'You've been shopping,' he said, nodding at the bags in her hand. He felt his face move into a grin, something it didn't do that often. It felt strange and wonderful all at once. This woman and her boy made his days brighter when their paths crossed.

'Joggers for DJ. He is like a weed at the moment. Growing constantly,' Ruth answered.

'I was about to go in for a coffee. Would you join me?' Tom asked. He had to stop himself crossing his fingers that she would say yes.

When Ruth did not answer immediately, he said, 'I would like to buy you a glass of milk. I'll ask them to serve it extra cold.'

She smiled at this and walked into the coffee shop.

'Come on, gal.' Tom gently tugged on Bette's leash and

she wagged her tail in delight. If things went Bette's way she might find some crumbs fallen onto the floor.

As he made his way through the small coffee shop, towards the counter, Tom felt the eyes of the diners follow him. A small child reached out as they passed her table, her short pudgy arms grabbing Bette Davis by her collar. She squealed in delight, 'Doggie, doggie, Mammy, look a doggie!'

Bette Davis, ever the Oscar-winning actress, wagged her tail and nuzzled the little girl's hands. Bette yelped in annoyance when the child's mother pulled the girl back, whispering something into her daughter's ear.

And while Tom got it, accepted it, understood it even, he felt irritation creep its way around him. And embarrassment that Ruth was witness to this. He tugged on Bette's lead and moved on to place his order, closing his ears to the child's cries of dismay.

'Cappuccino, please. Large. And a glass of cold milk. With ice, if it's not from the fridge.' Tom placed his order to the young girl behind the counter.

She remained silent, then frowned as her eyes looked him up and down.

It's going to be like that so.

He pulled out a crumpled euro from his pocket and laid it on the counter top. She snatched the money, still cheerless, still silent, but at least rang his order up.

'You go find a seat,' Tom said to Ruth.

The girl behind the counter began the task of making his coffee. He watched her pull the lever sideways on the coffee machine and smiled when Bette's ears pricked up as the familiar click of the grinder alerted her that something nice might be coming her way soon. Tom stuffed his change back in his pocket and felt his earlier irritation disappear as the rich aroma of the beans filled the air. He was about to have coffee with a friend. It was a good day.

Ruth had found a small table at the back of the coffee shop and he sat down, grateful for the seat. He stretched out his right leg, trying to take pressure off the knee that continued to give him trouble.

Why are you whipping yourself? Making life harder than it needs to be? Why don't you find a way to live out of the cold? Take better care of yourself.

He chose to ignore the voice in his head that demanded answers to a question he did not want to examine. Bette Davis rested her head on his ankle and raised her eyes to him in silent plea. She'd spotted the small shortbread biscuit that sat on the saucer his coffee rested on. She'd banked that there would be one.

'Good job I don't have a sweet tooth,' Tom said, then broke the biscuit into two small pieces, placing them in the palm of his hand. It took her a nanosecond to lick his palm clean.

'If only all things in life could be solved with the simple pleasure of confectionery,' Ruth said.

'Ain't that the truth,' Tom replied.

Satisfied that she'd had all the good stuff on offer, Bette Davis settled down for a rest, lying by his feet. He looked down at his chocolate-brown hiking boots, scuffed and worn from many years of walking the roads of Ireland. He'd not noticed their disintegration until this moment. His appearance had been of no matter to him for nearly a decade. Until recently.

Bette's new fan, the little girl, came running towards them. Before she had the chance to cuddle Bette, who was waiting with wagging tail, her mother clutched her back into her arms. She made a face to a couple who were seated a few feet in front of them. They watched the drama unfold with interest.

Their heads nodded in sympathy. While no words were spoken, Tom understood the message that passed between them all.

Stay away from the dirty old man. The tramp. The beggar.

His very presence, despite the fact that he had not spoken a word, or caused a single moment of trouble, disturbed them. Offended them.

Some days his stubborn self would take over and insist that he drink his coffee slower than normal. Just to piss them off. Other days, like now, their presumptions saddened him. Did they ever think that the offence was his to take, not theirs?

Tom pulled Bette back towards him, away from the child.

'Bye-bye, doggie,' the little girl said.

And Tom replied softly, 'Bye-bye, little one.'

Ruth had watched the scene silently, taking it all in. She saw embarrassment and anger flash across the doctor's face.

'Does that happen a lot?' she asked.

He shrugged, feeling belligerent. The brightness gone. He finished his coffee in three large gulps.

'So much for taking time to smell the coffee,' Ruth said.

He ignored her and used his teaspoon to scoop up the

sweet frothy milk that sat at the bottom of his cup; he was not leaving that behind for anyone.

'What would Cathy say if she saw you now?' Ruth asked.

He ignored her question.

'She would be upset that you have decided to live your life like this.'

He threw his teaspoon onto the table, the sound of the clash making Bette jump.

'Whatever happened cannot be so bad that you live on the streets. I can call my housing officer and arrange a meeting for you. She can help you. Find you emergency housing.'

Tom replied, 'Leave it alone, Ruth. I am where I want to be.'

'You need to get your knee sorted.' Ruth pointed to his outstretched leg. 'I have noticed you limping.'

'It gets stiff sometimes,' Tom replied.

The girl from behind the counter came over and picked up his coffee cup, saying, 'All done?' She glanced pointedly at the door.

The inference was plain to see. *Get out.*

'Another coffee, please,' Ruth said. 'For my friend Dr O'Grady. We are in no rush. Are we, Dr O'Grady?'

The girl scowled but went back to make the drink.

Tom sat in silence while they waited for his next coffee to arrive. His head swarmed with thoughts all jumbled up into one big knot. Somehow, since DJ and Ruth crashed into his life, everything had changed and become more complicated.

'Cathy would not wish this life for you,' Ruth continued, refusing to give up. And to his horror he felt tears bite his eyes.

'No. I suspect you are right,' he replied. 'But it is how things are, all the same.' Before Ruth had a chance to pursue this train of thought, he asked her, 'What is your wish, Ruth? What do you want?'

Ruth answered without missing a beat. 'To have a home of my own that nobody can take from DJ and me.'

'I would say that's not too much to ask,' Tom said.

'You would think so, yet I seem to find it difficult all the same. What about you, Dr O'Grady? What is your wish?'

Tom knew that the one thing he wanted, nobody could give him. So he said, 'We've met most days for lunch or a chat for a couple of weeks now. And I think we've become friends. Right?'

'Yes. That is correct,' Ruth concurred.

'I wish that you would call me Tom, or Doc if you prefer. But please, not the full title any more.'

'But that is your name. Why would I stop calling you Dr O'Grady?'

'That's not who I am any more.'

'Yes it is. I think that you have lost yourself out here on your own.'

He nodded, a tear finally escaping and rolling down his weathered cheek. 'I am lost,' he admitted on a whisper.

'It is OK, Dr O'Grady. I will help you find your way back. I promise.'

And somehow she had done it again. Ruth Wilde had made his day brighter.

30

RUTH

'Did you hear the goings-on in number 125 last night?' Aisling asked when Ruth walked into the kitchen.

'If you mean did I hear the continual banging of a headboard against the wall, then yes,' Ruth said.

'They were going at it hammer and tongs. The noise of them!' Aisling said. 'And I wouldn't mind, but they have two kids in the room with them. I mean, it's not right. I can't even bring myself to think about my parents having sex, never mind be in the same room.'

'Unless you are adopted, your parents did engage in intercourse at least once. And the likelihood of getting pregnant on the first time is less than twenty-five per cent. Which would mean that it's likely that they have had sex on numerous occasions.'

'All right, all right,' Aisling said. 'You're making my eyes bleed with those images.'

Aisling sighed, as she glanced down at her body. 'If we're talking numbers, I would say the likelihood of me ever having sex is less than five per cent with this monstrosity.' She wobbled her stomach and laughed. But the sound fell flat and the tears in her eyes confused Ruth. She did not look happy. Why laugh if that was not the case?

In the short time that Ruth had known Aisling she had brought up the subject of dieting several times. Aisling *was* fat. Should she agree with her? She bit her lip to refrain from saying the wrong thing. She knew that her bluntness offended people. And since they had moved into The Silver Sands Lodge, Aisling had been kind to Ruth. She did not want to upset her.

'I put two pounds on this week. There's something wrong with me,' Aisling moaned, her eyes still on her stomach.

'Then you must go see a doctor,' Ruth stated. 'What are your symptoms?'

Aisling cocked her head on one side, peering closely at Ruth. 'You're a curious one. I didn't mean that I'm ill, I meant that . . .' She couldn't find the words to finish.

'You are not very good at dieting,' Ruth suggested.

'Yes!' Aisling laughed. 'That's exactly it!'

Ruth laughed with her, without really understanding what was so funny. But it felt good to laugh.

'I envy you,' Aisling said.

This surprised Ruth. She didn't think she'd elicited that emotion from anyone in her entire life.

'You have a lovely figure. I bet there's not an ounce of fat on you,' Aisling exclaimed.

Ruth took a step back in case Aisling decided to investigate that statement.

'What's your secret?' Aisling asked.

'I do not have one,' Ruth shrugged.

'I've seen you cooking and I can't put my finger on what diet you follow. It's not Atkins, that's for sure. You pack away ridiculous amounts of potatoes,' Aisling said.

'It is not a diet; I just keep to my rules,' Ruth answered.

'Maybe I should keep to your rules, too. What are they?'

'I only eat white food. Mostly. I like white food,' Ruth said.

'Don't we all,' Aisling answered, pointing to her stomach. 'Carbs are like my abusive husband. I keep taking them back no matter how much hardship they put my poor body through.'

That was funny. Ruth liked Aisling and found herself looking forward to coming to the kitchen, hoping she or Kian would be there.

'Do you have any other rules?' Aisling asked.

'Foods must never touch each other. I do not find it acceptable when food groups collide.'

Aisling sighed. 'So that would mean no massaman curry? That's my favourite. Have you tried the Thai place down the road? So good.'

Ruth shuddered. 'I would rather chop my hand off than eat a curry or stew.'

Seeing the look on Ruth's face, Aisling believed her. 'Well, maybe I should try your rules, see if I can lose some weight that way. Because something has to give. Other than my bloody pants. This morning, the button popped on my jeggings. Jeggings, for goodness' sake! Made of Lycra. With give. Lots of it. And still my lardy arse and fat stomach broke them. That's a talent.'

'Just buy a bigger size,' Ruth said.

Aisling laughed at that and shook her head. 'You're a gas ticket. Sure I can't keep on buying a bigger size. No. It's time for action.'

'I run,' Ruth said. 'You should run, too.'

'Oh, I couldn't do that. The state of me!' Aisling said. 'I'd love to be one of those people who get a high from exercise. Take my sister, she's on her fifty-first Park Run. Do you do those?'

Ruth shook her head. 'I like to run on my own. I run on the way back from DJ's school most days. I can show you how, if you want.'

'Can I think about it? I wasn't much good at sport in school,' Aisling said.

'Neither was I,' Ruth said. In fact, school and the sports programme they ran there caused only trauma for her. Her parents and teachers were all adamant that she should try out for everything – basketball, football, camogie – and all had led to humiliation. Her co-ordination, or lack of it, resulted in her spending more time on the ground than on her feet. For years, as a direct result of the trauma of that time, she avoided any kind of physical activity.

'I was always the last person chosen when teams were being picked,' Aisling said. 'Not that I blame them as I was the slowest. But still, would have been nice to be picked first just once.'

'Schools and I do not seem to mix well,' Ruth said.

'Oh, I hear you. There are so many cliques at Anna's school. I'm forever in FOMO mode.'

'FOMO?'

'Fear of missing out.'

'I think I miss out on plenty at DJ's school but I give zero fucks,' Ruth said.

Aisling roared with laughter. 'Oh, I love you! Seriously, I need to be more like you. If only I could find some of your dedication and go running every day like you. I'd be too busy for any FOMOing!'

Ruth looked at her in surprise. Aisling seemed to be genuinely in awe of her. This was a new experience for Ruth. She was used to being the butt of people's jokes, rather than a source of inspiration. It felt good.

'I shall be running in the morning at nine o'clock, as it's Saturday. You should come with me. Wear runners and bring a bottle of water,' Ruth said.

This was moving a bit fast for Aisling, who started to get nervous. 'I get tired walking to the end of the corridor. My joints are in bits. I'm not sure my knees are up to it.'

Ruth nodded. 'The force on our knees when we walk is approximately one and a half times our weight. And if there is an incline involved, the pressure is even greater, up to two to three times your weight. So if you are 200 pounds, the weight on your knees is 300 pounds. You weigh more than that.'

'You don't mince your words, do you?' Aisling said, trying to decide if she should be insulted or not. She continued, 'I'm beginning to get a handle on you. You say what's on your mind, good, bad or indifferent. Right? There's a lot to be said for it. I don't know about the running, but let's hang out again some time. OK?'

Ruth asked, 'Can you define what you mean by that? What would be involved in the hanging out?'

Aisling said, 'We could have lunch together some day

when the kids are in school. Or go for a walk. You can build me up for a jog! Better still, we can walk and talk with a coffee in hand.'

Ruth shook her head, 'Too many choices. Just say one. Please.'

Aisling replied, 'OK. Coffee and a walk tomorrow at 11 a.m. Let's meet here.'

'That would be most acceptable,' Ruth said, and when she walked out she began to hum 'When You're Looking Like That', her absolute favourite happy song.

31

TOM

Tom spent the afternoon hovering outside the squat that Sheila and Bobby lived in, hoping she might come out and he could try to talk some sense into her. Hours passed and there was no sign of anyone coming or going, until a gang of lads arrived, around five. They spotted Tom and paused to give him the stink eye. Then one of them swaggered his way over to Tom.

'You that doc?' he said.

Tom nodded. He took a guess, correctly as it happened. 'And you're that Bobby.'

They sized each other up.

'We don't need you or your kind around here. Fuck the fuck off,' Bobby said.

'I just wanted to check that Sheila was OK,' Tom said.

'The first time I ask nicely. The next . . .' Bobby looked behind him and nodded. Two lads walked towards Tom.

Tom held his hands up and said, 'I'll leave. But tell Sheila I'll be in the usual spot if she needs me.'

He was still fretting about her and her unborn baby

when he settled down to sleep later that night. Bobby's pupils were so dilated, they were big black dots in his eyes. What if she went into labour in that squat, with only him to help her? *Oh, Cathy, what a mess.* He closed his eyes and remembered another baby, another time . . .

Mikey came into the world screaming with defiance and attitude.

'A bruiser, like his father,' Tom said with pride to Cathy who, despite her herculean efforts in labour, was as jubilant as he was at the arrival of their little man.

Tom had found the past couple of hours particularly difficult. Not that he was in any way comparing his discomfort to his wife's, but as a doctor he knew too much. Every monitor, every check-up made him nervous. What was this baby doing to Cathy? Why was her blood pressure so high? Why wasn't labour progressing quicker? Of course Tom had kept all of his worries to himself. Instead he quizzed his new colleague, Annemarie, who'd begun working alongside him a few months back. He fretted and he made bargains with God that involved a delivery from a stork of a perfectly formed, healthy baby, with no pain or suffering for Cathy.

In the end it all went perfectly to plan. And Cathy took every pain in her stride, remaining focused on one thing only – the safe delivery of their child. Tom realised with acute clarity that this woman was a thousand times stronger than he would ever be.

When Mikey was placed on Cathy's chest, skin to skin, Cathy's face changed. Tom felt privileged to witness it. He had felt pride in his life many times – when he graduated from medical school, when he watched his bride walk down the aisle towards him and their new life, the first time his medical intervention resulted in a saved life. But this moment, in that small labour suite that smelled of blood and sweat, was the proudest of all.

They settled into their new normal very quickly. Weeks became months and Tom and Cathy continued to be besotted with their life. They had listened to friends bemoan the state of their marriages once kids came along. It wasn't like that for them. Instead, it was as if Mikey solidified the love they had for each other.

Of course Tom and Cathy fought the odd time. They could go weeks, months sometimes, without so much as a cross word, then something small would trigger one of them off. Tom knew that he could be a grumpy sod sometimes. He liked a bit of a barney. Felt good to let off some steam, shout a bit.

Cathy would say, 'Don't be a dick. It doesn't suit you.'

Tom would in turn make her remember that he was indeed a charming fecker.

And so, their lives went by in a happy flash.

Until they didn't any more.

He opened his eyes and blinked back tears. He felt . . . anger? No. His rage was long gone. Disappointed. Yes, that was how he felt. Disappointed in himself. In Cathy. In how their life had ended up, him on this bench, with only his memories and nothing else. Before he could allow the darkness to overcome him, Bette Davis barked and ran up the footpath to greet DJ and his two pals from the hotel, Cormac and Anna. And a thought jumped into his head that surprised him. If he wasn't on this bench, then maybe he would not have met Ruth and DJ again. Curious, that.

32

RUTH

Since she broke her promise and told Mr O'Dowd about their housing situation, Ruth and DJ had managed to maintain a somewhat uneasy truce. But it was tenuous and the slightest thing seemed to set them at each other's throats. This morning DJ pulled on his school tracksuit bottoms, which the previous day were clean but were now covered in thick mud from his arse to his knee.

'What on earth happened?' Ruth asked.

'I was out playing with Bette. I fell,' he answered. That chin of his was back out again, daring her to have a go.

'I specifically asked you to change out of your school tracksuit before you went to the park,' Ruth said.

'I forgot.'

Ruth frantically went through the laundry basket that was now beginning to take over the room, searching for a less dirty pair of tracksuit bottoms. 'Here.' She threw a pair at him. 'They will have to do. Marginally better than the ones you have on.'

More scowls as he walked into the bathroom to change again. 'Why don't I have any clean clothes any more?'

'I shall find a launderette today,' Ruth replied to the slam of the door.

Things had been easier when he was younger. He accepted life as it was presented to him. His questions were easier to answer. And that was saying a lot, because he had some corkers back then.

'*Why is the sky blue, Mam?*'

'*Where does colour get its colour, Mam?*'

'*What happens to water when it goes down the drain, Mam?*'

And now he was still testing her because last night he came home from the park with the one question Ruth found impossible to answer.

'*Where is my dad?*'

She tried to shut her mind from that question. But it was becoming increasingly difficult. When she left Wexford she may not have said it out loud, but the reason she chose to go to Dublin was because that was where DJ's father, Dean, was from. And for the first couple of years she looked for him. Everywhere. She would walk the streets each day taking a different path, pushing DJ in his pushchair. Hoping that luck would be on her side, fate would shine a light on them, and they would bump into each other. What happened after she found him was cloudy. Because if that happened, then she would have to accept the fact that he had never loved her; that their lost weekend was just a fling. Nothing more. But no matter how much it seemed just like that, neither her head nor heart believed it to be true. Dean had loved her. She knew it. She no longer looked for him, but she never lost her hope that one day he would return.

Ruth remembered the day on Curracloe Beach so clearly, it felt like it had just happened . . .

With an ice-cream in hand, Ruth placed her coins in the slot, then pulled back the red velvet curtain to sit in front of the turban-clad statue that would dispense her fate at the arcade. She had been on the beach reading for the past two hours, the afternoon sun now in the mid-twenties. Ireland was in the throes of a heatwave. It was a universal truth that the Irish sun would come out to play whenever schools returned after their summer break. She crossed her fingers as she heard the machine hum and vibrate as it decided her fate. Be a good one.

The machine hissed and spluttered, then spat out a card.

YOU WILL MEET YOUR SOUL MATE TODAY.

Ruth's heart began to pound. In all the years she had used this machine, she never had a fortune about soul mates. Never! Ruth traced the words of the fortune with her forefinger. She jumped up and shook her head to banish her mother, letting dreams that she rarely dared to believe take up residence instead. All because of the card in her hand. She pulled back the red curtain and stepped out into the arcade, promptly crashing into someone.

'Hey!' a man shouted.

Her ice cream tumbled towards the floor followed by the fortune, which fluttered to the ground in slow motion, finally resting in a puddle of vanilla ice cream.

'I'm so sorry!' The man was quick to apologise, seeing the look of dismay on the young woman's face.

Ruth's eyes never left the card on the ground, the fortune's black ink beginning to melt away. 'It was my fault. I was distracted.'

'You OK, Ruth?' Pat's voice shouted over from the ice-cream counter. 'I'll make you another. Don't fret. On the house.'

Ruth kneeled down and picked up the sodden fortune. The man with shiny, black, lace-up shoes inched closer.

'Was it a good fortune?' Shiny Shoes asked.

Ruth peeked through her sunglasses, taking in the man dressed in a grey suit and red tie, which looked like it was strangling him, the sleeves of his shirt cuffed on each arm. His attire jarred with the beach. Jarred with her.

'What did it say?' he asked, trying to make out the words, which were now almost melted to oblivion. 'Meet . . .'

Ruth replied, 'It said that today I would meet my soul mate. I have never had that fortune before. It was a most excellent fortune.'

'Most excellent indeed,' Shiny Shoes acknowledged. He pulled out some change from his pocket and said, 'Maybe it will come out again. Let me try for you.'

Ruth shook her head. 'The odds of that happening are highly unlikely.'

He pushed his coin into the machine, then sat in behind the red curtain. And once again it hissed and spluttered, then spat out a card.

YOU WILL MEET YOUR SOUL MATE TODAY.

Ruth heard the man laugh out loud as he picked up his fortune. 'Well, I'll be darned. Look at that.'
Ruth looked up from the floor and their eyes met.

Ruth had found herself laughing with that strange man dressed in a grey suit on a hot September day, not just about the impossible odds that they beaten but so much more too. And because of this chance encounter, Ruth's life was about to change and shift more than she could ever imagine.

33

RUTH

Then

'Any good?' Shiny Shoes Man asked, pointing to her book and blocking the summer sun.

Ruth looked up, recognising the voice. He was smallish for a man. Skinny, too, but with a round face. She liked his face. It was kind. And handsome. He was holding his shoes in his hand, his grey slacks now rolled up to his knees. His white shirt was now open at the collar and he had pushed his sleeves up past his elbows. She moved herself up to a sitting position to answer him.

'It is most excellent,' she replied.

'My name is Dean, too, you know,' he said, pointing to the author's name on the book.

'If you say your second name is Koontz, on top of the fortune earlier, I may just have to marry you,' Ruth replied.

He started to laugh and said, 'Ha! I'm tempted to say it is, just to get a proposal. But I am a huge fan. Of his. Not just because we have the same great name, either.'

'He is my number-one favourite author. Followed by Stephen King,' Ruth said.

'Very precise. I like it,' he said. 'Can I sit down for a minute?'

'If you wish.'

He plonked himself down on the sand beside her. 'That's better. I finished work early today, and just couldn't face driving back to Dublin. Thought I'd take advantage of the Indian summer and have a walk on the beach.'

'It is unusually warm and dry. Met Éireann have forecast another three days of temperatures up to twenty degrees.'

'The sunny south-east is living up to its reputation,' Dean said. 'It always seems to be sunnier down here than in Dublin.'

'Is that where you live?'

He nodded. 'What is your favourite Koontz?'

She waved *Odd Thomas* at him. That was an unnecessary question.

'Doh!' he acknowledged. 'An excellent choice, although I would probably have to pick *By the Light of the Moon*. I've read it a few times and get something different from each read.'

'I am the same with *Odd*,' Ruth admitted. 'I have read it seventy-two times to date.'

'Wow. That's a lot of love for one book.'

'I do not like to waste my time on things that do not interest me. When I read *Odd Thomas* I feel happy. Odd is my friend. He makes me feel good about myself.' Ruth stopped suddenly. She had just shared something with this stranger that she had never told anyone else. She waited for him to sneer and laugh.

'That makes a lot of sense to me. I always think of book characters as real people, too. Or at least the ones from the good books,' Dean replied.

His response made Ruth feel all funny inside. Her stomach began to flip and flop. She popped a knuckle to try to quieten it down. Dean seemed to sense her need for silence, so he sat quietly beside her and they watched the ocean in front of them.

After a while he turned to her and said, 'I like your hair.'

'So do I,' Ruth agreed, reaching up to touch her short pixie cut.

'You look like Audrey Hepburn,' Dean said.

'I hope not, because she is dead,' Ruth said.

'Cute and funny, too. I like it,' Dean said, laughing.

Ruth had never had anyone compliment her like this before. It was uncharted territory. Her mother had been horrified by her haircut, telling her she looked like a boy.

'Do you live around here?' he asked.

She nodded. 'I live with my mother. Not far from here. In between Curracloe and Screen village. I like to spend my time on the beach when I can. I come here every week.'

'It's beautiful,' he agreed, wondering what colour the girl's eyes were behind her big sunglasses. He bet they were the same colour as the sky. He very much wanted to find out. 'You never told me your name.'

'You never asked,' Ruth replied.

'Mystery girl on the beach, with the cool haircut and funky sunglasses on, who happens to have impeccable taste in books, what is your name?'

Now it was Ruth's turn to laugh. 'I am Ruth.'

'With a cool name, too! You're making my head turn,' he said, with sincerity. 'So Ruth, do you work or are you a student?'

'Neither. I was fired yesterday. I have yet to tell my mother,' Ruth answered. 'I'm not looking forward to that.'

'Ouch, sorry to hear that. Do I take it your mother will not be impressed?'

'She will not be surprised. I do not have a good track record with jobs.'

'What happened?' he asked.

'I have been working for a PR company over the past couple of months. They were running a promotion for Budweiser this month. My job was to hand out free bottles of beer yesterday in a beer garden.'

'I bet the bar was jammers because of the Indian summer! Nothing like a hot day to send the droves to the pub!' Dean said.

'Exactly. But I do not think I am cut out for PR.'

He laughed, thinking that this girl could sell anything to him. He was enthralled with her every word. 'What happened?'

'Some guys were being arseholes. One of them asked me what did he have to do to get a kiss from me.'

'What did you say?' Dean asked, feeling irritation at these faceless guys who tried to chat up this woman who had intrigued him from the moment she stepped out of the fortune booth.

'I said to him, "I could kiss you, but I would rather kiss a pig's backside." His friends laughed. Turns out he did not like being laughed at. Also turns out that he knows my now ex-boss. He complained that I was stuck up. My boss agreed. He said that he found it hard to put up with my quirks, as he called them. My candid interactions were not appreciated.'

'You shouldn't have to put up with that shit in work. Sounds like you are better off out of it,' Dean said. 'As for being candid, I think it's like when people ask for advice. Really they just want you to pat them on the head and agree with everything they've said!'

Ruth nodded in agreement. She liked that Dean understood her. She liked chatting to him. And, unusual for her, she did not mind that he was interrupting her reading time. She felt Odd's approval.

'I'm curious about these quirks that your boss didn't like,' Dean said.

'I like white food. I am not sure why this bothers anyone else, as it does not bother me when they eat food all the colours of the rainbow. But it seems to put people out,' Ruth said.

'When I was a kid, I did my best to avoid any food with colour. Like broccoli and carrots,' Dean said. 'You know, I can't eat halved or broken peanuts. I have to separate them into little piles, and only the complete ones get past the Deano radar!'

Ruth said, 'I do not care for broken nuts either.'

'Noted,' Dean said. They both giggled at the innuendo that sat between them.

'Tell me more,' Dean said.

'I am not very good in big crowds,' Ruth said.

'Overrated. Agreed.' He swivelled his bum around till he was facing her, wishing she would take her sunglasses off. 'I'll let you in on a secret. You might not do well in

249

crowds, but you are doing very well with me. I feel like I could tell you anything.'

'Then do. Tell me something about you that no one else knows,' Ruth said.

'Like what?' Dean asked.

'Tell me the worst thing you have ever done,' Ruth said. 'Shock me.'

Dean gave the question some thought, which Ruth admired.

'OK, here's my most dastardly deed. I've not confessed this to anyone before.' He went on to tell Ruth about a time when he snuck over his next-door neighbour's garden fence and broke into their shed. Mr Murphy kept a stash of booze there, some beers and wine. And Dean was going to a party with no money. There was a girl there he wanted to impress.

'There usually is,' Ruth said.

'The weird thing is, I can't even remember her name now. But at the time, it seemed of the utmost importance that I be the big man, arms full with beer.'

'And did you get the girl?' Ruth asked.

'Yes, I did as it happens. We went on a few dates after that party, but whenever I saw her, all I could remember was the stolen beer. The Murphys were nice people. I shouldn't have done it,' Dean said. 'I swore after that I'd never steal a single thing again.'

'And have you kept that promise?' Ruth asked, crossing her fingers that he said yes.

'Yes. I have.'

Dean had never spoken so honestly about himself before, but somehow with Ruth he felt the need to tell her everything. He wanted her to know him. All of him. The good and the bad.

'We have all done things in our pasts that we shouldn't have,' Ruth said. 'When I was in primary school there was this boy in my class who was bullied by his classmates.'

'A friend of yours?' Dean asked.

Ruth shook her head. 'He was just a boy in my class. But he had a rough time of it. He was not from a well-off family. His clothes were always that bit too small or too big, hand-me-downs. A little bit shabby and dirty. And he often smelled. I would say now, looking back, that he was lucky to get a bath in his house.'

'That's bloody awful,' Dean said.

'The kids in my class used to brush by Paul, then touch him, squealing at everyone else, "I've got Paul on me." Then they'd all run away, playing a cruel game of tag, passing "Paul" onto each other.'

'Kids are savage,' Dean replied. 'Do you feel guilty because you played along, too?'

'I was not included in any of the games my classmates played. But I watched. I never intervened,' Ruth whispered.

'You were a kid,' Dean jumped in, quick to defend her.

'A kid who knew better, who knew what it felt like to be on the sidelines, bullied for being different. I should have said something, shown him a kindness, been a friend to him. I should have screamed at the kids, "Fuck the fuck off!"' She felt Dean's eyes on her and looked up to meet his gaze. And she did not feel anxious. But the flip-flops were back in her tummy.

Pop, pop, pop.

'Where is he now?' Dean asked.

'No idea. Last I heard he had gone to the USA on a J-1 visa.'

'What would you say to him if you could?'

'I would promise him that if I were lucky enough to have children of my own, that I would teach them every day to be kind. To stand up for the underdog. To avoid being a sheep.'

'I think a kid would be very lucky to have you as a mother,' Dean said.

They sat side by side on the sandy white beach and continued to swap stories until the sun began to go low. Others packed up their things to go home. Until it was just the two of them.

'Will you take your sunglasses off?' Dean asked, his voice a whisper on the evening breeze.

She did as he asked and he said, 'I knew it. Exactly the same colour as the sky.'

His words made her smile, and for the first time in her life she felt like someone who could grasp a happy-ever-after.

'If we kiss, that will be it, you know,' Dean told her, when it was almost dark.

Every word he spoke was a solemn promise that made Ruth's stomach flip. She nodded because she recognised the truth in his statement. She had no idea what lay ahead for them both, but she knew, with every ounce of her being, that Dean was part of her future.

Her soul mate. She had fallen in love with this man in just a few hours. It was that simple.

Dean leaned in and kissed her hard. His nose banged against hers and their teeth clashed.

'Shit!' Dean yelped. 'Ignore that kiss. I do way better kisses than that.'

'I should hope so,' Ruth said in disappointment.

He steadied himself. Then moved in, slower this time, and took her head in his hands. He kissed her like it was the last kiss he would ever give in his life. She felt her body move into his until she no longer knew where hers began or his ended.

She did not remember the kiss ending, but she knew that this time it was perfect.

Dean never went home that Friday evening. He checked into the Curracloe Lodge Hotel and without any need for speeches or promises, Ruth went with him. They continued the kiss that they started on the beach and afterwards, when they lay back on his hotel bed, Ruth realised that in this moment, in his arms, she felt happiness for the first time in her life.

34

RUTH

Now

They ate their breakfast in silence, with DJ's question still hanging between them, like rotten fruit. The scowl on his face only disappeared when Anna and Cormac walked in. One good thing about their move to this hotel was the friendship that was developing between the kids. Most evenings, the three of them went to the park to play football, or throw a stick for Bette Davis.

After breakfast Ruth packed DJ's lunch into his school bag and found a note. She opened it with shaking hands. *Please do not let it be another event that involves parent participation.* She still shuddered when she remembered the disaster that was the coffee fundraiser the previous year, when she managed to upset Dev and his mother. And DJ, too.

Dear Ms Wilde,
    I hope you are well. I have been thinking about our conversation and have a suggestion to make. DJ

may stay in school an extra hour each afternoon to do his homework. I am in the school until 4 p.m. every day anyhow, planning the next day's lessons. I appreciate that a hotel room is not the most conducive environment for him. Let me know if this sounds acceptable.

Yours, Mr O'Dowd

Ruth smiled as she reread the note. Mr O'Dowd was full of surprises.

She broached the idea with DJ, who thought it sounded like the most heinous suggestion he had ever heard. She wrote a note to thank Mr O'Dowd, saying she would give it some thought. Which is exactly what she did as she ran back to The Lodge from school later that morning. And somewhere along the route an idea began to form. When she got back to her room she grabbed the laminated sheet of rules and scanned them to find the item she was looking for.

A communal room is available on the ground floor. Guests must ask reception for the key.

She thought she had remembered that correctly. Where was this communal room? She had not come across it, or heard any of the other residents mention it.

She would ask Kian! He knew everything.

She found him in the kitchen eating a breakfast roll with gusto. She kept her eyes on the ground, shuddering at the thought.

'Hello, love,' Kian said mid-mouthful. 'How's she cutting?'

Ruth had no idea what he was talking about. She ran through possible reasons why he would ask her that. She had nothing. 'I do not understand. I am not cutting anything.'

Kian bellowed laughter at this. Aisling and Ava walked into the kitchen, their faces curious as to what was going on. 'What are we missing?' Aisling asked.

'This one. She's hilarious. Loves her, I do,' Kian said, taking another bite of his sandwich.

Ruth was surprised by this statement. *Should she say she liked him, too?* 'I am not sure how I feel about you yet, as I have not had enough opportunity to make an informed opinion. But early indications are that I like you, too.'

At this, Kian doubled over, holding his hand up, saying, 'Stop . . . you're killing me.'

Aisling said, joining in the laughter, 'I told you. She's funny.'

'People laugh at me a lot,' Ruth said.

'We're not laughing at you, love,' Kian said. 'We're laughing *with* you. There's a difference.'

Aisling filled the kettle and they each took a seat at the table.

'Have any of you been in the communal room before?' Ruth asked.

They looked at her blankly.

She held up the laminated rules and pointed to number nineteen.

'Jaysus, it's months since I looked at those rules, I'd forgotten that was even there,' Kian said.

'Me, too,' Aisling said.

Ava added, 'I did look for the room when we moved in, but never found it. Erica was vague when I questioned her. I assumed it wasn't available any more.'

Ruth shook her head. 'But the rules say that it is there. So it must be. I am going to investigate.'

She made her way to reception. Erica was sitting in her usual spot.

'Good morning! Isn't it a lovely day? I swear those clouds are full of snow. I said to my Billy this morning that one of these days we'll wake up and the ground will be white,' Erica said.

'Does Billy actually exist?' Ruth said.

'I beg your pardon?' Erica replied, as she seemed to do a lot when she spoke to Ruth.

'I asked you if Billy was a figment of your imagination. Because I have never set eyes on him. Is he just someone you talk to in your head?' Ruth smiled. 'I have one, too. Odd Thomas.'

'It is you who is odd. Honest to goodness, Ruth, the things you come out with. I can assure you that my Billy is most certainly real,' Erica said.

'If you say so.' Ruth did not believe her. 'May I have the key to the communal room? Please.'

'There's no lock on the kitchen, so no key needed.'

'I am aware of that fact. I am talking about rule number nineteen on the laminate.' Ruth held up the sheet. 'It states that there is a communal room for the guests. Guests must come here for the key. I would like the key. Please.'

Erica's face went from puzzled to understanding. 'Oh! That room. I've never been asked for the key before, to my recollection. And to be honest with you I'm just as happy. The room is little more than a dumping ground. My Billy has had plans to clear it out for years, but he does suffer with his back.' She looked at Ruth and dared her to question Billy's existence again.

'The rules say that if I ask I can have the key,' Ruth insisted.

'You and the rules,' Erica said. 'Well, you can have the key if you want, but don't come complaining to me about the state of it. You get what you see and that's just the way it is. And if you have an issue you know what to do. Take it up with the council.'

'I will not complain. I would just like to see the room,' Ruth said.

Erica got up from her seat and grabbed a key from one of the drawers. 'It's just past the dining room on the right-hand side. You can't miss it.'

Ruth walked out of reception, pausing at the last minute to call back, 'Thank you.'

'Happy to help,' Erica shouted after her. Ruth was an odd one, no doubt about it, but you couldn't fault her manners. Her Billy always said, you can get through life with bad manners, but it is a darn sight easier with good ones.

One, two, three, four . . .

Eighteen steps. Ruth had passed the door many times without thought. *What if it is a portal to another world, Odd?*

Only one way to find out, he answered. She unlocked it with shaking hands. It swung open with a bang.

Erica had not exaggerated. If this was a portal, the only place it led to was to a rubbish dump. The room was crammed with black rubbish sacks, cardboard boxes, stacked tables and chairs. Her eyes took in the cobwebbed ceiling and the dirty carpeted floor. With every detail her heart sank. While her expectations were low, this was worse than she had envisioned. It would take a lot of work.

But that was something that Ruth was not afraid of. She grew up in a messy and disorganised house. Her parents' lives were so busy that they never seemed to take a moment to stand still. Ruth's bedroom was the only space that remained uncluttered and pleasing to her. And that was all down to Ruth. Her earliest memory was wiping down her doll's house with a damp cloth she'd persuaded her mother to give her.

Marian had laughed, saying to Alan, 'Where did we get this one from?'

She could not work out why her parents did not just organise themselves better. Why could they not work harder to eliminate the things in their lives that caused the chaos? Why put themselves through so much every week? They constantly shouted to each other, to the children, 'Where is my coat, my keys, my book, my shoes?'

When her father left, Ruth took over pretty much all of the chores in the house. Mark teased and called her Cinders. But she did not mind. She liked to clean. She enjoyed bringing order to things around her. Bit by bit, she removed piles of newspapers from counter tops, took books that had toppled over into heaps on the hall floor and placed them in their bookshelves, untangled clothes that peeked out from under beds.

So, this communal room in The Lodge, that might

to some seem like a hopeless cause, did not faze Ruth in the slightest. *I can do this.* She flipped open one of the boxes closest to her. It was full of cups and saucers, all plain white. Dusty, but in good condition. Another box had saucepans. Then she found several that contained books. This made her happy. She grabbed the nearest one to her and whooped out loud when she discovered it was a Dean Koontz. She looked at it in awe. It had to be a sign.

I'll be just like Odd. An unlikely hero. I can do this.

35

RUTH

Ruth ran back to reception. Erica was mid-mouthful of mince pie. 'One of the nicest things about November is that the shops start selling these. You simply have to try the Salted Caramel ones from Lidl. Or Aldi. I can never remember which. Delicious.' She stuffed the second half in her mouth.

Ruth shuddered and said, 'I would like to clean the communal room.'

Erica brushed some mince-pie crumbs from her mouth. 'You, young lady, need to slow down.'

'May I clean the room?' Ruth asked again.

'Why?' Erica asked, suspicion written over her face.

'So that we can use it,' Ruth answered. 'It says here in rule nineteen . . .'

Erica held her hand up. Those rules would be the death of her. 'I know what it says. I personally laminated them myself.' She took a moment to go through the pros and cons of Ruth's request. She couldn't think of a single objection. Yet still, she was fundamentally against the idea.

'No.'

Ruth looked around the hotel lobby and said, 'Imagine having a quiet space that your residents could retire to in the evening.'

'Go on,' Erica said, putting down her second mince pie.

'What if the unused communal room became The Silver Sands Lodge Library?' Ruth said, inspiration hitting her.

'A library?' Erica repeated. She had to admit that did sound rather grand.

'Just think what that would do for The Silver Sands Lodge. A boutique hotel with its own library,' Ruth said. She noted with satisfaction the look on Erica's face. Erica liked the idea.

'What's in it for you?' Erica asked.

'The children need a quiet space to do their homework in. It is impossible for them to concentrate, study or write in their bedrooms. So the room has to be used by all guests. Not just the "normal" ones. Somewhere they can read a book or newspaper, have a cup of tea . . .'

Erica raised her hand, 'There is no budget for your proposed project. My housekeeper and her team are already at full capacity and do not have the time to take on the cleaning of another room.'

'What if I clean the room every day? There will be no additional responsibility for your staff because I will take care of it all,' Ruth said.

'I can't pay you,' Erica shouted after Ruth, who was already running down the corridor.

Ruth was too excited to wait for the lift so she ran upstairs two at a time, heading straight for the kitchen.

Kian, Ava and Aisling were still there, plus Melissa from room 131, who had a toddler in her arms.

'I found the communal room,' Ruth said.

'Praise be,' Kian replied.

'Good for you,' Aisling said, elbowing Kian.

'It is very dirty and full of rubbish,' Ruth said.

'Course it is. Typical of this dump,' Kian said. 'Look at the state of that wall.' The once-white paint in the kitchen was now grey.

'I am going to clean it,' Ruth said.

'The kitchen wall?' Kian asked.

Ruth looked at that and shrugged. 'Maybe later. But right now, I am going to clean the communal room. And I hope you will all help me.'

Ava made a face. She had just painted her nails. They weren't really dry yet.

'I'm not sure, Ruth . . .' Aisling said.

'The children need somewhere to do their homework. I have already been called into DJ's school to discuss the decline in his homework quality. It is impossible for him to concentrate in the bedroom. And there is no desk for him so he ends up working on his bed. It is unacceptable,' Ruth said.

Melissa added, 'My daughter Ciara is doing her junior cert this year. There are five of us in our family room. It's an impossible situation.'

'So your idea is that this communal room downstairs is going to be a homework room?' Kian asked.

Ruth nodded.

'What's the point of doing that, though?' Melissa asked. 'This hotel is just temporary for us all.'

'I like the idea of a homework room. Won't lie. But why should we have to clean the hotel, do their bleeding jobs for them?' Kian said.

'Exactly,' Melissa agreed.

'Playing devil's advocate here. Just say we do clean the room up, what then? Who says Erica will even let us lot use the room?' Aisling asked.

'I have spoken to her about that. The room will be renamed the Library, to be used as a quiet room for all residents.' She looked at Kian. 'No more hiding behind the palm tree when you want to read the newspaper. No more balancing their maths homework on their knees. A proper homework area with desks. Erica has agreed to it as long as it does not cost the hotel money to create or maintain. I have told her I will do all of that.'

Ruth looked around at them all, staring at her with varying degrees of shock and surprise on their faces.

'It's a waste of time, something I don't have spare,' Melissa said, walking out.

'I don't know, Ruth,' Aisling said. 'I think you are being taken advantage of by Erica. You'll do all the work, clearing the room out. Then she'll say it's only for her "normal" residents.'

Murmurs of agreement moved through the room.

Odd whispered in her ear, as Ruth's shoulder sagged with the weight of her disappointment. She cleared her throat then repeated one of Odd's lines. '*Perseverance is impossible if we don't permit ourselves to hope.*'

'Come again?' Kian said.

'It is a line from a book I love. *Odd Thomas*. It's my mantra when curveballs are sent my way. I believe that we have to keep trying, persevering, pushing for our children's sake. And the only way I can find the strength to keep doing that is believing and hoping that it will all work out in the end. For DJ's sake, I have to hope that.' She walked out of the kitchen and made her way back down to the communal room.

I can do this on my own. I do not need anyone. Why then, did she feel so disappointed?

Standing on her tippy toes, she reached up to pull a chair from a tall stack.

'You trying to kill yourself?' Kian's voice said, making her jump.

She turned round in surprise to see him standing there, with Aisling and Ava by his side. 'You came.'

'My diary was wide open today so you chose a good time to make a speech,' Kian said.

'Anna needs somewhere to go other than our bedroom or the park. I figure that if we do this, maybe it will be like good karma or something,' Aisling answered.

'I like the idea of a library,' Ava said. 'I read about these free libraries popping up around the world, outside cafés, in villages, towns, even in people's front gardens. A free book exchange – take a book, leave one back. I've got a few bags of books in storage I can donate.'

Ruth said, 'I found a couple of boxes of books in here. We could have a section for children and for adults.'

'There is some serious shit in these boxes,' Kian said, peering through open box lids. He picked up a plastic green turtle and threw it back in again.

'I've got lots of kitchen stuff over here that could be useful.' Aisling held up some saucepans. 'We could do with a few of these upstairs. Someone burned the bottom of a couple of the pans in the kitchen last week.'

Kian held up a kettle. 'Couldn't we make a little hot-chocolate station for the kids, too? Cormac would love that.'

Ruth smiled. 'DJ loves marshmallows.'

'I'd say this place hasn't seen a duster in years,' Aisling said.

'I like to clean. I just need help with the furniture,' Ruth said, afraid that they would leave again. And she did not want that. She found she liked having their company.

'Many hands make light work. Let's get going so.' Kian began unstacking the chairs one by one.

'I'm going to take some of this kitchen stuff upstairs. That way we are clearing as we go,' Aisling said, sorting a box out.

'Where do you want this table?' Kian asked, and they looked around the room, trying to work out how it would all fit.

'How about over here for a homework station for the older kids? They need space for all their books,' Ruth said.

'And over here, we could have a few tables for the small 'uns. Melissa's kids are forever running around the hall. They might sit still for five minutes if they had somewhere to do it,' Kian said.

'That's a lovely idea,' Aisling said.

'I've been known to have a few,' Kian winked.

Ruth noticed Aisling blushing scarlet and turning away to hide it.

'We need a bookshelf,' Ava said.

'Why don't you use the windowsill?' Kian suggested. They walked over to look at it and all agreed it was perfect as it was so deep.

'Ah, lads, I'm on fire today, what?' Kian said, and the room filled with laughter and hope. 'You happy with the plan, boss?'

'I am not the boss,' Ruth answered, startled, when she realised he was talking to her.

'Oh, you are, no doubt about it. This is all you. I'm just the muscle.' He flexed one arm and Aisling pretended to swoon.

The four of them worked well together in companionable silence, with Kian cracking the odd joke. The furniture was moved to new positions, the rubbish stacked out the back with the bins.

Ruth collected a vacuum cleaner and some cleaning materials from the housekeeper.

'Give me a go of that bad boy,' Kian said when she came in dragging a Nilfisk behind her. 'I'm parched. Why don't you all go for a cuppa and I'll be up in five minutes when the floor is hoovered?'

Aisling, Eva and Ruth watched him for a few minutes, delighted to see an acceptable red carpet revealed under the layer of dust. Then they walked upstairs to the kitchen.

'Kian is really lovely when you get to know him,' Aisling said.

'I never thought I would ever agree with that statement. But he's been all right today, I suppose,' Ava replied.

'He is a man of many contradictions,' Ruth said.

They looked at her with interest. Ruth continued, 'Well, he curses a lot, yet he is also polite, well mannered. He looks lazy, yet he is not afraid to get his hands dirty. And despite his tendency to rant and rave about the injustices of the world, his arguments and views are valid and well informed.'

'Wow,' Aisling said. 'You really nailed him!'

Ava made a pot of tea and poured Ruth a glass of milk.

'Who would have thought cleaning could be so much fun?' Aisling said.

'Kian is like a one-man stand-up show,' Ava said.

'He made me laugh occasionally,' Ruth said.

Kian walked in at that moment, 'Ladies, ladies, I know you are talking about your favourite subject, *me*, but would you ever pour this hard-working man a drink?'

Ava did the honours, then said, 'I've texted Brian and he's going to get our books from his mam's house on the way home from work. I'll start sorting the books from the boxes below when we go back down.'

'They must be in alphabetical order,' Ruth said.

'I think I can manage that,' Ava said, throwing her eyes up to the ceiling.

Aisling said, 'You do know that five minutes after the kids arrive, they'll mess up any order you put them in?'

'Sometimes, I go into Eason on O'Connell Street and sort their books out for them,' Ruth said.

'I bet they love seeing you,' Ava replied, laughing.

Once they'd drunk their tea they all got back to work. And within a few hours they were done. They stood side by side and looked around the newly transformed room, with satisfaction and pride.

'It's beginning to look like a library now,' Ava said, and everyone nodded.

'Gas thing is, I can't stand books myself. I'd much prefer to watch stories than read about them,' Kian said.

'You are missing out on so much!' Ruth said, shocked at his admission.

'Like what?' he asked.

'*Odd Thomas*, for a start. A race against time. Good versus evil. It is truly excellent,' Ruth said.

'I've visited so many different cultures, more than I could ever visit in a lifetime, all through books. Just with the flick of a page,' Ava said.

'Like Pico Mundo in California,' Ruth said.

You know that is a fictitious town? Odd whispered.

It is real to me, Odd.

'Last night I was in Hawkins, Indiana, courtesy of my auld pal Netflix. With the flick of a remote-control switch! Not sure it's a place that you'd want to go to, though. Stranger things happen there, get it?' Kian started to laugh at his own joke and Aisling joined in.

'Anna and I love that show, too. How talented are those kids?' Aisling said.

'You should watch it together some time. It is obvious to everyone that you have taken a fancy to each other. Kian, you cannot keep your eyes off Aisling. And, Aisling, you start to giggle whenever Kian is around. Watch the programme together.' Ruth carried on cleaning while she spoke.

'Who needs Tinder when you have Ruth around?' Ava said.

'I didn't think we would get this done by tonight, never mind before lunch.' Ruth was oblivious to the reaction her words had made.

'I can't wait to show Cormac,' Kian said, stealing a glance at Aisling.

'And me, Anna,' Aisling agreed, flushing under his gaze. 'We could have a little party to show it to them? Get some crisps and pop? I can go to the shop to pick up a few bits.'

'Great idea. I'll go with you if you like,' Kian said.

'I'd like that very much.' She beamed a smile in his direction and they walked out, shoulder to shoulder.

Ruth looked around the room with satisfaction. For the first time in months she started to feel hope begin to dance its way around her again. Whatever amount of time they had to spend here, she would do all in her power to make it a better place for them. A home.

36

RUTH

Back at the park, on what was now their bench, Ruth handed Tom a napkin with two carrot-cake muffins inside. 'They are from the breakfast buffet. I would not normally condone taking these but yesterday it came to my notice that all unused breakfast pastries and cakes were thrown out. I had suspected as much, and when I investigated the matter, I was most disappointed.'

'That's a crying shame,' Tom said. 'I want you to know that I appreciate how good you are to me, Ruth.'

She waved aside his thanks, handing him his flask that she'd filled for him.

'I would like you to get out of your clothes before you have a coffee,' she instructed.

'I beg your pardon!' Tom exclaimed. Had he heard her correctly?

Ruth placed a Bag for Life onto the bench that had become their regular spot for lunch every day. 'I have made an approximate guess as to your size, but I am reasonably confident that I have chosen well. They are

273

from a charity shop but are in perfect condition. In fact the sweater is new, with tags on still. An unwanted gift donated, I would imagine.'

She passed him a pair of blue denim jeans, a T-shirt, a roll-neck sweater and a waterproof jacket. A hat, scarf and pair of gloves completed the haul.

'You got these for me?' Tom picked up each item and examined it. He had not received a gift from anyone since Cathy left . . .

'I enjoy our lunchtime chats, Dr O'Grady. But you smell.'

Tom's initial reaction was to laugh. Then offence followed, stopping his laughter in its tracks.

'I wash every day,' he protested.

'You may very well wash yourself every day, but you do not wash your clothes. And they smell. It is unaccept-able. You can have your coffee and muffins when you are changed.'

Tom got up and grabbed the bag of clothes, then made his way to the public toilets. Bette Davis, the traitor, stayed with Ruth, ever hopeful that a treat might be passed to her, too.

Everything fitted perfectly. But Tom refused to get rid of his overcoat. It had two deep pockets that especially pleased him. He could hold treats for Bette Davis in those. He placed his hat, scarf and gloves on and even though he had no mirror to check himself out, he felt good.

And for the first time in weeks he felt warm, too. The cold that had seeped into his bones began to disappear.

'You look different,' Ruth said, when he walked back. He might even have swaggered a bit. Bette Davis ran towards him, barking in delight that her master was back.

'I've had a makeover,' Tom said, ruffling her ears. 'Do you recognise your old pal?'

'Where is the new jacket?' Ruth asked.

'Under my overcoat,' Tom said. 'I'm not giving that up. It's non-negotiable.'

Bette barked her approval when he pulled a dog biscuit from his pocket, which he'd placed there earlier.

Ruth told him, 'You will be too warm with both.'

But she poured him his coffee all the same. Tom liked having her fuss over him. He felt a lump threaten to choke him as it grew bigger and took up residence in his throat.

'Do I smell better?' he asked.

'Yes,' Ruth said.

'I am more grateful than you could ever know. It's difficult keeping clean; perhaps I let the standards drop a bit. Most of the public showers don't want the likes of us using their facilities. We're too "dirty", apparently. That's always been a puzzle to me. How the hell are we to keep clean if they won't let us in the doors to use their facilities? I don't know, some people are just stupid.'

'Stupid is as stupid does,' Ruth said.

Tom replied, 'I ain't no Forrest Gump.'

They both smiled in contentment at the pleasure of sharing a joke, made famous in the Tom Hanks movie.

'Maybe I can sneak you into the hotel to wash,' Ruth said.

'Don't put your place there at risk,' Tom said. 'Now, what news do you have today?'

Ruth told him all about the new hotel library and homework room, her excitement shining from her.

'Good for you! Sounds like you are making some friends.'

'I have never had friends before. It is a whole new world. I like it.'

'And it sounds like they like you.'

'It is a most unusual feeling. Most people do not seem to care for me,' Ruth said.

'You have just been hanging around with the wrong people,' Tom said. 'Or maybe, from what you told me, you've been on your own for so long, you've not given people a chance to get to know you.'

Ruth frowned. It was true that over the past ten years she had spent most of her time alone or with DJ. 'I have had some bad experiences,' she said, in an effort to explain herself.

'I don't doubt that. If you are too much for some people, then maybe they are not your people. Simple as.'

Ruth thought about Denise and the other mums at the school gates. Not her people.

'You've found your tribe with Kian, Aisling and Ava, by the sounds of it. Hold them close, don't let them go,' Tom said.

My tribe. She liked the sound of that very much.

'You are part of my tribe, too, Dr O'Grady,' Ruth said.

Tom felt inordinately happy with that statement.

He ate his first muffin in two bites, then halved the second one for himself and Bette, washing it down with his coffee. 'DJ has been asking me a lot of questions again. About your parents. And his dad.'

Ruth put her hands over her face. Not this again.

'I'm sorry,' Tom said. 'I don't want to upset you. I'm not being nosy. It's your own business. I just want you to know what the lad said.'

'Go on.'

'When he thinks about his dad he feels sick and gets a knot in his stomach,' Tom continued. 'I told him he should talk to you.'

'Thank you,' Ruth said. 'I wish I could give him something else to help him answer those questions that make him ill. But I do not know where his father is.'

'Do you want to find him?' Tom asked.

'Of course. I loved him. Or at least I felt I did. I am sure most would think I was stupid for falling for a man in one weekend. And maybe I need to accept that they are right, because he never came back.'

'I don't think you were stupid. He's the stupid one, letting you slip through his fingers. For what it's worth, I fell in love with Cathy in one moment. We were just meant to be.'

They sat in silence for a few moments, both lost in thought.

'When I was a little girl, I overheard my parents talking one night,' Ruth said.

'No good comes from eavesdropping, that's what my dad used to say,' Tom replied.

'But when you hear someone mention *your* name in conversation it is impossible to walk away.'

'And I'm assuming whatever you overheard wasn't good?'

Ruth remembered the pain her mother's words caused, like it was yesterday. Some cuts never heal. 'Mam told Dad that she hated reading to me. The thing was, I loved story time. Sitting at her feet, leaning into her legs.'

'That must have been hard to hear,' Tom said.

Ruth felt her heart rate begin to accelerate as it always did when she thought about her parents. She sighed, 'I should have walked back to my bedroom, but I was so upset. I asked her why.'

Tom wanted to reach over, to touch Ruth, offer her some comfort. But instead he nudged Bette gently, who took the hint and nuzzled in close to Ruth. She began to stroke her coat, and Tom was sure Ruth's breathing evened out. 'She told me that she hated reading fairytales to me, because I would never have a happy ever after or fall in love with a Prince Charming.'

'That's ridiculous!' Tom spluttered out.

'I asked her why for the second time.' Ruth leaned in close to Bette, till her cheek was touching the dog's fur, then whispered, 'She said that Prince Charmings never fell in love with freaks.'

Tom had seen and heard a lot over the years. Had thought that nothing much could shock him anymore. But this . . .

Ruth nodded, her eyes on her plastic cup.

'Oh Ruth,' Tom whispered. 'I am so sorry.'

'For what? You did nothing wrong. I thought I proved her wrong when I met Dean. Sometimes, I think I imagined him. I made up a fairytale.'

'Stop that. Whatever happened to him, he should be helping you with DJ. Paying maintenance.' Tom wanted to hunt him down and tell him to get his sorry arse in touch with Ruth and DJ. He wasn't sure who he was more annoyed with, her parents or Dean. All of them.

'I have tried to search for him online many times. But

with the only information being Dean, Dublin, Sales Representative . . . I click on the same images that I have clicked on hundreds of times before, hoping for a different result, hoping that this time Dean's face would appear but it never does. I don't know enough about him.'

'What if you find him, what then?' Tom asked.

'I do not know, Dr O'Grady. Sometimes I imagine a different truth for DJ and me. A world where he never left and I am married to Dean.'

Tom felt his jaw clench. 'I don't want you wasting your life dreaming about your past, instead of living.' *Like I do?* Tom pushed the thought away, refusing to acknowledge it, but knowing he wanted so much more for this woman and her kid than he had for himself.

'I know that salvation does not lie with DJ's father. It is up to me to find a way to make DJ happy again. Find us both a forever home.'

Tom leaned in close to Ruth. 'And I have no doubt that you will succeed. But your mother got it so wrong. Happy ever afters come in all shapes and sizes. When you least expect them. Some last a lifetime, others only a fleeting moment. But the point is, they happen. This world is not done surprising you yet, Ruth Wilde. I am sure of it.'

37

TOM

Bette Davis moved away from Ruth's embrace, her ears pricked up, looking into the shadows of the trees.

'There's a woman watching us,' Ruth said.

'You know her?' Tom asked Ruth, as the woman began walking towards them.

Ruth shook her head then joked, 'She probably finds you attractive in your new clothes.'

'Ha! She's coming over so let's see if you are right!'

The middle-aged woman wore jeans, runners, a light rain jacket and a frown. She cleared her throat when she reached Tom's side, then whispered, 'Are you Charlie Sheen?'

Tom felt laughter gurgle its way inside him. Of all the things he thought she might ask him, that was not one of them. 'Once someone said I had a look of Brendan Gleeson. That was around the time of *Braveheart*. Great movie. But I have to admit that it's a first that anyone would mistake me for Charlie Sheen. Maybe his dad, Martin, at a push.'

Her face fell and he saw her eyes water up. She blinked hard to stem the threatened tears.

'Are you OK?' Tom asked.

She shook her head. 'Charlie Sheen said I was to be here at twelve thirty.'

'You know Charlie Sheen is an actor. He's unlikely to come here,' Tom said. This woman was clearly in distress and he wondered if perhaps she wasn't very well.

She looked at him in irritation. 'I know that's not his real name. I don't suppose I'll ever know his real name. I'm not sure I want to know it now.'

'You are not making much sense.' Tom was lost and still wasn't sure that the woman wasn't, too.

She looked from Ruth to Tom and then whispered, 'You're not an undercover detective or anything like that, are you?'

'No. I'm just Doc. And this is my friend Ruth.' He tried to look unthreatening. It must have worked because she took a seat beside him on the bench.

'I'm sorry about all of this. I'm Lorraine and quite clearly out of my depth!' she replied.

'You have me intrigued.'

'Charlie Sheen is a drug dealer,' she replied. 'I've shocked you, haven't I?'

She looked around her once more as if, by saying the words out loud, she'd incite someone to swoop down and arrest her.

'You have shocked me,' Ruth said. 'But then again people shock me most days.'

Tom looked at the woman a little closer to see if there were any of the usual tell-tale signs of drug abuse.

She wouldn't be the first housewife to become addicted to prescription pills. He'd seen it many times over the years. No. Nothing. If she was using, she was hiding it well.

'The drugs are not for me. They are for my husband, Dan. Although, to be honest, I could do with something right now for my bloody nerves.' She held her hands up to show them shaking.

The poor woman. What on earth had driven her to the streets to look for drugs? 'And what are you in the market for?'

'Cannabis. Or is it marijuana they call it now?' Lorraine answered.

'I think either name works,' Tom replied.

'Dan and I both got through our teens and most of our adult life without touching so much as a cigarette. I don't know how we ended up here.' She looked bemused.

'Sometimes life throws us off course,' Ruth said.

'No truer word,' Lorraine said. 'Dan was diagnosed with multiple sclerosis in 1997.'

'That's rough,' Tom said.

'Every day has been a new challenge for Dan. And me,' she replied. 'He was in remission for nearly ten years, so we both got complacent. I began to think that the doctors got it wrong. A misdiagnosis.'

'It came back?' Tom asked.

'About a year ago now.'

Tom had treated several patients over the years with MS. It was a horrific disease. Dermot, one of the men he knew from the Peter McVerry Trust, had it. He'd deteriorated rapidly in the past year.

'He's developed secondary progressive MS now. And

that comes with severe spasticity. I massage his legs to try to help, but late at night he can't sleep with it. Then a neighbour gave him some weed and the stiffness eased. I make a tea for him with it. He likes that. But last week my neighbour moved. Every day I lose a little bit more of the man I married. So, here I am out on the streets trying to score drugs at fifty-six years of age. If my children could see me now . . .' Lorraine ended on a sob.

Tom shook his head in sympathy. This was wrong. 'How many kids do you have?'

'We've two. A boy and a girl. Well, they're all grown up now. Both are great and I wouldn't be without them, but they live too far away to be of much help. The burden – and I hate saying that word, but it feels like that – is all mine. I've got to find a way to make this disease bearable for him. Our doctor says that it won't be long until they legalise cannabis oil but I can't wait that long. Neither of us can,' Lorraine said.

Tom recognised desperation when he saw it. He'd seen it before. Hell, he'd felt it before. 'How did you find this Charlie Sheen?'

'On Facebook,' Lorraine laughed. 'Imagine that. On bloody Facebook!'

Tom shook his head in amazement.

'I'm one hundred per cent serious. There is a private closed group that I asked to join, called Friends of Cannabis. It took me two days to get the nerve up to ask the question, and when I did I expected the hand of the law to come out through the computer screen to arrest me. But someone pointed me in the direction of this fella.'

'Lorraine, if you don't mind me saying, this is quite a risk you're taking. You don't know who or what you're getting yourself mixed up in. Plus, I'm here most days and nights and I've never heard tell of that guy,' Tom said.

'What do you suggest then? I can't go home without this sorted,' she said.

Tom wanted to help her. But how? Then an idea began to sneak its way around him. He walked to the pay phone and called directory enquiries, hoping his contact was still at the same address and listed. She was. Yes! 'Don't move. Give me five minutes, OK?'

'Hello,' Caroline answered before the third ring, her voice firm, no-nonsense as she had always been.

'Hello, Caroline. It's Dr Tom O'Grady here.'

'Dr O'Grady. From Spawell Road? I thought you were dead!'

'Alive and kicking.'

'You just upped and left years ago. I assumed you'd corked it.'

'Nope.'

'Well, I'm glad to hear it. You didn't call to swap pleasantries with me after all this time. What do you want?' Caroline asked.

'Do you still have that special plant?'

She took a breath, but answered without hesitation. 'Yes.'

'I have a woman here with me whose husband has multiple sclerosis. She's in trouble, Caroline. She needs help. Can you help her?'

Again, no hesitation. 'You can vouch for her?'

'Yes I can,' Tom said with ease. He may have just met this woman, but he trusted her.

'Give her my number and I'll take care of it.'

Tom hung up, jubilant. 'Good news. An ex-patient of mine is going to help you. Her husband had multiple sclerosis too. He died a few years ago, but like you she had to find a way to help him when he was alive. She's a feisty one, and not many would take her on. But even so, she knew she couldn't traipse the streets looking for drugs. So she started to grow her own.'

Tom couldn't help but feel chuffed with himself when he saw both Lorraine and Ruth's faces. They were obviously stunned by the direction this day had taken. He realised he liked surprising them. He was still needed. He could make a difference.

'If you can get to Wexford, she'll look after you,' Tom told Lorraine.

Once the words had sunk in, that help was there for them, Lorraine started to laugh out loud. She leaned in and kissed Tom on his head. 'You may not be Charlie Sheen but you are saving my life! I cannot begin to thank you.'

When Lorraine had walked out of the park, Ruth turned to Tom and said, 'Oh, yes, I can see now that you were correct before. You are most definitely not Dr Tom O'Grady any more. Not one little bit.'

There wasn't a single thing he could think of to say in rebuttal.

38

TOM

After Ruth had left, Tom couldn't help but think about the man he used to be when he knew Ruth, and the man who slept on this bench. Who was he now? The street bum who occasionally gave some medical advice to the homeless? Or the same Dr Tom O'Grady from Wexford? The thing was, he knew it wasn't just the geography that changed when he left home. He felt something give inside his head and heart. The first fracture was after Mikey . . . but then Cathy finished the job.

But this past month, with Ruth and DJ, his world had become a little brighter. And he felt himself changing again. He didn't know if he liked it. For ten years he had not thought beyond each hour he was living. But now . . . bloody hell, his head was full of tomorrows and what they might bring. *Damn it to hell. Damn you to hell, Cathy. Why did you have to go leave me?*

He wouldn't think about it any more. He'd close his eyes and go home, because there was another word that he used to be called, and that was his favourite one of all . . .

Mikey's first word was 'Dada'. Tom had never heard a more beautiful sound in his life. Cathy pretended to be happy that the cards had fallen this way. But he could see the disappointment in her eyes.

'Dada . . . dada . . . dada . . .'

'Children say "dada" first to keep us interested because we all know the truth. It's all about the mama!' *Tom had heard that before, he was sure of it. He couldn't take his eyes off his son. His beautiful, clever son.*

Cathy shushed him, smiling through tears as she watched Mikey. 'I'm not upset, I'm happy! Our boy has just spoken his first word and he is not even a year old.'

They stood side by side and laughed in delight as Mikey continued to show off his new trick.

'When he says "mama", I'm going to record it and make it my ring tone!' *Cathy said.*

'Annemarie has approached me about buying into the business,' *Tom blurted out.* 'She's been left some money by an aunt who died earlier this year.'

'Wow. I didn't see that coming,' *Cathy said sarcastically. They had both been expecting as much.*

'Well, her aunt instructed her to do something useful with it. She wants her own practice. But she likes working with me.'

'You being a charmer and all that,' *Cathy interjected.*

'Exactly!' *Smiling, he pushed a leaflet towards Cathy.* 'Remember that house we loved last year?'

'The one that was out of our price range? The one that we said under no circumstances could we afford?'

'Well, the thing is, if Annemarie buys into the business, we can buy it. She's also suggested that she rent this place, when we move out. The rent would help pay the mortgage.'

'Does she not want to buy her own place?' Cathy replied, ignoring the fact that Tom said 'when'. Clearly he had made his mind up. He always was impulsive. When he made his mind up, it was hard to make him divert from his course of action.

'That's what I said to her. But she wouldn't have the money to buy into the practice and buy this place. Apparently Sam and her are not at the proposal stage yet. Whatever that means.'

'It means he's being a typical bloke with commitment issues. Silly man. If he doesn't hurry he'll lose that woman.'

'I'll tell him when I see him next. But what do you think about the house?'

'You love this flat. Are you sure you are ready to leave it? You've lived here a long time, Tom,' Cathy pointed out.

'We've outgrown it. Or are getting close to that. It was perfect for us two. But it's not ideal for a family. Mikey is already crawling; his first birthday is coming up. Imagine celebrating that in the new house. We can watch him take his first steps in that big living room.'

Cathy glanced towards the nursery in their two-bedroomed flat, which was little more than a boxroom. With the baby-changing unit in there and the cot, there wasn't much room for anything else.

'It's a great location. Just down the road,' Cathy said. When they said no to it last time, it was their heads talking, not their hearts. Could they afford it now? 'I suppose it wouldn't hurt to go back and look at the house again.'

Within eight weeks they moved to their new home.

For a few months everything was perfect. Should Tom have seen it coming? Could he have stopped the unspeakable horror that was racing towards them? These were questions that still haunted him to this day.

39

RUTH

Despite her best efforts, Ruth could not persuade Aisling to take up running. Instead they began walking in the park each afternoon, once the kids finished their homework after school. Most days Ava joined them, too. DJ and Anna would play on the swings while they did a few laps in the park.

It was a few days since Ruth had last seen Tom and she scanned the park once again for a sight of him but he was nowhere to be seen. It was as if he'd disappeared off the face of the earth since they'd had lunch last Tuesday. DJ was withdrawn and sullen again. He blamed Ruth for Tom and Bette Davis's absence, as well as everything else.

'You must have said something to him to make him leave,' he'd accused. Ruth had gone over every conversation they'd had and fretted that she'd offended him when she gave him new clothes to wear.

'Things any better with DJ?' Aisling asked as they walked. Ruth shook her head.

'It's a funny age,' Aisling replied. 'Neither a kid, nor a teenager. I feel for them. Anna burst into tears the other night. When I asked her what was wrong, she said she didn't know. She just felt frustrated and fed up.'

'Welcome to the complicated world of womanhood,' Ava said.

They all giggled at that.

Aisling said, 'Speaking of womanhood, you know our noisy neighbours in number 125? Well, Kian filled me in on all the gossip there. Turns out their kids are staying with their grandparents, who have a huge house out in Dun Laoghaire. Those two chancers are only pretending that they are homeless so that they move up the list quicker.'

'They lied?' Ruth asked, incredulous.

'Yep. Sure they're having the time of their lives. Shagging morning, noon and night. It's like a fecking holiday for them.' Aisling shrugged.

'That is downright despicable,' Ava said. 'If they get a house ahead of me and Brian, I'll swing for them. And don't get me started on that Melissa one.'

'What has she done?' Ruth asked.

'Well, to start with she's turned down three houses that I know about. For someone who is forever moaning that she had to sleep in a car for weeks, she's fierce fussy about where she goes next. You'd think that with four children in one room with her she'd be desperate to take any house. Especially with Christmas coming,' Ava said.

Hearing the stories of the other social housing residents was a revelation to Ruth. She took people at face value and was shocked to hear about some of the shenanigans going on.

'Speaking of Christmas, we should decorate the Library. Wouldn't it be nice to have a tree there? It's not as if we can fit one in our hotel bedrooms,' Aisling said.

Ruth replied, 'I love a well-hung Christmas tree.'

'Don't we all?' Aisling joked. 'I'll talk to Kian about that later.'

'Ooooh, I bet you will . . . well hung, is he?' Ava teased.

Aisling flushed a brighter shade of red, which did not go unnoticed by her friends.

'You're going scarlet!' Ava said.

'I'm just knackered from this walk, that's all. Slow down, women!' Aisling said.

'You're fooling no one,' Ava said.

Aisling whispered, 'If you must know, he asked me on a date!'

As Ruth watched Ava and Aisling jump up and down with delight, she felt happiness bubble its way up inside her. For the first time in her life she felt like she belonged in a sisterhood. She'd watched other women in groups bounce up and down with delight over some shared good news. And she'd always been on the outside, wondering what it would feel like. Warm and fun, that's what it felt like.

'Where will you go?' Ava asked.

'It's tricky. We are both in the same situation that we don't have any family who can take our kids. And as we are not allowed to go for a drink in the bar downstairs we can't leave the kids on their own in their rooms. So it's gonna have to be a family date.'

'That is unacceptable,' Ruth said.

'You don't think I should go on a date with Kian?' Aisling's face fell.

'That is acceptable, but bringing your children with you on a first date is not. I will take them to the National Museum of Ireland. Then you can have a drink or dinner, just the two of you,' Ruth answered.

'I can't ask you to do that!'

'You did not ask. I offered,' Ruth said.

'Ah, Ruth. What would I do without you? You're a pal.'

A pal. Nobody had ever called her that before. She felt a rush of emotion and could not wait to tell Dr O'Grady later on. He would be so happy for her. If she saw him again.

Where are you, Dr O'Grady?

'Spending all that time with Kian cleaning the Library, well, it made me realise how great he is. I mean he's got a mouth on him, but his heart is good,' Aisling said.

'I shall find more cleaning jobs for you all. Maybe by the time you finish the next, he will propose!' Ruth joked.

Aisling and Ava shrieked with laughter at that.

'Speaking of cleaning, what's Erica been like over cleaning the communal room? Bitch, right?' Ava asked.

Ruth shook her head. 'She gives clear direction. I like that. However, I do not like all her chitchat. She talks a lot.'

Aisling snorted. 'My Billy this and my Billy that. Sure we have never seen sight nor sound of him. Maybe he's worn out with all of her chatter!'

As her two friends talked on, Ruth began to panic that she would do something wrong that might cause them to leave her.

Just like her father. Mark. Cathy. Dr O'Grady. And Dean. Always Dean.

Without realising, Ruth started wringing her hands.

Pop, pop, pop.

'Ruth?' Aisling's voice cut in. 'You OK? You're doing that thing with your knuckles again.' She turned to Ava and said, 'She does that when she's upset.'

'What is it, Ruth?' Ava asked.

Ruth looked at the two women who stood in front of her. Concern on their faces.

Find your tribe and hold them close. Do not let go.

'I want to be understood,' Ruth blurted out.

'About what?' Aisling asked.

Ruth struggled to form the words.

Pop, pop, pop.

'I want you to know who I am,' Ruth continued.

'Well, tell us then,' Ava said. 'We're listening.'

'I always say the wrong thing. I upset people. I am an Aspie!' she blurted out.

'Is it like a disease or something?' Aisling asked.

Ruth shook her head and wished that it was as simple as that. 'It is a syndrome. Asperger's is part of the autistic spectrum. I am not very good with people. I get things wrong a lot. I do not mean to upset anyone, but sometimes the words I say come out wrong. And I do not want that to happen with you both. I like our chats and walks. I do not want to lose you both.'

Pop, pop, pop . . .

'Why didn't I cop that? I should have copped that,' Ava said. 'It's so fucking obvious now that you say it!'

'Is that like yer man, the guy from the movie, what was he called? The rain man guy?' Aisling asked.

'As in, will I take us all to a casino and win us all a fortune, so we can get out of here?' Ruth asked.

'Yes!' they both answered, grinning.

'No,' Ruth replied. 'That is just in the movies. And it is not how it is for most people who are autistic.'

'Pity. I could do with a few bob to buy a new dress for my date!' Aisling said.

'Tell me about it! Are you wicked clever then, Ruth?' Ava said. 'Sorry if that's another generalisation.'

'If you meet one person on the spectrum, then you have met one person on the spectrum,' Ruth said.

They let the words sink in, nodding as they got it.

'You are clever, though,' Aisling said. 'Anyone can see that.'

'Correct, I am cleverer than most. And I do have a superpower. Or at least, that is what DJ calls it,' Ruth told them.

'What?' Aisling squealed. 'You're not going to start flying or anything, are you?'

'You've been watching too much television, you nut,' Ava teased. Then she looked at Ruth and said, 'You're not, are you?'

'Sometimes I flap a bit when I am really stressed. But no, I have never actually flown. But I can guess the weight of things,' Ruth said. 'I realised this when I was a child and correctly guessed how many balloons were squashed into a vintage car at a fair.'

'No way!' Aisling exclaimed. 'Show us, show us!'

Ruth thought for a moment then looked Aisling up and down and said, 'Based on the assumption that you are five foot two . . .'

'That's exactly what I am,' Aisling said. 'See, clever.'

'. . . I normally like to lift things, to confirm the exact weight, but you are too fat for me to do that.'

'Awkward . . .' Ava said.

'You weren't lying when you said you could say anything . . . jeez . . .' Aisling said.

'Should I stop?' Ruth asked.

'No, go on . . . just don't talk about my weight in front of Kian. I prefer to hold onto the thought that he only sees a supermodel when he looks at me.'

'OK. I estimate you are between 244 and 246 pounds,' Ruth said.

'What's that in stones?' Aisling asked.

'It is just over seventeen and a half stone,' Ruth confirmed.

She looked at Ruth with eyes wide in awe. 'I wish you were wrong. But, Lord above, that's bang on the money.'

'You carry the weight well,' Ava said, patting Aisling's arm in sympathy. 'Bloody hell, Ruth. That's some super-power to have.'

'If you ever need me to go with you to a village fair to help you guess how much the oversized turnip weighs, just call me . . .' Ruth joked.

'You are one funny lady,' Aisling said.

Ruth's arms flapped, but this time in delight.

'Well, I for one am delighted you told us a bit more about you,' Ava said.

'Me, too,' Aisling agreed. 'And who cares if you say the wrong thing every now and then? Friends don't mind about that.'

Friends.

'Yeah. Let's stick together, right?' Ava said. 'We'll get through this bullshit situation together. I have to tell you ladies, you've been such a tonic to me lately. I was so low only a few months ago, but now I feel like I've got people who are on my side. Who've got my back. It's getting me through this nightmare, it really is.'

Stick together. 'I never had friends before,' Ruth whispered.

'Never? Not even in school?' Ava asked.

Ruth shook her head. 'People do not like others who are different. My mother told me that. In my experience she was right about that.'

'You are less different than you believe or have been told before,' Aisling said. 'For goodness' sake, we've loads in common.'

'We are all homeless, for a start,' Ava said.

'And you and me both failed epically at school sports. Right?' Aisling asked.

'True,' Ruth confirmed.

'I was bleeding brilliant,' Ava told them.

'Show off.' Aisling shoved her good-naturedly.

'And let's never forget that we're all beautiful,' Ava said. 'Here, come here, you beauts. Let's do a selfie.'

'I have never done one of those before,' Ruth said.

'A selfie virgin in Dublin? Jeepers! Didn't think they existed!' Ava exclaimed. She manoeuvred them into the perfect position and snapped. 'I'll insta that later. #besties. #mytribe.'

'Tag me,' Aisling said. 'And there's another thing we have in common, Ruth. You and I are both single mums.'

'Where is DJ's father?' Ava asked. 'If you don't mind me asking.'

'I wish I knew,' Ruth replied.

'What was he like?' Aisling asked.

'Funny. Kind. Good. Strong. We were soul mates.'

Ava and Aisling looked at Ruth in sympathy. She had it bad.

'I met him on the day that I was supposed to meet my soul mate.' She told them the story of the ice cream and the fortune-telling machine.

'That's so romantic,' Aisling said.

'My world in Wexford was jam-packed with Seans and Jacks. I never met a Dean before until he walked into me with his shiny black shoes,' Ruth said.

'You like that name?' Ava asked.

Ruth nodded. 'My number-one favourite book is *Odd Thomas*, written by Dean Koontz. I have read it two hundred and thirty-one times so far.'

'Wow,' Aisling and Ava said in unison.

'Was he gorgeous then, this Dean?' Aisling asked.

Ruth scrunched her nose up and said, 'He was short with a round face. He had scrawny legs.'

'You're not selling him very well,' Ava remarked.

'I had never been kissed until I met him.'

'My first time was with Don McIntyre in the back of his car,' Aisling said, shuddering. 'I cannot for the life of me work out why I ever agreed to that. Worst five minutes of my life.'

They all had a giggle at that.

'He had long eyelashes,' Ruth said. 'When he was asleep, they rested on his round cheeks like two caterpillars.'

'Aw, that sounds so romantic. Was he a great ride?' Aisling asked.

'The first time was not as good as I hoped it would be. But by the time we got to six times, it was most excellent.'

Aisling spluttered, then said, 'Oh, I do love you, Ruth.'

'So what happened then? Did you split up when he found out about DJ?' Ava asked.

Ruth shook her head. 'The last words he said to me was that he loved me and would see me the next weekend. I am still waiting for that to come.'

Aisling and Ava moved closer to Ruth, who was now standing on the gravel path, lost in her memory. Aisling touched Ruth's arm gently and Ava stood shoulder to shoulder with her. Ruth did not mind. In fact she liked it very much.

40

TOM

The day started off wet so Tom spent the morning in the public library. He had been avoiding Ruth and DJ. After Ruth gave him new clothes, his initial joy and gratitude for her kind gesture gave way to something else. Panic. Fear. And when he tried to find Cathy and Mikey in his dreams, they refused to co-operate. Instead, his mind was full of Ruth and DJ, and he did not like that. He felt angry – irrational, he knew – at them both. His life was perfectly fine before they came crashing into it.

But the more he kept away, the harder it was for him to find peace in his dreams, like he usually did. And he realised that he missed Ruth and DJ. He missed their chats, their company, their care.

So this morning, it was most serendipitous when he found Jackie Lynam, the librarian knee-deep in a stock check. Part of which involved the culling of books to make way for the new books on the block. A plan formed. A way to make it up to Ruth for disappearing.

To Ruth's surprise, when she made her way out of the

hotel to meet Tom for their usual lunch, she found him hovering by the side entrance. With four large boxes of books at his feet.

'What on earth . . . ?' Ruth exclaimed.

'I have books for the Library,' Tom said. He'd pleaded his case with his librarian friend, who had happily agreed to donate books.

'Where have you been? I waited for you for every day for seven days at your bench. DJ went looking for you every afternoon and evening. And you just turn up here with books?'

Tom shrugged.

'I asked you a question. Do not be rude,' Ruth said.

'That's rich coming from someone who spends her life being rude!' Tom exclaimed.

'I have Autism!' Ruth said.

'That's a reason, not an excuse,' Tom batted back. Why was he being so mean to Ruth? She had showed him only kindness. He was guilty. And he was doing what most did when they felt that. Attack. He felt a flush of shame. She deserved better. 'I'm sorry.'

'I was worried I had offended you. Did I?' Ruth asked.

'No! Look, Ruth, I just took off for a bit because I was feeling sorry for myself. Stuff on my mind about Cathy.' He did not know how to explain to Ruth how he felt because it did not make any sense to him.

'Do you want to tell me about it?'

'Not really. Don't be mad at me. Please. I am sorry for worrying you.' Tom realised that now he was back it mattered a great deal what this woman thought about him.

'I accept your apology, Dr O'Grady.' Ruth's face broke

into a smile as she took in the boxes of books on the ground. 'How on earth did you get them all over here from the library?'

'My librarian friend, Jackie, gave me a lift.'

Together they carried the boxes into the Library, in two trips. It took nearly three hundred steps. Unfortunately Erica decided to call into the Library at the very moment they laid the last boxes down. Her surprise at seeing a dog was doubled when she saw Tom holding onto the end of his leash.

'Get out!' she squealed.

Despite Ruth's hasty explanation, Erica was indignant and could not be swayed. 'We have standards at The Silver Sands Lodge!'

'This is Dr Tom O'Grady. He is my friend,' Ruth said.

'I do not care if he's Mickey Mouse, he has no business being in my hotel. Out!'

Tom knew that people were afraid of rough sleepers. They assumed they were addicted to something or had a mental illness. And of course some were dangerous. But most who chose to live on the fringes of society were just people who were broken in some way. People like Erica preferred to walk on by someone they saw huddled on the ground. Ignore the invisible and then maybe they will go away. Someone else's problem. Most days Tom accepted this. Not today.

'You know, earlier today I was in Pearse Street Library. And they had a table near the counter with books all covered in brown paper. Written on each book were just three words to describe the hidden book. No title. No author. Just three descriptive words.

'I thought that was such a great idea, because normally,

based solely on a cover, people decide whether a book is or is not for them. As a result, so many great books are overlooked. Wouldn't life be so much better if people took the time to open a book up, no matter how it looked on the outside?'

Tom was not the type of person who made speeches. But he was doing lots of things that he would not normally do recently.

'Everybody has a story,' Ruth said to Erica, who looked bemused by Tom's outburst. 'You might be surprised to hear Dr O'Grady's.'

Erica mulled over what she had just heard. Doctor, indeed. A likely story. She arched her back and said in her most authoritative voice, 'The Silver Sands Lodge Library is for residents only.'

Tom thought about arguing some more. But he didn't want to get Ruth into trouble. So he left without any further comment. There was a time that he was a respected member of society and now everywhere he went he was sent on his way, like a bad smell. And despite Ruth's comments, he smelled bloody good, if he said so himself. He pulled his collar up, to protect himself from the strong winds blowing from the Atlantic, then made his way into the city, to Aungier Street. It used to take him a little under an hour to do this walk, but old age had slowed him down. It was closer to two hours now. Just before he reached Summerhill Parade, he noticed a bundle of cardboard boxes next to Sackville Gardens. He walked a little closer to check it out and saw a young man huddled under a box, which he had made his makeshift home for the night. He opened his eyes in alarm when he saw Tom peering down at him.

'What you want?' His words were slurred. He'd been drinking.

'Not a thing,' Tom replied, taking a step back. 'It's going to be a cold one tonight. You might be better off heading into one of the shelters.'

''S fine here . . .' The man rolled over and turned his back on Tom.

Tom placed his rucksack on the ground and reached in to pull out his sleeping bag. Without a word, he gently placed it over the man's slumped body, then picked up his rucksack and continued walking.

'Hey, mister!'

Tom turned round to look back at the man who was now on his feet.

'Thanks.'

Tom nodded and continued on his way to the shelter. It was crowded because the temperatures had dropped. Bones and Lash were there. Lash was having a go at some poor schmuck who accused him of stealing his shoes. Which he most likely did, because he was light-fingered. They all knew that.

Tom had a restless night and not once could he find his way to Cathy and Mikey in his dreams. Part of the problem was the noise in the hostel. But that wasn't the only issue. His mind was full of Ruth and DJ: worrying about them and their situation one minute, then grinning like an idiot as he remembered their earlier conversations and what it felt like to have real friends. He wanted the day to begin again so that he could see them.

And then irritation would come a-knocking. He preferred being on his own, reliant on nobody. It was better that way. Maybe he should move on from the park. Break the ties that were beginning to form with them both. Before someone got hurt. *Him.*

But the following morning he found himself walking towards his bench with purpose. He wanted to see if the kid had made up with his mam yet. He was a loose cannon with all the worries of the world on his little shoulders. Tom wanted to have another chat with him, make him see that his life wasn't so bad.

But something caught his eye that made Tom stop in his tracks and forget all about DJ and Ruth for a moment.

What the hell is that?

Tom made his way towards a box that sat on top of his bench.

Fyffe bananas?

He scanned the park, but it was empty, bar him and Bette Davis. The hairs on the back of his neck stood to attention when he heard a whimper. It was coming from the box.

'Bloody hell, Bette,' Tom said. 'Stay here, girl.' The box made another whimper. *That's a baby's cry.* His heart hammering, Tom broke into a run, throwing his rucksack to the ground. He fumbled with the lid, all the time praying the child inside was OK.

Oh sweet Jesus. The poor little mite. Nestled, naked, in a blanket was a newborn. Only a few hours old by Tom's reckoning. Pink in colour: that was good. Tom pulled the baby in close to his heart and held it there, whispering over and over, 'It's OK, it's OK, it's OK . . .'

But it was anything but OK. Someone had left a baby on a park bench. In November, for goodness' sake. The child could have perished in the cold! Who would do such a thing?

Sheila. Of course! Oh, you silly girl, what have you done?

He stood up and scanned the park once again. Then called out her name into the wind. 'Sheila! Sheila, are you there? Let me help you, Sheila, please.'

She must be terrified, maybe she needed medical attention. *Think, Tom.*

He felt eyes on him, or at least fancied he did. He did a three-sixty turn and scanned the area once again. Was she out there watching him? He didn't believe that she would leave the baby and not make sure that Tom was here to take care of it. He thought he saw a shadow move from under the oak trees on the other side of the park. He held the baby close and broke into a run, again calling, 'Sheila' over and over.

But there was no one there. If the girl had been there, she was now gone.

He walked back to the bench, Bette Davis trailing after him, and sat down, clutching the baby. 'Now what am I going to do with you, little one?'

He walked out of the park to the phone box down the street and called the emergency services. He had no choice. This little baby was on its own now and needed medical attention, a bottle, a cot in the warmth. He returned to his bench to wait for the paramedics and the gardaí.

Oh, Cathy, what a bloody mess.

He tried to work out what his wife would do if she were here. She'd look for Sheila and make sure she was OK. That's what. Once the baby was safe, he'd find her. The infant began to whimper again. So he rocked her back and forth in his arms, singing a lullaby that he once sang every day to his own little boy.

Somewhere over the rainbow way up high . . .
And the dreams that you dare to dream really
do come true.

The words came back to him as if it were yesterday that
he last sang them. And as he sang the last line with tears
in his eyes, he heard sirens make their presence known.
The noise of them brought him to a place that he could
not hide from. That was the problem with memories, they
were unpredictable. No matter how hard you tried to push
them away, hide them in a corner of your mind, they came
back to bite. He looked down at the little one in his arms
and only saw Mikey. And his heart splintered once more.

How many times can a heart break? Agony, fresh and
raw, sliced through him.

He didn't hear the paramedics until they were upon
him, in a flash of luminous yellow and green.

'Sir, you found a baby?' One of the two paramedics
spoke. He reached over to take the baby, but Tom held
on. He couldn't let go. Not to this baby.

Tom looked at him, tears steaming down his face.

'I'm Declan Cunningham. And that boyo over there is
Steve Holloway. We're paramedics. You called about this
baby you found, sir.' Declan took a seat beside Tom on
the bench.

'I found her in this box,' Tom said, remembering himself.
'A quare kind of banana . . .' He nodded to the Fyffe's
banana logo that was stamped on the brown lid. Declan
and Steve laughed, for a moment.

'Any idea where the mother is?' Steve asked, looking
around the park.

'No,' Tom replied. He looked down at the child in his arms and made a promise. *I'll find your mama, I promise.*

'Can I take a look at the baby?' Declan asked, and Tom handed her over. He looked down at his empty arms. *All gone.*

'The guards will be here shortly to take a statement. All right, bud?' Steve said.

Tom expected as much. 'Where will you bring the baby?'

'The Rotunda,' Steve answered.

'Well, this little one seems remarkably healthy despite her entrance into the world,' Declan declared, wrapping a silver-foil blanket around her to keep her warm. 'Even so, we need to get her to hospital.'

Before they left, Steve laid a hand on Tom's arm. 'The baby was lucky it was you who found her. You did good, buddy.'

The guards arrived moments later and Tom made his statement. There wasn't much to tell. Once they moved on, Tom took several steadying breaths. He didn't have time to sit here feeling sorry for himself. *Bones.* Find Bones and then he would find Sheila.

It didn't take long to locate Bones. He was sleeping off the previous night's cider in his usual spot, down by the waterfront, alongside Lash. Tom found them under a cover of brown cardboard boxes. A bark from Bette stirred them.

'I need you to help me find Sheila. She's had the baby. And I'm worried about her,' Tom said.

Bones sat up without a word. He kicked Lash and told him to take care of his things, then made his way back to the town. Tom had to practically run to keep up with him. They went to the squat and Tom asked Bones to go in and make sure Bobby was not around. He did not want to come face to face with that fella.

'She's in there. Asleep, by the looks of it,' Bones said. Then he grabbed Tom's arm. 'Don't be here when Bobby comes back. He's gunning for you. Mouthing off about you sticking your nose in. I don't trust him, Doc. He's off his head most of the time and is a loose wire. Watch yourself.'

Tom nodded, then followed Bones along the side of the house. Sheila was in the front upstairs bedroom cradling a pink babygro in her arms. Asleep, as Bones said. Then he saw it and the blood drained from his body, making his knees buckle. There was a needle sticking out of her left arm.

'Ah, Sheila, no.' Tom kneeled down beside the girl and felt for a pulse.

'She's alive. Barely.' He pulled out his phone and dialled 999 for the second time that day and prayed for a second miracle. *Keep this child alive, please.* Because that's what she was. A child herself.

'Will she be OK, Doc?' Bones asked as he paced the room. Sheila reminded him of his own daughter, one who didn't want to know him any more, but was never far from his mind. 'She never took drugs before, Doc. Never. I swear, she was clean!'

Tom knew exactly what had happened. He'd seen it hundreds of times on the street. Sheila had given in to the hopelessness of her situation. And took the only way out she could think of.

310

41

TOM

When the ambulance took Sheila away, Tom's body began to tremble. The day had almost done him in and he felt every bit of his sixty-odd years. And no matter how hard he tried, Sheila's overdose and the little baby sent Tom into the darkest part of his mind. Memories, dreams of a time in his life that he fought to avoid, overcame him. This was a home he did not want to revisit, but his mind found its way there all the same . . .

Tom dropped his toothbrush to the floor when he heard Cathy's voice scream out. He wiped the foam from his mouth as he ran towards her voice, terror, horror, heartbreak laced in every scream.

It only took seconds for him to reach Mikey's room, but it felt like an eternity. As he pushed open the white door, as it swung open wide, Tom had the urge to slam it shut once more. To run away from whatever horror lay on the other side causing his wife to howl like she did.

Nothing prepared him for the truth on the other side.

Cathy lying on the ground holding Mikey in her arms, kissing his face over and over, begging him to wake up. 'He isn't moving. He was on his tummy face down when I came in, Tom. Why isn't he moving? I need to warm him up; he's so cold.'

Tom's mind screamed No! over and over. Yet somehow he managed to calmly say to Cathy, 'Give Mikey to me, love. Let me do my job and see what's wrong with him.'

In the end, he had to peel her hands away from him. She couldn't let go. Tom laid his son down gently on the floor. His tiny body was cold and lifeless.

No!

He refused to believe that he could not help. He was a doctor. This was his job, to save people. To save children. To save his son.

'Do something. Please, oh, please, do something . . .' Cathy was on her knees, as if in prayer, sobbing hysterically.

'Call 999,' Tom instructed. Then he began CPR, blowing gently into Mikey's mouth.

Time stood still and they waited for a miracle.

God damn it, Mikey, breathe. Don't you dare leave us.

Cathy watched him with hope and fear stamped onto every nuance of her face.

Mikey did not move. No answer to their prayers. No miracle.

The paramedics arrived within fifteen minutes. They found Tom still trying to resuscitate his son. Gently they asked him to move aside. And to Tom's shame he felt relief that he could now hand over the responsibility to someone else. Let the paramedics perform a miracle that he could not muster. They continued CPR and they injected Mikey with adrenalin.

Tom fell back and leaned against the white cot that only a few short months ago he had put together. His mind refused to accept the reality of the nightmare that was in front of him.

Over and over he screamed inside, No! No! No!

The silence in the room thundered around them. Tom closed his eyes, unable to watch as the paramedics began to shock his baby's heart.

Cry, Mikey, cry for your mama and dada. Cry . . .

But all around them was that thundering, fucking sound of silence.

'We need to bring Mikey into hospital now,' the paramedic said kindly. She had tears in her eyes and this made Tom cross. No tears, no crying for their son allowed. He was going to live. He had to live.

They picked him up and wrapped him in a blanket, walking out of the house to the waiting ambulance. Tom and Cathy ran behind them, clutching onto each other. Horror unlike anything they could ever have imagined ripping them into shreds.

'They'll put him on a drip or something. A life-support machine to help him breathe. Won't they?' Cathy shrieked at Tom.

Tom lied and said yes. Of course they would. But he knew all was lost. Because even if by some miracle they managed to bring Mikey back, all that time without oxygen to his brain would leave him severely brain damaged.

He felt sorrow begin to seep into him, working its way through his body, poisoning everything. Causing a lasting fracture in his mind that would one day snap in two.

42

RUTH

Now

Despite the fact that Kian could now read his newspaper in the new hotel Library he preferred to hide out behind the palm tree in the lobby. Knowing he was getting one over on Erica, on the system, on life, made him happy. And he had to get his kicks wherever he could.

And this was a good thing, because today he overheard Erica placing an advert for a temporary part-time cleaner at the hotel.

He was waiting for Ruth in the kitchen when she got back from her early morning run to fill her in.

'My track record with employment is abysmal,' Ruth said.

'I've been a bit hit and miss myself, won't lie,' Kian replied.

'Over the past five years, since DJ started school, I have worked in and been fired from over a dozen jobs. Inadvertently, I always manage to do something that causes my employers to lose patience with me.'

Ruth remembered her most recent jobs. The owner of the boutique in Swords Village at first loved her quirky style of dress, saying she was a perfect addition to their team. She changed her mind when Ruth's honesty back-fired. A customer asked her if her bum looked big in the tube dress she had squeezed herself into. 'Yes' was the wrong answer, but Ruth did not know that. When the woman left without spending a cent in the store, her manager took Ruth to task. Apparently she should have lied and let the woman leave with a dress that did her no favours.

Neither was stacking shelves in her local supermarket a success. It was the noise that bothered her the most: Tannoys booming announcements without warning. On the third occasion her manager found Ruth locked in a bathroom cubicle wearing her headphones to block out the noise, he sacked her.

'Maybe you have been in the wrong jobs before,' Kian said. 'You've been cleaning the Library every day for free. This kitchen, too, I'd wager. That mark has disappeared from the wall, the cooker has never been as clean and these cupboards have *you* all over them.' He pulled open a cupboard to reveal neatly stacked plates and cups. 'If you apply for that job, at least you'd be getting a few bob!'

With Christmas rushing towards her at breakneck speed and DJ growing an inch by the week, Ruth needed to bring in some cash. Luck was on her side because at the very moment she walked into the lobby to talk to Erica, the chef stormed out, refusing to cook another meal until someone came in and sorted out the mess in the dining room.

'It's highly irregular. I'm not sure I'm allowed to hire you!' Erica said.

'Why ever not?' Ruth was puzzled. 'It is not on the . . .'

Erica held her hand up to stop her finishing the sentence. 'So help me, Ruth, if you mention the rules one more time . . .'

'You wrote them,' Ruth pointed out.

Erica sighed and said, 'You may be on our social housing list, but you are still a resident.'

'But I am not one of your "normal" residents. Plus, at the speed the list moves I will be here for at least a couple more months. You saw what I did with the Library. I am a good worker. I like to clean. I like to organise things,' Ruth pointed out.

Erica glanced towards the bar and the restaurant that should both be serving lunch in less than two hours, but were still in a mess from breakfast. She needed to get her chef back. Pronto.

'If you can bring order to that dining room before lunch, we can talk.'

'I'll start in five minutes.' Ruth went back to her room to grab her headphones. She was going to need Westlife to get through this. DJ was with Cormac and Anna in the park. They'd left after breakfast, giggling about some story Cormac was regaling them with. Like father, like son.

Ruth worked fast, diligently moving from one section to the other, until order was restored with half an hour to spare. When Erica came in to check her progress Ruth could tell she was impressed. The chef returned to his kitchen, too, singing her praises.

'Minimum wage. 9 a.m. to 12 p.m., six days a week, take it or leave it,' Erica said.

'10 a.m. to 1 p.m., five days a week. Double time if you need me at weekends. Take that or leave that,' Ruth said. She had the school run to think about.

Erica looked at her with respect. White as a ghost and could barely look you in the eye, you'd think she was a pushover. But there was steel in this one. 'Done. You start Monday.'

Ruth threw her head back in delight. She called into the kitchen to have a celebratory ice-cold glass of milk.

'Did you get the job?' Kian asked.

'I most certainly did. Thank you for the tip. Incidentally, do you ever leave this kitchen?'

'You are welcome. Don't let Erica lord it over you too much. And ha ha, yes I do,' he said.

'I have worked for much worse,' Ruth replied. She opened the fridge and began to rearrange the contents until everything was in the correct order. Once they were back where they should be, she pulled out the milk.

A beep signalled the end of the dishwasher cycle so Ruth decided to empty it.

'A free sauna, eh?' Kian said, making her laugh, when the steam hit Ruth in the face.

She unloaded the dishwasher, then placed the delph and crockery in piles, colour co-ordinating them as she went.

'What happens if you mix the colours up?' Kian asked, mesmerised by her routine.

Despite a quickening of her heart rate Ruth shrugged. 'Nothing happens. It is just I like it this way. It pleases me to have things where they need to be.'

Kian said, 'Cool. I get it. It's all about control for you, isn't it?'

Ruth looked at him in surprise.

'There are things that drive me mad too if they are not the way I like them,' Kian said.

'Like what?' Ruth was curious. She didn't know this about him. She supposed she didn't really know him at all.

'I like doors closed. The problem is I spend a lot of time getting up and down like a blue-arsed fly, because Cormac thinks he lives in a barn with a bleeding swinging door! Door closing is my thing. Cleaning is yours. Or rather, creating order.'

Ruth closed the door of the dishwasher, winking at Kian as she did, then picked up her milk. She sat opposite him and took a sip. 'Have you ever felt like you were free-falling?'

Kian nodded. 'Fuck, yeah.'

'That is how I feel at some point, most days. But when I clean a surface, or colour co-ordinate my plates, then I eliminate some of the chaos in my life. It helps.'

'I get that. I do. Listen, whatever gets you through the day, I say. What's the gig with the food, though? I can't put my finger on it. You have some weird stuff going on there, too. Am I right?'

Ruth smiled at him. 'You are an observant man.' He knew and understood her better than her family ever had. 'I try to only eat and drink white things. These calm me. Other colours bother me. Bright ones, like reds or oranges, are particularly irksome and hurt my eyes.'

'Fuck them, whoever they are!' Kian said. 'I take people

as I find them. And you, Ms Ruth Wilde, are all kinds of all right.' He stood up, pulling his jeans back up to waist level. 'Laterz.'

Ruth made a couple of rounds of sandwiches and headed to the park. She found DJ sitting on Tom's park bench on his own. 'Where are Cormac and Anna?'

'Gone back to the hotel,' DJ said.

'Any sign of Dr O'Grady?'

DJ scowled and said, 'I saw him for a minute, but he said he didn't have time to stop and talk. He looked in a bad mood.'

'I made him lunch.' Ruth felt a jolt of disappointment. She wanted to tell him about her new job. She knew he would be happy for her.

DJ's stomach growled, so Ruth passed him the lunch box. 'Chicken sandwiches.'

DJ pushed the box back to her.

'You are not hungry?' Ruth asked.

'I am sick of chicken sandwiches. I am sick of potatoes. I am sick of pasta!' he shouted.

Ruth put the lunch box back in her bag, her own appetite lost now, too.

'I got a job,' Ruth said. 'The money is not much, but it will help coming up to Christmas. And I can get you a new pair of joggers. Some new trainers. We could go shopping now if you like.'

'What job?' DJ asked.

'At the hotel. I'm their new cleaner.'

He jumped up and kicked a stone out onto the path, his face scrunched up in anger.

'What is wrong now?' Ruth was at a loss.

'Why do you have to be the cleaner?' DJ asked.

'They need a cleaner. I need a job. Why not me?' Ruth replied.

'This will give everyone something else to laugh about,' DJ said.

'Who is everyone?' Ruth asked, puzzled.

'Everyone at the hotel.'

'They are laughing at me?' Ruth asked. Doubts started to creep in. Her hands began to twist and turn as they often did when she was upset or worried. And the only way to stop that was to . . .

Pop, pop, pop.

'Everyone always laughs at you,' DJ said. He looked up and saw the shock and hurt flood his mother's face. But he didn't care.

Ruth picked up her things and turned to go back to the hotel. She didn't want him to see her cry. 'Are you coming with me?'

DJ stuffed his hands into the pockets of his trousers and followed her, because he had nowhere else to be.

Mother and son walked in silence, both in pain and both unable to say what they really wanted. Or the unspoken words they should say.

43

TOM

Tom saw the disappointment on DJ's face when he told him he was too busy to stop and talk. He felt guilt weigh him down. Just like it had after Mikey died. Guilt that he could not save his son. Guilt that he could not reach his wife and bring her back from the horror she now lived in. He felt like he would drown under the weight of the guilt he felt. Now that he had opened a door in his mind to the memory of Mikey's death, he could not stop memories pounding at him continuously. He tried to keep moving, to keep busy, to stem the flow, but they came, no matter what.

Tom and Cathy sat opposite each other at the kitchen table. A new notebook and pen, the kind with the spiral top, sitting in front of them.

Beside the notebook sat a small white box.

A whole life was contained in that box. Mikey's birth cert. His first curl, snipped carefully by Tom, because Cathy was too afraid to cut him, her hands shook so much. *The small identity bracelet from his birth: 'Baby O'Grady. Parents: Cathy and Thomas O'Grady.'*

His first babygro. Simple plain white. Pure and innocent like their boy.

One more item was now added to the box. A death certificate: 'Cause: Sudden Infant Death Syndrome. SIDS.'

The silent killer with no explanation. Children should outlive their parents by decades. What is the actual point if not?

The point was a life too short, cruelly snatched away. The remains of that life lay in one small white box.

If Mikey had been sick they would have been prepared for the loss. But instead they had no answers. And just the one question.

Why?

They had not been the only ones asking questions. When Tom and Cathy returned home from hospital, parents without a child, their home had become a crime scene. Cathy's mum and dad awaited them, her mother stammering, 'They've . . . sealed off Mikey's nursery . . . I'm so sorry, I couldn't stop them . . .'

And even though Tom knew the authorities were following procedure, standard practice following the sudden death of a child, he was angry. Crime-scene yellow tape barred them from their own child's nursery and mocked them, accusing them of something truly terrible.

There was no foul play. The room was not too cold, in fact they were having a mild winter. Mikey wasn't co-sleeping with them, so there was no issue of either parent smothering him by mistake. No air pollution. No cushion or pillow in the cot that blocked his airways. No answers to that same fucking question. Why?

Their baby boy's heart had just stopped beating.

'There was no way you could have known.' That's what the coroner said.

But Tom should have. He was a doctor and he had somehow missed something. He should have saved his son's life. He saw the way that Cathy looked at him. She knew it, too.

They sat on opposite sides of their kitchen table, staring at a blank notebook page. Trying to find the words to go on Mikey's headstone. Words that conveyed to the world how much his life was worth.

Tom reached over to touch Cathy. His need to feel the warmth of her hand in his was overwhelming.

I need you. Please Cathy. Please . . .

His silent plea went unanswered. She pulled her hands back and placed them under the table. Cathy hadn't spoken a single word since their baby died. And he wasn't sure she ever would.

44

RUTH

Now

Ruth was dusting the front desk, trying to block out Erica's rant, which was now in its tenth minute.

Erica held up her newspaper and pointed to a headline, 'One in four in social housing reject the houses offered to them. Disgraceful.'

Ruth lifted the guest register and wiped the counter under it.

Melissa from room 131 walked into reception. 'We need more toilet roll, please.'

Erica sighed loudly, 'You go through toilet roll like nobody else in this hotel.'

Melissa replied, 'There's five of us in our room. More arses to wipe.'

'Well, there is no need to be so crude,' Erica said.

'It must be difficult, so many in one room,' Ruth said.

'There isn't a spare inch that doesn't have a pile of clothes on it. But it's better than my car . . .' Melissa replied.

'I got some plastic storage boxes from the St Vincent de Paul charity shop down the road. I keep our clothes in them, and stack them in the bath. Then take them out in the morning when we shower,' Ruth said.

'Nice one,' Melissa answered. Her two youngest boys came running into the lobby, crashing into Ruth.

'Luke, James, I told you both to stay in the room!' Melissa admonished.

'Sorry, Mam,' they both chorused.

'We wanted to show you our pictures,' Luke said, holding up a crayoned picture of a house with a big garden. A large yellow sun hung in the bright-blue sky.

'Look at my robot!' James said.

'Brilliant,' Melissa praised them both. 'Go on up to the room and put them in my special folder.'

'I want to stick them on the wall,' James said. 'That's what my friend does in his house.'

'No art work on the walls,' Erica said. 'Have you seen this article in the paper? I can't get a word from that one.' She pointed at Ruth, who was now dusting the lobby coffee table and chairs.

Melissa said, 'People have their reasons for saying no to property.'

Erica sniffed. 'I always say beggars can't be choosers. Just this morning I said that to my Billy. It says here that someone refused a house because they didn't like the colour of the carpet.' Erica shook her head in disbelief. 'And another one because they wanted somewhere closer to their mother. Well, boo hoo for them. I'd love to live near my daughter. But she's in America.'

'Where in America is your daughter?' Ruth asked,

hoping to steer Erica away from the subject of housing.

'She's in Maryland. Married to a state trooper. Lovely man. And I've got three grandchildren that are getting so big. Thank God for FaceTime . . . I told my Billy only last night that we'd miss out on so much if it wasn't for technology.'

Melissa coughed. 'You can't believe everything the papers say. There are plenty of valid reasons why people turn down housing, you know.'

Ruth and Erica turned towards her in surprise.

Then tears began to fall down her face in large splashes, hitting the counter top. 'I'm sorry,' she said in between sobs. 'I don't know where that came from.' She wiped the tears with the back of her hand.

Erica reached into a drawer in front of her and handed her a pack of tissues. 'Here you go.'

Ruth and Erica watched Melissa blow her nose noisily. 'I haven't had a good cry in nearly a year, because there's just nowhere to have one in private without the kids seeing.'

'I do enjoy a good cry, too,' Erica said. 'Last night I watched that show, *Say Yes to the Dress*. Cried my eyes out, don't mind admitting. This woman was there with her daughter. She had cancer. The mother, not the daughter. The saddest thing I've ever seen. I lost sleep thinking about her. Now Billy isn't a fan of the show, but then again he's a man and they don't get the whole wedding thing like we do. Am I right?'

Ruth felt dizzy listening to Erica sometimes. She turned her attention back to Melissa, who was now sniffing back the tears.

'Once the kids are asleep Ciara and I just read. The TV would keep the boys up,' Melissa said.

'I like to read, so that is not a problem for me,' Ruth said. 'But I understand about the lack of privacy. DJ is nearly ten and a half and it is beginning to feel unnatural. He needs his own room somewhere he can be without me. And I do, too.'

'I've been offered a house,' Melissa said. 'Last night. I got a call.'

'And that is making you sad?' Ruth was puzzled. 'It is good news.'

'It's nowhere near my requested locations. It's in Donabate,' Melissa said. 'That's practically in the countryside.'

Ruth felt envy snake its way around her. 'I would not care one iota where the location was, once they offered us a home.'

'Hear hear,' Erica said. 'What is the house like?'

'I haven't seen it yet. I don't think there is any point. It's too far out.'

Erica pointed to her newspaper and sniffed, 'One in four.'

'I spend all day looking at my mobile phone, willing it to ring. I would give anything to have an offer like yours,' Ruth said.

Erica heaved herself up from her chair and pointed a large stubby finger at Melissa, 'Well, missy, you better watch out that you don't lose your place on the housing list. And serve you right if you do.'

Melissa's face hardened. 'I am allowed to refuse an offer when it's on reasonable grounds.'

'Which you don't have,' Erica said. 'Have you heard of public transport? This one and her boy take two buses every day to get to his school! And I've not heard her complain once. Not once.'

Melissa turned on her heel and walked out of reception.

'I hope it stays sunny for her, is all I'm saying,' Erica sniffed. Then seeing Ruth's face, which had crumpled with disappointment and annoyance, she said, 'Ah, now. Don't be fretting. You'll have your turn.'

Odd whispered in her ear to hold onto hope. Ruth continued cleaning the lobby and tried to think of only good things. Every day since they lost their home she held on fast to something good that happened, so that she did not lose herself in a cloud of emotion.

Yesterday DJ brought home a note from school complimenting him on his homework that week. The Library and the homework club made a difference. She was proud of that.

She put her shoulders back and tried to smile as she wiped another smudge from the coffee table. *It is getting more difficult to hold onto hope, Odd. But I shall keep trying.*

45

TOM

Sheila died in the end. Another wasted life. Tom needed to get away from the park and his bench. From DJ's questioning every five minutes when he came across him. From Ruth always reminding him of the man he once was. He moved to the waterfront and sat watching the Irish Sea. It was bitterly cold and the wind bit his face, seeping into his bones. He didn't care. About that, or anything. He closed his eyes and returned to the darkness . . .

Life became one of two parts. Before and afterwards.

After the funeral, when family and friends had finally gone home, leaving their fridge and freezer overflowing with food and the house filled with flowers, it was just the two of them again. Tom was grateful but relieved when the last car, with his sister in it, drove away from their driveway. Cathy had not spoken a single word since they came home from hospital.

Shock, the doctor said. Give her time. Tom did not

leave her side. And all the time the crushing devastation of their loss crippled him.

His boy. Taken from him.

'Speak to me,' Tom begged.

If she heard him, she did not show it.

Days became weeks and still she remained silent. Tom cooked her breakfast, lunch and dinner. He made her coffee and he blitzed her favourite strawberry and banana smoothie. She took it all without a word. If he touched her, she got up and walked away.

Tom knew that his wife was locked in a world of pain and he had to find a way to bring her back. His own heartache he wore like a badge and he never wanted to lose it. Every waking second was for his boy. But he could not continue if he lost Cathy, too. Seeing her in turmoil gave him focus, reason to continue.

The breakthrough happened almost two months to the day after they lost Mikey. Tom awoke when the early morning sun found its way through the curtains and filled their bedroom with golden shadows. He turned to his left and saw the gulf that was now between him and his wife. The years of her pushing her bum into his tummy, his arm across her body, were gone. He missed those days. He was bereft, unanchored.

He turned his body on its side and moved close to her, pulling her into him. He felt her body stiffen in protest, but he didn't stop his insistent pulling of her, into his embrace. He never spoke a word, just silently put his arm around her. He felt the warmth of her begin to seep into him. She struggled for a moment, perhaps two, then relaxed into his embrace. He let his shoulders relax and he sank his head back onto the pillow. And they stayed like that until the alarm rang, alerting him that a new day had begun.

When he got up, she didn't speak, but she looked at him and he saw something give in her eyes.

For ten days he held her, despite her efforts to keep him away. If she remembered how they used to be, she might come back to him.

And finally she did. As he climbed into bed with her one night, flicking the lamp off as he did, she broke the silence.

'You wake up one morning and lose everything. Just like that. It's all gone.'

He wanted to scream at her that she'd not lost everything.

You have me.

But he didn't want to frighten her, make her close up again. So he simply said, 'Yes.'

'I shouldn't be here,' she whispered. 'I should be with him, wherever he is.'

'How can you say that? The only reason I keep going, putting one foot in front of the other, is for you.'

She was silent again.

'Do you blame me for not saving him?' Tom whispered.

Silence. Hesitation. Then denial. 'No.'

'I blame me,' Tom confessed.

Cathy sat up in the bed and reached out for his hand. 'In the past, when bad things happened in our lives, there was always light at the end of the tunnel. But now, there's only darkness. I'm not sure I can find my way back to the light.'

Tom had never heard anything as profoundly sad in his life.

'I don't know what to do. I don't know how to live, how to be me,' Cathy said.

'Neither do I, love. But we have to keep going, until we find a way to get through the day. We have to try to find a way to make the pain stop.'

'And until then?'

'We do the best we can to make it to the end of the day. We become each other's light.'

Tom looked around their house. Four bedrooms that would never be used. Two reception rooms, that they thought were so important to have, so that Mikey would have his own space when he got older, to hang out with his friends. The large dining room, to cater for all of Mikey's pals for birthday parties. All the plans they had for this house and now all of them seemed redundant.

The house taunted him.

'I miss the flat,' Tom said.

'Then let's go back there,' Cathy said.

Tom grinned. 'I could have an extra half-hour in bed if we moved back. Do you think . . . ?' He stopped, unable to finish the question.

'You want to know if we'll regret leaving the house that we lived in with Mikey?'

She always knew what he was thinking. 'I loved this house. But now, all I can see is a team of paramedics, with bright-yellow jackets. The neighbours at their gates, watching, wondering what the ambulance was for and the shock on their faces when they saw us. The nursery a crime scene. I see all of that.'

Those same images burned Tom. If he didn't find a way to put the fire out soon, he didn't think he could make it.

'I say we move. And if the flat doesn't work for us, we move again. We keep moving until we don't have to any more.'

Cathy came back to him. Until the next time the darkness swallowed her whole once more.

46

TOM

Now

They came at Tom fast. He opened his eyes when he heard the thud of their feet as they ran towards him down the boardwalk. Four of them. Dressed in black, hoods low over their faces. Two held large sticks, like clubs. Not a social visit, so. Tom sat up and held his two hands up in defence. Bette Davis bared her teeth and charged towards the first two. Before he could arrange the thought from his head into a reasoned sentence, to ask them to desist, the first blow hit his back. He fell forward, face into the cold concrete path as he saw Bette Davis fly through the air.

Heavy, laboured breaths filled the air. His? Or theirs? Grunts and shouts, from each, as they kicked and hit his body in continuous barrage. He felt his nose crunch and splinter, as a foot connected with his face.

'That's enough,' a voice said, breathless with exertion. Tom recognised that voice.

He kneeled down low, so that his face was inches from Tom's now bloodied mess. Recognition passed between the two. *Bobby.* Sheila's boyfriend. He spat on Tom, then hissed, 'Interfering old bastard.' He stood up, taking Tom's rucksack with him.

No! Not that. My things . . . No!

But Tom could not speak. All he could do was watch through half-closed lids as they rummaged their way through his rucksack.

They found what they were searching for. His doctor's bag.

'He's as good as dead,' a faceless hoody said, glee lacing each word. He bounced up and down, nervous energy abounding through him.

Where are you, Bette? Come to me. Good girl.

Bright lights filled the street. Headlights from an oncoming car. He saw Bette limping towards him, blood dripping from her face.

'Let's get out of here!' Bobby said.

They ran but not before giving one last kick to his abdomen. Tom felt another rib crack and closed his eyes.

The car slowed down and he heard voices.

'Is that man OK?' a young woman asked.

'He's probably pissed,' a man answered.

'Is he bleeding, though?' Her voice again, more urgent this time.

'Nah. He's just a bum.' The engine revved and they were gone.

Tom lay on the street, bloodied and bruised. He wanted to go home so badly.

But only darkness came.

47

TOM

Bette Davis was scared. Her master, her best friend, had not moved for the longest time. She licked him, nudged him, but he would not wake up. So she did the only thing she could. She rested her head on his legs and did her best to keep him warm.

Grief never leaves you. Tom and Cathy did not want it to. They clung to it, wrapping its sharp shards around their skin.

The sound of an ambulance in the distance made Cathy shake. 'All these years later and still . . .'

Tom nodded in understanding. It was the same for him. 'Part of our life will always be unfinished.'

Cathy looked at her husband and tried not to cry.

'When Mikey died, so much of the future we thought we were going to have died too,' Tom said.

'Not in my dreams,' Cathy whispered. 'Our future is much nicer there.'

'If only I could close my eyes and dream a different version of this life,' Tom said.

'*You can dream anything you want. Just close your eyes. Go on.*'

She placed her hands gently on his eyes and he closed them. He listened to Cathy's soft voice weave a story for him.

'*Can you see him? Blond curls, turning ash now that he's a little older. He loves the park. Look, he's walking between the two of us now, his little hands in ours . . .*'

'*We swing him between us!*' Tom said.

'*Yes! And Mikey is screaming, "Higher, Daddy, higher," and I say, "No, be careful," and you shush me, telling me I worry too much.*' *Cathy reached over and caressed Tom's face.*

'*Keep going . . .*' Tom begged.

'*He loves fruit, especially mangoes, but we can't get him to eat his vegetables. We've tried everything.*'

'*I never ate vegetables either. And look at me . . .*' Tom cut in.

'*Remember his first day of school – he was so brave! Even though he was scared, he wanted to be a big boy so badly, he just walked into his classroom . . .*' Cathy said.

'*. . . Like a boss! You had to wear sunglasses, because of course you were crying . . .*'

'*. . . and you tried so hard to pretend that it wasn't bothering you, but you left very quickly so no one could see your tears,*' Cathy said.

'*Who, me? Tough guy?*' Tom replied, with tears flowing down his cheeks. '*He's a clever one, isn't he?*'

'*Yes! He's articulate, his vocabulary is outstanding. He excels at maths and I don't understand that because neither of us is any good at it!*' Cathy said with pride.

'What does he want to be when he grows up?' Tom asked in a whisper.

Cathy leaned in close and whispered back, 'Why, he wants to be just like his daddy. A doctor.'

And Tom understood where his wife went to when the darkness took over and she became silent.

He learned that no matter how hard he tried to break through he could not reach her. Because she liked it in the darkness. Years went by. He learned to live with her silences, until they did not hurt him any more.

He worried about her state of mind, of course. He spoke to Annemarie, Cathy's parents, Breda. They all told him that if this was Cathy's way to deal with the loss of Mikey, so be it.

But he fretted. What if one day she decided to stay in her make-believe world and not come back to him?

Today was a good day, though. He was in his favourite chair in what had become their reading room. And opposite him was Cathy. Her legs were curled up under her bum and she was leaning onto a pile of cushions. Always with the cushions.

She looked up, aware of his eyes on her. A small pair of reading glasses perched on the bridge of her nose and he pushed his own a little further down his nose so she wasn't blurry. They had been through the best and the worst times of their life, together. And the invisible bond that was between them still felt like coming home to him. Their shared history – tears, joy, love, loss – was irreplaceable.

'What, my love?' Cathy asked.

'If someone saw us, sitting in silence here, reading, what do you think they'd say?' Tom asked.

'That we're a couple of almost blind, boring golden oldies?' They both laughed.

Their life after Mikey's arrival changed in ways he could never express. Their hearts got bigger. And then when he left, the joy went for a long time. But they found it again in the small moments in their lives. Like this. The raw nerves left open and bleeding from their grief had begun to heal.

Maybe this time he could make Cathy stay.

Tom leaned in and gripped her hands tight between his own.

She carried them to her soft lips and gently kissed them. 'You know what?' Cathy said. 'I'd like a drink.'

'But it's only 11 a.m.'

'It's the evening somewhere. I want a drink and I refuse to be a lush on my own.'

So they went into the kitchen and, like two college kids, began to make a cocktail. Cranberry juice in the fridge, with a shot of vodka and a squeeze of lime.

'Other than getting drunk on a Sunday morning, what do you want?' Tom asked his wife.

'You've been asking me that for nearly two decades now,' Cathy replied.

'And I'll keep asking you until you breathe your last breath. Because I want to give you everything.'

Her face clouded for a moment, dark, ominous. He couldn't give her the one thing she wanted most. Mikey.

'Don't go again,' Tom pleaded, shadows closing in again.

'Let's go *skinny dipping*.' Cathy surprised him for the one millionth time in their life, her smile sending the clouds away.

'Right now?' Tom asked.

'Why not? We'll drink our cocktail, then head to the beach.'

'But it's October. It's cold.'

'We live in Ireland – even if it were July, the water would be cold.'

'Someone might see us,' Tom said.

'I spent the first half of my life giving all the fucks. And so did you, Dr Tom O'Grady. For once, why don't we just do whatever we want?'

Tom put his glass down. He could not think of a single argument. He held his hand out to his wife and led her to the place of the zero fucks.

48

RUTH

Now

The Inner City Helping Homeless voluntary organisation will have outreach teams working again tonight and they can be alerted to anyone sleeping rough by calling 01 8881804 or 085 8389281.

Variations of this news bulletin filled every social media site as another cold spell hit Ireland. Ruth finished her morning shift and began making lunch for Tom. She had done the very same thing for days now in the hope that she would find him and Bette Davis sitting on their bench, waiting for her. She would give him a piece of her mind when he came back. She flicked the kettle on, for Ava, Aisling and Kian. They would be along any minute, too. Their newly formed gang had fallen into a habit of meeting up every morning at the same time.

Ava was the first to arrive. She walked over to the new A4 poster that was pinned to the noticeboard.

Residents are reminded that no photographs or artwork are allowed on the walls in the hotel rooms or common areas.

'Ha! Am I bovvered? All my photographs are on this,' Ava said, waving her phone. 'Check out my latest Instagram post. Another lie shared for friends to like.'

'You look beautiful. That is not a lie,' Ruth said. Ava was a natural beauty, with flawless skin and dark, thick hair.

Ava ignored the compliment and said, 'No one knows that behind that selfie, carefully taken at just the right angle, of course, the truth is we are in a hotel room, *homeless.*'

She began to pace the small kitchen. 'We are all creating the same lie, presenting a pretty package, with a filter that hides a multitude, at an angle that cuts out the nastiness. Because God forbid that we share the full story to the world. God forbid that people know our shameful secret.'

Then Ava began to cry, overcome with emotion. 'I can't do this any more. I can't airbrush the shit out of the mess I'm in.'

'Can you tell me what particular part of the shit you are talking about?' Ruth asked.

'Take your pick, Ruth. Today is our anniversary. We're homeless. And the best bit is . . . I'm pregnant and I don't know how to tell my husband.'

'You do not think he will be happy?' Ruth asked, stunned by the revelation.

'He's stressed out of his biccie. What if this is the final straw that breaks him?'

Ruth sat beside Ava and said, 'A baby is good news. And nothing should take away from that. Congratulations, Ava. You will be a wonderful mother.'

'You think?'

Ruth nodded.

'I needed to hear that. I'm just a mess right now. This morning I sat on our bed in the room and tried to envisage a cot there. I couldn't. I just couldn't.'

'You might be in your house before then. But if not you will make it work. Like we all do,' Ruth said firmly.

'It's not meant to be like this, though. I used to dream of how I would share baby news with Brian. But at no stage was it in this godforsaken place . . . How did this happen, Ruth?'

'You had sex, I would imagine,' Ruth replied, making Ava giggle through her tears.

'When we got married last year, we had so many hopes and dreams for our future. It was so romantic, Ruth. Brian's proposal was perfect. He arranged for my ring to be brought out by a waiter in a glass of champagne,' Ava said. 'And now, I think of all the money we wasted on champagne and our wedding. At the time, I thought it was worth it. Everyone said the beef was the nicest they'd had in years.'

'You cannot beat yourself up about things you have done in the past. I always see things clearer when I have the benefit of hindsight,' Ruth said.

'Maybe I should have been nicer to Brian's mother. We

stayed with her for a bit after we lost our apartment. But she never liked me. Nor I her.'

Ruth sat down opposite Ava and said, 'You have to tell Brian you are pregnant. You cannot keep this to yourself.'

'We had a row this morning because he wants to go out for a meal for our anniversary. I want us to save our money. We need every penny for this baby.'

'Hello, ladies,' Kian said, walking into the room.

Ava mimicked zipping her mouth to Ruth, then wiped her tears away.

'You are in a good mood,' Ruth said.

'I am,' Kian replied, making his coffee.

'Why?' Ava asked, suspicious.

'Morning,' Aisling said with a matching smile, as she walked into the room.

Kian pointed to her and said, 'I know I'm a short arse, but this one here makes me feel ten feet tall.'

When Kian asked Aisling out he expected her to say no. He'd never had much success with women. He talked a big talk, but it was all smoke and mirrors with him. You could have knocked him down with a feather when she said yes. And now, every day seemed a little brighter in this godforsaken hotel. The previous evening they had all squeezed into his room to watch *Stranger Things* together. Anna and Cormac sat on the floor, with a large bag of Doritos between them. Kian and Aisling lay side by side on the double bed.

'Last night, for the first time in a long time, I felt normal.'

'Me, too,' Aisling said. 'It was fun.'

'I think I might be sick,' Ava said, jumping up.

'Hey, no need for that!' Kian said.

'No, I mean it. I think I'm going to be sick.' Ava ran from the room.

'Hope it's not catching, whatever she has,' Kian said. Then he pulled Aisling in close, whispering something in her ear that made her blush and giggle all at once.

When they had their first date they swapped their stories. The intimate stuff that you only tell someone you know is special. He told Aisling about Cormac's mum. A woman whom he thought was out of his league but who seemed to enjoy his company. They dated and when she announced she was pregnant Kian proposed immediately. She hadn't needed to say no out loud. The look of horror on her face was enough. He spent months trying to change her mind, especially after Cormac was born. Every day she looked more and more depressed and trapped. She told him that she wasn't cut out for motherhood. Or him. She loved Cormac the best way she could. And in fairness, she saw him every week for an hour or two. She just had no interest in the everyday life of a mother.

Aisling had listened to his story and when he'd finished she told him he had it all wrong. 'You were never punching above your weight. Cormac's mum was.'

Yep, ten feet tall, she made him feel.

Ruth smiled at her two friends, happy that they were happy. But Ava's distraught face would not leave her. She had to do something to help.

'I have a plan!' Ruth declared.

'Another room makeover?' Kian joked.

'It is Ava and Brian's anniversary. I think we should

make it special for them. I shall need your help, though,' Ruth said.

'Now why doesn't that surprise me?' Kian said. 'What do you want me to do?'

'I want you to do an errand for me. At 5 p.m. Right now, I need to find my friend.'

'The rough sleeper?' Kian asked. 'Still no sign of him? Jaysus, I wouldn't leave a cat out on the streets right now. It was three degrees outside this morning when I dropped Cormac to school. The frost was leaving bite marks on the windows of our hotel room.'

'He's probably just moved on to another area,' Aisling said. 'I still don't understand how a doctor, of all people, ended up on the streets. What chance do the rest of us have?'

'Probably drink. Is he an alchy?' Kian said.

Ruth shook her head. 'I have never seen him drink. I do not think so.'

'Gambling, then. I knew a guy who lost his missus and his home on the throw of a hundred dice or so. Couldn't stop. And he was an accountant. You'd think he'd know better, working with money all the time. Shocking waste,' Kian said.

'I do not know what happened, but I do know for sure that he is a good man. His wife, Cathy, did, too. I owe them both a lot.'

Ruth heard Aisling say to Kian as she walked out, 'She's such a big heart.'

Then Kian replied, 'Which is about to get broken. That dude has gone. He doesn't give a shit about her or DJ. I warned her to be careful.'

Ruth knew Kian was wrong. When Dr O'Grady showed up she would talk to him, find out if he needed help. She sat on his park bench for an hour until it was time to collect DJ, her eyes scanning the walkways on either side, to no avail.

As she got up to leave she spotted Bones walking through the park. She ran over to him. 'Have you seen the Doc?'

'Not since yesterday,' he said. 'I've just come from the shelter. He wasn't there last night. Odd that, 'cos it was wicked cold.' Then he asked, 'Have you any money for a hot drink?'

She passed him the sandwiches she had made for the Doc and a couple of euro.

'Thanks.'

'Will you tell him that I was looking for him?' Ruth asked. And when he nodded, she asked, 'Are you OK, Mr Bones?'

He shrugged. 'I'm grand. Had a big fry-up for breakfast. Was right tasty. I'll go back to the shelter tonight. They said it might snow.'

A vision of the doctor lying on the ground, cold, covered in snow, sneaked its way into her head. She shivered and pushed it away. 'How's Sheila? She's been on my mind.'

'Bad news, I'm afraid. She had a baby girl last week. She left the baby here on the Doc's bench. Then over-dosed.' He wiped his eyes and whispered the final truth: 'She died.'

Ruth felt tears sting her own eyes. Erica had said something about a baby in the news, but she had tuned her out. The poor, poor girl.

'Bobby is gunning for Tom,' Bones said.

'Why?'

'Because he's bat-shit crazy and he loved Sheila. He loves the junk more, though. That's the way it goes. You see Doc, tell him to watch himself,' Bones said.

When she found the doctor she would have a lot to say to him, Ruth thought to herself. She did not care what Erica said about the rules, she was bringing him inside.

Later that evening, once his homework was done, DJ pulled his coat on to go to the park.

'I waited today for an hour and he did not show up,' Ruth said.

'He'll be back,' DJ said.

'Be back before dark,' Ruth said.

'Anna and Cormac are going to come with me, too. I'll be fine,' DJ said.

'If you find him, you tell him that I want to talk to him. Tell him that it's important.'

The communal room emptied as the last of the kids went upstairs to their room to watch TV. Time to get her plan into action. Ruth pulled a box out from under the homework table that she had stashed away earlier.

Kian walked in just as she was finishing her makeover. A white tablecloth now adorned the table and it was laid for two. She lit the tealights under the food warmer that sat in its centre.

'Looks great. I collected the food as you instructed, boss.' He held up the Thai takeaway.

He then passed Ruth a bottle of prosecco. 'Put that on the table for love's young dream. It's from the chiller in the supermarket, so it's cold.'

'That is kind of you,' Ruth said.

'I probably owe them both at least this,' Kian said.

'Help me light the rest of the candles,' Ruth said, emptying the food into the silver trays. 'I told Ava to bring Brian here at five fifteen.'

Together Kian and Ruth transformed the Library into a flickering magical room, with tealights on every surface. The fragrant smell of coconut milk and curry paste filled the air, and if you tried hard you could imagine you were in a restaurant.

'You did this?' Ava gasped when they walked in. Brian's mouth fell open in shock.

'It was Ruth's idea. I'm just the hired help,' Kian said quickly.

'But the prosecco is a present from Kian,' Ruth said. 'Happy Anniversary, Ava and Brian.'

Kian walked by them both and said to Brian, 'It's not lasagne. Sorry, mate.' Then he ran out the door before Brian clobbered him.

'Thank you.' Ava squeezed Ruth's hand and Ruth mouthed, 'Tell him.'

'That felt good,' Kian said.

They walked out onto the street and looked in the direction of the park for the kids. The street was empty.

'You can change the world by helping one person at a time,' Ruth said.

'I think you might have something there, Ruthie my love,' Kian replied.

'My friend Cathy told me that a long time ago. She was married to Dr O'Grady.'

'Well, you are certainly following her advice. You've

done a lot for us all here in the hotel since you arrived. More than my own family ever did for me. You're a good pal.'

'Thank you, Kian. And I have had enough time now to make up my mind about you, too. I like you very much. I should be happy to be your pal.'

'Well, that's settled so. Nice one,' Kian said. And they stood side by side watching the empty road. 'They should be back by now. I'm going to go get the kids. You go on back inside. I'll send your young fella up to you, promise.'

She smiled as she returned to her room, pausing outside the door to her pop-up anniversary restaurant for a second. She was gratified to hear the quiet hum of conversation and laughter. Of two people in love, about to begin a new chapter in their lives, as parents.

Tell him your news, Ava. It's too good to hide. Tell him.

As she stood there, her thoughts went to Dean. To their lost weekend together. *Oh Dean, come back to me, like you promised you would.*

49

RUTH

Then

Dean awoke with a jolt at 4 a.m., feeling an empty space next to him. His heart hammered as he clambered out of bed.

'So hungry,' Ruth's voice said in the darkness. She was sitting in front of the small hotel fridge eating cashew nuts. The only vaguely white thing the fridge held.

'Is there any chocolate in there?' Dean asked, as his stomach kicked in and started to growl in agreement.

She stuck her head in the fridge and pulled out a large chunky KitKat, passing it to him. When he offered her some she shook her head. He accepted her food thing without question. They sat, munching on their meal, cross-legged and naked on the floor.

'You know, yesterday started off so badly for me,' Dean said.

'Explain,' Ruth said.

'I hate my job,' Dean replied. 'I don't know how it

357

happened, but I never dreamed that one day I'd end up as a janitorial supplies sales rep.'

'What did you dream of?'

'As a kid, I always said I wanted to be a fireman or a transformer robot. Or maybe a ninja turtle.'

'All amazing life choices, as far as I am concerned,' Ruth said.

'Yep. Instead I spend my days driving around the country, talking about cleaning materials for hotels and hospitals. This week I've been in Belfast, Dublin, Cork, Waterford and now Wexford. It's why I stopped in Curracloe. The heat of the sun bursting through my window . . . it all got too much. So I found myself turning towards Curracloe. We used to come here as kids for our holidays. Best decision I ever made.'

'Make another one. Quit your job,' Ruth said.

'It's not that simple.'

'Why?'

'Well, you can't just quit your job for no reason,' Dean said.

'Hating it is a pretty strong reason, I would think.'

'But what would I do?'

'Positions for turtles and robots are hard to find, Dean. But there's no reason why you cannot be a fireman.'

'I can't do that!' Dean said, but he found himself grinning.

'Why not? Have you ever looked into what is required to become a firefighter?'

'No,' Dean admitted.

'For all you know they are recruiting right now,' Ruth said, stuffing the last of the cashew nuts into her mouth.

'Do not wait another day to follow your childhood dream. I think you would make a most excellent firefighter. You have strong arms.'

'You make it sound so easy,' Dean said.

'It does not have to be hard.'

'No, I suppose it doesn't. What about you? What are you looking for?' Dean asked, licking his fingers.

Ruth's mind raced with thoughts about the many things she had dreamed of her whole life. A library with a sliding ladder. A home of her own, away from Marian. Friends. A private Westlife concert, just for her. And more than anything else, to find love and understanding. But as always, the thoughts stuck in her head, jumbled up into one big hot mess.

'Come on, spill! What do you want?' Dean asked again.

'You need to be more specific if you want an answer. I do not do vague,' Ruth said.

He smiled, promising himself that he would always remember that. 'What do you want in a relationship?'

And in an instant, her thoughts clarified and she answered without skipping a beat. 'That is easy. I want to love and be loved. To understand and be understood. To find my soul mate,' Ruth replied.

They both looked over to the bedside locker, where their earlier fortunes sat, side by side. Ruth felt Dean's eyes on her, but she could not meet them. Her honesty lay between them, fragile.

'I'd like to try to give you all of that,' Dean whispered into the room. 'If you let me.'

Ruth felt her heart race with his words. Could it be true? Had they found their soul mates today, as the fortune predicted? 'We should get dressed and go back to the beach,' Ruth said, pulling him to his feet.

'It's not even 5 a.m.!' Dean said.

'I know. But if we are quick we might make the sunrise,' Ruth said.

They got dressed and Dean drove them back to the beach. They walked to the same spot they had sat on earlier. It was – unsurprisingly – empty. He grabbed her hand and they walked to the water's edge. The ocean was calm, gently rippling towards the grainy sand. The sky was grey, with orange hues on the horizon. In the distance they saw a boat silhouetted against the skyline.

'Look!' Ruth said, pointing to their left.

'What am I looking at?' Dean asked.

'See that small orange dot?'

'Yes . . .'

'Keep watching it . . .'

The dot started to grow, bright yellow, flooding the skyline.

'Oh!' Dean said, smiling in glee. The sunrise. It was spectacular. As was Ruth. Totally, unfucking-believably-spectacular. He had never felt so alive in his life.

With the sound of the gentle waves lapping the shore, they stood arm in arm as the sun rose into the sky.

'It's wonderful how the sun changes everything. The sand is now golden. The birds have appeared. Look!' Ruth moved from his arms, turning in a circle.

'Why are you single?' Dean blurted out as he watched her dance around the sand, waving her arms in the air. She was perfect. Almost too perfect. There must be a flaw. *Please don't let there be a flaw.*

When she didn't answer, a sudden thought struck him. She wasn't single. She had a boyfriend or a husband.

'You are single?' he asked.

'I hate that question!' Ruth finally replied. 'Why is it the be-all and end-all in life?'

She stopped dancing, fear making her tremble. Afraid to believe that her mother was wrong. That maybe she did have a chance at that happy-ever-after.

Dean felt his stomach flip, confused by her statement. Maybe she wasn't looking for a relationship. Maybe this was just a weekend fling. He should have kept his big mouth shut.

Yet, he didn't. 'I think you are spectacular,' he said, taking her hands and twirling her around in a circle in the sand.

'I do not think I am single, as it happens. Not any more,' Ruth said. She turned her face towards his and Dean realised what she was saying. He whooped out loud, before kissing her again, something they had got very good at.

'I told you it would be the end,' Dean said.

In one lost weekend together, they went from virtual strangers to madly in love. When Dean dropped Ruth home she knew that they would see each other again.

'I'll call you every day. I'll text you every day. Then I'll be back on Friday so we can spend the weekend together again,' Dean promised. 'Remember, there's no going back now. This is it.'

'This is it,' she repeated.

He grabbed her hand and placed something into it.

You will meet your soul mate today.

His fortune. She watched him get into his car and waited until he disappeared from sight. She felt calmer than she had ever felt in her life. Both her brain and body were in sync at last.

He rang her every day. Sometimes several times. He texted. Until Friday arrived, a day Ruth looked forward to so very much. But instead of more kissing and love, there was only silence. Dean disappeared off the face of the earth, as if they had never met.

No more Dean. No more sunrise.

50

TOM

Now

Bette Davis watched them load her master into the green van with flashing lights. She was scared. She was cold and she was hungry. And she wanted her family back. Tom had not moved for the longest time.

Cathy stood by their bed and said, 'We need to talk.'

Her words made his heart race. He'd always worried that one day she would work out that he wasn't a charming fecker after all. She wagged a small grey velvet cushion at him.

Relief flooded him, making him feel silly for doubting her. For doubting himself.

'What have I done now?' he asked, grinning.

'How long are we married now?'

'Ten years this October,' he answered.

'That's a long time for me to pick up cushions from the floor whenever it's your turn to make the bed,' Cathy said.

'*I put four pillows on the bed! Far as I can see, that's all we need.*'

'*What about the cushions?*'

'*It's like they're multiplying,*' Tom answered. '*Every time I look, there's another one on the bed, or on the sofa downstairs. I feel like I'm under attack.*'

He picked up a small grey oblong one and held it up, as exhibit A. '*This one wasn't here last week, and what on earth is it anyhow?*'

'*It's a jumper cushion. It adds some texture. And it's quirky. Feel it. Isn't it lovely?*'

'*It feels like an Aran sweater my gran made me when I was a kid. I hated that jumper. Made me look like Foster and Allen,*' Tom replied.

She fought a smile that was sneaking its way onto her face.

He continued, '*One of these days I'll wake up on the floor. The scatter cushions will have won the battle.*'

'*But they make the bed look so pretty,*' Cathy said.

'*But they have no use,*' Tom replied.

'*But make me happy,*' Cathy said.

Game over. Why didn't she just start with that? '*But then the cushions must stay.*'

She let the smile flood her face this time. '*No more throwing them in a corner.*'

'*Absolutely.*' They both knew this was a lie.

'*Like this,*' she said, arranging them in a way that made her happy. '*There. Doesn't that look much better?*'

Tom looked at the bed and for the life of him he couldn't see it.

'Infinitely,' he answered. 'Can I go to work now?'

She leaned up to kiss him on his cheek, shooing him out the door.

Their second-to-last conversation was about cushions.

51

Now

Homeless services in Dublin confirmed the body of
a man in a sleeping bag, thought to be an Irish
national, was discovered by a member of the public
before 9 a.m. on Friday.

Temperatures in the city fell to zero on Thursday
night. This is the first death of a homeless individual
in Dublin this year.

Ruth walked down the hotel corridor towards their
lift. A blast of cold hair rushed by her as the door to the
car park opened. DJ walked in leading Bette Davis on
her leash, followed by Kian, Cormac and Anna.

DJ looked at his mum and burst into tears.

'What happened?' Ruth asked.

'I'm sorry, love. But we just saw your pal the Doc being
loaded into an ambulance.'

'Is he OK?' Ruth asked, and felt her legs go weak when Kian shook his head.

Kian ushered them into the lift as they made their way upstairs to Ruth's room. He instructed Anna to go get her mother. Ruth had gone deathly white and the boy was crying. He felt ill equipped to deal with all of this on his own.

'How do you know he was dead?' Ruth asked when they were inside her room.

'I spoke to the paramedic. He died shortly before they found him. Nothing they could do,' Kian said.

DJ was huddled on his bed, clutching Bette Davis, rocking back and forth.

Kian was relieved to see Aisling and Anna arrive.

'How can you be sure it was the Doc?' Aisling asked.

Kian nodded. 'I'd recognise that dirty old overcoat of his a mile off. The paramedics said he'd died of hypothermia. He must have fallen asleep outside. In these temperatures, sure nobody could survive.'

'Mr Bones said he was staying in the shelter. Earlier today, he said that,' Ruth said.

'He must have changed his mind,' Aisling said, holding her friend tight.

'Where are they bringing him?' Ruth asked, pushing Aisling away. She would not believe that he was gone. Not Dr O'Grady. This could not be how it ended for him.

'To Beaumont Hospital,' Kian said.

Aisling said, 'Ah, pet, I'm sorry.'

'I was going to insist he get help,' Ruth said. 'That was my plan. No more living on the streets.'

'Bette Davis is bleeding, Mam,' DJ sobbed. He wanted the Doc. He wanted his mam to make this all OK again.

Kian took a look at the gash on the side of the dog's face. 'Superficial, but she's had a belt of something, by the looks of it. Poor fecker. I'll get something to clean it up.' As he walked to the door, he said, 'You'll be thrown out of here if Erica sees that dog.'

DJ shouted, 'I'm not losing her, too. Mam, tell him.'

Ruth walked over to her son and kneeled down on the ground beside him. She did not wait to be asked for a hug. Nor did she count as she pulled both him and Bette Davis into her arms. She simply comforted her son and promised him that she would somehow make this all OK.

'Aisling, Kian, can you take care of DJ and Bette Davis for me? And not a word to Erica about the dog.'

'Between the lot of us, we've all broken her bleeding rules. Don't worry, we'll help you keep this secret,' Kian said.

'I am going to the hospital,' Ruth said to DJ, popping her knuckles over and over.

'There's no point, love. He's dead, one hundred per cent,' Kian said, not unkindly.

'He is my friend and on his own. At the very least he deserves someone to identify his body.'

Kian grabbed a twenty-euro note from his pocket and pressed it into Ruth's hand. 'Get a taxi then. You're shaking like a leaf.'

Ruth looked up to thank Kian and he held his hand up. 'That's what friends are for. You go and take care of your pal; we'll be here waiting for you when you get back.'

Less than an hour later she walked into the lobby of Beaumont Hospital. 'Can you tell me where to go? I'm looking for Dr Tom O'Grady,' Ruth asked the receptionist.

'One moment.' The woman tapped the name into the screen and said, 'First floor. Room 160.'

Three hundred and three steps to the room where her friend lay. Ruth would never forgive herself. She should have asked more questions. She should have pushed him to go home. She should have done something to keep him safe. He was her friend. And now he was . . .

'Hello, Ruth.'

Ruth clutched the door frame to Room 160, unable to believe her eyes.

Sitting on the bed, very much alive, was Dr O'Grady. *Pop, pop, pop.* Shock, denial and then relief floored Ruth. *Dr O'Grady?* Joy came next and Ruth wanted to scream, to laugh, to dance and then scream again. He was alive!

'You are not dead.'

'I should hope not.'

'But I thought you were dead,' Ruth insisted, and then she began to cry large gulping tears, her body shaking as it went through an assault of emotions. She moved towards his bed, one, two, three, four steps. 'They found you in the park. The paramedics said you had died of hypothermia. It's been on all the news stations.'

'That wasn't me, Ruth. I've been in here for two days now.'

Five, six, seven, eight . . . and she was by his bed. She blinked her eyes, to make sure she was not hallucinating.

She reached out and touched him. He was here. Bruised and swollen. But here.

'Kian saw your overcoat on the body they put into the ambulance,' Ruth said. 'I do not understand.'

Tom's face crumpled. 'Ah, no. Lash! He stole my overcoat from the shelter a few days ago. The stupid fecker. Ah, no.'

'That is the best news I have ever heard,' Ruth said, then put her hand to mouth, horrified, saying, 'Not about Mr Lash . . .'

'I know what you meant,' Tom replied. 'Can you call the Peter McVerry Trust? To tell them about Lash.'

'I will take care of that,' Ruth said. 'You look like an extra from *The Walking Dead*.' Tom's eye was swollen and blood had filled the white of his eye.

'Few cracked ribs, a small concussion. Nothing major,' Tom said.

'What happened?' Ruth asked.

'Remember Sheila?'

Ruth nodded. 'Bones told me what happened to her.'

'Her boyfriend, Bobby, caught up with me.'

'Why on earth would he do such a thing?' Ruth said. 'You helped her. You saved her baby.'

'He wanted my doctor's bag. Looking for drugs, I would imagine. It's happened before.'

'You have to ring the guards,' Ruth said.

'Maybe. But I suspect they will not be too worried about two rough sleepers having a fight.'

'This was not a fight. It was an attack,' Ruth said.

'I need to get back on my feet to find Bette Davis. And my rucksack.'

'She is with DJ at the hotel,' Ruth said.

Relief made Tom shake. He had been so worried.

'We do not have your rucksack,' Ruth said.

'I have to get it back. It's important,' Tom said.

'You are alive. That is the most important thing.'

'It had my stethoscope in it. My parents gave me that. And a grey cushion. I don't care about anything else, just those two things.'

Ruth watched raw, visceral pain twist her friend's face. The room swelled with the unanswered questions. What happened to Tom that made him like this? A doctor, happily married, now living on the streets . . . She had to find a way to keep Tom inside once he left this hospital. While there was never a good time to be a rough sleeper, the current cold spell was disastrous for anyone stuck on the streets. She would not let this kind man end his days broken, bruised and perished.

Ruth said, 'I have some savings. The deposit I got back from my flat. And despite my best efforts I am unable to find a suitable flat in Dublin to rent. It's enough for you to take a room at The Silver Sands Lodge when you get out of here. That way I can take care of you while you recuperate.'

'I prefer to live outside,' Tom said, feeling close to tears again. Her kindness was unravelling pieces of him inside that had been tied up in knots for years. And he was no longer sure he knew what he wanted.

'You cannot sleep outside anymore. No argument. When you are able I will bring you to Parkgate Hall and you must present yourself as homeless. You have been rough sleeping for a decade, Dr O'Grady, and it is killing you slowly, one day at a time. You must end this before it ends you.'

Tom closed his eyes, feeling dizzy, elated, sick, happy, all at once. Ruth cared about him. She was everything he had hoped Mikey would grow up to be. Kind. Compassionate. Fearless. Strong. He wished she were his daughter. He would have been so proud to be her father. He should tell her that.

Ruth said, 'I do not care that you have gambled away your home.'

Tom opened his eyes in shock at the words. 'Excuse me?'

'Well, you do not drink, or take drugs. Kian offered gambling as a possible reason for your situation.'

'Ruth, I chose to sleep outdoors. Nobody forced me.' He knew he had to tell Ruth everything, to say the horror out loud. But he'd spent ten years denying this truth. He looked up and saw the bravest person he knew in front of him. And that gave him the strength to admit his truth. Their truth. Cathy and his.

'Cathy is dead.'

Ruth nodded. Somewhere she knew that this must be the truth. Dr O'Grady would never leave his wife. 'I am so very sorry.'

'After she died, our apartment was just a cruel shell filled with too many bad memories. Outside, there is no white noise around me, confusing me, distracting me. I can find my way home in my dreams.'

'You can dream inside,' Ruth said.

'I told you, there was too much pain inside. When I'm under the stars I find my way home every time.'

'Cathy would not want this for you,' Ruth insisted.

Tom ignored that and said, 'We used to talk about love a lot, Cathy and me. The longer we knew each other, the more it expanded. And if you are lucky, when you fall in love that person loves you back in the exact same way. That's the best kind of love, one that is received and reciprocated.'

Ruth wiped away the tears and the thought of Dean. 'That is everything.'

'Not the only everything. What you have with DJ, that's everything, too.'

'I wish I could be one of those mothers who says "I love you" every day. I think it, but the words get tongue-tied in my head.'

'What's more important is showing how you feel. You do that plenty,' Tom replied.

'I think about the day he was born a lot. When you placed him on my breast, my world expanded and shrank all at once,' Ruth said.

Tom felt tears sting his bloodied eyes. 'I think you are better at saying things than you think. You should tell DJ exactly that because every eloquent word you have just spoken is love.'

'He is so angry with me about his father,' Ruth said.

'You cannot give him something you don't have,' Tom replied. 'He'll work that out for himself in the end.'

'You would have been a great father,' Ruth said.

'I am a father,' Tom whispered.

Ruth looked up, confused by his words. She rifled her memories, trying to remember a mention of a child, by either Dr O'Grady or Cathy. She could not recall a single time.

'For a year we had everything. Then our son Mikey died. And when he went, everything changed. Cathy never really found her way back from her grief. Not properly.' He shook from the words he'd just acknowledged for the first time in ten years.

'What about you, Dr O'Grady? Have you found your way back?' Ruth watched his face contort in pain. She saw profound grief etched onto every groove and line.

He had chosen to step away from the world he knew. He hid himself in the park, one of Dublin's invisible. A rough sleeper filled with loss and regret. And now he was not sure if he could ever find his way home.

52

TOM

When Ruth left, with promises that she would return the following day, Tom's mind kept looking at all the roads he'd taken over the past ten years. He had spent so long thinking that this was the only way he could find his way home to Cathy and Mikey. But what if he was wrong? What if there was another way?

But to do that, first of all he had to be honest with every part of his story . . . Mikey's death was only the start. There was something else he needed to acknowledge, to tell Ruth about. For now, he was tired. He closed his eyes and dreamed, going back to the darkness.

'I'm getting old,' Cathy moaned as she moved her legs slowly to the ground. Her knees cracked as if to punctuate the point.

'I heard that!' Tom said.

'My hips aren't much better.'

'I felt you toss and turn all night,' Tom said, 'It's time to get an appointment to see what's going on.'

Cathy responded by throwing her eyes up to the ceiling. 'And they say women are the ones who nag!'

'I don't like seeing you in pain, that's all.'

'I know.' Cathy walked around the bed to her husband and kissed him. And to both their surprises the kiss grew passionate and all thoughts of hip and knee replacements vanished as they fell back onto the bed. Their lovemaking was slower, gentler now, yet somehow more beautiful.

'Not bad for a man getting close to his sixtieth birthday, eh?' Tom boasted.

'Not bad at all,' Cathy replied. 'I would say that like fine wine, we're getting better the older we get. But right now, I need to get a wiggle on. It's a big day for one of my kids from the centre. She's moving into her own apartment.'

Tom looked at his wife with pride. 'You have helped so many do that.'

'A team effort, of which I am proud to be a part.'

'Will I make tea?'

'Do,' Cathy said. Her face changed and Tom knew she was thinking about Mikey. He could always tell. He didn't want to lose her. His body still felt the touch of her hand and he was not ready to lose her to the damn darkness again.

'How is Ruth doing?' he fired at her.

'I am amazed at how quickly she is transitioning to motherhood. She's adamant she wants to leave Wexford, though. Her fear that her mother will harm her baby just won't go away.'

'I will miss her if she does. I have grown fond of her and DJ,' Tom replied.

Tom watched Cathy's eyes become dull. It was as if a switch had turned off inside of her.

'Don't go,' he whispered. 'I don't like it when you go.'

If she heard him, she didn't show it. She was upstairs, oblivious to his words, his pain.

He prepared her favourite poached eggs on wholegrain toast and brought them upstairs to their bedroom. She kept her back to him, lying on their bed.

He stood watching her for what felt like an eternity, but it was only a few moments. He left her with Mikey and consoled himself that a version of him was with Cathy in her dreams. That had to be something. When the centre rang looking for Cathy a few hours later, he kicked himself for not calling them to let them know she would not be in.

His mother had many odd phrases, picked up from her own mother, who no doubt picked them up from her own. One of them was 'Someone walked over my grave', something he uttered right now. He felt a shudder and began to shiver as an unexplained coldness seeped through him.

He ran up the stairs, two at a time, somehow knowing, yet not knowing.

He found Cathy lying on the bed, clutching the grey jumper cushion in her arms like it was a baby. Her face was ashen white and her eyes were closed.

Just sleeping. That's all.

But then he saw. A glass of water. An empty tub of tablets.

No!

He felt for a pulse that he knew was not there.

No, no, no! Not this. Not like this, Cathy.

Then he climbed onto the bed and pulled her into his arms, kissing her cheeks, her forehead. 'You're where my story began. You can't leave me.'

The silence that had engulfed him when Mikey died came back and this time it was not letting go.

53

TOM

Now

Tom awoke stiff with pain under his ribcage and on his right eye. His face felt tender and raw, from the hours he had cried the evening before. A decade's worth of unshed tears. He looked around his room again, re-orientating himself. It was a strange sensation being inside a room that didn't have rows of bunk beds side by side. He kept dozing off, which confounded him. He had not napped like this since he was a kid. It must be the warmth of the hospital ward making him drowsy, and the pain medication.

Then he saw her, sitting by his bed, reading a battered copy of *Odd Thomas*. Wearing a paper face mask just like the one she'd worn the first day she came to his doctor's surgery. *Oh, Ruth, I am so glad you never changed.*

'You came back,' he managed to croak. He felt a lump form in his throat, choking him, and tears stung his eyes once more.

'How are you feeling?' she whispered, lowering her face mask. She looked around her, as if expecting a swarm of germs to attack.

'Better,' he replied. He felt the strangest sensation over-whelm him. In this room with Ruth he felt healed.

He marvelled at her strength and was humbled by it. While she was struggling with the huge changes in her life she took time to take care of him, to reach out to support an old acquaintance. He realised that he could not love her more if she were in fact his own daughter.

'DJ is outside with Bette Davis. We had a plan to sneak her inside to visit you. It did not go very well.'

'Go on,' Tom said, grinning again.

'DJ's first plan was that I pretend to be blind and bring Bette in as my guide dog. I saw many problems with this so we moved on to his next bright idea.'

'I'm all ears,' Tom said.

'DJ borrowed a pram from his friends in room 131. I suspect their mother, Melissa, does not know. She is a most objectionable woman. I just cannot take to her.'

'What did you do with the pram?' Tom asked. Then his mouth formed a perfect O of surprise when the penny dropped. 'No . . .'

'Yes! We placed Bette in the pram and covered her with blankets. I think she rather liked it. It worked well until an orderly blocked our path as we made our way along the ground floor downstairs. Several people peered in to look at the baby. I thought Bette was rather fetching, albeit a bit hairy for a child. One pointy-nosed woman shouted out to everyone that Bette was a dog. As DJ swore blind that Bette was his sister, someone walked by with a McDonald's takeaway bag. One whiff of the Big Mac and Bette was up and out of the pram, chasing her next meal. I have to tell you it was quite a sight.'

'Stop, can't laugh, the pain . . .' Tom said, holding his side.

'I am sorry we did not make it in to you, but I thought you would like to know that she is close by.'

'I do, and I'm grateful more than you'll ever know. How is she? She's been through the mill too, poor little mite.'

'Healing, like you,' Ruth replied. 'DJ is taking good care of her. As are my friends at The Lodge.'

Her friends. Tom felt his heart leap in joy at hearing Ruth say this. She had friends. And what a boy DJ was. Funny and kind. The DNA jackpot. 'You have done a great job with that kid,' Tom said.

She blushed at the compliment. 'I had to make a lot of it up as I went along.'

'That's what all parents have to do, Ruth. And mothers with Asperger's have been raising children for ever. Just because it wasn't recognised years ago doesn't mean it didn't exist,' Tom said.

'I was so scared when I was pregnant.'

'I remember,' Tom said. 'But mostly I remember how strong you were. How excited to meet your baby.'

'I might not have DJ if you had not been there for us,' Ruth said, and they both remembered that moment at the foot of the stairs when he delivered her child.

'I have had a lot of time to think about that fall. I had just walked upstairs and the stairs landing was dry. Then my mother walked out drinking a bottle of soda. I believe my mother spilled her drink deliberately. To make me fall,' Ruth said.

Tom nodded. He believed that was true, too. 'I am so sorry, Ruth.'

'Me, too, Dr O'Grady. I do not want DJ to know this,' Ruth said.

'He will never hear it from me,' Tom replied.

'I keep thinking about your baby, Dr O'Grady. I am so sorry about Mikey. I would very much like to have met him,' Ruth said.

Tom knew that the time had come to share everything with Ruth. No more hidden truths. 'There is more to my story. I should have told you before now. But in truth I could not face it myself, never mind admit it to anyone else. Cathy didn't just die, she . . . she committed suicide.'

She listened to Tom tell her about the horror of finding his wife dead. And what came next.

'You want to die, too. I understand now,' Ruth said.

'No,' Tom replied, surprised by this. 'I'm ready to die whenever that time comes, but I'm not suicidal. At least, not any more.'

'Yes, you are. Because you will die if you continue on this road you have chosen,' Ruth said. 'Another Bobby will rob you and you will not come back from it. Or the cold will get you and you will perish, like Mr Lash did. And that is unfair, because there are people who care about you.'

Tom was silent.

'And that limp you have will only get worse. You are an old man now. You have no business putting your body through the hardships you are forcing yourself to face,' Ruth said.

'You said last night that the only way you can be at

home is by remembering Cathy and Mikey in your dreams. Outside under the stars. Well, I think that is a crock of shit. There are a thousand ways to find your road home. But you have to be brave enough to look for them.'

A nurse peeked her head around the curtain and said, 'Good news, Mr O'Grady. You are free to leave. Is this your daughter?' She smiled at Ruth.

'No,' Ruth replied at the same time that Tom said, 'I wish she was. I could not ask for a better one.'

'I will wait outside,' Ruth said, her cheeks flushed from his words. She wanted to tell him that she would like nothing better than for him to be her father. How different her life might have been, if fate had given her him, not Marian and Alan. But the words were tumbled up in her head, so instead she told him, 'You are coming back to the hotel with me. We shall check you into a room. I do not want to hear a word about it.'

Tom thought the idea sounded splendid all of a sudden.

An hour later, the three friends and Bette Davis walked through the front door of the hotel. Kian and Aisling were standing in front of reception waiting for an answer from Erica about putting up Christmas decorations in the Library.

They had chosen a bad day to ask. Because Erica had been feeling out of sorts for hours. She placed her half-eaten Subway roll back onto the reception desk. Then felt a sharp pain in her chest. When would she ever learn that chilli sauce gave her wicked heartburn? Her Billy would be cross with her when she told him.

She felt warmth sweep over her body and a bead of sweat lined her upper lip. She picked up her water bottle and took a swig. The phone rang and she answered it, listening incredulously. Someone was complaining about a dog barking the previous night. Whatever next? She was getting too old for this job. Always an issue with something or someone.

Ruth and DJ were moving towards her. With an old man. The same guy she had thrown out of the Library the other week. And was that a dog sitting in a pram? What on earth . . . ? She really didn't need this today of all days.

'Ah, howaya, Doc. Feeling better?' Kian asked. 'You didn't half give us all a fright.'

'Better than I've felt for years,' Tom replied.

'Dr O'Grady would like a room, please,' Ruth said.

'What's the story on the Christmas decorations before you check him in?' Kian asked. 'It's a miserable enough Christmas for us to be stuck here, but for the kids it's just not fair.'

Erica felt the blood pound in her ears to the point where she thought she might go deaf.

Aisling stepped forward. Had she been holding hands with the mouthy one just then? 'We'd like permission to decorate the Library, Erica. And the kitchen upstairs, too. It won't cost you any money.'

Kian put his hand up. 'Let's not be hasty, love. Erica might be feeling the Christmas cheer and want to donate a few euro.'

Erica held her own hand up, and said, 'I've no rooms for the likes of him. And I do not want any tacky decorations in my hotel.'

'Told you the auld bag was a bleeding scrooge through and through,' Kian said.

'Are you OK, Erica?' Ruth asked.

Erica had gone deathly white. She moved from the front desk and staggered towards the centre of the lobby. She began to stumble as a wave of dizziness hit her. 'I . . .' Her words ended in a gasp and she fell to the ground in an undignified heap.

'Is she locked, or what?' Kian asked.

Erica was astounded to find herself on the ground. She wasn't the type to faint. Was this a faint? She gasped as another pain shot up her arm into her chest. She found it hard to breathe. Erratic, irregular gasps filled the air. She looked around the lobby of her hotel and then felt the strangest sensation, like she was leaving her body. The last thing she saw was the tramp and Ruth running towards her.

'Erica, Erica, can you hear me?' Ruth shouted, kneeling beside her.

'Why doesn't she answer, Mam?' DJ said, his eyes wide open.

'She's having a bleeding heart attack,' Kian said. 'My mam was the same when she had hers.'

Aisling pulled Anna into her arms, in an attempt to shield her from the event unfolding in front of them.

Ruth watched in horror as Erica's body rose with each inhalation and then wheezed on the exhalation.

'Call 999,' Tom called out, then he gently moved Erica onto her back. He began CPR, thirty compressions to every two breaths.

'Someone stand on the street so that you can wave the paramedics in,' Ruth instructed.

'It is OK, Erica. You are going to be OK,' Ruth said, holding her hand. *Billy, she would want her Billy.*

'Kian, go find her Billy,' she shouted. If he existed, then this was the time for him to come forward. Ruth had never seen anyone die before. She began to shake as the real possibility that it was happening in front of her eyes overtook her.

'The paramedics are on the way,' Aisling said.

Then all at once pandemonium ensued. The infamous Billy ran in, paling at the sight in front of him. He took one look at Tom on the floor beside his beloved Erica and screamed, 'Get off her! What are you doing? Get off my Erica.'

'Billy, he is a doctor. It is OK,' Ruth said, moving aside so he could take up position beside his wife.

The sounds of sirens filled the lobby and the door swung open as the paramedics arrived.

When they kneeled beside Erica, Tom told them, 'I've been performing compressions for the past four minutes. Her name is Erica. This is her husband.'

It was the same team from a few weeks ago when he found Sheila's baby. Recognition flashed between them all.

'We'll take over now. Well done, mate. You've done great,' Steve said, then applied a shock to Erica's heart with a mobile defibrillator. The whole room jumped in sync with it, then held their breath, waiting for Erica to make one.

Declan checked Erica's pulse and said, 'Nothing.'

A second shock was administered to Erica's heart and the room swelled in silence and panic as they prayed for a miracle. Billy was mumbling the Lord's Prayer, on the ground beside them.

'Go again,' Declan said. And it was a case of third time lucky, because he shouted, 'We've got a pulse!'

The room erupted in a cheer and the paramedics loaded Erica onto a stretcher.

'You've done that before,' Declan said to Tom.

He nodded, then admitted, 'I used to be a doctor.'

'He saved your wife's life,' Declan told Billy. 'You were lucky he was here.'

'Once a doctor, always a doctor, mate,' Steve said, clapping Tom's shoulder.

'I will take care of The Silver Sands Lodge,' Ruth reassured Billy as he followed his wife out the door. She moved towards Dr O'Grady, who was being congratulated by the residents.

'Total legend!' Kian exclaimed.

'You were so calm. Incredible,' Aisling added.

'Way cool, Doc,' DJ said.

And Tom realised that he liked being Dr O'Grady again. He liked it a lot.

54

TOM

It turned out that time was not up for Erica. She'd had a mild heart attack. The doctors said it was a warning. Her mince pie-eating days were over.

Billy asked Ruth would she take over as temporary Hotel Manager, which she was happy to do. She was most surprised by this promotion, but apparently it was Erica's fervent wish. Erica would be in hospital for at least a week and Billy wanted to spend his time by her side. They were both shaken by their near miss.

Ruth handled the role of receptionist, manager and housekeeper beautifully. Partly because the hotel was quiet and partly because the staff rallied round to help out. When the chips were down, while they often moaned about Erica, they were all terribly fond of her. Aisling did some shifts on reception, too, picking up Erica's system quickly, which Billy was happy to agree to. 'Whatever you think best,' he told Ruth.

Tom did manage to check into room 19, which was the closest to the car-park door. He could bring Bette

Davis in and out for walks without going through reception. While Erica owed him her life, Ruth was not so sure what her policy was on dogs, paying guest or not.

Every morning Tom joined Ruth and DJ for breakfast. He did the school runs for Ruth, more than happy to ride the bus with DJ each day. This allowed Ruth to put in longer hours at the hotel. Tom loved his time with the kid. They talked about football and *Stranger Things*, which DJ, Ruth and he were now binge-watching together in their room. Some days they discussed the news, both here in Ireland and overseas. The kid was bright, and he soaked every word up. Tom had a suspicion that one day DJ would do something rather wonderful with his life.

One of the first things Ruth did when she was in control at the hotel was to speak to the chef about the leftover breakfast buffet food that went in the bin each day. It had bothered her for months.

'I plan to give it to the homeless,' she said. And he could not think of an argument as to why he should say no. Some days there was very little to donate, bar a few pastries. Other times, there were sausages and bacon, too. Under Ruth's instructions he packed it up into silver-foil parcels after the breakfast service each day. Tom would then take them to his park bench and wait for his buddies to come by.

Then Tom would spend his afternoons helping the kids with their homework in the Library. Bette flourished under the many cuddles and caresses she now had courtesy of the children. They adored her and she them.

But Tom also knew that what they had right now could be fleeting. Erica would come back, take over and more than likely ask him to leave. Ruth and DJ would get their council house. And he would go back to his park bench to live out the rest of his days. But that didn't have to be the only road for him? Did it?

Find another road home. That's what Ruth had said. He knew what he had to do. He would return to Wexford to face his demons so that he could move on.

'I think you should come with me,' he told Ruth when he filled her in on his plan. 'Maybe if you show DJ where he came from he won't feel so unhinged about his dad and that missing piece.'

'I do not want to see my mother,' Ruth said. When she became a mother she recognised the ugly truth of her relationship with her own parents. And she had come to accept that some things could not be changed. Marian and Alan might be her biological parents, but they were not her family.

'You don't have to. But you could show DJ where you started out. Where you met his father. That might help him come to terms with the fact that he'll likely never meet him,' Tom said.

Kian offered them his car, so the trio and Bette made their way down the N11 to their hometown, with Ruth behind the wheel. With each passing mile, Ruth and Tom became quieter, both lost in their memories.

Their first stop was Curracloe Beach. Ruth and DJ peered in through the locked glass doors of the arcade, which was now closed for the winter. She told DJ about the fortune-telling machine, Pat the ice-cream man and her many days spent here. Ruth and DJ climbed the dunes and found the exact same spot she had sat in when Dean came looking for her on that hot September day over a decade ago.

She held nothing back as she told DJ about that weekend and how they loved each other.

'Why didn't he come back?' DJ whispered into the wind.

'I have asked myself this many times. I wish I could answer it,' Ruth said. 'He would have been a good father. I am sure of it.'

'You are a good mother,' DJ whispered.

Ruth turned to him in surprise. 'You believe that?'

'I know that, Mam. If I had to choose a mother, I would choose you every time.'

'And I am enough for you?'

He nodded. Despite her emotions racing through her, making her arms fly and her head spin, Ruth found the words to say to her son what she thought every day. 'I love you, DJ.'

'I love you too, Mam,' DJ replied, reaching down to hold her hand. And as they watched the sea bounce back and forth from the beautiful sandy shore, he felt all his anger and resentment about his father disappear into the very air where his parents had met for the first time.

They said goodbye to the beach and drove by Ruth's mother's house, pulling into the side of the road opposite it.

'That's your family home?' DJ asked.

'It was never a home to me. Just somewhere I used to live,' Ruth answered.

'Where is home?' DJ asked.

'Wherever the people you love are,' Ruth replied.

'Then I'm home now,' DJ said, looking from Tom to Ruth.

Tom leaned over and said, 'There's nothing here for you. Let's go.' So they drove to Wexford town to see Tom's old house. He stood in front of the black railings and stared at the bricks and mortar that once housed everything in his world that he loved.

'Mikey died in there,' he whispered to Ruth and DJ.

Tom felt DJ's small hand move inside his big calloused one. And in this gesture, this kindness, the broken parts inside of Tom healed a little more. 'I wish you were my granddad.'

'Me too kid. Me too.'

Then they drove by Tom's old doctor's surgery, now run by Annemarie.

'Your mother caused a riot in there the first time she arrived into my surgery,' Tom said, and he delighted DJ by telling him all about the first time he met his mother.

'Do you want to go in, say hello?' Ruth asked when they had finished laughing.

Tom shook his head. Not now. But he thought that maybe another time he would like that very much.

Then Ruth parked up in the big car park outside Dunnes Stores and Tom told Ruth and DJ that he wanted a few hours to himself.

'What will you do, Doc?' DJ asked.

'I'm going to catch up with an old friend,' Tom said.

He hoped that he had not changed so much that his friend would no longer recognise him. Because with every passing day, he felt more and more like his old self. A man with a future once again. A man with a reason to live.

55

TOM

When Ruth and DJ walked away on the hunt for a whipped cone ice cream, Tom sat down on the monument in Redmond Square to gather his thoughts before he went to see his friend. As is sometimes the way, when you think of someone, you somehow magic them up in front of you. Because striding his way with a tray of coffee in hand was Ben. His friend. Time stood still as he moved closer and Tom felt the years fall away. Ben glanced in his direction, frowned, then swerved in a large unnecessary arc to avoid contact.

Disappointment crushed Tom. Ben hadn't recognised him. But then Tom put himself in Ben's shoes. Every face tells a story. What did his say to Ben? Red skin, weathered from sun and frost, older than his sixty-one years and unworthy of pause or recognition. That's what it said. He was one of the invisible.

You chose this life. You walked away from all who know you. You did that. This is on you.

Cathy's voice, nagging him in his head again. This truth

prickled him, made him uncomfortable. He had spent years only remembering certain parts of his past, but now he knew he had to remember everything. Including the day he left Wexford.

Tom looked at their super-king bed, which he'd shared with Cathy for two decades. They would start out every night in each other's arms and remain there all night. Even on the odd occasion they fought, the following morning they'd find themselves back together again, close, in a tangled mess of arms and legs. That bed represented love.

Not any more. Now all he saw was anger and pain.

He could no longer sleep in it. It was their bed. Not his. His sister suggested he change all the bed linen. He took the carefully co-ordinated sheets and pillow shams off the bed and replaced them with deliberately mismatched sets. He threw the cushions in the hot press and slammed the door shut.

When he sank his tired body into it, no matter the colour of the bed linen, it was still wrong. He was besmirching the memory of Cathy by changing her design choices. So he got up and stripped the bed bare, replacing the linen with Cathy's choice. He couldn't get it back the way it was meant to be. Her way. She never let him forget that.

'Are you happy now?' he asked the empty room, broken.

The walls began to shimmer and move. They were closing in on him. He picked up the small scratchy jumper pillow and rubbed it against his cheek. He packed a rucksack with some essentials, placing the pillow into it. He closed the door softly on their bedroom and walked downstairs to the kitchen. He checked the fridge. An empty milk carton, half a block of cheddar cheese, hardened and discoloured, a pear, a tub of cherry tomatoes and six cans of Heineken. He threw the contents into a black sack and placed that in the bin outside, which was waiting for collection later that day. He began to walk into Wexford town.

'Hey, Tom, how are you, mate?'

It was Ben. His friend reached out and patted Tom's shoulder, awkwardly, but none the less in kindness.

'Hello.' Tom found his voice, then went to move on.

'I almost didn't recognise you.' Ben gestured towards Tom's face.

Tom rubbed his newly grown beard. 'Shaving hasn't been top of my list lately. Didn't seem much point to it.'

Ben nodded. He understood.

They stood in awkward silence for a moment. Tom had got used to these uncomfortable moments. No one knew what to say to him. And in truth there was nothing anyone could say that could help take away his pain.

'How have you been?' Ben asked, then looked stricken as he continued, babbling, 'Stupid question, sorry.'

Tom felt both sorry for him and irritated by him in equal measures. This here, this awkward sympathy that he seemed to evoke whenever he came close to someone who knew him and his story, was intolerable. It was one of the reasons why he wanted to leave.

'It's just . . . we all worry about you,' Ben ended.

'I know,' Tom answered, and he worked hard to find a smile to reassure the man.

'You off somewhere?' Ben asked, nodding towards his rucksack.

Tom had forgotten about that. 'Yes. I'm getting away for a bit.'

'Good idea. A break would do you the world of good. Where you off to?'

Tom shrugged. 'I've not worked that out yet.'

Ben laughed, then stopped when he realised Tom was serious. His face scrunched up for a moment, then he continued, 'Listen, you know we have that place in Spain. Why don't you get a flight out there and take a few weeks in the sun? I can get the keys for you straight away. Come back to my place for a coffee and you can even look at flights there. Ryanair do great deals into Alicante airport.'

'Thank you.' Tom felt a lump clog his throat, making him gulp loudly.

'For nothing,' Ben replied. 'I think of you often and when I do . . .' He paused for a moment, then continued, 'Well, let's just say, I don't know how . . .' He stopped again.

Tom understood. He couldn't find words to articulate the horror of his life either.

'So what do you say?' Ben asked.

'I say thank you. I appreciate your offer, more than you can realise. But I'll pass. For now,' he added when he saw the disappointment on Ben's face. He wanted to help; he got that.

They stood in awkward silence for a few moments. Tom hoisted his rucksack on his shoulder and said, 'I'll be off then.'

Ben raised his hand to say goodbye, then shouted after him. 'Wait!'

Tom turned back to look at his friend.

And Ben's last words, which were in the end a prophecy were, 'If you don't find something to light up the darkness, Tom, you'll get lost in the shadows.'

56

TOM

Now

Ghosts of a past almost forgotten continued to whisper to Tom as he made his way along the uneven cobblestones of Wexford town. His feet ached with each step he made. He shivered as another cold rush of air bit his cheeks and nose. He watched the fur on Bette Davis's body ripple. Sensing eyes on her, his faithful dog and companion paused mid-step and glanced his way.

'That's my gal,' Tom murmured, gently ruffling her coat.

He forged ahead, walking towards South Main Street. When he arrived at Deerings Solicitors he paused for a moment to collect his thoughts. Intuitive to her master's indecision, Bette Davis pulled on her leash, trying to move away from the possible danger that lurked on the other side of the door.

'It'll be fine,' he said to Bette, more to reassure himself than her. Ben hadn't recognised him. What if he turned him away? What if he said, 'Too late, mate'?

He leaned his shoulder into the heavy wrought iron that led to the large open-plan reception area. They both scoured the room, Bette sniffing the carpeted floors and Tom noting that the previously magnolia walls of his memories were now dove grey. Accent mustard shades were evident in all the soft furnishings.

You trained me well, Cathy. Years later and he still recognised a well-placed scatter cushion.

A woman in her fifties with greying fair hair looked up. She was new. But there again Ben went through receptionists faster than Trump did his cabinet. She frowned as she watched Tom make his way towards her.

I'm making a lot of people frown today.

The woman's eyes opened further, wide with shock when she realised that not only was a bedraggled man walking towards her but he had a dog by his side for good measure. It took her only a moment to recover and she stood up, leaning forward in consternation. She placed her two hands on the desk in front of her and said, 'Get out. You've no business coming in here. And you certainly can't bring that . . . that dog . . . into Mr Deering's office!' Her voice rose in indignation with each spoken word. Tom stood his ground. When she realised her words were falling on deaf ears, she moved towards them both, shooing them.

Tom sighed but it was a sigh of acceptance rather than annoyance. He took no offence from her reaction. He had long since hardened himself to the fact that people in the main judged others by their appearance. Looks matter. Clothes matter. It was difficult to ignore a person's appearance and not make a snapshot social judgement.

She was simply basing her opinion on how he presented himself to the world.

The receptionist filled in the blanks, as was human nature and without even knowing she had done so, decided that Tom was a down-and-out, possibly dangerous but at the very least, up to no good. Her eyes finished their inspection and his offence slid away, replaced by shame.

Tom's voice was gruffer than normal. 'I have an appointment.' He made an effort to keep his gravelly voice low, soft and he hoped, calm. There was no satisfaction in frightening anyone, least of all this woman. The world they lived in, it often seemed like there was more evil than good to be found. He took a step backwards in an effort to reassure her, then continued, 'I'm here to see Ben.'

'That's Mr Deering to you,' she replied.

Tom pointed to his dog, who was sitting quietly by his side, enjoying the show. 'I can't leave Bette Davis outside. She doesn't like to be on her own. She's a good dog, though, house trained. And I can assure you that she doesn't bite.' He paused for a moment.

In for a penny in for a pound.

'And, for that matter, neither do I.'

His statement threw the woman. A nod acknowledged his intended joke. 'Your dog is called Bette Davis?'

'Her big eyes made me think of the song. My wife sang it a lot,' Tom said.

'Well, her hair is almost Harlow gold, I suppose,' she replied, referring to the song's lyrics.

Tom searched her desk until he found a sign with her name on it. *Janice Sutton.*

'What kind of a dog is she?' Janice asked.

Tom shrugged. 'I'm guessing she's a labrador and red setter cross. But that's just a guess.'

Janice nodded, taking in Bette's strawberry-gold glossy coat and dark-brown eyes.

'I'm not here to cause trouble, Ms Sutton. I just want to see Mr Deering.'

Janice felt herself soften. This man threw her. His voice didn't match his appearance. She took a closer look. He was of indeterminate age, but she guessed in his sixties. She noticed that he didn't look away; he accepted her scrutiny. In her two years as Mr Deering's personal assistant she'd never been faced with a situation like this. Even if it were true that he did have an appointment, they couldn't allow the dog in. Whatever next? Clients bringing their children to appointments?

Janice picked up her phone and pushed a button. 'Mr Deering. Your five o'clock is here . . .'

Moments later, a door to the right of her desk opened and Ben walked out. The two men looked at each other, both sizing up the cut of the other. Tom thought he saw a flash of recognition but it was fleeting. It might have been from earlier on the street. Ben's eyes rested on Bette Davis and he frowned again. Like before, he looked away. Tom felt disappointment nip him again.

Look at me, Ben. Don't look through me. Look at me.

And he did just that. As if Tom's thoughts had transmitted through the air between them in the office into his brain.

Ben moved closer and said, 'I'm Ben Deering.'

'I know who you are,' Tom said. *Look at me.*

The penny dropped at last and recognition dawned on his friend's face. 'Tom?'

57

TOM

Tom smiled at Ben, his old friend, and tried to summon the man he used to be. He felt vulnerable. Unsure.

'Is it you?' Ben's voice had gone up an octave on his question.

Tom had forgotten that Ben had a habit of becoming a soprano at times of supreme excitement.

'The one and same. It's really good to see you again, Ben.' Tom realised the truth of this statement and it nagged his conscience.

Ben found the use of his body and leaned in to clasp Tom's shoulders, laughing as he did. 'I'm so sorry I didn't recognise you straight away. Forgive me, it's been a long day. I can't tell you how good it is to see you. Really good to see you,' he repeated.

'You know this man?' Janice made no attempt to hide her shock at the new development. She looked between the two men, who were now grinning at each other like long-lost brothers.

Ben turned to his receptionist and said, 'Indeed I do

know him. This is Dr O'Grady. A dear friend of mine. You can finish up for the day. I'll lock up when we're done.' He shook his head as he muttered, 'Who would have thought it? You never know what the day will end up with, do you? Come on into my office . . .'

'What about Bette Davis?' Tom asked. 'I won't leave her outside. She gets nervous without me. If Bette isn't welcome, I'll have to leave, too.'

Ben walked over and looked down at the dog, stroking her velvety ears. 'Cathy was always singing that song, wasn't she?'

'You remember,' Tom said.

'Of course I remember. We are friends,' Ben said. 'Come on, Bette Davis. Bring your lord and master with you. We've a lot to catch up on.'

'Hollywood royalty or not, if that mutt makes a mess, you're cleaning it up,' Janice called after them.

'I bet she keeps you on your toes,' Tom said.

'I'd be lost without her. I'm sorry if she was rude to you.'

'I liked her. She reminds me of Breda,' Tom said. He sat down on one of the two leather chairs that were positioned in front of Ben's large Victorian writing desk. He placed his rucksack at his feet. Bette Davis dropped to the ground and rested her head on Tom's feet as she always did.

'How long has it been since we've spoken? Gosh, it must be . . .' Ben's forehead creased as his mind tried to work out the maths.

'Nearly ten years,' Tom replied.

'That long? I didn't recognise you, Tom. The hair, the beard . . .'

Tom laughed. 'I woke up one morning and realised I had started to resemble Santa quite a bit.'

'Without the paunch.' Ben nodded at Tom's skinny frame.

'You, on the other hand, haven't changed at all,' Tom said.

'Less hair.' Ben fidgeted with his receding hairline. 'Want to send some of your long locks my way?'

Ben's laugh was a little too loud, heightened by his nerves. He had no idea why Tom was here, and now that he'd got over the surprise he was thrown by his arrival. 'I never connected the dots when I saw your name in my diary. I'm sorry.'

'Nothing to be sorry about. It must be a shock for you to see someone that's not been in your sight or mind for years.'

'I wouldn't say that,' Ben replied. 'I've thought of you now and then. Especially around the milestone moments of the boys . . . you know . . .'

Birthdays, graduation, first kiss, first pint – oh yes, Tom knew.

'When did you get back to Wexford?' Ben asked.

'This morning.'

'You should have called to let me know. I would have met you as soon as you got here.' Reproach made Ben's voice thin.

Tom felt a flash of shame. When Cathy died something snapped in his mind and he pushed everything from his past life away. Including his friends. But sitting here in this chair, the same chair he'd sat in many times before a decade ago, made him question everything he thought to be true. He missed his friend.

'Will you come home with me this evening, stay the night?' Ben asked, trying to block out the worried face of his wife, Orla, whom he knew would be unsure about having this version of his friend stay.

'I appreciate the offer, I really do, but I'm good. I'm going back to Dublin this evening.'

'Are you in trouble, Tom? Is that why you're here?' Ben asked, leaning in towards him. He could see the end of a bruise on his face.

Tom shook his head. 'I do need your help, though,' he replied.

'You need money?' Ben opened a drawer in his desk and pulled out a black leather wallet. 'How much do you need?'

'No!' Tom held his hand up in protest. 'Thank you, but no, I have money. It's a legal matter that I need your help with.'

Ben laughed, looking at the sign on his desk, *Deering's – Solicitors, Notaries, Public.* 'Ha! Sometimes the cat really is just sitting on the mat, eh?'

'Or the dog,' Tom replied, grinning and looking down at Bette.

'How can I help?'

'It's a long story,' Tom said.

'Well, I've got all the time in the world. You were my last appointment of the week so we won't be interrupted. I've a single malt here that's pretty decent.' He stood up and walked to a cabinet that sat to his right. 'Like the old days. Do you remember?'

'I remember. I'll join you in a drink,' Tom said. How many times had they sat in this very room, talking politics, sports, family and life? All with a single malt in hand.

Ben opened the cabinet up and revealed a row of crystal glasses and several bottles of whiskey. Tom had never been much of a drinker and, despite any preconceived notions of a drunken homeless man, he couldn't remember the last time he'd had a drink. He didn't like the way it dulled his senses.

'I've never found anyone else worth ending the week with,' Ben said softly, his eyes glassy with emotion. Then he looked away embarrassed, rifling through the bottles, deciding on which drink to choose. 'This single malt has sat in the cabinet for years, untouched.'

'Don't open it for me!' Tom protested.

'Sure, who else would I keep it for?' Ben cracked the top open, lifting the bottle to his nose to sniff. 'Aah . . . yes, I think this will do nicely.' He poured two measures into the cut-crystal glasses.

'Denny Crane!' Tom said, lifting his glass in the toast they always made in tribute to a much-loved character in *Boston Legal*, a show Ben always loved.

'Denny Crane,' Ben replied laughing, lifting his own.

How many times had Tom and Ben sat side by side, on a Friday evening, once their last client and patient left? This inside joke made them smile every time back then and it still did now, ten years later. Tom once again felt something niggle at his conscience. When he'd walked out of his life, he'd not thought of the impact on his friends. As he looked into the amber liquid, he remembered so many times where Ben had been the best of friends. Listening to his guilt over Mikey's death. His worry over

Cathy's declining state of mind each time he lost her to the silence of her dreams.

Tom took a sip of his whiskey to gather his thoughts. 'You were right, you know. I did lose myself in the shadows, like you predicted.'

'I know, mate.'

'But I've found something that's brought me back.'

Surprise flickered in Ben's eyes, followed by delight. 'Can I ask who she is?'

'It's not a she, it's a them,' Tom answered, finding a grin landing on his face for no reason other than the fact that he was thinking about Ruth and DJ.

'Tell me everything,' Ben said.

'I'm not sure where to start.'

'At the beginning. That's as good a place as any.'

Tom took a deep breath and began to talk.

58

RUTH

The realisation that the chance of a happy-ever-after house before Christmas was off the table for most of the social housing residents of The Silver Sands Lodge gave them all the motivation they needed to start decorating. They had got side-tracked after Erica collapsed, and had lost the inclination to follow through on their plans, but now, with the holidays looming closer, Operation Christmas Makeover was in full swing in the Library.

A few lucky ones would spend Christmas Day with their families. Some had unofficially left the hotel already. But for Ruth, DJ, Tom, Aisling, Anna, Kian and Cormac, the hotel would be their home for the holidays.

They were going to have a big Christmas dinner, *Waltons* style, in the Library.

Kian kicked open the door whistling 'White Christmas'. He was hoisting a large Christmas tree over his shoulder.

'Where did you get that?' Ruth asked.

'Ask no questions and I'll tell no lies,' he responded

with a wink. Cormac trailed behind him carrying a box of brightly coloured baubles.

Aisling and Anna followed moments later. They were rarely apart these days. She turned on Christmas FM on her phone app and put the volume up to its highest. As they tacked tinsel to the ceiling and wrapped more around the tree, they all began to sing along to 'Grandma Got Run Over by a Reindeer'.

Kian's phone rang and he told them, 'With a bit of luck this is my mate John. He's sorting some lights for us. Back in a minute.'

'You look so happy,' Ruth said to Aisling, who watched him leave with adoring eyes.

'Is it that obvious? I didn't think I would feel like this again,' Aisling said. 'It's the real deal, Ruth. It really is.'

'He is your soul mate,' Ruth said solemnly. She looked over to the kids where much merriment was underway. Cormac and DJ were busy wrapping a piece of tinsel around Anna, who was giggling hysterically. Ruth suspected – correctly – that both boys had a crush on her.

The door burst open again, banging off the wall. 'It's a Christmas bleeding miracle,' Kian shouted. His face was flushed bright red.

Aisling ran to his side. 'You got the lights?'

'Guess again. Better than that,' Kian said, grabbing her by the hands.

'You won the lotto,' Aisling joked.

'Lower your expectations, love. Not that bleeding good,' Kian replied. 'But honest to goodness it's deadly, it really is. Because never mind your Christmas number one, Ed Sheeran, my number has only gone and made it to the top spot.'

'You're not making any sense,' Aisling said.

'He rarely does,' Ruth replied.

'Ladies, ladies, brace yourselves. The Kiano has only been offered a house. That was the council on the blower. They've got a house for me with three bedrooms and a garden!'

'No!' Aisling screamed, jumping up and down.

A strangled sob came from the mass of tinsel in the corner where Cormac was now entangled, revenge dished by Anna.

'Cormac lad, get over here. They've only offered us that house in Donabate that yer woman Melissa turned down,' Kian said.

Cormac looked at his father in disbelief, shards of silver tinsel hanging off his ear. 'This isn't a joke, Da? For real, we've got a house? A real house?'

'Yes, son. A real house! Out in the bleeding sticks, too. Looks like we're going to be culchies. Get your wellies, lad, get your wellies!' Kian pulled his son into his embrace.

'You have taken it?' Aisling said, tears in her eyes. 'Course you have taken it. You have to take it. It's wonderful news.'

Kian started to laugh. 'I never thought in a million years this would happen.'

'It's going to be very quiet around here without you,' Aisling said, smiling bravely even though she suddenly felt very tearful.

'It's got three bedrooms. And has a "bijou" garden. Which means in reality the garden is the size of a postage stamp. But sure, what harm?' Kian grabbed Cormac's shoulders and said, 'It's walking distance to the schools. And they are meant to be the business out there. Gillian was at pains to tell me it has a regular train service into Dublin. We can be city slickers every day, if we want.'

'Sounds perfect,' Aisling said.

'Not quite,' Kian replied. He disentangled himself from Cormac and stood face to face with Aisling. 'But I know how it could be.'

'How?' Aisling whispered, then crossed her fingers behind her back.

'If you come with me, that's how. The kids can have a room each. That's if you don't mind sharing with me, eh, eh?' He nudged her.

'Are you serious?' Aisling asked. He nodded at once. 'We'd have to talk to the children.'

'Forget about them for a minute, love. This can't be about the kids. I made that mistake the last time. I thought I could make someone love me for Cormac's sake. And we all know how that worked out. I love the bones of *you*, Aisling. I don't want to go anywhere without you and Anna. But the question is, do you want to come with me?'

'Oh, Kian,' Aisling whispered, covering her face in her hands. Was this really happening to her? Her!

'I mean it. I love you. And if you let me take care of you and Anna I promise I'll never let you down. I'll never walk away and leave you on your own. Together we can move bleeding mountains. What do you say?' Kian was wiping away tears furiously with his sleeve but they refused to stop coming.

'We've only been dating a few months,' Aisling said, but she inched her way closer to him.

'What's the point in waiting? I know how I feel. That's not going to change,' Kian said.

'Say yes! Say yes!' both Anna and Cormac shouted, already on board with the idea.

'YES!' Aisling shrieked, and then suddenly Kian was jumping up and down, spinning her around in a circle, then running over to Ruth to give her a spin, too. 'That's two bleeding Christmas miracles! Can you believe it?'

'I have only one thing to say to you, Kian . . .' Ruth said. She paused for a moment, then finished, 'You jammy fecker!'

Kian bellowed laughter, remembering their earlier conversation when he told her to say that very thing should he ever get a home. 'That I am. That I am.'

'Is there a party on and no one thought to invite me?' Erica's voice cut in. She hobbled in on her crutch, smiling at them all, not in the least bit put out. 'This place is beginning to look very festive. We have some decorations in the attic. I'll get my Billy to get them for you later on.'

'Take a weight off,' Kian said, pulling a chair out for her. 'Don't want you keeling over again!'

'What's all the excitement about?' Erica asked.

'Well, apart from seeing your lovely face again,' Kian joked, 'I got some good news.' He turned to Aisling and said, 'You tell her.'

'No, you tell her,' Aisling replied.

Ruth tutted and said, 'For goodness' sake, I shall tell her! Kian and Cormac got offered a house. And Aisling and Anna are going to move in with them.'

'Oh, my,' Erica said. 'Well, isn't that wonderful? As I said to my Billy last night, love is all around, you just have to open your eyes to see it.'

'That is quite a beautiful sentiment,' Ruth said.

'I sometimes surprise myself,' Erica said. 'And speaking of surprises, there's one coming for you, too . . .'

On cue the door creaked again and Tom walked in, leading Bette Davis beside him.

Anna, Cormac and DJ fell to their knees to grab some licks and kisses from their pal.

'Kian, can we get a dog like her when we go to Donabate?' Anna begged.

'Course we can, love,' Kian said. 'Look at that, she's already got me wrapped around her finger, what?'

Erica said, 'I wish my Billy were here, but he's a martyr to his sciatica. He's out in our mews having a little rest. Are you going to add to the celebrations, Dr O'Grady? Go on, tell them your news.'

Tom beckoned Ruth and DJ over to him and they sat down, side by side, around the homework table. 'When I left Wexford ten years ago, I had no plan, just a sense that I had to leave. Over the years, I moved from county to county based on whims or whispers in my ear. And then one day I ended up here in Fairview. I didn't understand what this whole journey was about until recently. Then it all became clear. I believe I've been moving towards this moment, to you and DJ, all along.'

'Are you getting all mushy on us?' DJ asked, pretending to shoot himself.

'Brace yourself, kid, because I am. Last week I remembered something Cathy used to say. "You can change the world by helping one person at a time."'

DJ moved his chair closer to his mam, who was beginning to pop, pop, pop.

'That's what you do, Ruth. You help people. It's extra-ordinary,' Tom said.

Murmurs of agreement echoed through the room, the truth of his words in every change made in this very room they stood in.

'And you helped me most of all. The darkness has gone. The sun is back, shining bright for me. That's because of each of you,' Tom said. He gently patted each of their knees.

DJ started to shuffle awkwardly in his seat. He was mortified by Tom's words in front of his friends. And he was beginning to feel all emotional. There was no way he was crying with Anna watching him.

'Now it's my turn to make a difference. Cathy has done her job and guided me here to you both,' Tom said.

Erica said, 'I thank God that he guided Dr O'Grady my way. My Billy said to me last week that he thought he'd lost me. And I won't lie, I thought I was a gonner, too. I get quite emotional when I think about it all.'

'I'm happy I was close by when you needed me,' Tom said.

'Well, I don't mind telling you that it put things into sharp perspective for me. As my Billy said, what are we doing wasting what little time we have here on our own, when we have a daughter and grandchildren over in Maryland, just waiting with open arms and hearts for us? And then just like in a movie – that's what I said to my Billy, just like in a movie – the phone rang. A solicitor. Asking us if we were willing to sell this place. Imagine that. Well, I don't mind telling you we both got quite the shock by that call.'

'You are selling The Silver Sands Lodge?' Kian asked.

'Yes. In fact, the sale is already made,' Erica replied.

'Thank the bleeding stars we're getting out of here, love,' Kian said. 'We'd be on the streets.' Then he turned to Ruth and added, 'Jaysus, sorry, love. Listen, if they don't put you anywhere decent you can come and bunk in with us. We won't let you down.'

'Absolutely,' Aisling said, squeezing her hand.

Ruth could not speak. All she could do was pull at her hands nervously, pop, pop, popping her knuckles some more. She couldn't breathe.

DJ asked, 'Does this mean we have to leave here, Mam?'

Odd whispered to her, *It will be OK.*

No it won't, Odd. All my hoping and persevering has been for nothing.

But she was wrong because then the next thing Tom uttered changed her world for ever.

'I've bought The Silver Sands Lodge. The solicitor was acting on my behalf.'

Gasps of shock came from every part of the room.

'You bought this place?' Ruth eventually squeaked. She never in a million years could have dreamed this. 'With what? How?'

'Contrary to popular belief, I never lost my money gambling.' Tom gave a pointed look to Kian, who started to study the carpet intently.

'I had a house, flat and surgery once. Which each sold for a nice sum. The money has been sitting in an account since then. I've had no use for it. Didn't want it. Until now.'

'You've been sleeping on a park bench with all that

418

money just sitting in a bank? You are one crazy dude.' Kian was incredulous.

Tom spoke softly, trying to make them understand. 'Ten years ago I walked out of my home, with only a rucksack on my back. Home had become a living hell for me. Every cup and plate, every soft furnishing, every scuff on the floors from the wear and tear of life, every scent and smell of Cathy and Mikey infused into the very fabric of the bricks and mortar, tortured me. I didn't know how to live any more. The new normal that had been thrust upon me was intolerable. And I knew that if I stayed one more day it would be the end of me.'

Ruth said, 'When I get upset or scared, I have to put my headphones on, to switch off the white noise. Living outside was that for you. A pair of headphones.'

'But then I met you and DJ again. And day by day, I began to realise that I didn't need headphones any more,' Tom said.

'You really can't judge a book by its cover,' Aisling said, shaking her head in disbelief.

'I knew there was something about Dr O'Grady the moment I met him. I said that to my Billy. There's something about that man.'

Ruth replied, 'You said he was a tramp.'

'Not in those words. No,' Erica blustered.

Kian walked over to Tom and said, 'Well, if you are looking for some staff, Doc, I'm on the lookout for a job. I could be a deadly porter. I did loads around here when herself was in hospital.'

'You need to discuss that with the new owner. Not me.' Tom placed his hands over Ruth's and said, 'I asked you what your wish was a few months ago. I'm making it come true. You have your own home that nobody can take away from you. For Christmas. For ever. The Silver Sands Lodge is yours, Ruth Wilde.'

Ruth was not sure who was screaming but the noise in the room was at fever-pitch level.

'Things like this do not happen in real life,' Ruth said, feeling her hands begin to fly.

Tom said with great tenderness, 'I told you your mother was wrong. You do get to have a happy-ever-after. Just not the one you thought you were going to get.'

'As I said to my Billy, if anyone can run this place after we go, it's Ruth Wilde,' Erica said. 'You might be as odd as dishwater sometimes, but you are a right little worker. And I've never seen anyone take to a set of rules as much as you. A lot to be said for that.'

Ruth remained silent.

Aisling said, 'You changed us all, Ruth. You made a difference in all of our lives. One room at a time. And now it's your turn. Tell her, Kian.' She looked over to her boyfriend, who had his head in his hands. 'Kian, are you crying?'

Kian had not had many exceptional days in his life. Most were average, with the occasional good one thrown in. But today was beyond exceptional. And it had quite undone him. 'That's three bleeding Christmas miracles.'

While everyone began chatting excitedly about this news, DJ watched his mam panic. He rummaged through her handbag and pulled out her headphones, ready to switch on Westlife to help calm her down.

Tom put a hand on his shoulder and said, 'Wait a

moment, kid.' He turned to the room and said quietly, 'Everyone, bring it down a notch. Give Ruth a minute to take this in.' He laid his two weathered hands on top of hers. Then DJ placed his two hands on top of Tom's. A tower of love in that pile of hands. The room fell silent and waited until Ruth's breathing normalised.

'I am not dreaming?' Ruth eventually asked.

'It's all true. I promise. If you would prefer to sell up, that is perfectly fine. But I think The Lodge suits you,' Tom said.

Ruth closed her eyes and took a deep breath. Odd whispered in her ear, jubilant that he was right. *Remember what I've told you for years. Be happy, persevere.*

Ruth wanted to say so much but, as always, her mind got tangled up and she could not get the words out. She looked at her family and friends, all watching her with love.

'Say something, Ruthie,' Kian said.

'I suppose if I am the owner here, this is one job I cannot be sacked from!' Ruth joked.

Be happy. Persevere. Yes, she rather thought she would.

EPILOGUE

Six months later

As is often the way, one good deed sets off a chain reaction of further good deeds. Tom's gift to Ruth and DJ made changes for all the residents of the first floor in The Silver Sands Lodge, past, present and future.

With a fixed address that nobody could take away, Ruth called Mr O'Dowd, DJ's teacher, to ask for help in selecting a new school. He began his first term after the Christmas break. Once again DJ could walk to and from his school. But now he did so with Tom and Bette Davis by his side.

Ruth said goodbye to the Queen Bee Denise and her mean girlfriends, happy never to see them again. She still laughed when she remembered their faces as they learned she was the new owner of a boutique hotel.

Ruth discovered that she was very good at being a hotel landlady. Her first official act of management was to cut up the laminated rules. Social housing residents were now allowed to access the hotel in any way they wanted. And they were welcome in the bar and restaurant, too. The homework club continued in the Library and an unofficial buddy system grew where parents took turns to supervise the children, so that they could have a break if they needed one.

Raising a child took a village. Simple as.

Ruth did introduce a couple of rules, though, which were non-negotiable. She formalised her No Food Waste policy. Some leftovers went to Fairview Park, to Mr Bones and anyone else that needed it. And some went to the Peter McVerry Trust and Focus Ireland, who made sure it made its way into the hands of rough sleepers, courtesy of their volunteers. Tom held unofficial consultations on his park bench and made 'house' calls to those that needed him.

The second rule Ruth set was to keep her old hotel room vacant. She filled the wardrobe with a range of clothes she acquired from the St Vincent de Paul charity shop. She kept the bathroom stocked with shampoo and soap. And when Tom came across someone who needed a bed for the night, they were invited in. No questions asked.

Erica and 'my Billy' moved to America, as they said they would. They got to Maryland just in time to spend Christmas with their daughter and grandchildren. Erica stayed in touch and sent regular instructions on how Ruth should run the hotel. And more often than not, her advice was helpful.

Ruth and DJ moved into the mews that sat at the back of the hotel. Tom listened to them both list all the reasons why he should unpack his rucksack for one final time and move in with them. He didn't need persuading, though. Because now when he closed his eyes he saw not only Cathy and Mikey, he saw Ruth and DJ, too. Being inside did not hurt or torment him. And when he walked into his new bedroom, sitting on top of the bed was a pair of navy Converse runners. He took his boots off and threw them into the bin as DJ cheered behind him.

For Ruth, having a kitchen of her own once more eliminated a lot of stress from her day. It was exactly as she liked it. Everything in its place. She got to eat mashed potatoes any time she liked. And most evenings, while she prepared dinner, she watched Dr O'Grady and DJ do their homework together. She did not take any of this for granted. She knew how lucky they were, that they found each other, just at the right time. Odd Thomas still spoke to her, but his visits were infrequent. And that was OK, too.

Tom never did find Cathy's old cushion, but maybe that was how it was meant to be. There were a lot of things he had to let go of, and that was one of them. But Ruth and DJ surprised him at Christmas with a wonderful gift. They bought him a new stethoscope, with a new engraving on the silver chest-piece.

A fine doctor but an even finer man. With love from your family, Ruth and DJ

And that's what they were. A family. Maybe an unlikely one, who found each other in the most extraordinary of ways. But one that worked so very well.

DJ loved having his own room again, but every now and then he climbed into Ruth's bed during the night and wrapped his arms around her. He still had those unanswered questions about his father, but he reconciled himself to the fact that he would probably never know what happened to Dean. And that was not his mother's fault. His Christmas present to Ruth was to frame his father's fortune from the day Ruth and Dean first met. Tom helped him. And it now sat behind reception. Ruth and DJ both liked this. It was as if Dean was with them in some small way.

Ava and Brian had a little girl, who looked a lot like her mama. And Ava got her wish too, because she got to bring her baby home to a crib in their new flat. They were offered this four months before they became a family of three. Every week, Ava called in to see Ruth and Aisling, and they would laugh and giggle as only friends can, who have seen both good and bad times together.

Aisling and Kian were on the payroll now. Aisling worked mornings on reception. And Kian worked weekends as the night porter and did odd jobs during the week, as their maintenance man. Their bright smiling faces and quick banter made all new residents feel welcome when they walked through the front door. Then when they took the train home to Donabate, they continued smiling, knowing they were going home to each other and their children.

Ruth got used to having her photo taken too. And when Aisling posted a selfie on Instagram of Ruth, DJ, Tom and Bette Davis, standing in front of their newly painted hotel, with a correctly hung sign, the photo went viral.

This Aspie mum, young boy and doctor may have been homeless, but together they changed their world and are now the owners of the The Silver Sands Lodge! #miracle #changetheworld #findyourtribe #family #friends #love #homelessness

It was the exact feel-good story that the world needed. Within weeks it had been shared on social media nearly a thousand times. Then the *Irish Daily Mail* sent their journalist Linda Maher to interview Ruth and Tom. She sensitively teased their story from them, layer by layer.

Three homeless people and a dog have found their tribe in the most unusual of places.

Homelessness does not have one face. Most assume it means a rough sleeper with dirty fingernails and clothes, living in a cardboard box with nothing but a bottle of Jameson for company. And yes, it can be that. But it can also be a well-dressed woman who leaves her hostel early every morning to teach our children in school. It can be the teenage boy who flees a dangerous family home, preferring his luck on the streets rather than that with his abusive family. Or it can be an average family, just like mine or yours, who have found themselves with no place to call home.

Yes, homelessness has many faces.

I'd like to introduce you to three of them.

Rough sleeper Dr Tom O'Grady who called a park bench his home. Aspie mother Ruth Wilde and her young son, DJ, who found themselves living in emergency housing in The Silver Sands Lodge Hotel. Homelessness changed each of them. It gave them something that they had been missing from their lives for a long time. A family. A tribe. A place to call Home.

Together these three ordinary people continue to do extraordinary things in The Silver Sands Lodge Hotel, that they now own and run together. This is their story . . .

The feature along with a photograph of them standing proudly side by side, made the front page of the *Irish Daily Mail*'s weekend magazine, *YOU*.

And that's when the biggest chain reaction of all happened. One afternoon, as the sun was just setting, a man with navy-blue trainers walked into reception. 'Hello, I'm looking for Ruth Wilde.'

Ruth had never been one for 'feelings', but she was suddenly aware that something important was about to happen.

Dean?

Ruth stood up and walked out from behind the reception desk, as if in a trance.

'You've grown,' Ruth said, her heart hammering so loudly she thought the whole hotel could hear it. He was taller by several inches than she remembered.

'And you are thinner, too,' she continued, puzzled, because he was the same but he was different.

Could it really be him? Ruth raised her eyes to look at her soul mate. The disappointment was crushing.

'I thought you were someone else.'

'I've been mistaken for my brother many times,' the man replied. 'I'm Finn. It's very nice to meet you, Ruth.'

Ruth had dozens of questions running around her head. The room began to spin as she tried to understand what was happening. Why was Dean's brother here? Where was Dean?

'Dean talked about you incessantly. He came home after that weekend in Curracloe a changed man. He said he was going to marry you.'

Ruth watched the door, waiting for her soul mate to return.

'Every day he told me something else about you and your lost weekend, as he called it. He read out every text message you sent him.'

Ruth walked past Finn, out onto the street, looking for him. Had Dean sent Finn in to check out her reaction? She ran through the many scenarios that had kept her awake at night over the years, as to why Dean went missing. Amnesia, illness, kidnapping.

'He's not out there,' Finn said, standing behind her.

Ruth knew bad news was coming her way. She supposed she always knew it had to be like this. Because despite what her mother said, if it were anything other than bad news, Dean would have found her.

'Dean is dead. I'm so sorry, Ruth. I really am.'

When she'd watched Dean leave her driveway in Wexford all those years ago, she began counting the hours until he came back. And she had been counting ever since. All these wasted hours, weeks, months and years, counting, waiting, for a man who was dead.

She felt her arms start to fly, her breath getting heavier.

Finn led her back inside to the brown leather chairs

that sat in the lobby. She wanted Tom. And, as if by magic, he appeared. Tom took one look at her face and walked over to sit beside the girl who had become his daughter. 'Take a moment. It's OK.' He placed his hands over hers and the warmth of them calmed her until she found her voice once more.

'This is Dean's brother,' Ruth said. The questions she had lived with, unanswered for a decade, were finally getting their reply.

'Where is he?' Tom asked Finn, hovering his arm around the back of Ruth, ready to protect her from whatever was coming her way.

'He died in a car crash on his way home from work, ten years ago. They said he was killed instantly, which is something. The other driver was on his phone. A split second, that's all it was. A split second of inattention on the road to take my brother's life.'

A split second to change everything.

Tom watched Ruth process the news and wished he could find a way to make it easier.

Emotion floored her as the abandonment and loss of over a decade crashed down.

Finn pulled out a folded magazine page from his pocket. 'A friend saw this magazine article and phoned me up saying there was a kid in the paper who looked just like me and Dean. It stunned me when he showed it to me. It was like looking at a photograph of my brother when he was DJ's age. I'm not mistaken, am I? Your son, DJ, is Dean's son, too?'

Ruth whispered, 'I named him after his father. Dean Junior. Or DJ, as he is to us.'

Finn had hoped for confirmation but now that it was here he was overwhelmed. 'I'd like to meet him. And so would his grandparents, aunts, uncles, cousins.'

Ruth began to rock back and forth as the shock hit her.

'Ruth has spent years trying to find your brother,' Tom said, unable to keep the accusation out of his voice. 'She never knew his second name. It was a hopeless task.'

'And we didn't know Ruth's full name either. My family and I were just reeling from Dean's death and, to be honest, we just didn't put much thought into the girl he had only spent one weekend with.'

Ruth stiffened at this and said, 'It was not just one weekend. It was everything. To me. To us.'

'I am so sorry, Ruth. I had no idea you had a child. Had we known . . .'

'How will I tell DJ?' Ruth asked Tom.

'We'll tell him together. It will be OK,' Tom said, and she believed him.

When DJ walked into the lobby with Bette Davis, Ruth called him over and said, 'DJ, I'd like you to meet your uncle . . .'

And later that night, when DJ went to bed, his head full of the promise of reunions with a big noisy family, his dad's family, Ruth sat beside Tom on their couch and felt at peace. There are a thousand ways and a thousand roads to take, when searching for home. For Ruth, DJ, Tom, Bette Davis and now Dean too, the search was over.

At last they had found the right road home.

A Note from the Author

Hello my lovely readers,

Some of you have been with me from the beginning, others I've picked up along the way. But all of you are in my heart. Every time you get in touch, on Facebook, Twitter, via the website, or in person at an author event, to let me know how much you've enjoyed my books, you give me a gift. You really do. So, the first of what will be many thanks (brace yourselves), goes to you! I hope you've enjoyed *A Thousand Roads Home*. Waiting to hear your reactions is both terrifying and exciting!

I have to confess that this book holds a very special place in my heart. Researching and writing *A Thousand Roads Home* has been an unforgettable experience that has had a profound effect on my life. I've found myself changed and looking at those who are affected by homelessness with fresh eyes. While this book is fiction, over the past eighteen months, these characters have become special and real to me. The idea for Ruth's character has been bubbling away in my head for nearly a decade now. Ruth's character was inspired by someone in my life who was diagnosed with autism as a young child. I'll just call her 'A', because she's young and her story is hers to tell, not mine. But I can share with you that unlike Ruth's character, A has always had the support of incredible parents and siblings who ensure she gets to live her best life. *Every day.* I've watched her parents fight to ensure she gets professional help both in and out of school. I've watched them make changes at home, some small, others bigger, to ensure that A lives in an environment that is not stressful for her. And as a result, this young girl, whom I love dearly, is growing up to be pretty spectacular. A testament to her family, who are warriors of love for their child.

My research into autism brought me into contact with many diverse and interesting people. And I learnt this truth: *When you meet one person with autism you have met one person with autism.* Each individual manifests autistic characteristics in an unique way. There are of course many traits that are relatively common, some of which you might recognise in Ruth. I did borrow a couple of A's habits – the knuckle popping, the need for order and place, the obsession with books (we get that, right?!). A's favourite is Harry Potter. When I decided that Ruth should also love one book more than any other, I looked to my own library at home and scanned the titles of my favourite reads. Hundreds of books that I'll never part with. And then I saw the perfect book – my first edition, hardback copy of *Odd Thomas* by Dean Koontz, bought in 2004. I've not read it quite as often as Ruth has, but it's one of the few that I go back to every few years. *Be happy, persevere,* is advice that I try to remember in my life. Sincere thanks to Dean Koontz, for giving me permission to use Odd references in my book. But more than that Dean, thank you for giving me so many hours of joy through all of your reads.

Homelessness is one of the central themes in the story – both from the perspective of a rough sleeper and a family in emergency social housing. With almost 10,000 people without a home in Ireland and almost 1.6 billion without adequate housing worldwide, it was easy to find people to talk to during my research. I was deeply moved by the personal accounts I heard and I did my best to understand. There's no doubt that the causes of homelessness are complex – a big pot of poverty, lack of affordable housing, mental health issues, addiction and family breakdown. Ruth, DJ and Tom's stories are just one spoon out of that big pot, but do reflect some of the issues that the homeless face every day. I would like to thank Francis Doherty and Father Peter McVerry from the Peter McVerry Trust. To learn more about the incredible work they do for the homeless, please visit www.pmvtrust.ie, where a small donation of money or time can make a difference. Thanks also to Valerie Whitford, who helped me understand the processes involved when you present yourself as homeless to the council, as Ruth and DJ did. Dr Annmarie Kavanagh, of Whiterock Family Clinic, thank you for taking the time to answer my strange and awkward enquiries about life as a GP in Ireland. As with all my books, despite my many months researching the issues, I'm sure that there are some errors. All mine! Please forgive me for any that jar.

Recently, Eugenie, my agent, called me a method author, because of the lengths I went to in my research for this book. Here's a couple of examples: To get into the head of Ruth, who you now know is socially awkward, I spent a weekend avoiding eye contact with everyone I met. And as a result, I realised that I spent a lot of time looking at people's shoes! And, in order to understand how hard it is to find affordable housing, I took on Ruth's persona and situation, pretending I was about to be evicted. I spent a month trying to find a two-bed flat in Co. Dublin. At the time, there were 596 properties available, of which three were in my price bracket. Two were house shares and would not accept children and the last flat was gone when I rang to enquire. I broadened my search, looked at one bedroomed flats, extended the location, but each time came back with nothing. With sinking realisation, I knew that had I been Ruth, without any family or friends to support me, I too would have been homeless.

During Storm Ophelia in 2017, I was working on edits for *A Thousand Roads Home*. My heart and mind were preoccupied with the rough sleepers. I have nothing but awe and respect for the many volunteers who relentlessly helped and supported those at risk, then and now. In Wexford, small and big kindnesses got us through the big snow storm. Us H's were stranded behind seven-foot snow drifts until a lovely neighbour, John Roche, rescued us! Thank you, Catherine and John! And speaking of rescues, two men – Declan Cunningham (Advanced Paramedic) and Corporal Steve Holloway (Irish Defence Force), did something quite wonderful that I felt deserves mention. They trekked through snow drifts to help a little boy who was extremely sick and trapped at home. They then carried him back over the drifts, on foot, to the awaiting army ambulance that sat 3kms away. The two paramedics in *A Thousand Roads Home* have been named in their honour, a small thank you for their kindness and bravery. Also, the librarian who helps Tom is named after the wonderful Jackie Lynam, a librarian at Pearse Street Library. And the journalist who writes a life changing story about Ruth, DJ and Tom is named after *Daily Mail* editor Linda Maher. Both ladies I admire and respect. I hope they enjoy being part of this story. And Marian McBay, Emma Smith and Marie O'Halloran helped me name The Silver Sands Lodge when I reached out on Facebook for inspiration. Thank you!

I would like to thank the clever book retailers, media, book bloggers and libraries who work tirelessly to find new ways to get books into the laps of readers. Your passionate love of books helps authors like me, every day.

My publisher HarperCollins will always have my gratitude. The Irish gang: Tony Purdue, Mary Byrne, Eoin McHugh, Ciara Swift and the UK gang: Charlie Redmayne, Kate Elton, Kimberley Young, Lynne Drew, Kate Bradley, Eleanor Goymer, Elizabeth Dawson, Jean Marie Kelly, Jaime Frost, and Eloisa

Clegg. I visited the Harper offices in London recently and while I was hugging everyone hello (I'm a big hugger!), Kim said to my agent, 'Carmel is family to us.' It meant a huge deal to me because that's how I feel too.

I've deliberately singled out Charlotte Ledger, my editor & friend, here. Her support, advice, encouragement and insightful edits have pushed me gently and firmly to make this book the very best it can be. I trust Charlotte implicitly and know that when it came to the editor lottery, I hit the jackpot.

To my agents Rowan Lawton and Eugenie Furniss and all at James Grant Group, your expert guidance is appreciated more than you could ever know. Special thanks to Eugenie, who has worked so closely with me on this story, and helped me more than once tease out a plot line.

Keeping me sane while I juggle struggle are my co-founders of The Inspiration Project and besties, Hazel Gaynor and Catherine Ryan Howard. We seem to find a way to talk on WhatsApp everyday about books, life, family and occasionally gin. When we teach our workshops, we tell our attendees about the importance of finding your tribe in the writing industry. And I've got a damn fine one! In addition to Hazel and Catherine, I am grateful to all of those who make me smile whenever we get together – Claudia Carroll, Debbie Johnson, Shane Dunphy, Louise Hall, Caroline Grace Cassidy, Caroline Busher, Sheila Forsey, Fionnuala Kearney, Sinead Moriarty, Alex Barclay, Cecelia Ahern, Margaret Madden, Maria Nolan, Sophie Grenham, Elizabeth Murray, Madeleine Keane, Vanessa O'Loughlin and Tracy Brennan. Special thanks to Marian Keyes, for ticking off one of the items on my bucket list, by endorsing this book. It means a huge deal.

Thank you to the talented writers at The Imagine Write Inspire Group, keep chasing your dreams. And thank you to my friends on the Wexford Literary Festival committee. It's always fun when we get together. To all at TV3 on the *Elaine* show, but in particular, Elaine Crowley and Sinead Dalton, thank you for letting me be a part of your gang.

If success in life is measured by the quality of friendships, well, I should take a bow, because I've done good! Fiona and Philip Deering, Davnet & Kevin Murphy, Gillian and Ken Jones, Siobhan and Paul O'Brien, Sarah and John Kearney, Catherine and Graham Kavanagh, Caroline and Shay Hodnett, Liz Bond, Siobhan Kirby, Maria Murtagh, Margaret & Lisa Conway – you are all wonderful!

And saving the best to last – it's time to thank to my family. There's lots of us, which means that there is a whole lot of love and laughter when we get together. Tina and Mike O'Grady, Fiona, Michael, Amy and Louis Gainfort, John, Fiona and Matilda O'Grady, Michelle and Anthony Mernagh, Sheryl O'Grady, Ann and Nigel Payne, Michael and Rita, Evelyn Harrington, Adrienne Harrington and George Whyte, Evelyn, Seamus and Patrick Moher, Leah Harrington, Ann Murphy (who the book is dedicated to) and John, Ben, Abby and Sean Furlong, Eva Corrigan, my beautiful step-daughter, my children, Amelia and Nate, who make my life a brighter place every day, and last but never least my husband Roger, Mr H, who has been my constant since the day we met. Tom's character has a date that is special for him and Cathy: 18th October. Well, it happens to be a special one for us too – our wedding anniversary. When HarperCollins set this date as Publication day for *A Thousand Roads Home*, I got chills. A good omen, right? I hope this date is as lucky for the book as it's been for me.

Before I go, just one more thing. If you find yourself lost on a thousand roads, for whatever reason, my wish for you is that you get to find your way home soon.

Be happy, persevere.

Carmel x

Book Club Questions

1. Discuss the meaning of the title *A Thousand Roads Home*.

2. Carmel Harrington's stories always have a strong message, offering inspiration and hope. Has this novel changed you or broadened your perspective? What do you think are the key themes in the novel?

3. Homelessness is an issue that affects us globally. Did the book's depiction of rough sleepers and families in emergency social housing change your opinion in any way? Have you learned something new or been exposed to different ideas about people who find themselves without a home?

4. Ruth did not have the support and understanding of her family as a child and young woman. How did this impact her life as an adult living with autism?

5. Loss plays a key part in Tom's story. Discuss how his personal trauma leads to his eventual depression

and break from society. Was there any moment surrounding these events that you empathised with?

6. DJ has never had a strong male influence in his life until he meets Tom. As their friendship develops and strengthens in what ways do they influence each other?

7. How do the connections between Tom, Ruth, DJ and the residents of The Silver Sands Lodge make a positive impact on each of their lives?

8. Ruth does many small acts of kindness throughout the story and the ripple effect reaches not just Tom, but also many of the residents of The Silver Sands Lodge. Have you ever experienced a random act of kindness?

9. Which character did you relate to the most and what was it about them that you connected with?

10. Have any moments in the book inspired you to reach out to anyone?

11. Who saves who in this novel?

12. How did you feel about the ending? Is it what you were expecting?